Storm Path

For Sharon and Brian

STORM PATH

G. L. Brookover

G. L. Brookover

*May your horizons be
touched by
sunshine
May the winds
of life blow gently
May you
always have
shelter in the
storm*

Q quarrier press

Charleston, West Virginia

Q quarrier
press

Quarrier Press
Charleston, WV

©2011, G. L. Brookover

Library of Congress Control Number: 2010941023
ISBN-13: 978-1-891852-74-9
ISBN-10: 1-891852-74-4

10 9 8 7 5 4 3 2

Printed in the United States of America.

Photographs from the collection of the author.

Distributed by:

WEST VIRGINIA
BOOK COMPANY

West Virginia Book Co.
1125 Central Avenue
Charleston, WV 25302
www.wvbookco.com

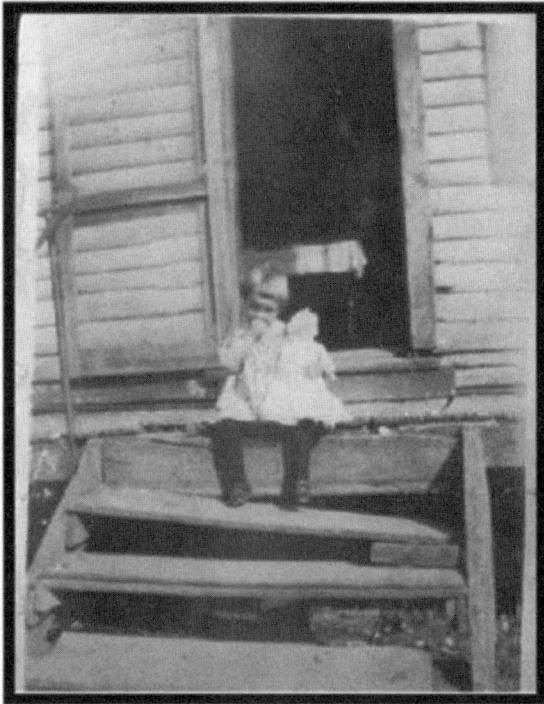

Dedicated in Memory

of

Mom

ACKNOWLEDGEMENTS

I owe gratitude to so many people who have extended words of encouragement as I stumbled along the path to publication of this historic novel.

For my husband, Gene, thanks for your input, your gentle criticism, your support as I traveled to distant horizons in search of historic facts, and for your unrelenting belief in the merits of this story.

For my toughest critic, Luke, thank you for your affirmations and honesty. I respect your opinion more than any other one. Dear friend, Phyl, I sincerely appreciate your hard work as you flew around the world with my manuscript in hand, editing grammar, spelling, typos, and composition. Bertha, your meticulous feedback was invaluable. What a gem I found when I discovered your extraordinary gift for detail. Marilyn, there are no words to express my gratitude for your patient listening as I prattled on and on through our many brunches.

For Curt, Dolly, Luke, Jackie, Denise, Seth, Katlyn, Ashley, Josie, Kaydee, Rebecca, Kelsee, Lyndsee, and Darrian, thanks for your work on the road photograph. It was a special meeting of cousins the day we got together for the long walk "home." You were great storm kids. We shall remember that walk.

A special word of thanks is extended to my friend and professor, Dr. John Shibley, whose generous accolades have been moving beyond words. I particularly want to acknowledge the enthusiastic assistance of folks at the Ellington Library, the Reynolds County Historical Society, the Sallie Logan Public Library, the Jackson County Historical Society, the West Frankfort Library, and the Princeton Public Library. To all the cordial staff people at the small-town public libraries and historical societies along the storm path, I am deeply indebted.

PART I

EXPLORING THE PATH OF '25

1

He was just a dead farmer. And, dead is dead. He had walked through the grassy meadows where cattle and horses now grazed. He had no name. It did not matter. At least, that was the way history was telling the story.

Elena's pain was gone for the moment. The Ozark Mountain sun was steamy, even early in the morning. It was a peaceful walk past strange rows of knobby rocks that marked nameless graves of souls long since forgotten. There was no way to identify some who had been buried in the Old Redford Cemetery. If Elena were going to get the work done, it would require a concerted effort on her part and some dumb luck thrown into the days and miles ahead of her. In another hour, the library in Ellington would open, and she would need to study diligently through archives and then move on toward Annapolis by afternoon.

She swatted flies away and wished she had swished an insect-repellant towel across her clothes and ball cap. Too late. She was alone with the swarming boogers and ghosts in a houseless town with two graveyards, one church, a county fairground, and apparently no people. At least no living ones. She had smiled as she drove past the Redford green-and-white lettered sign, and realized she could see the opposing sign at the other end of town. It was reminiscent of some lame joke she had heard from condescending storytellers who poked fun of Appalachian hillbillies. Redford felt like home.

Elena batted the air with flailing arms and scanned the wind-blown grass around the cemetery. She wondered if he had ridden his horse here. She could not know with certainty where he was, but she looked for him, for some sense of who he was in this peaceful place. It hit her. It was true. They were at peace. Like a revelation, the well-manicured graveyard, sprinkled with rainbow-colored, fake flowers, shouted to her, "He is at peace. You don't need to know his name."

"Perhaps not," she uttered quietly.

Who had taught her reverence when walking among the dead? Why was she whispering between tombstones? It was not as if anyone would have heard her if she shouted. God would not open up the sky and strike her dead for being loud and obnoxious among His deceased children. But she walked softly and spoke to herself in whispers, nonetheless. It was not fear of God that kept her gentle. It was just learned behavior. A habit. Oh. It was Bessie who had taught her to be very still. When they took real flowers to gravestones of relatives Elena never knew, it was Bessie who said to be quiet. Grandma Kizzie Jane Thomas, whom Elena called Grandma Tom, had been there in the home cemetery too, placing field daisies underneath Sherman's name. Grandma often bloodied her arms when she rode with the car window down. As the car crossed the Short Hill dirt road, she reached out to the enveloping banks to pluck spring flowers for a bouquet. Bessie would growl at her to get her arms inside the car, but Grandma Kizzie loved flowers so much, she never felt the thorns enough to stop making bouquets. Elena stopped looking for the farmer and paused, understanding, in this unfamiliar territory, that she was one of Kizzie's flowers. She smiled. What would Grandma Tom think of these fake roses gently laid on graves in Missouri? It did not matter. No more than the farmer's name.

What a perfect morning to be alive. The warmth of the midsummer sun pounded through her long-sleeved, checkered shirt, soothing the scar tissue that had replaced healthy tissue in the weeks after the wreck. In her assessment of humankind, Elena was fast concluding that everyone liked to bellyache about "high humidity." How tiresome it was to listen to the bellyachers wish they could be someplace else. If only they understood the soothing feel of sauna massaging away the pain that hovered over her every day. Pain had settled upon her life like a dark cloud which she ferociously fought as she forced herself out of bed each morning. But here, the Ozark sun-blanched meadow was a soothing spa where pain was eased and curiosity enhanced.

Yet, there were matters of practicality. Elena needed to finish the quick survey of the lot and head back to town. There was a water bottle on the seat of the Windstar, but without knowing the whereabouts of a public rest room, she thought it unwise to load up in the rural cemetery. With the temperature approaching ninety, she would need to bebop down the road and head for the library anyway. The nice young man at the store had been most cordial in giving directions, but Elena fully expected to make a wrong turn or two before finding the small branch library. Time was of the essence, and her thousand-mile journey had been tiresome. Maybe the farmer should just remain anonymous.

She walked toward the back fence and brushed by marker after marker. She scanned dates and wearied to think that she had imagined that she could just randomly drive through the country, stop at a cemetery, and stumble across answers to the beginning of a horrific puzzle. A puzzle she would piece together with great regard as if he did, indeed, matter. It was a quest, an adventure, and most perplexing, an oddity to pursue.

None of the dates registered, so she picked up the pace, blowing out a sigh of futility. Two more rows and she would have covered the logical place to begin her research, more or less. The booger flies seemed to have begun uniting in gangs to attack her, and she wondered if they had mistaken her for a horse. She had no desire to be overtaken by eyelid-attacking assailants of any description. Whatever pleasure flies derive from dive-bombing other beings did not interest Elena. She threw her arms about erratically and briefly thought about having fit of profanity right there on hallowed ground. No one would hear. She growled instead, and then squinted her eyes trying to speed-read the tombstones left in the row.

Elena took longer strides and viewed the van out of the corner of her eye. A dingy, blue car passed by, but the driver gave no indication that he thought twice about a lone woman in the cemetery. Then, just as she turned to watch the vehicle, something else caught her attention. To her immediate left, a gray marker with a double headstone stopped her in her tracks. She trembled like a frightened child as she read and reread the names on the tombstone.

Just above the neatly arranged, pink silk flowers on the granite base, the inscription spoke silently but unmistakably to her: March 18, 1925. She could wait a little longer to get back to Ellington. Elena stood motionless. Her breathing was shallow. Stunned and struck with serious doubts about the reliability of her senses in the suffocating heat, she read the date a third time to be sure she was not imagining it.

March 18, 1925. It could not be. The odds were unbelievably slim that she could have stumbled across it. No. She was in a hurry and probably making a mistake in her haste to get back to town. The tombstone was clearly marked, March 18, 1925. But, maybe, with all the fatigue of driving, she had somehow become confused about the date. Samuel M. Flowers. Absolute silence grounded her to the parched grass in the middle of this serene place of rest. She stared at the neatly etched name.

"Mr. Flowers, are you my missing farmer?" she whispered gently.

Maybe. Other Redford people could have died that day in 1925. There was a good possibility that this Mr. Flowers perished of tuberculosis or heart failure, knowing nothing of the neighbor farmer's circumstances. It was irresponsible to jump to conclusions, and Elena was determined to get the facts straight. She even doubted her recall. Was it the eighteenth? The notebook in her file folder had the answer. She would document what she could and then go into Ellington to check her facts. First, she would double-check the date with her files.

In a moment, her hands fumbled with the metal gate latch. She left the graveyard door ajar and scurried toward the Ford. She twisted the key in the lock on the driver's side and wished her damned hand would stop shaking. Finally, she was safely outside the cemetery where she reckoned her hand was damned for the time being. Her heart beat relentlessly beyond its normal rhythm, and she suddenly felt parched and faint. She reached for the water bottle next to the console. Just a sip to keep her mouth moist would not be a problem in the short time she had to get to Ellington. After a couple of swigs, she tossed the bottle toward the passenger door. The *Daily Sentinel* reporter yanked an accordion file folder out of the plastic bin behind the passenger seat. She flipped through the loosely stacked Internet pages. March 18, 1925. It was the right date. Not so fast. Was he—Mr. Flowers—the right person?

Elena grabbed the camera and discreetly palmed it beside her leg as she returned hurriedly past the ivy-covered tool shed. A small, rusted plow in the high grass jutted into the thick air. Normally, she would have paused and meticulously framed a rustic pictorial scene with the ivy-covered wall of the former caretaker's cottage. But, for the moment, the plow was barely noticeable. A power far greater than a rural scene of old farm equipment compelled her to bypass the solitary reddish brown collage. If her written notes failed her, a photograph would not. She had twenty AA batteries in the glove compartment to ensure faultless documentation. She breathed deeply and focused on calming herself.

Nevertheless, chilling ripples of nervousness shook her entire body. As she positioned herself before the headstone once more, she looked slowly over both shoulders. There were no signs of cars or neighbors this time of the morning, so there was no need to worry about the peculiar act of photographing a tombstone. As she raised the camera, she felt a tinge of shame for somehow desecrating this lovely eternal repository. But, somehow she felt also that if Sam and Mary only knew why she were there, they would understand.

Quickly, she snapped the camera shutter-release button and glanced down to ensure that the picture "took." Yes. She now had documentation of at least one person who had died on that day. Beyond her heart's fierce thumping, something else pounding inside her told Elena that Sam Flowers was the farmer without a name. She knew it.

Mary was his wife. The marker indicated that she had lived until 1996. Hers had been a long life that carried the memory of that day in her heart, every day. A moment in time, such as March 18, would not be one to forget. Elena wondered if the date was a haunting every year for the ensuing decades, or if Mary found a place of personal peace in the green countryside. Today, a constant breeze gently swayed Queen Anne's lace by the thousands, and Elena imagined being quite at peace here. Despite the extreme heat, she could see the potential for a lovely life in these rolling Ozarks.

As soon as she had verified that the picture was secure in the five-megapixel digital camera, Elena once again palmed the wallet-size Pentax and quickly turned away from the grave. She felt uncomfortable in a way that defied common sense. She regretted not having stopped for some appropriate, real, cut flowers to leave as a gesture of honor for the person whose story sauntered through her brain. The first stop, and she found him. Good journalism required absolute verification, but she knew. She knew.

Her head was tilted downward as she lumbered toward the gate for the last time. A tug of reverence and regard seemed to pull her back toward the grave, but the clock was ticking, and she could not spend any more time in the isolated, rural cemetery, not if good work were to be done farther down the road.

She turned the ignition and pulled slowly onto the Reynolds County road. Again she drove past the silent fairgrounds, studying the pavilions and picnic tables, and past a tiny chapel toward the back of the grassy lot. This was Bible Belt country, for sure. Every turn in the road had evidence of hardworking people with an abiding faith that held them on course through all life's adversity. Sam was probably a Believer.

One small, blue-and-white sign she had spotted somewhere continuously recycled through her thoughts. Every time she wanted to tear loose with some fiery, offensive language, she paused to remind herself where she was. This was not church. But it might as well have been, because it was the Bible Belt. She smiled as she remembered the strange message that glared at passersby from the side of the road. The sign read, "REPENT OR PERISH."

An abrupt, unexpected sensation of choking preceded a tear that welled on Elena's eyelid. She tapped the brake, waiting for her sight to return to clarity before resuming a normal speed. It was not the flies that had blurred her vision. Not fatigue or fear. It was the reality of this awful, beautiful place. It was history that had drawn her here. There also was some other purpose she did not understand. She would discover that her quest for understanding began in these highlands. The story began with a farmer. And a horse. Elena was alone in the middle of nowhere. Except for his horse, a farmer had been alone too. Had Sam been that farmer?

"Dear God," she murmured, "this is the beginning of the path."

2

The Ellington Branch Library was pleasant. It was neat, clean, well maintained, and apparently funded adequately for the small community. Rows of well-organized books afforded visitors good reading material, but Elena had no time to browse. It could take hours of work to uncover every horrible detail ever published about the monster. The power of this story was both exhilarating and maudlin for her. It was hard for her to understand why she fiercely pursued this work, traveling halfway across the continental United States to read about strangers she would never know. Her savings account had taken a hit to underwrite the trip. No matter. Evil had been in this place, and she would find its soul in the old files. At the same time, she would find irrefutable goodness personified far beyond the Ozarks before it was all over.

Elena settled quickly into the rolling, gray office chair in the archives room. She was at ease searching through the microfilm, although it was a bit of a jolt to have to crank the film feed by hand. She was not sure she had ever cranked a microfilm reader in search of material. But energy was running high as she knew she would uncover alarming information not readily available on the Internet.

As feature story writer for *The Sentinel*, she had learned from experience that work in the field was still essential to a good story. Despite popular belief, the best information is not necessarily published on the Web. She believed a good reporter had to taste the local food, feel the meadow breeze blowing strands of hair across her face, drive the winding turns, and chat with the locals to get a true sense of time and place. Even though the time was far removed, the essence of the people, their vulnerability, and their fierce determination echoed through the hills that held the secrets of that day. Her editor, Charles, was eighty years old. He always advised reporters to travel as much as they could. Elena had listened attentively and bought into the creed of the savvy octogenarian: "Go to the story, wherever it takes you."

Here, in this small building in the heart of Reynolds County farmland, Charles' sense of place was absolutely on target. Perfect advice. She would not forget it. Far more than she expected, she felt an immediate awareness of the ease with which she could put herself back in time. It was as though she were standing in that field north of town. She could feel the farmer's presence as she drove the paved roads of Ellington today. Her only direct connection to him now was the printed press. Newspapers were the Internet of the day, and they preserved the era well.

The librarian had been very kind and enthusiastic about the research Elena pursued. It was curious to move through the files of the coveted archive room and wonder if any records were left at all to contemplate. After all, it had been eighty-two years since the lone man was attacked in the rolling hill country. Perhaps the records had been purged years ago. Why keep them on file for a century? What purpose could they serve? Elena sighed and hoped she could uncover some well-documented facts about how it all happened. Was he turning soil in preparation for the seeding of the family vegetable garden? Perhaps he was mending a fence to keep in some stubborn cow that got out every chance she could.

For some reason, Elena envisioned the farmer working out in the field, with no shelter, no help from neighbors, and no protection. She hoped the archives would clear up her questions. Possibilities raced through her brain like water through a cragged mountain canyon. Her thoughts flowed so fast and so intensely that she could not sort them in a logical fashion. She exuded a hodgepodge of curious notions about who he was and where he was when he died. But it was the reason he died that was at the heart of the mystery. It drove her.

The attack had been vicious, totally undeserved, and absolutely unforeseen. Whoever he was, the farmer must have been bewildered by his wholly baffling moment of death.

Before traipsing through the Old Redford Cemetery, Elena had come into Ellington just as morning coffee sippers gathered at the local restaurant-gas station. The sweet waitress at Wendy's in Poplar Bluff had assured her that the mountain roads would demand a good two-hour drive to reach Ellington, and she had been very close to the mark for the post dawn trip. Ellington was an impressive community. Elena liked it almost immediately. The Internet pictures by the Chamber of Commerce were inviting, but it had been hard to tell clearly what to expect. She was far out of her home territory, and with West Virginia license plates, she was a conspicuous target for imagined troublemakers who could follow her along isolated roads.

To her pleasant surprise, no one seemed inordinately concerned about the blonde stranger with West Virginia tags coming into town. When she entered the little restaurant for some chocolate milk and a water bottle, she had felt unnerved by her own presence. Her instinct was to turn around, get in the car, and drive sixteen hours, or whatever it took, to get back home where she would be safe and welcome. But, that was too cowardly for a feature story writer. This series would run for several issues of The Sentinel, and she needed some perspective that others would never see online.

She tried not to stare as she walked into the restaurant. An old man in suspendered overalls sat at a table with a coffee-drinking friend. The old geezer's eyes settled on her immediately, but she thought he was merely curious. She was not a threat to him, or to anyone else for that matter. Not knowing the local customs, she hesitated to make much eye contact, thinking it might be considered rude. The young man behind the counter seemed comfortable with her presence. Elena quickly purchased a local newspaper, her breakfast milk, a bag of ice, and a water bottle for reserve as she prepared to explore the back roads.

She thought it best to justify her presence to the locals. A deputy sheriff was bellyaching to the clerk about some lawyer getting a worthless guy off with a plea bargain. He groused that he would just have to arrest him again, and the next time it would probably be worse. No-accounts in the Ozarks too, Elena thought. Well, speaking up in the presence of the law would be a good test of how she would be received.

She smiled and spoke as warmly as she could imagine.

"Mornin'! I'm doin' some research about the tragic death of the farmer here in 1925. Wonder if you could give me directions to the library?"

She nearly choked on her cornpone dialect and vocabulary. Did she sound as phony as she thought? A Phi Beta Kappa who had hosted family members of the United States President in her home, talking cornpone to strangers in a mountain community where she had no friends. Here she was: Miss Corn Pone Hillbilly West Virginia "researcher" in front of Barney Fife or, at least his colleague. This was sure as hell an uncomfortable moment.

As soon as she explained her presence, the deputy nodded his head up and down, almost as though he were saying silently, "Oh, yes—the farmer. Yes."

Elena immediately felt welcome and unafraid of the bona fide locals. They understood all too well her interest in archives that would elaborate on the events of March 18, 1925. The memory was embedded in successive generations with the depth and certainty of genetic encoding. No one in Ellington ever would have forgotten that moment in history, even though it belonged to their grandparents. She was sure that the youngest grade-school children knew the story. Also at that moment, she was certain that the nodding, uniformed lawman was accepting her as a trustworthy outsider. He said, in his silent response, "You're no problem here, Little Lady. It's a terrible and compelling story, a moment that will interminably hold its place in the hearts of Ellingtonians. There is work for you at the library, Little Lady. They have all the facts there."

Her next smile was a genuine one as the clerk raised his arm, pointing toward the window between her and the gas pumps. She was just a few blocks from the library, but he thought it did not open until ten o'clock. So, at that moment, Elena realized she had enough time to drive up to Redford where the farmer had lived. The morning was breezy, clear, and sunny. Traffic was very light. Even though the air blanketing the fields was beginning to feel steamy, the van air conditioning would give her a comfortable diversion from the nuts and bolts of data gathering. Better to gather some sweet-smelling, Ozark Mountain air before beginning the hours of work it would take to sort through old newspaper microfilm records.

She had gone full circle that morning from Ellington, through the fields and hills up to Redford, and back down the streamlined road. Now here she sat, twisting the crank in the back room of the library and hoping she might find even a small paragraph about the day. She suspected the now-defunct *Ellington News* would have covered it as the front-page, bold-type headline, and the events would be spelled out in vivid detail. She held her breath and hoped that the film had no breaks. This was as close as she would ever come to 1:01 p.m., March 18, 1925.

How did they know it was 1:01 p.m.? Did he have an old stopwatch that cracked and stopped when he died? Who had the 1:01 p.m. precise measurement that had been quoted for eight decades? The precision of the documentation that accurately recorded the day that hell wrenched the heart of Reynolds County but somehow managed to leave out the farmer's name was as perplexing as Elena's deep-seated preoccupation with the story. Remembering clocks and forgetting people was vile, from Elena's point of view. What civilized person documents time and excludes the name of a living, breathing being? Well, it had not been the first time in history that man's priorities, and she did mean man's priorities, had been skewed in favor of intangible concepts. She knew better. It was time to put a name with the story.

Her arm was aching slightly from rotation of the old film machine crank. Time to give it a rest, she thought. At that precise moment of rest, the one-column story reached through the glass screen and seized Elena's heart by way of her throat.

"Oh, God."

She was immobilized by irony. Thumps of heartbeats pounded intensely against her rib cage. She stared straight ahead, trying not to appear insane to the library staff and patrons. The lady with long, black hair poked her head through the door, and Elena was vaguely aware of her presence.

"I wanted you to know that they're over at the Historical Society today. I'd be happy to call them for you, if you'd like to talk with them," she said.

"Oh … uh … well, I saw that there was a "closed" sign in the window today. I hate to bother them if they're working. That would be nice … just a few minutes to see if they have any records you don't have here. Thank you so much."

"Are you finding anything in the records?" the librarian asked.

"Yes, thank you. I have found something. It's a good start. I'll make notes on my laptop here, and then I can run next door, if they have a few minutes to spare."

"I'll give them a call," the book lady added.

Elena wondered if her shaking hands had been noticed by the library manager. She was embarrassed by these recurring outbursts of adrenaline-based shakes and heart palpitations. It was totally out of character for her to lose her composure. If Grandma Kizzie could be here, she would tell her not to get her wits in a tangle over something that had nothing to do with her. Ol' Grandma was long gone. Just her memory of that day in 1925 had propelled Elena along the interstates to the blaring Ozark newspaper headline that loomed in front of her.

SAM FLOWERS KILLED IN TORNADO WEDNESDAY

3

<u>March 18, 1925, Reynolds County, Missouri.</u> Sam had finished most of the chores about ten that morning. With the milk buckets washed and the cows back out grazing, he had plenty of time for an easy ride into Ellington for supplies. Mary had gathered the eggs and was washing them at the pump when he began to saddle up Joker. It was warm for March, and that could be a sign of a good growing season. In the cellar there were still plenty of green beans, sliced peaches, and canned corn, but the tomatoes and apple juice were getting low. They had plenty to get them through to canning time, but then there would be many torrid summer days with long hours of cooking and sweating over the wood stove to boil up food reserves for the next winter.

Warm gusts of wind whipped brown strands of Mary's bangs in front of her eyes. She pinched the metal tabs of a wave clip on the back of her head. She moved the clip to her forehead to catch the playful strings of hair that snapped like tiny bullwhips across her brow. With a few more eggs to go, she slowed her pace to give her time to watch Sam and Joker get ready for their ride down Logan Creek. There was always more work to be done than could be done, but they had a good life on the farm. Sam was a good provider, and they never went hungry like some folks they knew.

Still, she felt ready for a trip into Poplar Bluff to look for some material to make a new dress. Maybe next Wednesday. They could hitch up the surrey and pack a picnic basket for a ride to the city. Easter Sunday was just down the road. It was the one time of year Mary treated herself to a new dress. She wanted to have plenty of time to sew in extra pockets and make a row of hidden hooks for the tatted white collar she had worked on during the frigid winter. She hoped snow was done for the year. The McNail girl over at Vinson Branch was a hard worker who they could get to do the milking, so they could head out early in the morning. Mary had all kinds of plans to get away from the farm, just for a much-needed break from long months of being holed up in the wood-frame house. She had plenty of time to talk it over with Sam. Mary knew that when she brought up the subject of a Poplar Bluff excursion, he would be up and ready to go. He was as weary as she was of blizzards, bone-freezing temperatures, cutting wind, and long gray days on the farm. It was time for an excursion.

Sam nudged Joker's ribs with his heels and tugged the rein in the direction of the creek. It was a good morning to ride into town. The sky was light blue, and a handful of white clouds blocked some of the sunlight that was already warming up the air. While the horse moved toward the creek road, Sam twisted around in the saddle to look at Mary. She was smiling. Sam had a hunch there would be sweet and warm corn pone with melted butter waiting for him when he got back home.

He smiled and looked down toward the crate he had mounted firmly behind the saddle. Some cheese, homemade butter mounds, and three dozen fresh eggs would make good bartering at the general store. He needed some half-penny nails to mend the fence that had sagged after the winter snows. After getting a sack of nails, he would have a little pocket money left over. He planned to bring home some sugar. Sugar cookies were his and Mary's favorites, and their girl smiled as he had never seen a child smile when she helped her Mama cut out the dainty, flat, sugar cakes. Before the baking was all over, Mary's blue-ribbon-winning apple cookies would probably be stacked with crunchy, blonde, sugar biscuits in the red ceramic cookie jar.

As Sam and the horse rounded the bend, Joker whinnied and nervously pawed the rutted road. It was too early in spring for varmints to pose a threat to travelers on horseback, but Sam sensed something in the young horse's behavior that was out of the ordinary. He stroked Joker's neck and tightly seized the reins to ensure control. "Easy, boy, easy," Sam murmured.

Joker shook his head, trying to resist the strain of the tightened reins.

"Whoa, now," Sam spoke sternly.

He was not about to lose perfectly valuable eggs and butter to the whims of a contrary horse. In spite of Joker's jerking movements, the crate stayed firmly in place. Sam continued to soothe the warm neck of the horse with flattened, gentle smacks from the palm of his right hand. After a couple minutes, the rider managed to get the feisty young horse to step steadily forward on the quiet dirt road. Once they got to Ellington, Sam would take a look at the bit in the drooling mouth of his mount. He might need to forego the acquisition of sugar in order to spare money for a new bit if it looked as though Joker's mouth were being irritated. As far as he knew, the rein and bit fit Joker well. Why the horse was acting a little contrary was puzzling.

"C'mon, boy," Sam urged, "Let's make a little time here, if we can."

The farmer dug his heels into Joker's ribs with just enough pressure to propel the two of them down the slope at a steady pace and consistent stride that had been missing in the previous few minutes. Sam had had plenty of years to learn the curious antics of animals. A good horse could be contrary one minute and placated the next. And there was not necessarily a good explanation that worked one time and would explain all the other times too. A fellow never knew what a horse would do if the mood to act up came over him. Sam reckoned they were something like people, in that regard. He garbled a deep chuckle when he realized he was seeing the same qualities in Joker that he saw most mornings when he looked in the shaving mirror. They were two of a kind. Working hard one minute, and balking at chores the next. The horse could easily have been called Sam, and the rider could have been called Joker. Mary often lightened the load after a hard day's work, saying she was never sure if it were the horse or her husband that was carrying on at the supper table. It was one of the things she loved about him. And he loved her gentle teasing.

With a stop for water and a check of the saddle, Sam and Joker made it into Ellington in a little more than an hour. The town was quiet, and that was the way Sam liked it. Getting supplies in the middle of the week was always preferable to Saturdays when everybody and his brother descended on the rustic village. Today was a good day to check on seed for spring planting, and there was plenty of time to wrangle for a fair price on the eggs, butter, and cheese. Sam usually picked up the mail once a week, depending on the weather and his mood. He would always pick up a treat for his ladies, usually some hard candy that rode well in a gunnysack attached to Joker's saddle.

Sam dipped a small, tin pan in the rain barrel on the corner and gave the horse a long drink before tying him to the hitching post by the feed store. He was in no hurry to get back to the farm. He would have plenty of time for chewing the fat with some of the long-winded storytellers that huddled over a checkerboard-topped, nail keg in the middle of the town meeting store. The Meetin' Store was what some folks called it. Not only were dry goods, baling twine, lamp oil, horse gear, and sewing paraphernalia sold there, but the old town store was always the best place to kill time with anyone who was not too eager to get back to work.

Sam had a good reputation for always putting in long hours in the fields and working on the home place. That was certain. But he also knew how to rest and work the neighbors toward a friendship that would pay off. If the time came down the road that help was needed more than a game of checkers, Sam had a long list of feed-store friends who would come running. He was not devious in his socialization, just practical. He had helped out more than a few folks in his day, and the country ways of the Ozarks were such that there was a fundamentally shared notion that, "You get what you give … in time." He did not need anything. Certainly did not want anything. That was not the point. The time would come when they would all need something or other. You never knew when life would turn on you.

Sam dug through the nail keg, scooping up six handfuls of nails. That would be plenty for the work he had planned in the next few days. Only a few boards were loose or down along Upper Logan. Some springs required that he hire a neighbor boy or two for making repairs, but he was confident that he could make the needed fixing on his own this year. A lady in an ankle-length riding skirt sorted through bobbins of thread and a bin of loose buttons as Sam plunked the pan of nails down on the counter top.

"Mornin' Miss Emmy," he said.

"Well, good morning, Mr. Flowers. How are you and Mary these days?"

It was good to hear such kind regard from a neighbor whom he and Mary encountered only a few times a year. She was a polite, young widow woman, who had struggled to hold onto her small farm a little way out of town. Her husband had died several months before in a farming accident of some sort. Sam could never get straight exactly how it was that he had died, but dead is dead. Ozark women left on their own with children to raise often had a hard time, and he wondered how she was doing a year since the accident.

"We're doin' very well, thank you, Miss Emmy. It seems like each winter is longer than the last one. I think we're ready for a warm, long summer," he replied.

"I guess we're all ready for a good, long summer," she chuckled.

The storekeeper handed Sam some bills and a brown sack containing the nails. Sam unfolded a canvas bag, and the spectacled, bald man placed the mail, the bag of sugar, and some hard cinnamon candy in it. Now there was time to visit with the two men sitting beside the four-paned window in the corner. They were jumping kings and barking out victory cries with each successive jump. He recognized John Lawrence as the reigning Reynolds County checkers champion, but the skinny young man across from him did not look familiar.

"Harold, is that you?" he asked.

The skinny man stood up and extended his hand for a shake.

It was that puny little Anderson boy. He must have shot up a foot since Sam had last seen him. Harold had been one of the hardworking boys who had worked on the Flowers' farm occasionally, and much like his part-time employer, he was a diligent worker who still had enough sense to play a round of checkers or two when the opportunity presented itself.

"Hello, Mr. Flowers," he smiled. "Yep, it's me all right. My mother says she's never seen ironweed grow as fast as I have. My pant legs are shrinking every time she does a wash."

The trio laughed and stared at the boy's work socks that conspicuously poked out of the space between his ankles and calves. Sam smiled and reckoned the boy was well on his way to becoming a farm worker with a lot of promise. He had a strong body to do all the heavy lifting needed on his home place. Harold had made it through the eighth grade, and that was enough schooling, as far as most folks reasoned, if a family needed the boy home for chores. Pride in a good day's work on a farm was prized as much as a good head of cattle.

"Will you be needin' me to do some work for you this year?" Harold asked.

Sam nodded and squinted his right eye as he contemplated the question.

"Well, I may need some help gettin' the crops planted here shortly. If we get a lot of rain this year, I may call on you to help turn the soil and get the seedin' done. You never know about the growin' season from one year to the next. I'll probably ring your Mama here in a week or so, if it looks like we need some help. But, I tell you what, I'll keep an ear open. If anyone around needs a worker, I'll be sure to put in a good word for you."

The young man smiled, knowing he could trust Sam Flowers to do exactly as he said he would. Playing checkers did not pay anything, but sometimes the opportunity to strike up a deal for work presented itself smack-dab in the middle of a good game of checkers.

Just then the distinct checker sound of "click, click, click," resonated through the air. He had been jumped three times in the little bit of time it took to drum up a reference from his old friend and employer. He rolled his eyes toward the ceiling, and challenged Sam to a round of checkers. John leaned back on a wooden crate as Sam and Harold set up the board and contemplated maneuvers through a three-game playoff. When the games ended, Sam excused himself, indicating that he had a few more errands to run before he headed back home. Mary would be looking for him, and he was looking forward to that pone he knew would be hot out-of-the-skillet about the time he got there.

He spent some time at the feed store, checking on supplies of grain for his cattle that needed fattening up. The large burlap sacks of grain could not be managed on horseback, but he would get the Model A truck out of the barn in a week or so and come back for the bigger haul. He spent some time studying the tack and remembered that he needed to check Joker's bit before heading back out of town.

He stopped at the bank, where he deposited half of his money. He and Mary tried to keep a savings of whatever could possibly be spared, just in case a rainy day came along and extra money was needed. They had seen more than their share of hard times in the lives of neighbors in the small community. Living frugally was not easy, but it gave them much security for a bad growing season or for the occasional ailment that cropped up. And there was always a little spending money they could spare for an excursion or two on warm summer days or a new dress or shoes as needed. Sam had his eye on a light blue, cameo broach in the glass case at the general store. It would be a special present for Mary's birthday. He reckoned it would be a fine investment for the lady who made the best corn bread in the county.

The noonday sun had barely begun leaning toward the western sky, when Sam mounted Joker. He had checked the horse's mouth and saw no need to adjust the bit or rein. He double-checked the belly strap of the saddle and the blanket beneath it, looking for a bur or jagged object that might be a source of irritation for the equine companion. Everything looked all right where Joker was concerned. So Sam held a tight rein and smacked the horse gently again on the neck as they rode past the old block-building store and out of town. He had made the trip home more times than he could count. Yet today was different from all the others. This ride would never be completed. The Ozark Mountains held Death in their grip. Sam never saw it coming.

4

12:45 p.m., March 18, 1925, Reynolds County, Missouri. The
wind whipped up twigs and leaves from the banks of Upper Logan.
The loose plant pieces brushed the face and chest of both the sorrel
and his rider. Although the breeze was warm and the temperature a
balmy relief from previous weeks, Sam was annoyed by the increasing
difficulty of controlling his horse. But he reckoned March was a time of
high winds and erratic gusts. It was a far cry better than drifted snow
over the road that could block him and his family from going to town
for days and, occasionally, weeks at a time. This day was right on track
with the almanac for spring weather. Sam fumed and huffed with self-
recrimination. He had known better than to wait too long in Ellington
before heading back upstream. He now realized he had spent too much
time at the checkerboard, and not enough time paying attention to
changes in the air outside the general store. This was typical aggravation
as March afternoons often coughed up showers and thunderstorms in
the Ozarks.

Sam and Joker had blue sky in the north, but the low clouds in the
southwest spelled rain for Reynolds County. Nevertheless, the farmer
and horse had time to make it to the Redford farm and tie up in the
barn before the downpour came. Sam was sure of that. He smacked
the rump of his horse in an attempt to speed up the ride through the
highland gorge, and Joker complied to the extent that the rough terrain
allowed him to trot. The air grew increasingly hotter, and Joker's rippling
coat gleamed with slick sweat.

They had gone only a few minutes at the faster pace, when the sky
suddenly transformed into an inverted boiling vat of ebon cloud layers.
Out of nowhere, suspended bowels of dark billows howled a deep,
deafening moan. Hell was headed dead center for Reynolds County, and
it was aiming right for Sam Flowers.

The downward thrust of layered air grew blacker and blacker in a

21

matter of seconds. Although Sam was well versed in the signs of serious storm trouble, he had never seen anything this abrupt and threatening in all his days in the mountain highlands. In all too many cases a twister could snuff out the life of anyone caught in its path faster than a person could react. He knew that. And, he realized then that Joker had smelled the stench of death charging through the air long before he had. Instinctively, Sam patted the horse's neck as affectionately as he had done a thousand times before.

What had been a bright, spring day had callously shifted into an ominous, black cauldron of doom. There was little time to act. Sam jerked the reins, bringing Joker to a sudden halt. He threw his right leg over the saddle horn and slid to the ground, holding onto the reins with his right hand. Glancing around, he noticed a wooded ravine with a small tributary that fed into Logan Creek. It was the closest place to hope for protection against the killer wind that was honing in on him and Joker. He tugged at the horse's leather straps, moving steadily toward the hollow that would give the two of them shelter. With any kind of luck, it would all blow over in a matter of minutes, and they could resume the trip home. They would be a little wet and worn from the experience but able to forge on, probably in sunlit skies.

Joker screamed a horrifying series of piercing cries, and his head fiercely jolted in sheer terror. The descending, bellowing monster tore loose with a full assault of ice pellets that hammered the thick-coated horse unmercifully and pummeled Sam's head and shoulders. The hailstones felt like death-intended stones hurled by Satan himself. Sam glanced at his right hand and saw blood on his knuckles that oozed with each successive blow. A twig jabbed the side of his neck, and he momentarily loosened his grip on the reins. In that brief second, Joker pulled loose and stormed frantically away from his master. Sam glanced at the horse for a mere second, and then he realized that Joker would know how to escape the torrent of hail, wind, and piercing debris.

A wall of white suddenly blinded Sam as a lightning bolt crashed into Logan Creek. He became disoriented and stumbled erratically, trying to get his bearings in the general direction of the ravine. As his vision returned, the strength of the wind had increased so much that he had to force his legs to carry him another fifty feet in the direction of the deep hollow. He leaned forward precariously, nearly doubled over. He was absolutely compelled to reach safety and bury himself low in the hollow where the winds and lightning would most likely not assail him.

"Oh, dear God, help me," he bellowed. But the roar of the wind was louder than his cry, and he doubted that God had heard him at all. "Oh, dear God in Heaven …," once again he prayed. Suddenly, an absolute peace rippled through him. A strange sense of warmth and calm swept over him like the comforting first winds of spring. Unbelievable strength surged through his legs, and he powered himself once more toward the gully. He was determined to find safety among the banks and trees above Logan. Mary was waiting for him.

Just when it seemed as if things could not be worse, the nightmare reached new heights. Sam covered his ears to the ungodly sound of trees snapping into pieces all around him. Enormous trees, deeply rooted in the hills for a century, were being plucked from the earth as casually as Sam plucked tomatoes from their vines.

Sam dropped to the ground and crawled toward the rim of the gully. Once on the edge of the embankment, he stretched out prone, wrapped his arms over his head, and rolled downward toward the safety of the embracing banks. He thought the sounds of earth yielding to the hellish attack would surely leave him insane once the tornado passed. Once again, it was more than he could bear.

He moaned as he crouched in the narrow ditch at the bottom of the hollow. He covered his head and neck with folded arms. A tree trunk landed on his left knee, knocking him to the side. Within a few seconds, another powerful blow of wind lifted the same tree off his leg and hurled it farther down the crevasse. He was stunned, but he did not think the leg was broken. His arms were locked firmly against his skull and ears, and his fingers held tightly to opposing hands as he curled into a human ball of fear.

"Dear God ... my family. Please ... watch out for my family ...."

His voice wavered, and the feeling of peace once again embraced him. It was his time, and he knew it. A presence was in that hollow. Some enormous power far beyond the ruthless force of the black sky descended upon him. He held firm to his position, staying nearly flat to the ground, protecting his head the best he could. What was meant to be, would be. It would not be long now.

His last thought and his last word were the same.

"Mary."

5

As Elena drove away from Ellington, she glanced intermittently in the rearview mirror. There was something compelling about the beginning of this somber journey. The roads of such awful history were pulling her toward the northeast country of southeast Missouri. She wanted to stay longer. The little motel had looked very pleasant, and she might have gleaned much more information, could she afford to tarry. But she had quite enough information for the beginning of her research. The sun was shining, and the air conditioning was keeping her most comfortable in the blazing July heat. The red Windstar was running well. She felt very safe—a hell of a lot safer than Sam had been.

She replayed the conversation she had had with Lee at the Historical Society. No obituary for Sam Flowers. It was not uncommon for simple folks to be omitted from obituaries of the early twentieth century. Had he said there was no death certificate? Why had she not written that information clearly in the notebook? She knew better than to omit details of this sort, and yet it all seemed too much to comprehend. With a thousand miles between her and home, she had found her farmer and placed a field and moment in time with him and his family. Once the studious volunteers at the Historical Society gave her a photocopy of all they had, which was one newspaper article that had been hung on the wall in the back room, she tossed a twenty onto the glass display case, and moved through the narrow aisle toward the windowed front door. The largest poster of Franklin Delano Roosevelt she had ever seen stared her down as she headed toward the front of the little building. She had to press on. It would be necessary to make the most of the opportunity to see what the next town held in its own archives. She would finish out her afternoon in Annapolis. Then onward she would press through more farmland toward the Mighty Mississippi.

Once again her thoughts raced as she scribbled notes in the spiral notebook on the passenger seat. She could drive with her left hand, watch for lazy curves in the road ahead, take notes with her right hand, and scan the bucolic countryside all at the same time. She smiled. In the meadow to her right, a rust-colored cow was cooling herself very nicely. The motionless bovine stood alone smack-dab in the middle of a fish pond, up to her belly in cool water. The cow had no place to go and gave no indication of any desire to move at all. Elena smiled even more, concluding that animals somehow know the obviously best ways to live when people are not always so blessed. Horses grazed on the hillside above the pond.

Her smile waned as she imagined Sam's family seeing the riderless horse barreling toward the house that night in 1925. Sweating, terrified, and wholly alone, Joker eventually figured out what he needed to do— go home. Elena gripped the steering wheel tightly as she felt her jaw clench with the thought of the men forming the search party to go on hunt of Sam. The Flowers' neighbors on Vincent Branch knew nothing about the missing farmer until his daughter knocked on their door that night. She said a search party of men was going on hunt of him. Elena suspected they had little hope of a good ending to their quest.

At 4:00 a.m. on March 19, 1925, the small search party found Samuel M. Flowers doubled over deep in a hollow, stilled for eternity. His arms were locked tightly over his head in rigor mortis, evidence of a futile effort to protect himself from the tornado's fury. *The Ellington Press* printed that he had died from a "hard lick on the back of his head." The memory of Sam Flowers had almost died in that hollow with him, except for a few artificial flowers on a headstone in the Old Redford Cemetery in the year 2007. Now he had a name and a place in history that carried an admonition for future Ozark dwellers and their children: be careful when the winds come in fast from the southwest.

Annapolis, Missouri was a different story. It would take Elena a good forty-five minutes to wind through the Ozarks to reach the small town of three hundred or so. The tornado of '25 had crashed full force into the community in less than fifteen minutes after tearing up farmland, barns, and orchards north of Ellington. Much like Sam's experience, the people of Annapolis and the nearby mining town of Leadanna had little warning of the approaching monstrous storm. Elena had looked diligently through public records for some remaining signs of Leadanna, but the U.S. Census Bureau showed no such record, and the official state road map of Missouri likewise showed no such place. She suspected that operations had shut down long ago, and the mining camp was only a blurred memory in the brains of a few old-timers.

Elena knew there was a small branch library in Annapolis, and she would have a pretty good opportunity to add yet more information to her Tri-State tornado files. It would most likely be similar to Ellington's library, and she fully expected enthusiastic staff to assist her with the work. The events of the warm March afternoon in 1925 constituted too great a moment in time to expect anything less. Elena was certain that she would find more information than she could ever use for the feature story. Annapolis was an exciting destination, and the July weather was perfect. Only the intense heat made the day slightly uncomfortable, but even for the times she was outside the van, the warm breeze was the perfect balm for her aching back. This day was certainly nothing like Sam's last one, when a boiling black sky pummeled down atop so many innocent people. That day was difficult to imagine.

Current annual income for Annapolis households was modest, less than $20,000 according to the Census Bureau. But homes were neat, and there was a sense of quiet resolve along the smooth paved road toward Iron County. It was not stereotypically poor like many of West Virginia's counties, and Elena found that refreshing. Although her home in Monongalia County was relatively expensive, some West Virginians seemed to work hard to uphold the image of an impoverished, backward state. Elena had strived diligently for her education and for a place in the hills that defied even the most hysterically funny, Letterman stereotypes. Her writing and photography screamed in favor of intellectual prowess and fiery determination of such West Virginia greats as Pearl Buck, Chuck Yeager, John Nash, Challenger astronaut Jon McBride, and U.S. Constitution scholar, old

Senator Byrd. Even intellectual carpetbaggers like Jay Rockefeller had brought dignity to the beautiful hills of the Little Mountain State. And, of course, there were all those Rhodes Scholars from her alma mater who served as a reminder of greatness amidst poverty.

This trip, with its focus on another people, was off course for her. She wondered why any of this mattered, eight decades after the fact. Clearly, it was where she wanted to be, and it was a story she wanted to tell. But how much did it have to do with West Virginia or any sense of intellectual prowess? The connection was vague, but the truth was compelling.

Here she was in the hill country of Missouri, appreciating the simple beauty of an easy drive northeast toward Annapolis. Northeast. Northeast. The common direction of most tornadoes, and the absolute direction of the one that killed poor Mr. Flowers. Elena glanced from side-to-side through the windshield, trying to gain some perspective on a day that could never be relived. She craved understanding with an intensity that most people would liken to insanity.

Her new NOAA radio crackled static gibberish as she tested it once more to double-check on weather conditions to the east. The signal had been strong until she reached the Poplar Bluff area the previous day. She was exasperated to realize that the one security plan she had had for a good night's rest in unfamiliar tornado territory had rendered itself useless in the Ozark Mountains. She was fit to be tied. Her fifty-dollar investment in a useless radio with an alarm she obviously would never hear in the middle of the night was worse than having no warning system at all. She had no idea when she could or could not rely on it to blare the screeching siren, even for nothing more than a thunderstorm.

Forget a tornado warning. It was the one huge disappointment of her carefully laid plans that was both unsettling and maddening. Why the hell could she get a cell phone signal perfectly in this area, but no NOAA radio signal? These wonderful people of Reynolds County and beyond absolutely needed and deserved first-rate, immediate access to storm information at all times. These were murderous mountains.

Everyone knew that. Missouri had more tornadoes in 2006 than any other state of the union. It seemed to Elena that the modern families of southeastern Missouri were not much better off than Sam Flowers had been in 1925. And that was a crime of renowned proportions. Madness in an era of technological genius.

But her mind needed a break from worries about the static-screeching, gray radio. She turned it off and moved her attentions to the immediate environment. Such a beautiful drive. The absence of trash along the Missouri road stood out as a lovely contrast to some litter-strewn rural roads of her home state. And there was always Morgantown with its drunken escapades of couch-burning victory parties ... nothing short of embarrassing. Letterman had gone after that one too. So had ESPN.

Elena loved West Virginia nonetheless. She would never leave. But here she was in Missouri. Pangs of homesickness stabbed her throat from the inside out as she maneuvered the van along gently tilted roads. She wanted to get the work done efficiently and skedaddle back to Heron Creek to cuddle up in the king-size bed at home. Greg was waiting for her. He waited for her nightly calls and daily emails in which she outlined her expected itinerary. Few great men of the world happily embraced their loved one's dreams of going off alone to explore unfamiliar roads in tornado territory.

Elena smiled. The last advice Greg had whispered was for her not to damage her Windstar in the hail and debris of some wild twister-chasing adventure through the Tornado Alley. It was a joke. Ludicrous. First of all, the tornado season had already moved north into northern Illinois, Iowa, and the Dakotas. Even though apprehension about improbable meteorological madness pursued her like a panther in the night, she had great respect for the forces of nature and no intentions of coming close to an encounter with a killer storm. That was why she had bought the radio with the emergency alarm system, worthless as it was. Her mind strayed to thoughts of her departure only two days before. Greg had stood beside the mailbox as she drove away. She thought she had seen him laugh and wink as he waved goodbye. He would be waiting for all her stories when she drove back home in a couple weeks.

6

<u>1:05 p.m., March 18, 1925, Iron County, Missouri.</u> He was sweating
just as much as the other men who were working to fill in the ruts
and trenches that had been washed out by early spring rains and snow
runoff. Four of the men were digging debris from the culvert beneath
the road. Road work was hard, but it was honest work. It was a good
day's work for a day's wage. Preacher Ben Johnson was determined to
save every dime he could toward building a little farmhouse on a small
patch of land in the Ozarks. He did not need much in this world, but
like most men, he wanted a home, a family, and a spot of ground for a
few cattle, chickens, and a garden. This would come together first, and
then he would take a wife. At least, that was his plan.

His morning devotions had been briefer than he had hoped. Ben
had overslept and had but a few moments to pray and pore over God's
words. On some mornings, he just let the Bible fall open where it
happened to fall, and that was the extent of his study. On this morning,
the familiar "Yea, though I walk through the valley of the shadow of
death …" had been a quick read before he gulped a glass of milk and
grabbed a fried egg sandwich from the hands of the boardinghouse
lady. Her girl, Alpha, had Ben's lunch bucket packed and ready for his
workday with the road crew.

He had a ride eastward with some of the boys on the crew, and he
never liked to keep them waiting. The young preacher man still had a
few days to prepare his sermon for Sunday, but in the meantime, money
was to be made repairing washed out sections of the road over toward
Annapolis. He hoped he would find a good woman like Alpha someday.
But for the time being, he was determined to save souls and build roads.
Alpha was always ready to help out her folks, but she still managed to
get in lessons for school and have time left over to help boarders like
Ben and neighbors like Sam and Mary Flowers.

Now here he was slinging a mattock into the uneven mountain

terrain and filling road ditches with broken rock. It was the hardest work a man could do, but there was something gratifying about making a smoother surface for those traveling between Reynolds and Iron Counties. Good for the soul, he thought, but hard as hell on the back.

The heat was taking a toll on the whole crew, but they had plenty of water from the hillside spring. Taking a break or two before and after lunch was no sin, as far as he could tell. Even though they had eaten lunch in the shade of trees along the road bank less than an hour before, it was time to announce another break for water and a brief rest. The heat was sneaking up on them faster than a mad dog, and they could not afford to lose work time because of someone collapsing from heat prostration.

The scripture words scurried incessantly through his head, like dogs chasing a rabbit with no intention of stopping until the killing was over. By this time of the day, Ben was usually feeling enough aches and fatigue that his brain had little space for much of anything, let alone scripture. Maybe it was because they were working alongside the valley road just west of Annapolis. He had long ago concluded that the brain does what it wants to do, and he just needed to take care of his responsibilities, no matter what thoughts jumped into his knobby skull.

"Let's have a water break, boys," he yelled.

The sweat-soaked shirts of everyone on the crew sent a clear message that more water would be carried today than most days in March. The men threw down their shovels and mattocks and headed for the large oak that tilted slightly over the embankment. Old Bill was not the fastest worker on the crew, but he was the best water carrier they had. The silver-gray bucket was filled to the brim only momentarily. The men scurried to dip tin cups and small canteens into the cool mountain water. A couple of men sat on the ground, waiting for the most heated workers to quench their thirst. Just a few minutes of easy breathing could muster strength for afternoon laboring on the road. They had a little reprieve from the sun. Besides the shade of the oak tree and the cool spring water, a snapping breeze blowing back and forth helped cool down the road crew. They savored the short time to catch their breath.

"Storm movin' in, Preacher," Bill said.

The skinny Reverend stood to look in the direction of the old man's gaze. Out of nowhere, a billowing dark gray cloud was moving out of the southwest from the Redford area. It rolled steadily across the meadows in the direction of the men. No one seemed alarmed. Clouds and showers were all too common for March. Some of the men had closed their eyes in quest of a momentary withdrawal from their tedious work. But Ben saw something that was out of the norm. The dark cloud was on the ground. He saw signs of tree limbs, dirt, and rocks being hurled erratically by the ebon mass. He did not see a tail or a funnel, but the black cloud spelled trouble.

He dropped his cup and yelled at the top of his lungs, "The Devil is coming. On your feet, boys!"

The closest building with a cellar was a quarter mile away. The men did not have enough time to make it to the Henning homeplace. The tornado would be on top of them before they could even break into a full run down the road. Besides, that direction would drive them straight into the monster's grasp. They had to act quickly or die. In a matter of seconds, every man understood that lethal winds were the only thing that mattered, and they looked to Ben for answers. He quivered inside to think that his faith would somehow be perceived as a direct line of communication to God. Did they really believe he had all answers to life and death? No such insight existed, but the frantic stares of the horrified crew demanded maturity and wisdom that he knew was far beyond his years. He had had some experience with downbursts and tornadoes in the two decades of his life, but he could not recall anyone ever talking about a killer storm exploding through the sky from nowhere. This was not the way storms moved in. It was too fast and too violent, as far as he could tell. They were all lined up for death, unless he, Preacher Ben, had answers which the others could not muster.

"In the culvert! Get in! Now!" Ben yelled.

His arm shook nervously, as he pointed toward the pipe that ran underneath the road toward the hillside runoff from the very spring where they had quenched their thirst.

"In the culvert!" he yelled again more loudly.

One by one, they scurried into the slimy, wet drain that only moments before they had cleared of winter's runoff debris. It was long enough for all of them and was buried well below the rocky road surface. The culvert was all the hope they had. Ben looked over his shoulder as dust and small rocks stung his crouching body.

"Valley of the shadow ... Thy will be done," he whispered.

In a second, the sky was black. No sun. No color. The pitch of night had crashed atop the road, and an ungodly howl descended in a roar on the preacher man. He was the last one to make it inside the culvert. Ben hugged Bill's ankles and doubled up his legs in an effort to encase every possible inch of his body. The sound of Hell's door opening in the Ozark Mountains was one that would last a lifetime for all the men in the pipe. They could not see the intense vortex that passed directly over of them, but they felt Satan's screams reaching underground to assault their very souls. In less than two minutes, it was gone. The nightmare vanished as quickly as it came. Once the air was perfectly quiet, the men crawled out. They stood aghast, staring at topless tree stumps sticking like jagged kindling wood toward a calm blue sky. The oak tree was gone, ripped from the earth that had held it tightly in place for a hundred years. A part of their hearts went with it, and the drenched, dirty men said nothing. It was time to go on hunt of their families.

7

Elena's mood was buoyant as she drove through the Ozark hills. Tree after tree lined the roadside. It was beautiful. She wondered how much time the road crew of '25 had had to escape death's grip as they crawled inside the culvert pipe. Blind spots notched between steep wooded embankments would have yielded no warning whatsoever. Yet, if the workers had been in one of the intermittent rolling fields, they could have seen the storm coming and had more than enough time to crawl into underground safety. With flickering glances, she eyed the hilltops and wondered what she would do if a black mass came hurling over the tops of the trees in a matter of seconds. Did she have the wherewithal of Ben Johnson and his friends? She knew it would not happen today. The statistical probability of being engulfed by a Missouri tornado in July was relatively remote. That morning she had studied the Weather Channel online before leaving the hotel. She heard reports of tornadoes hammering Iowa and South Dakota the night before, but she was well south of that turbulence. Nevertheless, she reached for the weather radio, just in case. Again, only incoherent scratching sounds emanated from the palm-sized black receiver. She flicked off the switch and refocused her brain on the exciting path she was pursuing.

This was the most exhilarating research project she had ever undertaken, and she could not wait to take on every small-town library between the Ellington Ozarks and Indiana's cornfields. She admitted to herself that some sense of danger accompanied her on the trip. It was precisely this minutia of fear that made her heart race and smile, both at the same time. This trip was something comparable to a natural roller coaster that facilitated belly flops.

She was spun back in time to the sparkling Ferris wheel of the Wadestown Fair in West Virginia. Driving this historic path generated the same feeling she had once a year as a little girl when they came around the turn by Bertha Taylor's store. The lights of the carnival rides jumped through her eyes and straight to a racing heart. Elena sighed. Would that so many children knew the joy she remembered from those perfect days. Unlike those sweet childhood moments, this exhilarating experience would be one she would not hold quietly behind a diminutive smile. This was a story she would shout from the mountaintops.

The discovery of details of the storm fascinated her. She was onto something extraordinary. It was becoming clear that the sudden onslaught of life-extinguishing wind was a phenomenon she had never experienced, and probably never would. Some awful power of that monstrous day stirred her gut, like nothing from her past had come close to doing. She was on the edge, but very safe at the same time.

Perhaps her next Sentinel feature story would analyze the underlying psychological forces that compel thrill seekers to scale snowcapped mountains or to crawl through bat-filled caves in search of unmapped sections of a mysterious earth. Mystery teased her here too, amidst the trees and hillsides of Highway 49/72. A road that appeared to be a small state road called simply K would have been a more accurate path to follow, but Elena had decided early in her trip planning, to stay on the main roads just in case she needed assistance. It had been years since she had changed a flat tire, and she dreaded the possibility of having to jack up the van on an isolated road deep in the Ozarks. Circling north, east, and then south through Iron County was close enough to the monster's trail for her purposes. Inexplicably, Elena changed her mind. She swerved onto Highway K. It was a good road.

Soon, Elena was rumbling over the railroad tracks below Annapolis. She could see the town on the knoll ahead. Suddenly, in the middle of great anticipation, she shivered and gasped for air. She had never in her life been one to hyperventilate. She was a cool, calm, levelheaded reporter for whom objectivity was paramount. But here, in this quiet little town, some force unleashed itself on her. Like the citizens of Annapolis in 1925, she never saw it coming. It was the ghosts of that day who were descending on her. At least, that was what it felt like. She realized exactly where she was. It happened here. On these tracks. She could almost hear the cries of panic-stricken women and children who rushed the relief train.

"Oh, God. It was here," she mumbled. "Calm down. You're a reporter. You know better."

She stared straight ahead and inhaled a long, deep breath. The real story started in this community. It was mind-boggling, intriguing, and bothersome to dig up the past. She wondered what peculiar notions anthropologists have as they dig through the past, unearthing the bones of civilizations long ago deceased. What bones lie here in Annapolis that represented the life and laughter of the innocent people of 1925? What more lay ahead? She slapped the back of her left hand and smiled as she recalled a movie line of Cher, in which the character yelled, "Snap out of it!" Elena came back to the present and maneuvered the Windstar toward the small business section of town. Once again, she was a reporter and a researcher, back in 2007.

Elena would have plenty of time to retrieve the town's records of the tornado. By mid-afternoon, she could cross the Mississippi. She would settle into a Super 8, well before dark. Elena looked for a sign with the standard white-and-blue reader symbol, certain that the regional library location would be well marked. To her surprise, she found herself driving out of town in a matter of minutes, having seen no clue about where to conduct research. How had a building as conspicuous as a library eluded her? She turned the van around and once more drove slowly through the small community. By the time she reached the train tracks, she realized she needed directions. She stopped at a small grocery store, bought some crackers and cheese, and asked the whereabouts of the library.

A dark-haired lady with an overflowing cart of groceries smiled and started explaining the location of the small book reserve. At the same time, the young clerk behind the counter chimed in, quickly giving her directions, as though the stranger had not heard the woman at all. Elena had a quirky feeling that the two of them were competing for some courtesy-of-the-year award. It was impossible not to smile.

Elena loved the friendliness of the good people in Missouri. She felt welcomed here too. She was just a block-and-a-half from the library. It was behind City Hall.

But her good feelings did not last long. By the time she twisted the key in the ignition of the Ford, a black-and-white had picked up on her West Virginia plates. The cop frowned and stared out the patrol-car window as she pulled away from the store. She winced and hoped there would be no harassment. Her motives were genuine. If necessary, she would pull out her credentials to wave in the face of the suspicious officer. Why could not all cops be like the good officer in Ellington? She pondered whether being a woman were an asset or a liability in a strange town. Women are easy to harass but not likely to commit any crimes. That was statistically the case. But one traveling alone was still an anomaly, even in the twenty-first century. Elena hoped she would not have to think about it for more than the second it popped into her head.

Again she became sidetracked. A large cemetery off the main road stood out as a conspicuous silent tribute to the past. She slowed the van to a respectful speed and entered the sacred site underneath a towering archway. She drove past headstones, wondering if there were any traces of the storm victims. It was so bloody hot she could stand to walk among the tombstones only a few minutes at a time. At the moment, the van air conditioner was more satisfying than water, a good meal, and a good night's sleep all put together.

She parked beneath an oak tree at the top of the hill and looked down over the town. A sparse gray area with high structures towered between the valley and a hillside just beyond town. The old lead mine? It was hard to tell exactly what was over there, and with the police officer eyeing her like a drug dealer, she felt sufficiently unwelcome so as to refrain from asking too many questions. She would look around the cemetery and, later, see how the library staff responded to her. Then she might ask questions about the old lead mine location.

The walk through the cemetery was not productive. The luck she had had in Redford ran out. None of the dates seemed to correspond with the tornado day. She needed to check her notes to see what the death count had been in Annapolis. *The Ellington Press* reported that 6,000 people drove to Annapolis the Sunday after the tornado, curious to see the aftermath of the worst tornadic catastrophe in the history of meteorology. Even the newspaper society columns of the day listed the prominent names of elitists who had informed the publication's staff of their travels to the devastated community. The same community where mothers and small children, overwrought with sheer terror, overtook train cars that pulled into the decimated town. Eyeing the remains of the terror-stricken town and its people was a morbid fascination, but quite the thing to do.

The ladies and gents were probably wearing their Sunday best for the outing. Lovely women with bouffant upsweeps, flower-trimmed black hats, long skirts, and high collars and men in waistcoats, crisp white shirts, and polished boots. It reminded her of the historic accounts of giggling Sunday churchgoers who took noontime picnics to the hilltop overlooking Manassas, Virginia, in 1861. They dined while watching Confederate and Union soldiers slaughter each other in the bloody battle that made Stonewall Jackson a household name.

Dressing up to see other people suffer. Elena concluded that unconscionable inquisitiveness is inherent in the minds of everyone of every generation. Sick curiosity is universal. She winced to realize abruptly that she easily could be seen as a perverted storyteller of people's sufferings. Her motives would be challenged. She wondered if she could make a compelling argument for the validity of her work. She could, indeed.

It was, in fact, the innocence of everyone who had fallen prey to the torturous weather system that earned them a meaningful place in history. Their names, their lives, and their place on earth held value and purpose. Elena would be sure of that. They were good people to be remembered in *The Sentinel's* feature story. Not one lost child would be forgotten if Elena had anything to do with it. And she did.

8

Elena was munching on crackers and cheese when she saw the police car pass by the cemetery drive at the bottom of the hill. The frustration of having wandered unproductively through the graveyard was magnified now by the conspicuous surveillance of which she was obviously a target. She needed more information though. Leaving town was not an option. Only one thing was left to do: stifle the cat-and-mouse game. She would become the cat. She pulled the gearshift knob into drive and snaked along the paved road back down to the valley and side street above the church. The black-and-white had vanished, but she knew he was lurking somewhere nearby.

After a few turns around the small street blocks of Annapolis, she eased her way into the parking lot behind City Hall. Even though she did not feel like smiling, it was time to act friendly and respectful in order to take control of the situation. She approached the white door that was marked "Library" and momentarily frowned as she squinted to read the operation hours. With no windows and only a solid door to access the back of the building, the library appeared to be about the size of a walk-in closet. More importantly, it was open only two days a week. There would be no access and no research in this town today.

In its heydey, this small city consisted of four hundred buildings. Only seven were left standing on the night of March 18, 1925. Elena wondered how many buildings made up the town today. Obviously, Annapolis nowadays was hanging on by a thread with limited resources to manage a local library.

Elena turned the corner and walked through the side door where the words "CITY HALL" identified the center of police operations. A lady smiled and looked at Elena. Did anyone in Missouri have a bad day when a frown was the best they could offer a stranger? The local culture was almost as intriguing as the famous storm. It was still pleasant.

"Hi, can I help you?"

"Hi. I'm doing some research on the 1925 tornado and hoped I could find some records at your library, but I see it's closed today."

The clerk behind the counter shook her head, indicating that no one would be available to access the local records. It would have been a terrific place for in her search for facts and stories about the storm, but Elena was feeling discouraged by each turn she made in the town. Maybe there was some other way to pursue local historic events, even without formal records. She wondered if the community had much information at all. Perhaps it was a moment in time that local folks wanted to bury in the years long since past. The population of Annapolis in 1925 was about 1200. Today, only 300 citizens remained settled into the warm and easy days of the Ozark community. Perhaps the legacy was too painful and left to fade away. Elena smiled and nodded cooperatively in the direction of the town worker.

"Do you know if there is anyone around who might be able to tell me about the storm?"

Just as the lady was ready to respond, a little blonde girl walked into the office, followed by a man whom Elena assumed was her Dad. The girl's face lit up as she looked straight at her mother.

"What about that old man that's always telling me stories?" she asked.

"Oh … maybe. He is old, probably old enough to remember the storm," the mother added. The father chimed in and warned Elena with a grin that once the elderly fellow started talking, she would have a hard time getting away.

This was encouraging. Someone old enough to remember the storm was a bonus in a day when most survivors had passed away. Elena fluttered her eyes in the direction of the family trio. She jotted down directions to the old man's house, thanked them, and hurried toward the van. The family had said that the elderly resident had a clear, sharp mind and that he was an excellent story teller. Now that she had made her intentions clear and had demonstrated respect and polite discourse to the three Town Hall folks, perhaps she could pin down some more information with less suspicion than she had raised by just driving around anonymously. She counted on the family to relay her intent to the patrolling officer.

Again her heart rate was picking up as she slowed the Windstar on the side street. She parked under a row of maple trees, reached for her notebook, and checked to see if the house number was the one she had scrawled with the quick directions given to her only minutes before. As she opened the van door, a sudden gust of wind snatched the door away from her grasp. Elena gulped, wondering how the unpredictable burst of wind was generated. Her nerves were on edge, and somehow she did not have the good feelings she had had in Ellington.

Every stop could not be perfect, but this town … this town had been flattened in a matter of minutes by the '25 tornado. Every person here had been left homeless in an explosion of natural forces as no man, woman, or child could possibly have imagined that day. The storm was violence beyond belief, and people had to have maintained some record of a grandpa or great uncle's horrific moments on March 18, 1925. When a town disappears in less than five minutes, the survivors must have relayed some of the facts to someone along the way. How could that not be the case?

She knocked loudly on the front door of the white house, expecting that the gentleman might be hard of hearing. A skinny, somewhat stooped man opened the door slightly, but made no offer to invite the pretty stranger inside. She was relieved that he was a little wary. She could probably get as much information as necessary in a matter of a few brief questions. Once he understood who she was, his face took on a cordial expression, and his kind demeanor was a source of optimism for Elena. She was poised with her pen to jot down anything he could offer about the storm. She told him about the little girl at City Hall who had described him as a good storyteller. That was the hook for trustworthiness she needed for the interview.

Old Man Martin looked to the side as he thought about the history of the community, but apologized that he could be of no help. Elena was perplexed and clearly disappointed by the unexpected disclosure. It turned out that he had moved back to the community in 1946 and was not privy to firsthand knowledge about the storm. Then he went on and on about his work at the local church with the children who knew him well, but whose names he did not always remember.

Elena politely nodded, genuinely appreciating the fact that here was an old geezer who still made time for kids and obviously made productive his remaining days on earth. That was how she envisioned getting old … living, laughing, telling stories to kids, and giving something back to her West Virginia home. But, for now, if she did not land something about a town that was horrifically wrenched from the face of the earth in 1925, her report would fall far short of the details she hoped to convey to thousands of *Sentinel* readers. She flipped the notebook shut and thanked the gray-haired man for his time.

She walked down the steps and traipsed along the small flowerbed that he obviously tended beside the picket-fenced lawn. Erratic whips of wind whisked hair strands across her face. She tucked her hair behind her ears and vowed to dig out her Scrunchies as soon as she was back in the Ford. She had kept her look plain and wholesome for the small towns along the path, wearing only a touch of foundation and pink lipstick. Pulling her hair into a ponytail at the nape of her neck made her appear ordinary and purposeful. She missed sleeking on heavy eyeliner that deliciously accentuated her hazel eyes, but looking delicious would not open doors to information about the storm. At least, it would not open the right kinds of doors.

Once more a gust of wind from the southwest hit her and momentarily threw her off balance. She looked up at the sky before opening the van door, but saw nothing more than a few billowing, white cloud formations in the northeast. The southwest sky looked quite clear, and she reminded herself that she was in the center of one of the most churning weather patterns in the mainland United States. No one around the town seemed to think anything about the whipping breeze. Cars drove by with radios blaring from open windows, and kids were skipping rope down on the corner. Clearly the people of Annapolis were used to these modest spurts of air and made no ado about any of it. Elena reassured herself that the locals would act differently if they smelled trouble. Obviously no one gave the wind a second thought.

Once inside the van, she brushed her hair vigorously into a single clump at the back of her head and twisted the black Scrunchie twice around the ponytail. But, before starting the Ford, she tried the weather radio one more time. Holding it in her right palm, she waved the static-screeching black unit in all directions of the van. When she held it toward the right back corner of the van roof, a slightly wavering voice recited the latest report. It was something about an unstable air mass … spotters may be needed ….

There was no telling when or where the report was made. She could not hold the signal in one place long enough to get any more information. But it was early afternoon, and the skies looked pretty clear to her. She had lost a great deal of time wild-goose chasing around Annapolis. Elena had enough daylight to hit one more library before lining up the next night's stay in a hotel. Depending on what information she could find in the Fredericktown library, she might make it across the Mississippi by early evening. She began thinking about the possibility of staying the night in Fredericktown if she got bogged down in archives there.

For now, it looked as if she would have to pass Annapolis and try to piece together storm facts about the quiet little town from other sources instead of the locals and the small archival collections, if these existed at all. It was not the best way to document the tragedy of '25, especially since Annapolis was blasted beyond recognition at the time. But information was sorely lacking in what should have been obvious research oases within the town.

She turned off the static-squealing NOAA radio and drove past the store where the two locals had amicably vied to offer her directions. The good feelings she had had about studying Annapolis' historic natural catastrophe had been sinking for the last hour. She had no place else in Annapolis to go. Fredericktown was close enough, and possibly big enough, to offer exciting details about this little community in its neighboring county. It was the only logical place to continue her work. As she passed the town sign beyond the little store, the black-and-white patrol car pulled to the side of the road behind the Windstar.

9

<u>7:00 a.m., March 18, 1925, Leadanna, Missouri.</u> Mattie Jane Kelley was stirring around before the rest of the household. She had laundry to do today and fresh bread to bake before evening if they were to have good meal fixings for the next few days. She sighed with fatigue, but thought how grateful she was to have a few quiet moments to work on her own. She and her eldest daughter Opal had traded shifts during the night caring for Freda who had been running a fever for several hours. They had dipped a rag in cold water from the well and soothed the teenager's forehead with the cold compress for the biggest part of the night. She reckoned that the younger ones would be coming down with whatever ailment Freda was carrying, and the week would be a long one. For the time being, the house was quiet, and everyone had fallen into a restful sleep, except for Mattie Jane.

She looked out the window and stared briefly at a pleasant, gray-blue sky. Shades of pink and amber streaked horizontally just above the mountain ridges, and Mattie Jane breathed softly. Easter would be here before she knew it, and there would be much to celebrate at the local church services. Winters were always drab in the small, lead-mining community, but her family had done fairly well this year. This morning, the sunlight was easing over the western horizon, and golden tones glimmered on trees just beyond the gray dusty village. Life could be harsh at times, but Mattie Jane always seemed to find a chord of grace where the beauty of the sky touched the green, rolling ridges near Annapolis.

The soft-spoken mother tiptoed out to the porch to empty the dishpan of water that she and her oldest daughter had relied on to comfort the sick teenage girl through the night. She wrung out the cheesecloth rag and shook it with the vigor of a good dust-mop shake. A warm breeze snapped the damp cloth in a northeasterly direction. The wind was soothing. Spring always carried a sweet fragrance into the otherwise drab community of Leadanna.

The children would be off to school in an hour or so, and today would be one of the fun days when they could run bases around the softball field at recess instead of being confined to inside play. If Freda's fever had broken, she would be sent to school too. Mattie Jane hoped that the few quiet hours were a good sign that the ailment was fading with her second daughter. Children needed fresh air, in Mattie Jane's mind. It was good for their lungs and souls to breathe air other than the brownish-gray dust clouds that stirred up in the road in front of their little shingled house. The schoolhouse was just far enough away that they could enjoy clearer air. Better for them to be there than here, she mused.

Cicero was not working at the mine today. He and his twin brother Oscero were planning to make some repairs to the roof that had been leaking for most of the winter. Buckets and a medium-sized wooden barrel had been placed at the edge of the porch. They had come in handy for catching the frequent strings of rain that seeped and dripped through the ceiling of the row house. Oscero lived just three houses down, and when repairs of this nature needed to be done, it was good that the brothers were nearby to assist each other. They were a close pair, and through thick and thin, they were always there for each other. Mattie Jane peered at the barrel. She wanted to put it out back and not have it taking up space on the porch, but she reckoned there would be plenty of rains through March and April. She would just wait to see how good the roof repair job was before tipping the barrel on its side and rolling it out to the shed.

Behind her the sound of footsteps distracted her from rain catchers and beautiful sky. It was Freda. She was staggering slightly as she ambled toward her mother. Her face was flushed as pink as the morning horizon, and Mattie Jane knew immediately that the illness would have a hold on her for awhile longer. No school today for pretty Freda. Mattie Jane just hoped the other children were not coming down with the fever before she could get this one better. One sick child at a time was plenty.

Mattie Jane tilted her head to the side, studying her pretty daughter's rosy cheeks. She extended her right hand to the girl's forehead and then sighed a low moan. The girl was burning up again, and this time she felt hotter than the night before. Freda began to cry softly, and Mattie Jane wrapped her arm around her bony shoulders.

"Mama, I'm awful thirsty," she whispered.

"All right, sweet lady, it's time to work on that fever some more," the mother replied.

She gave the pump handle a hearty jerk and lifted it as high in the air as she could take it. In just a few seconds, she had a tin cup of icy cold mountain water pouring over the brim of the mug that had hung on the nail beside the door. As the daughter sipped the cool water, Mattie Jane soaked the cheesecloth rag once more and wrung out the excess water on the stoop.

"Let's get you back to bed. I'm goin' to fix you some chicken broth and we'll keep workin' on that fever of yours. Let me get a rag to wash you down a little. That will help you feel a little better."

Mattie Jane gently coaxed the girl back into the kitchen, leading her toward the daybed across from the kitchen table. She hoped that what Freda had was not catching, but thought again about the unlikelihood of that being the case. She went to the back room and dug out a soft white gown from the bottom of the oak dresser. Soon, the mother and daughter were wrestling with bedclothes, a warm washcloth, and a thin towel, trying to make the situation as comfortable as possible. Once the sponge bath was finished, Freda lay her head against the fresh pillowcase her Mama had put on the daybed. She was still hot as a teakettle in July, but it was comforting to have special, fresh clothes and clean bedding in which to rest. Her Mama began working immediately, tossing chunks of coal into the cookstove. The smell of chicken broth and coal smoke wafted through the little house from ceiling to floor.

Soon the other children were up, scurrying around the kitchen, playfully snatching pieces of bread from each other's hands. Mattie Jane questioned the siblings to see if they were well, and the resounding affirmations gave her a feeling of relief. She could manage the chores for the rest of the day, napping when Freda dozed, and kneading dough in the big, brown crock she kept under the table for baking days. She had half a notion to make ten loaves of bread, with the intention of sharing them with Oscero and the poor widow lady that lived on School Street in Annapolis. There would be plenty to go 'round the table, plenty for Opal, Carl, Freda, Jewel and Herbert, all of whom were growing faster than bad weeds.

She put on the pot for Cicero's coffee and stirred up some eggs, giving him the last piece of white bread she had in the cupboard. She would open some canned tomato soup for herself once she got the children and husband out the door. Freda lay still, patient in the middle of the chaotic morning routine. It seemed to take way too long for the others to get out of the house, but not much could be done about it. She swabbed her face with the damp rag and waited for the noise to settle. Then Mama would serve her salty broth.

Cicero kissed Mattie Jane's head and explained that he was off to Oscero's to bring him over to the house to work on the roof. He was sure they could both manage to get their other chores done for the day if they flew into it and nailed tin sheets to the parts of the roof that were leaking. As Cicero walked down the chalky road, he spoke repeated greetings of "Mornin'" to the miners coming off nightshift. The weary workers' paths erratically crisscrossed with lines of lumbering, fresh-scrubbed day workers. The wind was stirring up dust, and Cicero wondered if it were just a little too much disturbance for fixing a leaking roof. Well, they would give it a good start and see how it went.

The morning went by pretty much as planned, and the twin brothers managed to get new strips of covering over the key roof areas that had dripped for the biggest part of the winter. Freda's fever began to come down some, and Mattie Jane managed time to work with her kneading. She would have more than enough bread to meet the family's needs for the next week. There would be a little left over to share and a little she could roll up with some butter, brown sugar, and cinnamon for a special sweet treat for the children. By midmorning, she covered the dark crock of dough with a clean tea towel and began sorting through some of

Cicero's work clothes that needed to be washed out. But with plans to bake so much in the coal stove, she decided that the work pants would have to wait for another day. Freda was beginning to show signs of spots on her delicate white skin, and the discomfort of the high fever was going to be rapidly replaced with maddening itching for a few days to come.

Then Mattie remembered. She had heard someone at the Annapolis store say something about chicken pox, only a day or two before. She had not given it much thought at the time, but now it was coming back to her, and it was destined to make a bunch of Kelley children very uncomfortable before it was all over. It was certain that the spots would be going all through the school, churches, and homes of the area. By forenoon, Freda had begun to scratch.

At lunchtime, Oscero ate some beans and wieners with his brother and wife and then excused himself to head back to his house for some chores there too. On his way out the door, he laughed and looked at Mattie.

"I never was much of a mind reader like some of those fellers in the carnivals that come in up at Farmington, but I think I got some notion 'bout what's goin' on with you."

"Oh, you do?" Mattie Jane asked.

The hardworking brother nodded and grinned a sly glance. He answered with surprising insight.

"You can roll that barrel out to the shed now. There's no more rain comin' into your house this year, Miss Mattie Jane Kelley!"

"We'll see about that!" she chuckled.

Mattie Jane slapped his shoulder, and Cicero thanked his lanky brother for the help. Oscero disappeared through the kitchen door. Freda was glad he was gone.

10

<u>12:15 p.m., March 18, 1925</u> Cicero washed up at the pump, put on a fresh undershirt, and walked purposefully into the house to check on his little girl. Freda was twisting and fussing, as he knew any sane girl would do if she were itching to death. Mattie Jane had just applied Arm and Hammer poultices to both of Freda's arms, and that seemed to calm the teenager to some extent.

"Punkin, you need to be careful not to pick at those spots," Cicero explained. "You don't want to get worse sores than you already got. Try usin' your water rag to take away some of the itchin'. I know it's worse than a herd of bees in a horse's tail, but it won't last too long. Your Mama and I had chicken pox too. We remember it like it was yesterday!"

Freda smiled at her father and dipped the cloth into the fresh, cool water that was on the floor beside her. She silently blamed that Henderson boy at school, who showed up with a fever a few days before and probably had a bunch of kids scratching like lunatics by now. It did no good to bellyache about her belly itchin', so she just draped the cloth over her face one minute and moved it to her neck and chest the next. She figured that her dad really did understand, and just knowing that made the red demon dots a little less bothersome.

Cicero went into the back room and returned with an armful of pillows. His bed pillow, Mattie Jane's bed pillow, and a couple of others were a strange sight from Freda's perspective. She had no idea what he was doing, but she guessed it had something to do with making her a little more comfortable. Without a word he began tucking the pillows around her, nudging them tight against her sides. Once more, it was the comforting gesture that gave Freda enough distraction that she momentarily forgot about the itching. It was still there. It just was not driving her to a mad fit which, a few minutes before, seemed inevitable.

"Young lady, you stay in bed. And don't get out. The more you rest the better you'll do tomorrow. Try to sleep a little if you can."

There was no sleeping for Freda. The irritation of every miserable splotch kept her wide awake. She could see out the side window and noticed that the gray dust was a little thicker today. The wind was picking up a good amount of grit from around the mine, but the air inside the little house was fairly clear, in spite of a few cracks in the ceiling. Both of the green calico curtains on the kitchen door wavered back and forth like crisp, green, grass blades in the field she walked through most days on her way to school. She would give anything to be in the meadow at that moment instead of stuck in a cocoon of pillows and damp rags.

Cicero and Mattie were talking softly in the back bedroom. Freda could hear parts of the discussion about how hot it was today. She had not noticed the heat so much outside of her own fever, which contrasted with chills that came when she hung the cool washcloth over her polka-dot skin. At lunchtime, Uncle Oscero and Papa were going on and on about a probable storm coming in that should cool things down and settle the thick residue in the air. Mama had agreed that it felt oddly warm for mid-March. But she still pined for breezy, warm spring days when she could spend a little more time visiting neighbors just up the road in Annapolis. Spring days were always unpredictable in the Ozarks, but the change from cool to warm and back again kept life interesting from her point of view.

Cicero was scheduled to go out on the midnight shift. He was planning to lie down to rest, but he continued talking with Mattie and looking out the window toward the other row houses. Mattie checked the dough in the large crock. It was rising nicely, and she was sure she could fire up the stove in time to get all the loaves baked before supper. She hated to stir up more heat in the house, but she could not let the bread dough go to waste. She laughed and told Cicero that she would fix him up a wet washrag like Freda's to cool him off. He had just opened his mouth to accept the amusing offer when a blast of wind hit the southwest corner of the house. Something was horribly wrong. He and Mattie paced back and forth between the bedroom windows and the kitchen door. Cicero's face suddenly turned as gray as the lead he excavated. He jerked his head around in the direction of Mattie first and then Freda. They were together, but that was not enough. They needed a safe place. It was too late. There was nowhere to go.

An exploding roar descended on the mining camp, and Cicero could see that Freda was crying out to her mother, but the sound of her girlish plea was overpowered by an unspeakable bellow above and throughout the house. Mattie Jane barely made it to Cicero's hand when the walls of the house began buckling with a blast of air as great as any TNT explosion at the mine. This was no TNT. It was a thousand times more threatening, and the Kelleys knew it could be the last sound they would ever hear. Pictures of the other children rushed through Mattie's brain as she eyed her daughter. Freda's feet were now dangling from the side of the daybed. There was no making it to her mother's embrace. It happened so fast.

The floor tilted sideways and the hand of God reached underneath the house, lifting the whole kit and caboodle slowly into the air. The thin walls held fast although it was clear that they were buckling and twisting with each ungodly movement. Just when the nightmare could not possibly be worse, the windows exploded into the room with the force of a shotgun blast. The three knew it was not God at all who had come calling. It was Satan himself whose killing screams shattered the air, the thin panes, and the Kelleys' hope of survival. Every thought, every piece of stick-wood furniture, and every dish in Mattie's cupboards and drawers were hurled at two hundred miles an hour in every which direction. Mattie Jane and Freda were crying out at the top of their lungs, but there was only one sound to be heard. It was not human. An evil force had been unleashed upon them, and they were thrown about the floor and air as inconsequently as a ball thrown by one playmate to another. Satan was having a good time. The Kelleys were dying.

Freda fixed her eyes on the gray-black movement outside the glassless side window. She was entranced by the horror and petrified by the power. She saw leaves and lumber flying past the window, and in a matter of seconds, she saw the shed that held Uncle Oscero's new car blown apart. Papa's Ford was beside Oscero's car. The black convertibles were rolling across the side yard. Before she could process the strange sight, the image of the vehicles tumbling down over the hill was intensified by the realization that the movable rooftops were severed from the autos. The brand-new cars had been the pride and joy of the twin brothers of Leadanna. Now they were expendable tin cans that would never be driven again. Freda saw the once-wonderful canvas tops torn away. She stopped screaming to study the scene as though it were nothing more than a distant dream.

The house hovered for what seemed to be an eternity and then began to rotate slowly in a counterclockwise motion. It felt like a slow version of the whirligig at the playground in Farmington. There, children held onto wooden beams that extended out from the axle of a great twirling wheel. When the Kelley children visited their Aunt Sally in Farmington, they would rush to the playground and spend the entire day spinning and giggling. The whole purpose of the spinner was for the playmates to hang on for dear life lest they be thrown into the dusty edges of the path that had been worn down by hundreds of racing feet that powered the wonderful, whirling toy. Once the spinning stopped, the children would rush into the grassy area where they staggered and repeatedly fell down drunk until their brains stopped spinning inside their skulls.

Now the Kelley house was turning. For a second or two, Freda felt exactly as if she were twirling on the spinner in Farmington. Her itching had stopped. Neither did she feel any pain from the blood that dripped into the lashes of her right eye. Her stomach felt as if it were lifted into her throat, and she was engulfed by some queer sensation of lightness, even as Hell's gates were opened for her and for her mother and father.

Suddenly, with no warning, there was terrifying silence. The Kelley house floated in a perpendicular fashion, back down to the very cinder blocks that had held it steady for years on the narrow Leadanna street. It landed with a gentle thud.

"Papa, your Ford is gone," Freda uttered.

"It's all right, Punkin. It's all right. Are you hurt? Are you hurt?" Mattie Jane cried.

"No, Mama. No. What happened? What ...."

Cicero crawled to his daughter and grabbed her shoulders.

"It was a cyclone, Punkin. We're all right. It was a cyclone."

Dazed and totally bewildered, the Kelleys exhaled, jutting quick breaths that merely mimicked breathing. They were alive. Cicero stumbled toward the kitchen door. When he opened it, everything was skewed between his eyes and his brain. The steps were no longer in front of the door. The house was not facing the road. By some unspeakable oddity, the Kelley home was twisted exactly forty-five degrees from where it should have been, but the house was on its block foundation. Boards, trees, telegraph wires, bedding, furniture, cars, and clothing were strewn in every which direction as far as he could see. Cicero stared at heaps of rubble and two, lone, standing houses. The house walls were intact, but the roofs had been blown away. Familiar property either was piled into heaps or was gone altogether. Erased.

The blood-curdling screams began.

"The mine ... it's gone! The mine!"

Cicero told Mattie to stay with Freda as he climbed down from the house to the side yard. His throat tightened as though he were being strangled by a hellish death grip. He stepped over piles of debris, moving intently toward the spot where Oscero's house should have been standing. He had to help his twin brother, Nellie, and the girls.

Cicero blared pathetically through the ruin, "Oscero! Oscero!"

Orville Shumaker was standing about fifty feet beyond Cicero, his hands cupped around his mouth. He was staring dead center at the distraught neighbor.

"Come here, Cicero! I think Oscero is hurt bad. Hurry!"

Forgetting about the protruding nails sticking upward from board after board, Cicero struggled to leap through the rubble as though he could jump his way to his brother and his family. But the sight of what remained of the house was overwhelming. Nothing was left of any room of his brother's home.

Shumaker grabbed Cicero's arm, and braced him for the inevitable. "I think Oscero is dead," he said.

"No! No, he is not dead!" Cicero screamed.

All that could be seen was a foot, sticking out from beneath a door. The two men dug through the demolished house, uncovering the brother who had, only an hour before, assured Mattie that no more rain would be coming into her house this year. In a heartbeat, his life was snuffed out, and Leadanna was completely destroyed. Cicero screamed the bellow of an insane man, and then calmed himself. His wails of despair had been buried in a wave of cries all along what had been the road that ran through Leadanna.

Cicero and Orville loaded the body of Oscero onto the door that probably killed him. Clasping the ends of the makeshift wooden stretcher, they stumbled silently toward the twisted abode of the living Kelley family. In Mattie's kitchen, the surviving brother fiercely kicked the unbroken crock of bread dough into the corner, and gently they laid the miner on the floor. Oscero's wrenched and muddy face mirrored Cicero's somber expression. His dear brother was gone.

From nowhere, another man came into the kitchen and began helping Mattie wash Oscero's body with water from a canteen. Cicero left his ashen, still twin in their care. The diminishing wails of terrified survivors echoed in the fading space behind him as he plodded along the road toward Annapolis. He knew he could get help for the others from people in town.

11

The train station had a bay window. Warm sunshine spilled through it into the waiting room, creating a cozy well-lit den for the passengers. It would be a good hour or more before the westbound train would be through, but the waiting room was filling up with an assortment of people who were dressed in their finest for the trip to Saint Louis. The depot was well swept and comfortable. Some folks frequented the old station often for an hour or two before scheduled departure time, apparently because they just liked to visit awhile in the sunny brown front room before boarding one of two passenger cars for their destination. Typically, the arrival and departure times could vary somewhat. No one wanted to be left behind. So it was best to be early. Today was a day just like all the others.

A skinny lady with a tightly cinched, black dress sat erect while pulling a little girl close to her right side. The four-year-old child did her best to be prim and proper, but her feet swung uncontrollably back and forth. The heels of her black shoes clunked against the oak bench as though her feet had a mind of their own. The dowdy mother juggled a frown and a smile as she listened to the woodpecker-like hammering of the little angel's feet whacking the bench. Just as her hand neared the kneecap of the little girl, she recoiled her fingers, tilted her head, and smiled. Except for a few scuff marks on the heels of the child's shoes, there was little harm that could be done by the wood-chopping beat of soles pounding the rock-hard bench.

Directly across from them, three men chattered about job prospects in Saint Louis. They spoke in cordial tones, with a conspicuous absence of cussing. Obviously, they were paying deference to the gentle lady and child. One man, whom the others called Earl, pulled a lump of yellow candy from his shirt and popped it in his mouth with all the playfulness of a ten-year-old. The little girl's mother nodded approval as he offered a second piece of candy to the staring, wide-eyed younger lady. The two new friends sucked the butterscotch lumps in quiet unison, smiling and winking back and forth at each other.

Sitting all the way at the end of the terminal was a young man in a tweed coat, white shirt, and baggy gray pants. He was reading The Herald Dispatch and nervously flicking the paper's top, right corner. His demeanor was subdued, and he made a particular point of avoiding eye contact with the other passengers. He turned the newspaper pages methodically, scouring each news item with the cunning of a swooping eagle about to devour an unsuspecting rabbit in a cabbage patch. When finished with one page of stories, the man began reading the page a second time. There was no telling what could be missed, if he did not check every column for accuracy at least one more time. He was a bit of an odd one to have separated himself so conspicuously from his fellow travelers, but he kept to himself, and that was fine with everyone else in the room.

The station master, W. C. Gunther, had moved toward the bay window with clean, white rags and a bucket of smelly ammonia and water. Having saturated one of the cloths with the pungent concoction, he began wiping the glass of each pane, first up and down, and then left to right. He grinned as the little girl wriggled her way toward the end of the bench. She moved closer and closer, eyeing his swipes at the filmy glass and marveling at the shiny, clear effect the cleaning solution had on each pane. She said nothing.

The window polisher reached into his back pocket and pulled out a dry, cotton rag. Within a minute, the girl was rubbing the cloth in circular motions at the bottom, right corner of the outwardly curved window frame. Together the two of them polished and smiled, and smiled and polished. They said nothing, but stopped intermittently to inspect their work for streaks.

Just as the last pane was restored to its original clear sheen, the stationmaster pulled his stopwatch from the tight pocket of his black, wool vest. He flipped open the silver timepiece, and stared briefly at the engraved message. "To W. C. on our Wedding Day. Anna. July 22,

1921." The watch was a source of great pride for him. It had been a reliable timepiece, always coming within two minutes of accuracy. He consistently made a point of taking care not to break it. He noticed his fellow window cleaner staring from the corner of her eyes, and he leaned down to show her the ticking, miniature clock. She tapped the engraved lid, and he read the inscription to her. It was 1:10 p.m. Within an hour or so, the train would be screeching its way into the station. After the exodus of passengers from the oak room, he would be alone to clean the small windows in the back storage room and the main station door. He reckoned those windows could wait until these passengers were on their way. There was not much need to be in a hurry in the middle of a Wednesday in Annapolis, Missouri.

As he turned toward the ticket window, Gunther heard the familiar sound of the steaming locomotive emanating from the distant horizon. He heard no whistle, but the roar of the train was getting louder by the second. He crinkled his brow and opened his mouth slightly, trying to figure out why the train would be nearly an hour early. Something was amiss. His watch was never wrong. Never. Could it be an unscheduled run by another engine? Not likely. Had he read the schedule incorrectly and improperly advised incoming passengers about their waiting time? That was even less likely. In all the seven years he had worked the railroad, he had kept a meticulous record for accuracy of the trains, routes, arrivals, and departures.

He walked toward the doorway on the side of the depot and peered into the distance. The black force hurling over the ridge toward the town bore no resemblance to an engine, but yielded a power far greater than any locomotive in the country. Blood drained from the otherwise rosy cheeks of the railroad man, and his eyes darted toward the little girl whose feet were once again tapping the bench on which she sat, snuggled close to her mother. Unspoken words throttled him, and his entire body began to shake. His brain was a jumble of emotions, and he struggled to react to the situation at hand. He had lost his wits. The conscientious manager of trains and train schedules was frozen in the doorway.

The little girl had been watching him the entire time. She jumped off the bench and ran toward him. It was the realization that she was innocently running toward a monster that had pegged the town and the station for destruction that extricated the station manager from his state of shock.

"Everyone! Down on the floor! On the floor! Now! It's a cyclone!"

He grabbed the girl, embracing her with both arms, and hurled himself toward the lady whose terror-filled eyes were fixed on the two of them. In a flash, he circled the woman's shoulders with his right arm and pulled her down to the floor. The ticket agent and the woman curled into a protective cocoon on their sides, with the four-year-old cushioned between them.

The newspaper-reading man ducked behind the ticket window and underneath the counter while the job-seeking men rolled underneath their bench, heads covered and bodies bent into fetal positions, minimizing the target of the anticipated assault. Two or three seconds of speechless abandon prevailed. The would-be passengers had nothing to say. The mother looked hopelessly at the young station manager who pressed her hand over her eyes in a gesture of last moment self-defense.

The roar escalated to an intensity of an explosion, and the effect on the railroad station emulated detonated dynamite. A blast of dust, wood, paper, exploding suitcases, and shattered glass filled the air. All the passengers in the station, except the little girl, felt the sting of glass particles penetrating their arms and legs. Wood beams, seats, and splinters pounded the bodies of the terrified, floor-embracing, human targets.

The man behind the ticket counter was hurled like a rag doll toward the back of the Depot, and he lost consciousness between the moment he left the shelter of the counter and the time he reached the back wall of the station, some fifteen feet away. No blow had been struck to his head. He had lost his senses and his consciousness from sheer fright of the experience. The benches were blown sideways, and all four walls simultaneously bellowed outward before the Annapolis Train Depot of the Missouri Pacific Railroad was blown to smithereens. In the last seconds of the assault, the ceiling beams crashed down on the victims, pinning them beneath a pile of rubble. It was over as fast as it came.

Gunther was conscious and aware that the woman and child were shaken but alert too. The strength of ten men welled within his skinny arms, and he hurled debris off the three of them. The smell of smoke was in the air. A fire was going to kill them, if injuries and shock from the previous batterings did not. He saw the cash drawer from the ticket counter now curiously positioned close to his right foot. Flames were shooting upward only a few feet away. He grabbed the empty metal drawer and half-crawled, half-ran to the place where the station door should have been. The pump handle of the well used to fill the steam-engine reservoir was all he could see. With a few quick jerks, he filled the cash drawer with cold Ozark Mountain water and hurled it toward the flames. After a series of tossed drawerfuls of water, the fire was extinguished.

Today, they would not burn alive. He doubled over in pure anguish, but mounted yet more strength as he quickly made his way back to the little girl who had helped him with the window cleaning. She was shaking, but alive and safe in her mother's arms. The three of them stared toward the eastern end of what had been the depot. Still standing was the slightly curved bay window, completely intact and panes unbroken, almost as though the storm had skirted around the window because it had just been so beautifully cleaned.

The trio of job seekers crawled through the rubble, and the four men went together on hunt of the newspaper-reading passenger. It took ten minutes to spot his tweed coat beneath a pile of beams, boards, and shelves, which once neatly organized supplies in the back room. Adrenaline was the underlying energy source for rescue in the depot. With bare hands and the use of one beam as a lever to remove heavy layers of ceiling atop the man, the foursome freed him just as he began to regain consciousness.

Then Gunther heard the awful sounds, more bloodcurdling than the tornado's roar had been. He trembled as screams of townspeople, some near, some distant, bellowed expressions of ungodly distress amidst the ruins of the unforeseen assault on their lovely town. Gunther froze again and wept, not knowing what to do. His knees buckled, and he collapsed in a state of inconsolable despair. The mother and child were beside him in moments. They embraced him and wept with him, unsure as well of what to do. Little did the people of Annapolis know, the nightmare was just beginning.

12

<u>1:15. p.m., March 18, 1925, Annapolis, Missouri.</u> Merle Stewart was just twenty-one years old when he died. He was crushed beneath the rubble of buildings that had been hurled into the middle of the main street. The Mercantile Company was obliterated before his eyes. It was more than he could comprehend. He had looked upward just as two juxtaposed black clouds merged and descended on the unsuspecting people of Annapolis. One villainous cloud had formed in the southwest. The other was moving inexplicably from the east. There was no rhyme or reason to this crazy weather pattern. Maybe if he studied it, he could figure it out. But it was too late for Merle, just as it had been too late and too fast for Oscero. Someone said that Merle froze as the boiling monster brazenly grappled every building and every living soul in the town. He simply stood there. His body would be uncovered after the sky cleared and the sun streaked down on what once had been Annapolis. None of the survivors believed he suffered. It happened too fast to have caused much pain.

The surreal images of an entire community erased in less than two minutes were simultaneously mind-altering and mind-shattering. Merle had felt his very breath pulled out of his lungs as the air pressure dropped during the heart of the storm. Yet there was another cause for suffocation. As he stared at the clapboard siding being ripped from the general store, his attention was pulled away to some bizarre happening he believed he could only be imagining. It was a flimsy rag doll passing over his head amidst clothes, lumber, bricks, and blurred pots and pans. He had slowly reached up his arm, but could not retrieve the doll. It was flying too high to be rescued. The little white arms and legs flailed wistfully, and the ragged toy tumbled aimlessly past Merle's head and out of sight. It was just a doll, after all. Nothing of great importance.

A block away, C. E. Pyrtle sat in his car watching the churning scene of an entire community's destruction. He was a traveling salesman from Kansas City, just passing through another small Ozark hillbilly town. All these towns looked the same to him. But within a period of thirty seconds, his gut was clenched by a spasm of sickening irreversible power. He knew that this town, on this day, would leave a searing impression in his heart for a lifetime. He would not be the same person he had been, now that he had been branded with horrifying sights and sounds that could never be undone.

That man over there—the one standing in the middle of the street—was nothing more than a marionette. He was dangling irreconcilably from some invisibly twitched set of cords. It was most unnatural. God was plucking strings of that skinny, dazed puppet of a man, casually pulling one arm straight up into foul air. Such futility in the middle of Hell. What could that poor being have possibly done to warrant such inhumane manipulation, such awful finality? Then it happened. It was like a javelin throw. C. E. saw the oak plank at the precise moment it penetrated Merle's chest, but he could not believe that his eyes were registering any semblance of truth. It must have been fear that compelled him to imagine the death of a stranger who had walked out of the General Mercantile ahead of him only a few minutes before. He would be back to the store another day. Surely.

C.E. sat motionless in the Model A. Perhaps if he did not move, it would all end on the other side of the street. Then, he could go on to the next town with his goods for sale, and life would be back to normal. Everything would be all right, if he just stayed in his car. He had no intention of being dangled beneath the hands of an angry Almighty, if he could help it. C. E. had no place to go anyway. He knew one thing most definitely. He would not fill the role of some pathetic, expendable character whose life was worth nothing more than fodder for the entertainment of Fallen Angels. Which was it? Fallen Angels? Or a vengeful God?

C. E. could have sworn he heard the roaring wind speak.

"Vengeance is mine," saith the Lord.

13

Elena was a gypsy, a snake oil salesman, and an anonymous traveler with an acute bout of wanderlust coupled with morbid curiosity. She was not sure. Fatigue and a paranoid power-obsessed cop had cut into her exhilaration in the early afternoon along the road to Fredericktown. She felt the first pangs of serious doubt. Her back pain was creeping through her. That did not help the situation. Since the research trail had gone cold in Annapolis, she drove mindlessly and munched on crackers, while contemplating spending one more night on the west side of the Mississippi. The closer she was to Annapolis to peruse library files, the more likely she would be to find details of its 1925 annihilation. The closer she would be to touch some awareness of death that merely started in the Ozarks. So far, though, she was stuck with indecision about time management problems and elusive information. The air outside the Windstar was clear, but she was driving in fog.

Preliminary work had indicated that other deaths occurred on this side of the river, but they were in very small communities and farms where a sprinkling of plain people fell victim to unprecedented winds. Nameless for eternity. As difficult as it had been to uncover Sam Flowers' identity, published reports about farms northeast of Redford were even more vague. None of the modern villages and fields bearing town names were big enough to have a library or any historical resources to add to The Sentinel reporter's repertoire. She would probably have to piece together facts from newspaper accounts and then continue to Illinois. Was that the truth? Or did she just want to outrun the wailing spirits of Annapolis? Raising the dead is an ominous undertaking. She choked on her cracker.

Elena realized Annapolis was the heart of the Missouri experience. Six thousand voyeurs had piled into buggies and cars four days after mothers had run screaming with their children toward the relief train that cut through the dark night of Annapolis. Such a memorable outing on a Sunday afternoon for heartless onlookers. It would be something they could tell their grandchildren. On the night of the 18th, men of Annapolis huddled for shelter in the few buildings left standing in the town. Women and children cowered inside train cars. Their cries filled the quiet warm air of the night. Whispering echoes of their suffering lingered in some mysterious way in the lovely town that was rebuilt and still thriving in 2007.

Elena's optimism for gaining insight had been tempered by an absence of record keeping and a general lack of knowledge evidenced by the few people she had encountered. They just wanted to live their daily routine, selling goods in the local store, sorting junk mail, and watching Dr. Phil in the afternoon. Perhaps that was enough. It was good to live in the present. Some tragedies are best left buried in the cemeteries on the hills. An evil force had imposed strongholds of power so permeating that the force has no place in the sane minds of living beings.

Now there was Elena's worthless NOAA weather radio with no signal in the midst of the deadliest spot in worldwide tornadic history! Some energy of anger welled uncontrollably inside her. She fumed and snorted like a meadow-grazing bull with its eye on an intruder. Once again she knew she was on track of some important quest. The pieces were not clearly coming together, but something was here. The temptation to cuss furiously built up pressure in her voice box like a Texas oil gusher ready to blow. This story was for the people who should be warned to take shelter today, not eighty years ago. It always came back to good people. How could there not be a contemporary, wireless, warning system that would work in the most treacherous cyclonic target in North America? It was shameless. It was a crime.

Elena nudged the accelerator pedal with the toe of her tennis shoe and realized that she could probably make it to the library in Fredericktown with sufficient time to retrieve the published highlights of the Annapolis leveling, possibly leaving enough daylight to make it to Cape Girardeau to rest for the night. Fredericktown was close enough to have good references, even though it was missed by the '25 storm. The tornado had ravaged everything right down to the dirt in the ground just five miles south of the town.

When traveling alone, Elena had a hard-and-fast rule to be checked into a hotel by dusk. Her 100,000-volt taze gun was her security blanket in strange lands, but the safety of a warm hotel room with a hot shower and a good night's sleep was always better. She had never had to defend herself on the road, and she did not relish even the thought of ever having to protect herself from assailants. But in a culture where violence seems to be casually justified against innocents, she had no choice but to be prepared for the worst.

That was all she wanted for people in and out of Tornado Alley: an opportunity to be prepared for the worst. The National Severe Storm Laboratory, NOAA, and the National Hurricane Center were doing extraordinary work, but people were still dying. Her retired friend, Rennie had been living only four miles from the twenty people killed by the Lake County, Florida, tornado only a few months earlier. Rennie had been called at two in the morning by her brother. With no shelter in their retirement, mobile-home park, they concluded that they had neither time nor opportunity to make it to a sturdy shelter. Rennie stayed in her small camper and waited out the storm; later she reported to Elena that a profound peace embraced her as she awaited her fate. She was at the mercy of nature. All she could do was accept her fate. She made it through the night, and in a matter of days, she volunteered with the Red Cross to aid and comfort survivors. People in cars and mobile homes continue to be at greatest risk everywhere the monsters kiss the earth. Now Elena knew why. Their damn NOAA radios would not pick up signals needed to alert them during deep sleep. Despite reassurances that parents give little ones, she knew very well that monsters creep through dark skies while children sleep. Time to slay the beasts.

The gas gauge was just below the halfway line as she neared Arcadia. Another strict traveling rule she had was always to keep more than a half-tank of gas in the Ford. She never knew when it could be several miles to a gas station or when she would veer off track to take in some historic view that would require more fuel than anticipated. A convenience store with four pumps caught her eye. She would load up on crackers, nuts, beef jerky, and water. The small restaurant next door looked inviting. She was due for a hearty meal before venturing farther east. She craved a full meal at the little restaurant but thought it best to keep moving along the tornado path. It looked as if she would be spending the night in Fredericktown, which would put her further behind schedule. But if it meant landing more details for the story, she supposed it would be worth it. Once there, she would grab a late afternoon research session at the library and then a hearty early supper to cover two meals with one shot. Nuts would do for now.

Elena parked at the end of the lot. She walked across the pavement as gusts of wind whipped hair across her face. It was noticeably difficult to walk through the blustery afternoon wind. It was still very warm. This was not West Virginia weather. Nevertheless, she shook her head and quietly reminded herself that she was preoccupied with death-spiraling tornadoes, which skewed her perspective on everything. She wondered if she were obsessed, but doubted it. Lots of writers bury their hearts in their work. She was as simultaneously passionate and sane as anyone could be. It was a little bit exciting to have to brace herself against the warm July wind. It made the trip real. It made the work authentic. Even in the Ozarks, the churning air from the Gulf Stream, coupled with cool downdrafts from the Rockies, was part of day-to-day living. People were going in and out of the convenience store without a care in the world. She could gauge reality by the locals. She was trained to eye the locals in order to win people's trust. She had to be normal and trustworthy, according to local rules. Only then could she effectively investigate a story. The wind was normal. But, as far as weather was concerned, she was out of her element.

Within a matter of minutes, she was barreling along Route 72 and wondering if the library in Madison County would have more information than she could cover in the few afternoon hours left. The emotional roller coaster she had been riding was once again pulling her back up to a new height of anticipation. She loved exploring every new part of this wonderful territory and could hardly wait to get to Gorham and Murphysboro the next day. Fredericktown was slightly off track of the storm path, but it was obvious that she could not tear through people's cornfields and wooded hillsides merely because the tornado happened to have gone that way. The county seat was close enough. She glanced at the road map again and smiled at the blue square that indicated a hospital in town. She was in good health and tried to be safety conscious, most of the time. But you could never tell about other people out there. Or anything else, for that matter.

It was just nice to find a hotel room where health care was immediately available … just in case. The probability of needing a doctor was small, but she likened her security to that of Greg and his snowblower. They had gone round and round about the snowblower. She was frustrated that they had spent over a thousand dollars on a machine that had new tags on it for three years and had never been out of the garage. He explained that it just made him feel better knowing it was there in case he needed it. Fredericktown was her snowblower in Missouri in July. She would be safe there.

14

The road toward Fredericktown was so much like West Virginia roads that it was hard for Elena to remember that she was far from home. The terrain was inviting, but this was the greatest distance she had traveled for a feature story, and something was unsettling about knowing there was absolutely no one she could call on for hundreds of miles around, if circumstances warranted it. Greg had double-checked everything on the van to be sure it would run safely and reliably. She was well prepared with her cell phone, two walkie-talkies, the bad black tase gun hidden inside the digital camera case, emergency flashlights, first-aid kit, and her favorite: daylight to guide her. Of course, there was the NOAA radio, which might be usable once she was back down near the river. Just not on this road nestled between these wooded, steep slopes.

The wind was picking up. Just when Elena began singing doowop songs with the radio broadcast, the van wavered unexpectedly from side to side. When the red Windstar was purchased, she had voiced some concern about a higher center of gravity, but versatility and comfort won out over concerns about a little less stability. She had promised Greg she would drive a bit slower on turns and treat driving with more caution than she had previously done with the Old Blue Chevy and Taurus station wagons. As Red jerked on road #72, Elena eased off the gas. She had plenty of time to hit the library before finding a spot to settle in for the night. No rush.

Suddenly, three loud, successive buzzes interrupted her sing-along with the Temptations. Her heart reacted with a jolt, and she went into danger mode as adrenaline shot through her body. She had not expected a weather alert. It was breezy and still sunny, as it had been all morning. Silence was the rule of the moment, and Elena's eyes rolled toward the radio dial. She wondered if she were losing yet another signal in the Ozarks. Then a droning, matter-of-fact robotic voice wiped the smile from her face.

"The National Weather Service has issued a thunderstorm watch for all of Reynolds County. Persons should be alert for severe weather in the area."

Then it was repeated.

"The National Weather Service has issued a thunderstorm watch for all of Reynolds County …."

Elena's brain was jumbled with weird notions of safety and security as she fought off the tendency to pay any attention to the blaring signal. She did not even know for sure that she was in Reynolds County. It was early afternoon. The sun had been shining all morning and was still warming the hills behind her. She sighed as the message became clear in her mind. All the research about the sudden attack of tornadoes throughout history resonated in a most disturbing way. Once she stopped singing and began wrestling with the weather watch dispatch, she saw something that had not been apparent on the drive. The eastern horizon was dark gray. The sky behind her was a starkly contrasting crisp, blue, window of light. She was not used to this weather pattern, whatever it was.

Still, it was a watch. And a thunderstorm watch at that. She was up in the mountains, so the probability of any serious consequences from a summer storm were mitigated by the lay of the land. She told herself everything would be fine. It was just a thunderstorm watch. In West Virginia, an advisory of this caliber meant low-lying residents needed to be on a lookout for floodwaters, and everyone should be alert for dangerous lightning. With her windows rolled up securely here in Reynolds County, the steady, red Star was a perfect Faraday cage that would fend off any bolts of fire from Heaven or Hell.

"Aaaah … overkill," she whispered, "keep your windows up. Drive a little slower. You'll be fine. It's just a thunderstorm. If it's worse than that, NWS would say so."

She breathed deeply and tried to rejoin the interrupted lyrics of an old Fifties hit. Her knuckles ached as her grip on the steering wheel tightened. The Oldies made her feel at home too. Especially now. But her singing faded to a humming whisper as she glanced out the windows. The horizon in front of her was growing darker by the minute. Every thirty seconds or so, she checked the rearview mirror and saw blue sky prevailing in the west. That would be her salvation if the weather advisory changed for the worse. She saw no houses, no gas stations, and no public facilities where she could lie on the floor and hug a commode if the gusty air churned into a hellish monster.

"Good Heavens! What am I thinking? Tornado season has moved north. It's Iowans and Dakota dwellers that need to have their guard up. Not here, you mindless idiot! The season has peaked and moved on. Calm down, twit! There's no tornado! There's not even a watch for one!"

No one was driving close enough to see her yelling at herself, and she was glad. She felt stupid and too blonde for her own good. Her reaction to the slightest inconvenience in weather was entirely inappropriate. That was all it was. An inconvenience. The blue hooded raincoat tucked behind the seat would keep her dry when she reached the library, and the town folks would be going about their business as casually as any experienced Midwesterners would be under the circumstances. She did not want to look like a hysterical, hillbilly tourist wandering through the Ozarks imagining monsters that were not there. Yet the idiocy of putting pride before safety was as perplexing as the weather. Which was it? Idiocy or pride? She shook her head as though she could shake herself into a rational state.

15

Elena estimated that she would be in Fredericktown within twenty, maybe twenty-five minutes. It was clear that she would be stopping there for the day, even though there remained more or less several hours of daylight. It was frustrating to have to cut short the day's work, but safety and calm needed to prevail. Her jaw tightened as she studied what quickly had become a purplish-black horizon. It happened so fast, she could not believe it was real. All her researched firsthand accounts of tumbling dark clouds rolling into towns from nowhere came to the forefront of her thoughts.

She had read hundreds of eyewitness accounts of tornadoes, and each one was replaying itself as though her mind had Tivoed every archive from her earliest days of library work in West Virginia. She definitely had watched more than her share of Storm Stories. Best friend Milly had joked that she should keep a lookout for Jim Cantore. Elena had even invested in a pumpkin-colored Storm Stories ball cap to "set the mood" for her research. For now, she could not imagine needing a ball cap to set any moods for solid research. At this very second, she would give anything to meet up with Mr. Cantore. He probably had a hell of a lot more sense than she had. She was in trouble and she knew it.

The van jolted back and forth as increasing darkness descended low on the hilltops. Cars were coming and going. Elena told herself that the drivers surely knew what they were doing. Each passing vehicle had Missouri plates. Not one driver braked or hesitated to continue traveling eastward. She vacillated between common sense and common fear, thinking that what she saw was horrifically exaggerated by inexperience. But with much of past success hinged on listening to a whispering inner voice, she found herself compelled to trust her own judgment more than that of anonymous drivers on the mountain road. Maybe they were all servants of the Devil, leading her into the bowels of Hell. Today was not the day she would go.

She flipped the turn-signal lever and slammed on the brakes. It was so dark within the few seconds it took to pull to the side of the road, she had to turn on her headlights. 2:36 p.m. and as dark as night. Where had she read that description? Shinnston Tornado? Night in the middle of the day. Was it Annapolis where darkness fell like a suffocating shroud before anyone imagined the tragedy that would befall them? Her capacity to recall night-day scenarios was so compromised by fear that Elena could not think straight.

A hundred possibilities for problem solving were tangled amidst billowing, dark, gray wind which provided no more regard for life than a bug Elena would squish underfoot. She trembled at the side of the road, overwhelmed by some weird memory. Several years ago, she had read an article in which it was reported that Albert Schweitzer refused ever to kill a single living creature, not even the smallest spider. He was a mere mortal. Were the children of '25 nothing more than bugs beneath God's heel? It felt so.

"Oh, God, what do I do?" she uttered.

She looked around for a farmhouse, but there was none. If she turned around and headed west, it would put her further behind with work she had barely begun. She simply did not have enough money in her savings account to justify heading in the wrong direction, if she were overreacting. Charles had already told her the paper could not advance her funds beyond the standard local mileage reimbursement up to $100.00. This trip was her investment. And she wondered exactly what it was that held her heart beyond the details of a feature article. Every story was a trek to another place, another time. But this quest gripped her very soul with a passion that simultaneously terrified her and drove her to this place.

Now she was scared. It was lonely on 72. The hills she had admired during her morning countryside exploration had become foreboding and unfriendly. This was no place for anyone, with or without Missouri license plates. Denial was at the heart of the mindless behavior of the other drivers. It was the only logical explanation. Finally, she was thinking logically, putting every notion of self-preservation at the forefront of decision making.

The radio DJ incessantly repeated the announcement that the Fredericktown area was under a thunderstorm watch. He made no mention of a tornado watch, but Elena knew "something" was up. She could hear it in his voice. The DJ broke into the normal program jargon after every song played. Yes, a thunderstorm watch had been issued by the National Weather Service, but he had new information too: cloud rotation. Every time he had open air he repeatedly cautioned listeners about cloud rotation in the thunderstorm.

"Hell! That's all I need to hear!" Elena mumbled.

Suddenly, everything changed. She was in slow motion, like an old movie edited for drama by purposefully slowed action that prolonged suspense. Elena pushed her chest forward until she was pressed against the steering wheel. She slowly raised her chin toward the high end of the windshield and stared at everything she had read survivors report seeing before losing consciousness and memories to boot. Leaves, small branches, and twigs were hurling through the air just above the van. It was that crazy scene in Twister: "We have debris!" This was no movie. Her hands were frozen to the steering wheel, and she pressed herself tighter and tighter against the air bag cover, hoping the lifesaving device would not deploy and crush her chest. Death by air bag before the tornado hit. Who would know when they found her body?

She checked the road twice in both directions before whirling the Windstar 180 degrees in the direction of blue skies. The number one driving rule under these circumstances is to abandon vehicles for shelter. She knew the facts, statistics, and safety procedures by heart. But, that part of her logical assessment was not persuasive. If a funnel touched down, it might just as well be on top of her. She was going to outrun anything that dared to embrace her with a death cloak. She could outrun it. And she would. All she needed to do was to head for blue skies. She floored the accelerator pedal and barreled away from the black clouds.

Everything was a blur except for the blue horizon. She was gaining distance quickly enough, but she could feel the wind whipping the sides of the van like an invisible bullwhip cracked through the air. Her concentration was broken slightly by the pretty, yellow Victorian house and large sign by the road. Bed and breakfast. Shelter. Protocol slipped in and she slowed to read: "Call For Reservations." A man was fiddling with something beside the truck in the private driveway. Elena was sure she was losing her mind. She thought it would be impolite to stop and ask for a room without calling ahead, so she kept driving. It would be rude to stop for a room without calling ahead first. She was losing it.

In a few minutes, she rolled back into Arcadia. Several cars were parked around the small restaurant, and the building looked like Heaven of the Ozarks. She was starved, yet wondered how much the anxiety was churning her stomach into a frenzy of craving. On the other hand, she had been munching on crackers and cheese most of the day. That was not enough to provide nutrition for the run to safety. It was time for a good meal and peace of mind to top it. The café probably had a storm shelter, and she would hang out there until the winds settled. She made a point of controlling herself, taking in deep, relaxing breaths with her eyes closed. For the first time in a good hour, she released her white-knuckle grip on the steering wheel. The folks inside the restaurant would be the barometer that would determine her next move.

Several older people were seated at tables scattered about the tile-floored diner. They were eating their early afternoon lunch as though it were just another sunny day in Missouri. Just like the folks in Ellington, the Arcadians all stared at her as she entered the restaurant. Elena managed a friendly smile. The muscles of her face were taut, but she flicked her famous eye-sparkle in the direction of the waitress and cook, who were behind the counter. Then her instinct to survive kicked in once more. Exhaustion and fear wrung her body into a state of limpness. A bed in a basement would feel great right now. The employees' faces quietly expressed what she had feared all along. The pretty young waitress and the cook were both huddled beside the radio that rested on the shelf between the counter and kitchen. Elena did not have to ask the obvious, but did so anyway as the smiling woman approached her.

"What's on the radio?"

"Oh, that —it's a tornado warning," she replied.

Elena did not need a mirror to know the color had drained from her face.

"Oh, not here!" the server emphasized. "We're okay."

Elena struggled again to smile and portray the demeanor of a cordial out-of-town guest.

"I'm traveling through town. Doing some research for a newspaper story. This weather is not what I'm used to."

"Where are you going to?"

"I was headed for Fredericktown, but I turned around."

The sweet smile of the young woman abruptly transformed into an expression of severe regard.

"Don't go there! Fredericktown is where the tornado is! It's not safe."

The feeling of a pounding hammer thumped inside Elena's skull. Lord, how close had she come?

"I need to get in out of this weather. I'm worn out. Is there a nice motel close by?"

Everything in the restaurant transformed into a dismal shade of gray, and Elena faintly heard something about an inn on a hill, or something. She felt disoriented, lost, and more vulnerable than ever.

"I'm sorry," she whispered. "I don't know this area. I'm afraid I can't find it. But, I did see a nice bed and breakfast just down the road. If I can borrow your phone directory, I'll call there and get a room."

The waitress retrieved a tourist placard from the drawer and pointed to the phone number for the B&B. Elena's fingers shook slightly as she dialed the number and whispered inside her brain, "I knew it. I knew it."

Her voice was strained as she explained to the innkeeper that she was alarmed and needed to get in out of the storm. The hostess was surprised to hear about a tornado warning. She had heard nothing. Nevertheless, she was in Ironton and would head back home immediately to check in the stranger passing through. She would be there in about five minutes.

"Thank you so much," Elena said.

She glanced at the menu board and decided to get something to go. This would be her lunch and supper combined. She did not want to overindulge in her state of nervousness.

"Could I get your cottage cheese? I wonder, do you have any fruit you could put on it to go, please?"

The waitress looked momentarily perplexed by a "special order" that was not clearly on the menu, but she nodded as she looked for options in the stainless-steel refrigerator.

"Oh, we have fruit cocktail. Would that work with cottage cheese?"

"Sounds good," Elena replied.

After a few moments of quick work by the young waitress, she handed Elena a styrofoam container that oozed with cottage cheese and fruit juice.

"That's $2.05," the waitress said.

It was a huge serving for the price. Elena was conscientious about paying a full price for service. But today was not a day to argue. It was time to get to shelter. She walked calmly out of the restaurant and eyeballed the southwest sky before getting into her van. She spread the Reynolds County newspaper on the passenger seat and set the overflowing take-out container of cottage cheese on the depicted face of some local official who made front-page news. She studied the distant black horizon and gulped to think she was driving back in that direction. If she could just get inside the house, she could relax, review her notes, and prepare for the next day. She could start writing that very afternoon.

The quick tour of the Victorian décor in the downstairs bedroom seemed incidental, but her host was determined to be charming and welcoming to the weary traveler. Little collections of elegant soaps, shampoos, creams, a spa shower, hot tub, pool, and a tea-brewing machine in the dining and library area were nothing more than godforsaken trivialities that would be blown to smithereens by an F-3. But her room was spacious and comforting. At last, she felt at ease.

"Where is the safest place in case of a tornado?" she asked.

Kathy was a gracious hostess but hedged momentarily, apparently pondering the question as though it were as out of place as a pig at a wedding.

"Oh ... uh ... I guess you'll have to come to our side of the house and go to the basement."

"A basement? Oh ... good, there is a basement."

Now, Elena's breathing was deep and assuring. Once Kathy left to return to Ironton where she was meeting a friend, Elena tiptoed to the kitchen and peered through the small doorway that led to the basement. She was absolutely determined not to snoop. She needed to know where the steps were. In case.

She brewed some Earl Gray, scanned the books in the library room, and headed for the front door. A flashed memory of a young man operating a weed eater down the road slammed through her skull. She had driven past him so fast and in such a befuddled state, the thoughts that prevailed now, "You have cloud rotation! You have cloud rotation!" beat her conscience like a sledgehammer smashing granite.

"Oh, that young man ... didn't he know? Why don't these people know there is death in the air? Maybe theirs."

She was alarmed to have seen the man weed eating when a tornado was nearby. She believed that in the twenty-first century, families were well informed and warned of threatening conditions. She was learning, in short order that warning systems work well in towns like Greensburg, but people in the country were on their own. So was she. Yet her host blew off her admonition of the storm, saying something like, "Maybe I'm crazy ...." Out the door she went.

Elena stared at the shaking boughs at the end of the stone walkway along 72. She sipped the warm brew. It soothed her soul like a silky balm. She was not alone. The beautifully-restored, yellow Victorian mansion was her new best friend. That was enough. At 3:15 p.m., she pulled the down comforter under her chin. The last thing she whispered before nodding off was not her most profound moment as a journalist.

"You're all fucking crazy."

16

Yount had been devastated by the cyclone. Its location was clear as a bell on the 2007 state road map of Missouri, but it was no more than a blur or a cornfield as Elena drove Highway J. She missed it, but the monster of '25 had hit it dead on. Now, it seemed to be nonexistent. Somewhere here, the monster split and became a double tornado. Biehle suffered the greatest loss of life in the state, with eleven people killed and at least fifty injured in March 1925. The 2000 U.S. Census Bureau indicated that currently eleven people resided in Biehle. 1925, eleven killed; 2007, eleven living.

Biehle had no library and little more than miles of fields and silence to displace the memory of the tragedy of that afternoon. Where were the libraries and historical societies? Gone, if they ever existed. It was just as well. Gorham and Murphysboro were waiting just on the other side of the river. But she had two stops to make on this side before finding the bridge at Cape Girardeau. Frohna and Altenburg offered no more information about Missouri's losses, even though both took the hit. A child in a small wooden school five miles north of Altenburg suffered fatal wounds from the black churning air. Elena kept driving. Research in this area was impossible. The little towns were too sparse. Too isolated. Too dead. At least that is what she told herself.

She reflected on her restful night at the inn. She had slept well. Sweet biscuits, an egg soufflé, and fresh fruit with Earl Gray tea closed out her brief visit. The other overnight guest at the inn was a gentleman traveler from Oklahoma. He and the host, Kathy, were engaging morning conversationalists. Kathy spoke briefly and somberly about two tornadoes that had hit since she had opened the B&B a few years earlier.

Elena thought it was odd that she had said nothing the day before when she drove off through gray howling gusts. The other guest, a second-career gentleman in his late fifties, talked about being turned away by the National Guard as he tried to get a look at Greensburg's aftermath several weeks before. He was an Okie with a history of tornado experience under his belt that could have intrigued Elena for hours. And a voyeur like she, to boot. Elena had lost too much time on the previous day's travel. She had to hit the road. This morning was again sunny and much calmer than the previous afternoon.

Absolutely, she would get across the Mississippi and tour the heart of the storm area. She planned to spend at least two full days in Murphysboro. Maybe more. Elena had no doubt about how much information she would glean from the larger libraries on the Illinois side.

Strangely, she felt some tug to stay in the Show Me State. Altenburg ranked slightly above average for tornadic episodes compared to the rest of Missouri. John Fulton was the child who died at the wooden school. But, where was he buried? Where was his kin? She had found Sam, but this child was not to be found, she reckoned.

Missouri had more tornadoes in 2006 than any other state in the country. Elena sighed. She was at the heart of Hell on earth. The hamlet of Altenburg was one of those pockets of trouble where Satan's winds came tearing through town with the disdain of an evil houseguest. It was true then. It was true now.

But Elena knew why people lived here. It was beautiful. She loved it and wanted to stay. How extraordinarily ironic. And how extraordinarily magnetic. When the sun shone, it gleamed with a warmth and gentility that defied heartless assaults from nature's most violent war chest. The good always outweighed the bad. Such was life.

Elena got her second wind as she drove down I-55 toward the Cape. The weather was picture perfect, with no more threat to her and the other commuters on the interstate than the man in the moon on a clear July night. Perhaps the worst was over. She checked the NOAA radio. To her surprise, a signal was coming through as she neared the Mississippi. Finally, she could count on the warning system she had needed so much the day before. The perplexing reality of inconsistent signal reception was baffling, but in some weird sense of equity, she forgave NOAA for branding the small black device as a weather radio, and accepted its fallibility. It was nothing more than an offensive bore.

She relaxed with the knowledge that, finally, a line of communication would alert her to impending danger. She popped the Beach Boys tape into the cassette player and was schmoozing along with Brian et al., "good, good, good—good vibrations—yeah ...." Her nasal rendition of the classic old song would make Mike Love proud. Perhaps not. Maybe, instead of Jim Cantore, she would bump into the Boys on the road in the middle of nowhere. She could temporarily divert her energy away from research and head down to Branson just long enough to join them in a few ditties in their next concert. She could harmonize with the best of them, or so she told herself. Finally, she smiled a spontaneous, happy grin. Such silliness for a serious, lone journalist. Inside her was a kid who always came to the front of every situation. She loved being a kid in an adult world. It was her best-kept secret.

The calm was not to be. Of course not. This whole trip had been a rush of emotions that inexplicably toyed with her soul. Warmth and excitement were part of the picture. Just not all of it. The black box began squawking. It screeched some raspy report about a National Weather Service's alert —forthcoming, afternoon, severe storms. Spotters would be needed. Spotters. They would not be looking for lightning. Elena was furious.

"No more!" she yelled. Then she glanced around to be sure no one saw the lunatic blonde yelling at herself in the Windstar that was barreling down 55.

"How do these people live with this stuff? I don't get it," she mumbled.

She studied the sky, which was clear and bright blue. For now, all was well. She would settle into her hotel by mid-afternoon, and then head out for more newspaper and historic record warehouses. After all, that was why she was here. With or without violent storms. The locals continued to work. She had no special claim on existence that superseded the lives of farmers and families in tornado alley. But maybe she had more objectivity. Knowing how to respond to stormy encounters was puzzling. She was having a hell of a time putting the pieces together.

Once again, her thoughts tumbled like boulders in an avalanche. She had to get to safety, but there was time for a brief respite at Trail of Tears State Park. She was not going to come all this way and miss a memorial to the great Cherokee people. The Hell with violent storms. It was time to change gears and contemplate other historic events of the lush, wide, river valley. She wanted to stand on that trail too.

Within moments or hours, she did not know which, she stood silently on the overlook above the powerful Mississippi. She strained to imagine mothers huddled with small children, shivering and terrified by soldiers that forced encampment below the ridge. Would that Old Hickory had been brutalized as much as the people he claimed deserved nothing more than slaughter, suffering, and ostracism. Not all American history was worthy of pride.

As Elena studied the Illinois riverbank, she saw vivid images beyond what her eyes could register. The storm had crossed these mighty waters. There was debate about how much water was lifted out of the river and dumped on the eastern side. Some accounts said the tornado jumped the river. Eyewitnesses at the time of the 1944 Shinnston (West Virginia) Tornado reported that the F-5 cut a swath through the Tygart River with such formidable strength that they actually saw the bare riverbed, temporarily dry as a bone. It was absolutely a myth that tornadoes do not cross rivers. The storm of '25 proved that. Two hundred nineteen miles of stripped earth was undeniable evidence, and it was well documented. Whether the storm jumped the river or lifted hundreds of thousands of water-gallons into the black cauldron was an ongoing battle of wits between scientists espousing irrefutable hard data in contrast to accounts told by irreconcilably terrified victims who lived through Hell long enough to talk about it.

Elena wrestled with claims on both sides. Her instinct was to side with the traumatized people even though she knew how well the brain could play morbid games with people's memory. At the same time, through her studies at WVU, she had developed a keen sense of contemplation which absolutely demanded hard evidence as a basis for formulating conclusions about any natural phenomenon. Somewhere in the mix was God. That was the biggest monkey wrench thrown into the pile of rubble that made up the storm, its human slaughter, and the aftermath.

The wind caused death and damage in Cape Girardeau, which was well south of the tornado's historic path. At this spot on the Trail of Tears, she stood a few miles north of the Cape. Clearly, multiple vortexes occurred beyond the split at Biehle. The expansive power was so horrific that she wondered if people believed it was the end of the world. Here, on the overlook above the roaring Mississippi, she stood between the historic paths. She was on yet another trail of human disaster. Too much suffering.

She whispered loudly enough for God to hear, "I don't understand."

17

2:20 p.m., March 18, 1925, Office of *The Democrat-News*, Fredericktown. The stories to go to press were laid out in a well-organized fashion, as always. Madison County readers were loyal to the local paper, and for good reason. It catered to their lives in very personal ways. Rebecca Matthews' birthday at her home in Highland Park would make a prominent front-page story on the nineteenth. All the children and grandchildren had gathered with "baskets full of good things" except for Justin who lived in Ureka, Utah, and John in Yerrington, Nevada. Democrat readers would thoroughly enjoy taking in the happy goings-on with Rebecca's family gathering in her honor.

But there would also be the sad story of twenty-nine-year-old Jesse Copher for whom surgery at the hospital in Saint Louis failed to save him from appendicitis. He would be laid to rest in the Methodist Cemetery. And the little boy of Mrs. Ora Cheek of Moore's Chapel had died. The dear child's father had been killed in a rockfall at Flat River only a few months earlier.

Greater space was given to more upbeat news in The Democrat. The Boy Scouts had enjoyed a dinner, "mess kit style," at the home of Mrs. Carrie Thompson. Mess call was sounded on the bugle by Scout Ralph Elders, and the boys lined up to partake of refreshments. A green-and-white motif, including green and white candles and crepe paper hats for the boys celebrated the Irish theme on Saint Patty's Day. Assistant Scout Master, Reverend T. E. Smith, had given a talk about his years of experience as a Scout leader. Following his talk, the boys enjoyed games and stunts. A list of all those in attendance was clearly laid out for inclusion in the front-page story.

Of great import for the town was the upcoming county spelling contest on Saturday, which was expected to draw a large number of people. Teachers and children in every school throughout the county worked diligently to prepare for the annual competition at Marvin

College. The winner would travel to Cape Girardeau for the regional championship. Pride in studies and hard work was evidenced in everything the community celebrated, right down to the endeavors of the youngest children in the smallest rural school.

A quirky story about Uncle Henry Arnett being arrested for going to church would be an eye-catcher for the local readership too. It seemed that old Henry had been caught breaking into the church house and, upon being apprehended, refused to sign a bond or go to jail as instructed by the sheriff and prosecuting attorney. A recent congregational squabble had erupted about the church being sold. Once the keys to the sanctuary were turned over to the new owner, Henry had decided to defend the home church by removing the hinges from the door and holing up inside with a shotgun until parishioners came to their senses. Arnett's good neighbors finally persuaded him to sign a bond for his appearance in court, and the heartbroken old fellow was turned away from what had been his place of worship for more years than most people in Fredericktown had lived. It was a moment in town history that would have the people sympathizing with the old geezer and buying an extra paper or two to boot.

The nineteenth's was a good front page that would have the town chatting amicably. Every day, local and regional news flowed into the small office faster than it could be transferred to print. Fredericktown was a busy community, and people were always living and dying, both of which made for good press and idle chatter at local businesses and church socials. This issue was as good as any, and maybe a little better than most.

Suddenly, a young man burst through the door. It was Reginal Graham. His face was pallid, and his eyes were bulging with terror. Beads of perspiration gleamed above his thick eyebrows, and for the moment, he appeared to be deaf and dumb. His shoulders shook violently, and it appeared that he would faint or drop dead smack-dab in front of Oliver Ferguson's desk. The bespectacled editor jumped from behind the desk and grabbed the young man's shoulder.

"What's wrong, Reginal? Here. Sit down and catch your breath."

Oliver kicked a wooden ladder-back chair in the general direction of Reginal's backside and held onto him until the young man slumped into a seated position. No one would be passing out in the newspaper office today. Oliver would be sure of that. His heart raced as he realized that something was terribly amiss to have shaken up the Graham boy this violently. Organizational wheels were spinning at breakneck speed in the editor's head. He had just enough space and time left to manipulate the front-page ensemble of stories to include whatever local crisis had knocked Reginal Graham senseless.

"It's gone! It's gone! Annapolis ...," he bellowed. "Oh ...."

"What's gone, Reginal? What in sam hill are you talking about?"

Reginal lifted his head and glared like a mad dog straight into the eyes of the editor. His gaze was so intense that all the years of covering every imaginable crisis barely prepared Oliver for the nightmarish look that assaulted him in his own office. He took a deep breath and spoke softly.

"Just catch your breath, Reginal. Slow down a little and tell me what you're talking about. Everything's all right now."

The shocked young man looked at the news desk as though the oak grain held some answers to the horror that overwhelmed him. When he resumed his stare at the editor, his eyes were filled with despair and disbelief. Words to explain the events of the last hour were tangled in his throat. He garbled an unintelligible utterance, swallowed, and started again.

"Everything is not all right. A tornado. It was a tornado. It hit Annapolis. Some man just came to our place. He was a yellin' about needin' help, and bleedin' from his head. The whole town of Annapolis is gone, Oliver. There ain't nothin' left."

The editor stared quietly at the young man, and tried to visualize a town the size of Annapolis obliterated by the storm that had passed through Fredericktown only a short time ago. It was certainly possible, but he reasoned that sometimes folks get overly excited. In the middle of frightening events, people in shock tend to believe things are worse than they really are. But he did not question aloud Reginal's assessment. He needed more facts before he could print a story about an entire town being wiped out by wind. He had his doubts. He would need more than the word of a hysterical man who was nowhere near the scene of this reported cyclonic tragedy.

Yet, it was not long before the reports came filing into the newspaper headquarters. Telegrams were delivered to folks around town, and three telegrams came directly to Oliver's attention within what seemed only moments of Reginal's report. It was true. Much work was to be done to get the word out and to decide how neighbors could render assistance. Oliver believed that the best thing he could do for Reginal was to give him some work to do in the middle of the crisis. It would keep the young man sane and productive despite the obvious tragedy that had befallen the friends in neighboring Iron County. In short order, Reginal was relaying reports, telegrams, and telephoned messages from folks all around about the power of the storm that leveled Annapolis.

It was terrifying. Oliver worked in a feverish, mind-swirling fog. His eyes scanned chopped sentence fragments on cream-colored Western Union Telegrams. He barked instructions to Reginal, and his bony fingers flew as he composed the most accurate report possible. After all was said and done, his readers' curiosity would facilitate a thirst for information, with *The Democrat-News* at the center of the county's communication. So much suffering was unimaginable. But, it was verifiable, or would soon be. Oliver's energy swelled with each report that came to his desk. On a normal day, he would work the daylight hours, and his brother Andrew would work late afternoon and evening, putting the paper to bed. Today, the real beds in Annapolis had vanished with a black broom of death that swept the town away or left twisted iron and splintered wood frames piled in vulgar heaps. By night, the beds for the Iron County residents would be the cold floors of Pullman cars for women and children, and a few haphazardly standing buildings for men and boys.

Andrew flew through the door of the newspaper office, shirt

flopping outside his pants, and eyes filled with amazement and daunting fear. They had been spared. Their work was intact. They were called to get the word out and to aid in any way possible. The two brothers did not always agree on editorial priorities, but every day they managed to work out problems of newspaper layout and publishing priorities. They managed business efficiently with shared ownership and co-executive roles. On this day, Andrew scurried around the small, wood-frame building, compiling notes and facts for the next printing. It was understood that errors would occur, as disasters inevitably distort perceptions of reality. The siblings agreed that their ethical responsibility was to do the best they could with what they had. And so they did.

Chaos rained down on eastern Missouri as the facts came together. The Ferguson brothers and the locals pulled together the beginning of the nightmarish report.

"Annapolis was practically wiped out …. We have been unable, before going to press, to trace the progress of the storm in this county farther west than the upper Twelve Mile country, where the Ebenezer schoolhouse was completely demolished." So read the opening paragraphs of *The Democrat-News*.

Illiterate townsfolk would gather around newspaper readers for days to come. They would listen to each word as though their lives depended on the latest reports. This was just the beginning. An awful beginning. Everyone heard unconfirmed rumors of great suffering as the tornado crossed the Mississippi River, but communication was sporadic and severed in many areas. Just as life was cut short for some Missourians to the west, so was information as to the whereabouts of suffering people and destroyed homes and communities far beyond Annapolis. It was more than enough to bear.

The storm damaged Ed Lampher's place. George Cook's car was damaged and he lost a barn as well as his supply of hay. The upper and lower farms of Roscoe Cook had been damaged. Fences were down everywhere. The outbuildings of Cecil Ramey and Mrs. Mae Shrum were damaged. A barn was blown down, and everything on the farm of Wes Cozean was totally wrecked. Hugh Shryock's house was blown off its foundation and would have to be rebuilt. The Prichard house was totally demolished and a cow, a calf, and a horse were killed. Reports of injured people continually filtered into the newspaper office as messages about the Dee Shrum buildings being crushed hit Oliver's desk. Of course, the mine at Leadanna was gone. Orchards were wiped out. Annapolis was clearly the worst hit, but time would show that Biehle had more than twice as many people killed. None of it made sense.

As the hours passed, radio reports indicated that the storm had continued through southern Illinois, but it was impossible to determine how much destruction had occurred.

Some people said it was a twisting wind. Others reported straight-line winds. People were killed all the way down to Cape Girardeau. Death and destruction were everywhere, or so it seemed. It was as though a hidden hand of evil brushed the face of the earth. It was the same hand that wrenched the life out of good citizens who only hours earlier talked cheerfully about the upcoming spelling contest.

The ones who lived through the destruction would struggle for years before finding safety and joy in the pleasure of a county spelling bee. Now the spelling bee was of no more import than the smallest complaint about flowers not budding the way they should. There would be beautiful life in the ravaged area again. But lives would not be spared weeks and months of children's sobbing in night's dark shadows. Oliver and Andrew wiped their eyes on their shirtsleeves as the first news coverage was laid in print on the night of March 18, 1925.

18

Elena shivered unexpectedly as she crossed the Mississippi at Cape
Girardeau. It was embarrassing not to know the correct pronunciation
of the town's name. What if she had to say it to one of the locals? Some
writer she was. It was not self-doubt that underlay the momentary
tremble. It was fear that muffled the repeated recitation of "Girardeau"
in her brain. Fear had been carried over from the black cloud threat of
Fredericktown. It also had carried over from some distant memory of
the Silver Bridge collapse in Point Pleasant. She could not afford to lose
her composure while hovering nervously above the waters that could
engulf her before she managed to crawl out the window of the minivan.
If she had to die, would death by tornado be preferable? Strange
alternatives. Horrible deaths. She had no choice. When her time came,
it would. Just like Sam. It was that simple … or was it?

"Not here," she whispered.

But, the Mighty Mississippi is wide water, and big rigs were a
heavy load for the bridge they shared, as she eyed the grassy banks of
the Illinois side. Touching tires on solid ground would feel peculiarly
reassuring. Anxiety had caught her off guard. Somewhere she had read
that the fear of bridges—gephyrophobia—compelled some people
to hire professional drivers to maneuver their vehicles over churning
waters. At least she was driving for herself. Engineers. MANmade.
Army Corps. All were loaded with heavy connotations of fallibility,
a notion which intermittently tormented unsuspecting victims
and phobics alike. She had yet to meet a woman engineer whose
responsibility it was to build bridges, and she wondered if a mother
would demand extra precautions when it came to securing suspended
surfaces over which her school-age children passed.

Kids are so trusting. They believe, at some fundamental level,
that grownups will know what to do to protect them. Mamas are
instinctively gifted protectors of little ones. So it registers in the sweet

little heads of smiling babes. It must have been like that in '25.

Only yesterday, Elena herself had smiled as little girls jumped rope on the side streets of Annapolis. They surely knew nothing of cloud rotation in Fredericktown. Would they know what to do? Were there sirens in Annapolis? Would the playmates scurry to safe basements of nearby homes or be hurled mercilessly into a tumult of airborne trees, fence posts, and chairs? Would they ignore the sirens, knowing that the sounds were so frequently part of their routine that they were no more significant than cars driving through the heart of town? But, if it happened ....

The scratching blare of the NOAA radio suddenly jolted Elena back to the Cape. In mere moments she was driving through town heading north toward Gorham. Repeated broadcast admonitions for spotters about an unstable air mass had the strange effect of simultaneously startling her and reassuring her. Finally, reports were active and continuous. Good. She knew and understood all too well the meteorological events that were coming to the heart of historic southern Illinois. According to the reports about forthcoming violent storms, she would need to have a strong sense of place tomorrow. She had a day to plan. Plenty of time. Her first thought was to settle into one centrally located hotel that would be her base camp for the next few days of research.

Once she got to Gorham, Elena would pull out the Illinois road map and plot her home place in the center of cyclone country. Her faith in the portable-radio alarm system welled. The signal was strong, and she knew she would have time to take shelter, if necessary. A smile spread across her pretty mug. She was close to the pulsating core of the disaster. Such beautiful country. It was lovely.

"I could live here in a heartbeat," she whispered.

Gorham was a surprise. Like many small towns of the Midwest, it seemed to be situated in a field of crops—like an earth island surrounded by vast miles of space and greenery. Elena saw the sign for the town and smiled thoughtfully. First Street was on her left. The railroad ran parallel to her paved path. The monster had been here. She knew that every town she would enter for the next hundred miles would echo solemn memories of a tragedy so distant that they hardly seemed real.

In fact, with the sun beaming through the windshield and bouncing a reflection of the dash onto her sunglasses, common sense told her it had probably been a fluke or a gross exaggeration. It simply was not possible for such fierce ripping torrents of air to rend the hearts of unsuspecting, hardworking folks. But was it not yesterday that she fled bulging, low, black clouds in quest of shelter? Had vile clouds not descended in a matter of moments? This was one hell of a roller coaster ride. No wonder some of these people lived in trailers with no basements. It was too easy to forget. Elena was already washed in a film of overconfidence.

Neatly mowed lawns of flatland were manicured like miniature parks for each homeowner. Someone had done a lovely job with the first marker Elena saw. She was in the right spot of flatland near the mighty Mississippi. It was not the traditional, little green town sign that she was used to seeing in similar-sized communities of West Virginia. Here, in this sunlit stillness, a craftsman or woman had artistically arched the words on a curved, solid-wood display that prominently extended greetings to anyone arriving in the once devastated community. Reddish-orange flowers had been meticulously manicured beneath the white and burgundy background of decorative beige lettering: Welcome to Gorham.

Low-lying flowering shrubs dotted the grassy margin between the road and the elevated tracks of the railroad line. It was peaceful here. No sign of violence, although Elena understood all too well how deceiving looks can be. We all decorate masks of one sort or another. Police officers who batter wives know how to inflict excruciating pain while leaving no marks as "proof" of assault. Serial killers live quietly and unobtrusively in small towns where they blend sweetly with the locals who say, "He was such a good neighbor … never bothered anyone." Not too much anyway. Cervical cancer cells masquerade as normalcy in the day-to-day routine of twenty-year-olds. Plain looking country girls manipulate foundation creams, coloring sticks, and eyeliners to create an image of beauty where no beauty exists.

Newspaper reporters are trained to secure the trust of old people in order to get the exclusives. They sit on the front porches of rotting houses, sipping lemonade with tottery old men. With microscopic precision, they excavate painful memories of days that victims bury in the deepest canyons of crackling brains. It all comes back. The reporter gets the story, and the old man is never visited again. Grandmas sign away their money to con artists and bloodsucking relatives who promise to take care of them. U.S. Army MPs fall in love and allow beautiful women to abscond with $50,000 in credit-card purchases. The schemers move on to collaborate with their accomplice boyfriends for the next "hit." Ex-cons boohoo about how much they have suffered and relish in the rewarding embrace of giddy female bank officers who forget they are being trained how to identify professional thieves. Conned by a con. All fakery.

Elena was too cynical for her own good, she thought. Such was the nature of the publishing business. Such was the nature of people. Everyone puts on a positive face for everything that truly matters in life. Human beings intuitively recognize their faults and compensate by instigating exquisite fraud. Universities teach students how to create a "good impression" for job interviews because an authentic representation of people, with all their warts and battle scars, is not good enough for the best opportunities. Communication studies professors teach "affinity-seeking strategies," so that students can manipulate people into believing they are something they can never be. Perfect. Small-town signs are disingenuous. So fellow reporter Jerry would say.

It was clear, here in the heart of Tornado Alley. As clear as the blue sky arching over the vast cornfields around her. Elena's objectivity and distrust were learned. It made her cautious when driving into a small Illinois town with West Virginia plates. As she pondered the risks of invasion into the hearts of people who were going about their daily lives, she promised herself she must get a Confederate flag window decal for her future assignments down in the mountains of her home state.

Now that she knew where the self-proclaimed, God-fearing Nazis homed in the exquisite hills of the Monongahela National Forest, an

NRA bumper sticker would bellow her militaristic allegiance façade in territory where a lone woman could be an easy target. Concessions like these were sickening, but necessary for self-defense … trust acquisition … and exclusive stories. It was the nature of the job, and no ethics were violated. Not for a good writer and reporter. It was not as if she were a bona fide, card-carrying, mindless paparazzo. She knew she was Little Red Riding Hood in a Windstar. The magnetic American flag slapped onto the hatchback door was corny, but necessary in God's country. So far, so good. Except for the bored Annapolis cop who had nothing more to do than harass out-of-town writers.

"Log out of my own eye," she whispered. "Oh, God!"

The view of the Gorham school smacked her like a ball bat between the eyes. Now she was in the moment.

"What the Hell? They were hit again?"

The school building was the biggest structure in the very small town. Windows were blown out or boarded over. Debris, consisting of bricks and boards, was strewn at the base of Gorham High School. Graffiti marred the sacred walls of learning. The grass was scruffy and the air smelled mysteriously pungent although it was the same air that greeted her only a couple blocks up the road.

She had already seen a few roofless, crumpling barns in Tornado Alley. They looked as though they might have succumbed to wind damage of some sort. They did not resemble the decaying, abandoned barns and farmhouses that dotted her Appalachian countryside. The structural damage was different. Roofs were gone. Walls had collapsed haphazardly into standing stalls. In spite of the knee-jerk reactions that bade her to stop and ask questions, Elena hesitated to approach people directly who may or may not have been able to raze the remains of sheds and cow shelters. Besides, her time was limited, and her budget was tight. She had to keep moving.

Here in Gorham, the high school was in need of a good razing. What had happened? Elena had the sinking feeling that she was closer to disaster than she wanted to be. Sadness choked her, until she felt as though her throat would swell shut. She struggled to keep her objectivity.

"Maybe, it's just an abandoned school."

The modern school administration trend is to consolidate, consolidate, and consolidate, notwithstanding the objections of parents who know better than elitist school board members. That would be the subject of her next feature story—after she wrestled with this one. This was a huge self-appointed assignment, so much more demanding than she had imagined. The distance, the costs, and the enormous power of the 1925 storm were bigger than her expectations. Something about this opportunity was engulfing her, as though the storm itself were wrapping savage winds around her soul.

The yellow-brick ghost school was the only thing of great import in Gorham, for the moment. If the town had a restaurant, she did not see it. Had the old restaurant reopened after 1925? Maybe. Today, there appeared to be no place to pause for reflection, contemplation, note-taking, and food. She saw no obvious presence of approachable people at the moment. Even the train tracks were silent.

Elena was hungry. Murphysboro was a stone's throw up the road. She knew there would be opportunity for food, conversation, rest, and creativity in the town that took the brunt of the tornado. She spun around the Windstar in the gravel margin below the railroad tracks, and skirted at thirty-five miles an hour along the gray road out of town. McDonald's would do and would certainly fit into her budget if that were the first eating spot she found in Murphysboro. She pulled the van off the road long enough to shoot a few pictures of Gorham. Elena hated to leave, but she had to keep moving. She could find detailed newspaper accounts at Murphysboro's library and the Historical Society. The news of '25 would fill in the gaps and answer questions about Gorham's horrific experience. Her thoughts were scrambled, and questions were multiplying exponentially. But getting answers was overridden by the most important demand of the moment: food in the stomach.

19

2:37 p.m., March 18, 1925, Restaurant in Gorham, Illinois. When
Judith came to, she could see sky straight out from her eyes. The
bellowing moan of a distressed cow was as near to her as her scrambled
eggs and fried potatoes had been just a few minutes earlier. She could
hear the muffled sound of men's voices hollering orders and yelling for
help, all at the same time. The screams of distant children hit her ears in
faint piercing punches. Stunned and bewildered, she reckoned she had
just been standing in the doorway of the café when the trains collided
or something. Her legs were numb, and she felt the weight of timbers
piled atop her torso as casually as Fred had stacked the morning dishes
on the sideboard in the kitchen. She tried to call out, but the braying
cow commanded what was left of the room where townsfolk gathered
every weekday for a bite to eat.

"Move these boards! Help me! Help …!" a man barked.

"There's a cow in here! Get it out!" another voice yelled. "Get it out!"

Judith listened with amazement. It was some kind of crazy dream in
the middle of broad daylight. Suddenly, planks of oak shifted abruptly
and pressed against the woman's left arm as the cow kicked fiercely
in unrelenting panic. The bovine kicked harder and brayed with ear-
piercing pleas as she gave her best to break free from the strewn lumber,
broken walls, tables, and dishes piled atop her. Judith groaned with each
shift in the cow's weight amidst the rubble. Lord, there was a cow in
the restaurant. Dear Lord, it was beside her. A cow had not been in the
restaurant when she stood in the doorway two minutes earlier.

"Move these boards! Help me! Get this cow outta here," a man
growled.

As Gorham men dug with their bare hands to pull boards and
tables off the dairy cow and Judith, screams of absolute despair filled
the village air. In only a matter of minutes, the bellowing air had
welled louder and louder with heart-wrenching cries. Suddenly, the

haphazardly flung boards of the restaurant walls shifted wildly as the cow rose to her feet and barreled toward the center of what had been the main road through town.

"Help me," Judith yelled.

Her plea was not necessary. The men had already seen her wavy hair beneath the brown planks, and they were digging furiously to relieve the crumbled restaurant press that threatened to squash the stunned woman. Gradually, the pressure eased, and two burly men with wildly hysterical eyes wrapped their arms under her legs and back, tugging at her until they had moved her to a crouching posture on a small, bare space of the floor.

"Ma'am, you all right? Are you hurtin' anywhere?" one asked.

"..uh ... I ... uh ... think I'm all right," she mumbled. "Was there a cow? I think I heard a cow ... What in the world ... I hear children ...."

The broad-shouldered man nodded and briefly brushed back hair from Judith's eyes. He was almost as numb as she, but what had happened to the town, in nothing more than a few moments, was coming into focus. Tears welled on the rims of sagging eyelids as he stumbled to put together some sense in the middle of unrelenting chaos. A lonesome moan welled in his throat, and he stared into the road where pans, clothes, boards, bricks, trees, glass, and lifeless bodies ... were strewn. A leg with no one attached was the bloody object of his gaze. His chin trembled as the horror of all he saw pummeled him with shards of agony.

"It was a cyclone, ma'am. The cow fell through the roof ... the cyclone let go of it right above us. Gorham is gone. It's gone—the children at school didn't have a chance to no more shelter than we did. We need to get to them. If you can manage on your own, we'll head over the way to try to help them. Can you stand? Is anything broken?"

Judith sighed, but sought courage even as she contemplated her complete bewilderment. She could do for herself as needed. She was alive. Just shaken up. She wanted him to stay with her, but she realized plainly that would be the wrong thing to expect. Part of her hoped he was injured. If his leg were smashed, he could not leave. Good God! There were children out there! What could she possibly be thinking! She had no need so great as to withhold comfort from little ones who cried out for comfort. She stared at the horrified eyes of her rescuer and nodded with all the strength she could muster. She lifted her shoulders by using her skinned elbows for leverage. Blood dripped from her right forearm, but as soon as she had she seen it, a girl from nowhere wrapped a curtain panel around it, managing to shut off the oozing scarlet fluid. Her body cried for comfort, but the children cried louder.

A cyclone. Was that the noise? Yes. She remembered now. She had heard a loud roar and then went to the door to see what all the commotion was about. The train tracks were lined with boxcars, but there was no sign of an oncoming engine. Without a second's notice, she had felt an invisible force shove her backwards into the small restaurant. She thought she remembered her feet coming off the ground but was not truly certain of exactly what had happened. She did know that she had wanted to run as far as she could, but the powerful hand of nature had other plans. The next thing she knew, she woke up, half-buried underneath planks, broken porcelain, and tin pans with a misplaced cow kicking furiously inside the rubble. Now she stood alone trying to figure out what to do next.

It did not take long to register the wails of pure anguish streaking through the air of the small town. With one foot strategically placed in front of its mate, she moved in the general direction of the Gorham school building. People were running all around her, but her ringing ears and dull head precluded her moving at a pace faster than a stunned slug. She froze for a moment, staring at all eleven boxcars that now were twisted and piled crazily beside the rail line. Wind alone could not possibly have caused all the disorder and suffering that enveloped her.

She stopped dead in her tracks as the sight of the collapsed school building came into focus. Bricks, mortar, glass, and papers were piled and scattered on the grassy lawn where children took recess every day at lunchtime. On this particular day, they had played chalkboard games and exercised inside the long corridors while gray rain drizzled outside the tan building. They never saw the likelihood of such devastation any more than did their teachers.

A little boy staggered in Judith's direction. She bowed forward instinctively and wrapped her arms around him. A crimson scrape across his right cheek was the only sign of injury she could see, but his eyes were glazed with fear and absolute bewilderment. As he looked up at her, tears poured down his dirty face. He clutched her waistline with such intensity that Judith feared she would lose her balance, fall, and hurt the two of them worse than they were already. She moved her right foot in the direction of where the town store had been, forcing herself to stand steadily for the young man.

"Mama," he cried, "Mama ...."

Judith shuddered and choked back her own tears. She had to be confident. Her thoughts were coming together, and she forced herself to assume a demeanor of strength and determination. It was her duty to help him and anyone else she could find in the rubble.

"I'll help you find your mama. Don't be afraid. I won't leave you," she whispered.

"I live on First Street," he bellowed. "My Mama is fixin' stew today. We're havin' it fer supper. I gotta get home."

The two new friends desperately clutched each other as they gazed in the general direction of where his home should have been. There was no sign of a woman who could have been the young lad's mother. There was no sign of anything.

"I won't leave you," Judith whispered again.

But it was little consolation for the third grader. He broke loose and bellowed an ungodly scream for his Mama. He sprinted toward a vacant street that held nothing for him but bare earth. Not even the grass was left in the tiny front yard. The monster vortex had consumed everything along First Street, right down to the roots of every plant and buried fence post. Judith suddenly found a burst of energy in her soul that propelled her toward the frantic child. She reached out for him as his bony legs crumpled underneath the weight of wrenching despair.

"Stay with me," she pleaded. "We'll keep looking for your Mama. We'll keep looking …."

She knew it was futile to hope for a positive outcome, but she had to keep her wits about her and hold onto her new friend. Together they would find answers to the awful questions pounding in their chests. Where was everyone? How could this happen? Where were their friends? Neighbors? Family? What to do now? What to do?

The boy and his schoolmates would later recall that their teacher vehemently ordered them away from black windows and to their respective desks. Suddenly the walls began to cave in, children in desks tilted crazily, and everyone screamed while they skated uncontrollably across the sloped floorboards. Glass and bricks pounded their arms, legs, and heads. Many would remember the screaming as the edifice wavered and collapsed in the black storm. It was not the walls that mattered. It was the good people of Gorham that mattered.

The New York Times would report seventy fatalities in Gorham. Later the official count would be thirty-four. Yet any intelligent person would realize that the death count was indeterminable. There was time only to live, not time to count the dead with meticulous accuracy. Bodies were stacked in a temporary morgue, the basement of Gorham School. The first floor had remained intact, serving as a roof for the grim body-storage room. Some of the dead were sent to Cairo for burial. Others were hauled in new boxcars to Saint Louis. It was impossible to know who was gone from the rustic community. Over half the townsfolk were either dead or injured. Outside medical help would arrive hours later only to find distressed villagers managing the best they could, rendering aid to each other.

That early afternoon, Judith held tight to a young man, whose name escaped her as readily as the town's buildings escaped their foundations. The duo rendered first aid to the broken limbs of suffering neighbors and friends who were totally or half-buried in the street of the obliterated town they had loved.

At the site of the Gorham school, a skinny woman in her late twenties called out for her son. She had walked to the post office some time around 12:20. A few moments later, she pushed the postmaster's shattered body from atop her. The school was all she had on her mind. She stood tall and strong beside yellow-brick heaps. The woman called out frantically for a third grader who had run through the street only moments before she could reach the crumbled mass.

"Jimmy! Jimmy! Where are you? It's Mama. I'm here Jimmy!"

20

Elena soaked in the cool air of McDonald's air-conditioning as she munched on the ketchup-covered cheeseburger. Part of her brain counted toward twenty-five chews as she tried her best not to wolf down food that would pile on the pounds quickly if she were not careful. Eighteen … nineteen …. Some days the slower eating worked well for on-the-road dining. On other days, it was a tedious distraction from facts she did not want to face. Today was that day. The part of her brain that was not counting sensed a solemn and enormous power like none she had ever encountered. This was where the heart of the storm generated its most evil throttle. The rebuilt town with little houses undergirded with block basements had a surreal quality. Basements … conceived after the storm. On one hand, Murphysboro was where Ozzie and Harriet could have lived. On the other hand, the streets held memories that hovered like historic shrouds, never to be forgotten. This was it. The vile soul of the tornado had raged here.

Elena sipped the 1% milk through the red plastic straw and wondered where to go next. Clearly she needed to spend a few days in the area. She would drive to the Sallie Logan Public Library, where she hoped to uncover archives by the hundreds. The Jackson County Historical society was nearby. It would be difficult to manage time here efficiently. There probably was entirely too much information to fathom. She would start at the library, get a feel for the files, and move on to the Historical Society the next day or two. But before doing the archive work, she wanted to get a sense of the community. How had the parents and grandparents of current residents pulled the town back together after the tornado and the successive fires that irreconcilably destroyed lives and homes? Some sense of dread shook her. Could history repeat itself? It often does. It was one thing to relish historic fact. It was another to live it.

The rattling sound of air and milk gurgling through the straw brought her back to the present. She felt safe. People were going about their workday with no regard for Elena's fantasized storms. She was convinced that nothing bad would happen here. The lawns were emerald green and the flowers were abundantly placed at the edges of homes, paved sidewalks, and businesses. This was a town secure in its place on the American map. It was an ideal place to live, no doubt. She had a warm feeling, even without meeting any of the good citizens of Murphysboro.

With the crackling paper wrapper and milk bottle deposited in Micky D's brown trash bin, Elena moved enthusiastically toward the Windstar. It was time to see the community where unspeakable suffering fell atop innocents whose ghosts lingered along now beautiful, tree-lined streets. She wished she had a week, but she knew that only a few days could be allotted to the history of the town. This was the community where 1,000 Boy Scouts had descended in droves to aid the American Red Cross in rescue and recovery efforts of storm victims. But not today.

It was more to comprehend than Elena's experience could approximate. What phrases could make this story plausible? Imaginable? The archives might tell it all for her and her readers. She hoped she could find the right words to do the town justice. For a moment, she doubted the possibility of conveying such horror with compelling linguistic portraits. What terror-filled faces could she paint with words? How could she convey dignity for those who died and suffered while describing details of the greatest tornadic assault in history? What did the townsfolk see? How could their experience be understood through mere verbal symbols? It was a challenge, and one that swelled her chest with absolute conviction as she drove toward Spruce Street. She would walk where schoolchildren stumbled. She would stand where devastated neighbors of all ages staggered for a sense of place and sanity in the midst of Hell.

Elena found a tree-shaded spot and maneuvered the van into the cool shadow. After cracking the front windows, she grabbed her notepad and slipped quietly from the vehicle. A middle-aged man was sweeping his sidewalk and looked at her curiously. She strolled confidently in the opposite direction, leaving him to wonder who she was and why she was in his neighborhood. She usually assumed a friendly persona in strange towns, but today, a whimsical feeling of mystery guided her steps. It was all right to leave a few people wondering about her presence. Somehow, the sweeper did not pose a threat as had the Annapolis cop with his insidious stalking behavior. Elena liked controversy, almost as much as she liked compelling natural phenomena. This was a fantastic trip.

But it was more than a feeling of mystery that moved her. It was the large, beige, brick building and the bronze, marble-like monument looming to her right that were drawing her across the street. She barely glanced over her shoulder to guard for oncoming traffic. It was quiet except for the man sweeping away behind her. There was a feeling here—a deep sense of some presence that pulled her inevitably toward the grassy lawn. What was it?

The building, clearly, was a school that bore an astonishing resemblance to her own high school alma mater. Yet its design and structure were strongly reminiscent of tornado pictures she had seen very recently. The building was strikingly similar to one of the schools that was pounded horrifically by three minutes of tumultuous air in 1925. Somewhere in the gray-toned photographs she had already logged was a bombed-out building that looked just like this one. The bomb was a tornado. The school was somewhere in Murphysboro. Was this a school that had been rebuilt? Was this the spot where students died as brick walls collapsed and floors plummeted onto skulls of innocent, unsuspecting readers in study hall?

"Oh, dear God …, she whispered. "I don't understand. I don't …."

She glanced at a bronze representation of some General John A. Logan. Logan was everywhere: school names, library names, street names. Here, he presided over the front lawn of Murphysboro Middle School. Logan was beside the point. Something had happened here that had nothing to do with either his memory or his glory.

She did not know what it was. She felt it. Something awful, and something wonderful, happened on every Murphysboro street along which she would stroll. It was as quiet on Spruce Street as it was at a Quaker worship service. Oh, for the prayers of Quakers on that day. She had nothing to say. Elena squinted and glanced over her shoulder to see if sweeper man could see her tears.

21

<u>2:20 p.m., May 18, 1925, Murphysboro, Illinois.</u> They were in study hall. They were at recess. They were in physical education class. They would run for their lives. These were the children of Murphysboro. Small children, gangly youth, and nearly adult teenagers would be stunned, mangled, dismembered, impaled, crushed, and in too many cases, slaughtered unmercifully by the voracious monster. It happened with a minute's warning. The sky would turn black as night. Later, written accounts of the mile-wide, lethal, ground-scraping cloud would portray the monster as an ebon sky ravaging the earth. The tornado had no funnel. It was far vaster than a funnel. It was Hell.

The schools of Murphysboro were in the direct path of the afternoon storm. This storm was seen as nothing more than a spring storm, like every other one that was slowly emerging from winter's grasp. The air was clear enough for play. Children were outside tipping up and down on teeter-totters and swishing with stiffly extended legs that punched through the air from oak-board swings. Older boys cracked balls against wooden bats on a makeshift diamond at Logan Grade School. They were on North 14th Street, only a few blocks from their homes. Shrieks of exhilaration filled the air as the clever, grade-school children ran full speed away from "It" in a game of tag.

A fast-running boy yelled at a little girl with carrot-colored, braided hair, "Tag! You're IT! You're IT! You're IT!"

His skinny, long fingers had brushed her right pigtail. Six other screamers doubled over, catching their breath, knowing they had a short reprieve from the chase.

The red-headed girl giggled, doubled over holding her sides with crossed arms, and nodded in conciliation that the role reversal would occur. She waved her hand in the air as though to say, "All right, all right … you got me. Just let me catch my breath. Then I'll catch you back!"

Two teachers smiled from the edge of the lawn, supervising the play, lest it get too rough for the little ones. They wistfully reminisced about their own laughter in the many games of tag they had played as youngsters. On some days the young lady with bobbed brown hair would break out of her role as teacher and join the hilarity of tag with children too sweet to imagine heartache in the midst of frivolity. She was prim and proper as a teacher when demonstrating how to print letters and add or take away numbers. But she was not afraid of laughing and frolicking with the children she loved so much. Recess was always a time for laughter. Ecclesiastes asserted as much. A time to laugh. A time to cry. Little did she know, a lifetime of tears awaited her laughing brood.

Tressia Schmallenberger positioned herself at the maple tree Base, and shouted at the top of her lungs, "Ready ... GO!"

Playmates, who had been frozen in place while gasping in huge bellows of stifling spring air, escalated the screaming once more and ran helter-skelter. The squeals were like sweet music to the teacher with close-cropped hair. She stepped forward to join the game but stepped back again as quickly as she had moved toward the delightfully agitated, screaming children. Only a few moments of recess were left, and she had a cautious eye on the dark clouds forming in the north. If a storm were brewing, she would need to maintain her authority to line up the students to enter the safety of the brick school. There would be other days to play tag with her Scallywag Gang.

Eugene Porter was the first one to make it to the maple tree, smacking its trunk with the flat of his hand while yelling, "Safe!"

Next came Martha Bowerman.

"Safe! I'm safe!" she bellowed as she extended her skinny fingers to touch the old maple bark.

She would not be safe for long. The sky grew darker with extraordinary efficiency. Suddenly, the skinny teacher vigorously shook the small, brass handbell. All the children stopped dead in their tracks. Play was over before the assembly had a prayer's chance to tag the tree or be tagged by Tressia. Still, there was an understanding that the game of chase would resume the next day, with Tressia leading the way as "It." No one wanted recess to end, but recess always ended. They would pound more book learning into their scrawny noggins for the rest of the afternoon and meander to their homes for chores and supper, and then for homework of reading, writing, and cyphering. They were smart kids. Every one of them. Although they all occasionally wearied of studies, they relished opportunities to play every weekday with the Scallywag Gang. It was a good trade and a fair one. A time to work. A time to play.

Blackish clouds to the north and west were ominous and unusually positioned over the town of 15,000. The two schoolmarms whipped their heads back and forth, briefly studying the southwest sky and then jerking their faces toward the north darkness. Lightning was visible in the distance, and they knew there was no time to delay. Whatever this storm pattern was, it was out of character and threatening all the same. The heavyset teacher clapped her hands against each other, sounding as though she were cracking a bullwhip rather than making contact of one hand sharply against the other. She cracked her hands again three times, and the children gummed their lips together, knowing she meant business.

"Line up!" she blared.

The boys fell into single file at the Boys Door, and the girls did the same at their respective door. Each day they marched like silent soldiers with stiff shoulders and solemn faces into the two-story, brick Logan School. That was the procedure, and none of the students wondered anything unusual as recess was only a few moments short of the full half-hour scheduled playtime. A ping of hail sheared past the tallest boy's head. Then another. And another.

"To your classrooms, quickly!" the schoolmarm barked. "NO RUNNING!"

Two older girls winked at each other, trying their best to stifle giggles that would surely land them with their noses in the corner if laughter burst out of their toothy mouths in the middle of the silent march. Mary and Barbara were best friends who spent every spare moment writing poems and then reading them to each other.

When the opportunity to write did not present itself, they talked about boys. Who would marry whom? Where would they live? Every day was a dream about the future, their hopes for lovely homes with handsome husbands, and the poetry book they would write together. They would be just like Miss Emily Dickinson, only they would never shut themselves away from the world or from each other. They would always be friends and literary colleagues. They would write beautiful odes to dear friends and loved ones that made their lives secure and reasonably content. There would be afternoon teas and time in the cool evenings to compose lovely lyrics for the world to savor. In the meantime, Mary and Barbara obeyed the teacher's rules and minded admonitions to work hard for rewards which they were promised lay ahead of them.

Suddenly, a loud crash shattered the silence. Barbara looked up and floated into a dreamlike trance as she watched sparkling shards of glass floating in slow motion overhead. She had no idea what was happening. Then, screams punctured the air of the long hallways. Some children froze and stared at the night that had gathered outside. Glassless openings had replaced windows, and stings of glass crystals stung the faces and arms of the tallest students. Some children ran. Others froze in place, unable to contemplate their fate or the safest response to flying glass. The student soldiers were children once again. They were together, but lost all the same. A formidable power had descended and engulfed the beautiful world of Logan School.

Mary hardly felt the tug of slashed skin that dangled above her right elbow. She turned to see Barbara wincing as brittle pieces of windowpane punctured her friend's face and scalp. Dots of red fluid oozed where only skin should have glowed. The rules be damned. They needed something between them and the cyclone's sweeping surge.

The other students' faces faded into the background as though their small lives were clouded by a sheer curtain panel. Nothing else mattered.

Mary and Barbara clasped hands, running toward the desks bolted to the floor in the fifth grade room. It was not their room, but it was the closest hope for shelter. Mary pulled loose.

"There! Let's get there! That wall is strong! Barbara ...."

But the rolling bellow of a thousand black trains drowned out the high-pitched plea. Her lanky friend was already balled underneath a side-row desk and could not free herself in time to make it with Mary to the outer brick wall. Mary cowered low in the corner, crying out for her friend, when horror overwhelmed every soul in the schoolhouse. Plank floors snapped like wooden toothpicks in the clenched mouth of Satan, and a roaring rumble of heavy walls exploded from the roof to the first floor.

Planks tilted sideways, throwing little bodies to and fro like dandelion seeds tossed by a breeze. Barbara held fast to the iron legs of the desk as debris as small as splinters and as large as bricks pelted and punctured her. It was as if bullets shot from all directions at once. She heard nothing and gasped in a desperate effort to get oxygen into her lungs. For a minute-and-a-half, she was completely alone, barely able to comprehend the power that seized her world. Suddenly, the wind stopped and rain poured into what little remained of the schoolhouse.

Only God knew where the roof was. The windows had been the first casualty of the pseudo-stalwart building. Not a sign of paned openings anywhere was to be seen. Only sparkling shards glimmered ironically amidst broken bricks, splintered boards, scattered books, spurned papers, and bloody children. The walls had crumbled into a pile of rubble that no one could have imagined mere minutes before. And then the screams. Then too, the silence ....

Eight-year-old Tommy Abbott was frozen in total terror as he found himself clinging to the highest remaining limb of the maple tree where the Gang had played tag. Tag was the last thing he remembered doing. Now, he was hanging in the tree. He was not even sure that he was safe. But he was conscious, and he had enough wits to hold on for dear life. How he got there was a total mystery. He knew only that he had to hold tight, lest he be carried to Franklin County by the next bout of winds he feared was on the horizon.

He looked down to see a misplaced two-by-four protruding from the trunk beneath him. Tommy knew with certainty that the tree did not contain a board inside it. He would have seen it at recess. He stared, as though looking at it would make it go away. It did not. Farther down on the ground, he saw two men with outstretched arms clasping children who were climbing down from what remained of the second floor on the east side of the school. At the other end of the building were only haphazardly piled bricks and lumber, with broken arms and legs jutting from the rubble, along with sky where walls should have been.

Desperate mothers were running toward the broken classrooms. More men gradually came and began digging with bare hands through the bricks. Slowly, a cortege of shaky children climbed down from the jumbled lumber and masonry mountain. One at a time they stumbled, while frantically clutching the hands and arms of their rescuers. One man cradled a little girl gently in his arms and took easy, confident strides down the brick mountain to safety.

Tommy saw a familiar, older girl emerge from the brick pile. She was the one who walked around with a pencil stuck behind her ear. That was the girl who was always reading her poems, whether he wanted to hear them or not. Now she was crying, but walking on her own. In the middle of the clamor of frightened, hurt children and the cries of overwrought parents, he thought he heard Barbara shouting for Mary, that other girl who read poems too. He looked for Mary in the small assembly of students emerging from the wrecked school. She was nowhere to be seen.

Could he disappear too? He had an alarming sense that no one would look for him at the top of the tree. The children who were being saved were buried or nearly buried by brick and mortar. Surely, he would not die at the top of the tree. He could not die there.

"Help!" he shouted. "Help me, please … help!"

Confusion reigned everywhere. His voice was not strong enough to obtain even a nod from the rescuers below him. Then he looked beyond Logan School. No wonder no one paid attention to him. The town was crumbled, ravaged, strewn in every which way, and in places on fire. This tree could burn down with him in it. No one would ever know that he had not been blown to Franklin County. All he could do was shout. So he did … until his mother and father called up to him from the walkway below. He was safe.

22

2:45 p.m., May 18, 1925, Murphysboro, Illinois. Eugene Porter
climbed down from the second story of Logan School. The people
around him were shadowed by a view that was stunning and distracting.
His thoughts were jumbled. All he knew to do was to go home. School
was out, and there was no purpose in staying at the collapsed brick
edifice. Children around him had begun to scatter in a frantic effort
to get to safety. Hysteria prevailed, but Eugene's head throbbed from
some blow that had been struck as he huddled near the blackboard in
the sixth grade classroom. He gently pressed his right hand against
a baseball-size knot on his forehead. He would have a whopper of a
headache when the shock wore off.

Sluggishly, he placed one foot in front of the other and moved
toward the street that would take him home. Each step produced pain
that struck him as being odd. He hurt in places he never knew he could
hurt. Standing still was worse. Standing still gave him time to imagine
dying. This would not be his day to die, if he had anything to do with
it. He had to move. Slowly and painfully, he plodded through heaps
of boards, downed electric power lines, splattered food, boxes, boards,
furniture, and occasional dead people.

He passed another boy who stood motionless in the middle of
what had been a passable street. Twelve-year-old Jack was shivering
and crying, but Eugene did not know what to do any more than the
other boy did. A tall man walked toward Jack, pulled off a heavy black
coat and tugged at the sixth grader's arms, pulling them through sleeves
that hung a foot below the boy's hands. The tail of the coat fell to the
rubbled ground on which he stood. It was a comforting gesture which
would help fend off shock, but answered none of the youth's questions.
What to do … what to do…?

Eugene pressed on. He had to get home. He would be safe there.
After trudging for what seemed hours, he reached what was left of the

family's little white house. He stared at destruction in every direction and wondered what to do. He was in no better shape than Jack. Nothing made sense, except to keep moving. Within moments, he found himself staggering away from home and back toward the Logan School. If he kept moving, he would be all right. As he neared the wrecked schoolhouse from which he had only minutes before escaped, a woman with blood all over her grabbed his arms.

"Eugene Porter, have you seen my boy, Jerry?"

Her eyes looked like they would pop out of her head if he could not account for her missing son. Eugene stared at the blood and, at that moment, realized that he too was bleeding just above his right eye. He had not felt it since his feet were back on solid ground. A numbness had set in and protected him from any discomfort and indecision about mending torn skin. The dear woman's face was twisted into a terrifying expression of total hysteria. She shook him gently and repeated her plea.

"I said, have you seen my boy? You know, my boy Jerry, you seen him?"

"Yes ... ma'am..." he spoke softly.

Eugene stared at the lady's eyes and knew he had to tell her where her boy was. She would not release his arms if he did not tell her where Jerry was. His lips parted slowly, and he searched for words to speak as broken buildings and snapped trees and running, crying children appeared faintly in the background where they should be playing tag tomorrow. He would yell, so that he would have to tell the crazy woman only one time. That would be best.

Eugene inhaled a deep breath of air that was somehow tainted with smoke, dust, and odors he could not decipher. For a brief moment, his eyes flickered away from the woman's stare. Then, with all the determination he could muster, he stared her straight in the eyes.

"YEAH! HE WAS KILLED," he shouted.

He felt his own eyelids widen, as they mirrored the distraught mother. Mrs. Grofsen released her grip on his arms, but Eugene was now uncertain that her response was the one he wanted. Her arms stretched toward Heaven as her wild eyes wrinkled in a tightly closed state of helplessness. A bloodcurdling scream surged from within her pathetic body as she fell to her knees. It was more than she could stand. At that very minute, she had no idea that she would not be alone in her state of being overwhelmed by too much suffering. Other children were gone from the lives of parents, siblings, and neighbors of Murphysboro. Other schools were in the cyclonic path.

Just two blocks from Logan School was located the stately Murphysboro Township High School. Jack's sister, Thelma, had donned her white middy blouse, black bloomers, and tennis shoes as she reported to physical education class. The girls had lined up in a row in the gymnasium as teacher Alice Frost spouted instructions for daily exercises. Thelma's arms were swinging rhythmically in time with jumping jacks when Miss Frost abruptly assumed a still-standing position. The girls' movements came to a stop as they waited to see if their teacher were changing the routine. Instead, Miss Frost looked away and appeared to be listening intently to some sound that had yet to register with Thelma and her friends. The gym had no windows and was tightly insulated. But some muffled sound made Miss Frost's face turn a shade of grayish white as she whipped her head back toward the assembly.

"Run, girls, run to the dressing rooms!" she blared.

The girls' dressing rooms were located underneath the bleachers where pep rallies met regularly to cheer on the basketball and football teams. Each room was a mere 3 feet by 3 feet. Pairs of girls huddled together in each dressing room. A girl Thelma hardly knew squeezed into the tight space with her, and they held onto each other as the sound of a "thousand and one trains" was pounded into their heads.

The other girl began screaming and flailing her arms as though she would suffocate in the tight space. She broke away from Thelma's embrace and strained to get out of the closet, inside which they would surely die. Thelma grabbed her by the waist and held on as the girl screamed and pushed on Thelma's bony shoulders in an attempt to break free. Steel girders were crashing onto the bleachers above their heads, and the boarded seats smashed into a thousands pieces. But the dressing room stalls held together, providing safety for students who would otherwise have suffered fatal injuries in the open span collapse of the gymnasium roof.

The next thing Thelma knew, she was walking through a hallway of the school in the general direction of the Spruce Street doors, or where they should have been. Broken glass lay everywhere. Walls and building parts were missing or piled crazily amidst boards, two-by-fours, papers, and desks. Lifting each foot, one step at a time, was an arduous task, but Thelma knew she had to get out. The other girl had disappeared, but was alive when Thelma last saw her. She spotted the opening to Spruce Street just as a hand thrust itself through a stack of boards and glass fragments beneath her. It seized her ankle like a vise grip.

A boy was buried in the rubble. He pleaded most mercifully, "Help me."

Thelma was lost and struggled to comprehend all that had happened to her beautiful school within three minutes. She looked down momentarily at the pathetic, half-buried boy. For reasons she later pondered, a well of super strength ran through her body. She forcefully jerked her ankle free from his grasp and walked away. She never looked back. Neither did she ever forget the details of the fellow student's grasp. It would stay with her for a lifetime.

Once outside, she headed toward home. Papa would know what to do. He was there peeling fruit he had bought that morning, getting it ready for Mama to can when she and Berneice got home from work at Brown's Shoe Factory. At lunchtime, Berneice and Thelma had walked to their home on North 16th Street and eaten a meal of tomato soup and homemade bread with their folks and Grandpa. Papa had invited them to sample the fruit before they returned respectively to work and to afternoon classes. The image of him sitting under the tree with a tin pan and basket of fruit was burned in Thelma's brain. It was the first place to go. Papa was there.

As she left the large brick building, she saw no one. It occurred to her that she was the only person still alive. But a sudden blare from a megaphone contradicted her perception. A voice called out a booming repeated admonition that somehow registered in her stunned brain.

"Watch your step, the power lines are live."

Over and over she heard the warning as it gradually faded behind her. She looked down at her feet with every careful step she made. It would be an awful shame to be killed by electricity after surviving a collapsed, school gymnasium roof. There would be no excuse for stepping on an electric wire and dying now. Papa would know what to do.

"Watch your step, the power lines are live," she mumbled.

She found a strange comfort in knowing that someone had called through the megaphone, even though she saw no one else ahead of her. She was not alone. It just felt as though she were. Thelma stayed as steady as possible but fell down a few times, narrowly missing nails that protruded through strewn boards. She made it past 17th Street and 16th Street, well on her way to 15th when a voice called out from the Stevens' porch. It was a familiar voice. She looked up to see Berneice and Mama standing alongside the Stevens family.

"Mama!" she yelled, "MAMA!"

She made it to the front steps of a house that miraculously escaped the storm's wrath. Mama's asthma had kicked in ferociously from all the confusion and terror. The shoe factory had been badly damaged, and the family car at the factory was too damaged to run. Besides, the streets were a mess of telegraph, telephone, and electric wires woven with debris of every description. Mama was trying to breathe slowly and deeply, but clearly she was having difficulty getting enough air flowing in and out of her lungs to keep her conscious. It was quickly decided that Berneice would stay with Mama, and Thelma would press on to find Papa and little brother Jack.

Minutes later, Thelma rounded the bend by the large, stone, Northern Methodist Church at the corner of Pine and 15th. The ruins of the Baptist Church to the north were a stark indication that she was close to Logan School. More energy flowed through her legs, and she marched forward, reenergized by the knowledge that Mama and Berneice were safe. If they were alive, Jack and Papa would be all right too. She knew it.

Suddenly, she saw a pile of beige bricks where Logan school should have been. Disregarding the live-wire admonition, she began running at full speed, her eyes unyielding in their search for a living brother. Then, a bizarre sight plastered a grin of amazement on her face. There he was. Standing in the middle of the street, surrounded by rubble, screaming and waving his arms. Jack had not moved since someone put the coat on him. He looked comical and sad all at the same time. But he was alive, with no discernible sign of serious injury. He was just terrified.

She placed a comforting arm around his shoulders, assured him that Mama and Berneice were fine and that they had to pull themselves together to go on hunt of Papa. Jack caught his breath, looked at her twice to be sure it really was his sister, and began the walk toward 16th Street. The two allies were disoriented by misplaced and vanished landmarks that should have marked the daily path to school. They glanced back at the school to get their bearings, but once it was out of sight, they had no idea where they were in relation to their home. Then an uprooted fir tree caught their attention. It was an unusual tree for Murphysboro, but they knew they passed it each morning on the way to school.

Soon they had found their barely recognizable father whose only response to them was an inarticulate moan. The forty-eight-year-old, 150-pound man of German descent lay scorched, blackened, and semiconscious in the rubble. Part of him had been on fire. His hair was singed, and he was suffering. His soft moans had guided them to his whereabouts within the debris. The lady next door was buried underneath her house, but she was dead. They knelt beside him in the middle of a tumultuous, unidentifiable neighborhood. Thelma and Jack cried. Then reason took hold, and they tried to figure out a solution.

Thelma could see the train tracks nearby, and she knew that if they could move him across the railroad tracks, they would be only a few blocks from the Stevens' house. That was the most direct way to get help, as far as they could tell. He was too heavy for the two of them to carry. They would need a way to move him. But how could a seventeen-year-old girl and a twelve-year-old boy move him? Jack began to stir through building remains looking for something they could use as a stretcher.

Jack found a bicycle, and the duo managed to mount Papa on the seat. Thelma walked alongside the bicycle, and Jack helped steer it through the rubble. They pushed him at a snail's pace through the wreckage.

It took an eternity to reach the train, which was still intact atop the tracks. The siblings were exhausted, and they had to lay their father gently on the ground as they studied how to get around the train. Clearly, they did not have the strength to push him around the end of the train so much farther down the tracks. In a split second, Jack had shimmied underneath the train, pulling the bicycle behind him. Thelma shoved her father's broken body as far underneath the boxcar as she could manage. Then she crawled on her belly to the other side. She and Jack pulled with all their might to drag their father to safety. Concern for Papa overshadowed any awareness of other schools and other children. That soon became a reality for everyone in Murphysboro. Every school in Murphysboro had been hit by the storm.

23

2:30 p.m., May 18, 1925, Murphysboro, Illinois. The colored children cried and huddled near the floor of the Douglas School as the roar of swirling winds deafened every other sound. A slender young teacher hurried her children toward the center of the room, shouting at them to get under their desks and cover their heads. Some of the girls were crying, but no tears or wails were heard at the moment of assault. The roar was engulfing. The teacher pressed her arm over the smallest ones closest to her and watched out of the corner of her eye to see to it that the students minded her and stayed in place.

Within a minute of the first sounds of the cyclone, a horrific roll of tin sheeting clamored overhead. The roof was peeling away, lifted by an ominous hand of a lethal power. The children shook in sheer terror, but obediently held their heads in their arms, rolling into tighter and tighter human balls on the plank floor. Papers flurried and whisks of air brushed the shoulders of everyone in the school. Then it was over. Fitfully frightened students sprang to their feet and ran from the building into devastation they could never have imagined.

At St. Andrews School, the roof was picked up above the housed children, and the scenario played out much as it was at the same time in the Douglas School. The only injuries of the children there were in their minds. May 18th would stay in their hearts and haunt their dreams for years to come. As they scurried into the school yard, they were disoriented by the sight of the school's roof in the very place where they had played just minutes before. There was no time to think about the roof. They were not hurt. Yet, they had to get home to safety.

No one was hurt at the Washington School, but its roof was gone in less than a minute. When the wind smashed into the school, it brought down part of the walls, but fortunately, the bricks did not fall onto the students' fragile skulls. Children had escaped the fate of death, and they knew it. It could come again. So they panicked. They cried, and they ran.

At the Lincoln School, girls and boys whimpered as the black sky settled on their town. Mary Bell was a third grader who cowered close to her best friend when the windows imploded. Everyone was pummeled with an unexpected downpour of cutting glass. She walked to her home, six blocks away, climbing over a tree and failing to register how a shoe and a leg could possibly be lying among downed trees, lumber, telephone lines, clothes, and other rubble. She thought her eyes were playing tricks on her. Probably she imagined it. She was just scared.

The roof that should have been on the house in the alley across the street was tilted sideways against a tree in her yard. Her chin quivered as she looked toward the house where she slept safely every night. The roof was gone someplace, but where? Every window in the house was gone. It was just like the scene she had left at Lincoln School. It was an image that played itself over and over every which way that she turned. She would never forget the sight of rain falling inside her house. Except for a few scrapes and bruises, her family had weathered the storm fairly well. Mother's arms were a tremendous comfort for Mary. She held on so tightly, she thought she would never let go again as long as she lived. Eventually, she let go, and she did live … a long time.

On the other hand, students at the Longfellow Grade School were not all free to run home. In a tangle of frantic reactions, children of all sizes were overwhelmed by the ebon cloud that smashed violently into the building. Located just a few blocks north of the high school, Longfellow held 450 children who were working hard at their lessons when teachers hastily ordered them to take shelter in their respective classrooms. They had hardly a moment to understand the seriousness of the situation. All adults made their best effort. It was just too much force with too little time to brace for the impact.

Howard was eight years old. He sat at his desk in the second row of the classroom with children whose last names began with C. A nub of a pencil was clutched in his skinny fingers, and he carefully jotted down the subtraction problems that were printed in large, white strokes on the blackboard. Howard was proud of his ability to subtract numbers in the thousands, borrowing as needed from adjacent numerals. He was a math aficionado, doing his very best to get every problem correct. He thought he might be a banker or a storekeeper someday. He dreamed of every possibility for working with numbers all day, every day. At the moment, he was concentrating with so much energy, he barely noticed any disturbance in the air outside. The students closest to the window-lined wall were twisting around in their seats, and the teacher had walked toward the view overlooking the playground.

It was getting dark very fast. Spring storms were normal for Murphysboro, and Howard took heart in knowing he was safe at his desk inside the Longfellow School. His one love was to finish all the problems as fast as he could while feeling certain that he had every answer correct. His mother had told him many times how smart he was to figure out problems using such speed and accuracy. Her words of encouragement only served to spur him forward with his studies. On some days, the teacher gave him an assignment to work with other students who had a hard time with arithmetic. He might be a banker. Or, he might be a teacher. In any case, arithmetic was the one thing he knew he did better than anyone else in his room. No problem was too hard for him to tackle.

Today was different. An arm of power was scraping the earth clean and was headed in Howard's direction. It was out to get him, his buddy Lewis, Mildred, Bertha, and the other beautiful children. No one in the Longfellow School was safe, but yet they counted on the teachers to keep them so. Everything would be all right. Until the last minute, there was no doubt that the grown-ups could shelter them from danger.

The plump teacher with a tight bun twisted at the nape of her neck turned ashen in a flash. She whirled toward the students, quaking as though she would implode from some mysterious onslaught of illness. Her arms flapped vigorously through the air as she yelped in desperation.

"Children, out! Get out! Downstairs, now!"

Howard lifted his floppy-haired head in curiosity. He had only a few more problems to finish. He scratched with his pencil in a flurry of calculations, and then he jumped to the back of the line of fellow classmates lined up at the window-paned door next to the hallway. It was a fire drill with no rung bell, one of those surprise alert responses they had practiced so many times throughout the school year. Line up. No talking. No running. Single file. Go to the grove of maple trees at the edge of the softball field. How many times had they practiced?

He was brave. He was obedient. He was a good student. He was a target of strength so evil he could never have understood it. No one could. Most of the children made it to the hallway when the bricks began pummeling the teacher and Howard. Wood splinters stabbed their backs, arms, and legs. A brick hit the teacher's shoulder, and she fell forward, even while reaching for Howard's hand. He was beyond her grasp. A little girl in the hall looked up in amazement. No one heard her startled proclamation. She did not understand a thing that was going on.

"It's raining bricks! It's raining bricks!"

At the moment Howard placed his right foot on the oak floor below the door casing, a queasy feeling in the pit of his stomach halted his progress. He was falling in slow motion as the second floor of the Longfellow School snapped in two. On top of dear sweet Howard, Bertha, Lewis, Mildred, and so many others, a brick thunderstorm pounded heads and tiny bodies with full force. Howard lost consciousness immediately. In seconds, his broken body was buried underneath what had been the walls, floors, and windows of his wonderful school. There was no one to pull him out. It did not matter. A single blow to his temple was lethal. He felt no pain. It was too quick to feel anything. Death was mercifully fast for the third grader. Many friends and neighbors of Murphysboro would suffer long hours before fading away.

About half of the Longfellow School children made it outside the building before the school imploded. The other half of the children was driven down by collapsing walls and floors. Some were only partly buried and were able to squirm out of the debris. Others lay alert or semiconscious, pinned by beams or heaps of misplaced bricks. Screams and cries penetrated the air as the roar of the storm moved beyond them. Some of the teachers had wits enough to begin digging, using their hands as shovels, pulling out students one at a time.

Within mere minutes, men from the Mobile and Ohio Railroad Shop arrived on the scene. Leaving behind thirty-five dead workers, they ran full speed to Longfellow. The men struggled to pull boards, desks, and piles of bricks off the children, laboring with no thought of their own safety. For hours, the excavation would continue. Later in the afternoon, a drove of Boy Scout volunteers would assist in the recovery of ten, innocent, beloved ones who were laid in a row beside the rubble. Mothers and fathers would stream by, praying for a better outcome. A throng of loving and courageous neighbors gave everything they had to save the children on the northwest corner of 20th and Logan Streets.

The students who had made it outside the school had scattered with great ferocity. Some ran in any direction that would take them away from the collapsed building. Others paused to get their bearings and figure out how to get to their homes. A few children waited underneath the maple tree cluster by the ball diamond, not knowing what to do.

Among the group waiting where maples should have been were three sisters and three brothers of the Carr family. They were scraped and bruised a bit, but stood tall, embracing each other for reassurance that the world had not gone completely mad. They were stunned, but willing to comply with teachers' instructions to wait by the trees for further instructions. Soon, they realized that there would be no further instructions. Not a single teacher approached them. But, they stood there anyway. They knew that they must stay together and that somebody would tell them what to do next. Clearly, they were safe. It was also clear in their minds that some of the children were not going to make it to the maples.

In the meantime, Austin Carr ran from the brick-factory remains to his home at 2115 Logan Street. Mrs. Carr was stumbling near the walkway when he extended his muscular arms to hold her. They cried together while staring at the space where their home had been. By some miracle, their Model A had suffered only a banged-up fender. Austin breathed in deeply, reaching for some strength he secretly doubted would sustain him. It did.

"We need to find the children," he whispered to his trembling wife.

"Yes … yes, the children …," she uttered.

"Are you hurt? Are you bleeding anywhere?" he asked her.

"No," she replied, "I was taking clothes down from the line. It happened so fast.

I don't know …."

Her husband guided her toward the automobile and comforted her with gentle pats as she sat cautiously on the velvet seat. His hands shook slightly as he closed her door and moved around the front of the car. Austin bent over to clutch a board which contained nails that spiked toward the cleared sky. He tossed it onto an upside-down tree in their yard. In a fit of rage, he kicked a branch to the side of the street and then proceeded to clear a driving path toward the Longfellow School.

The Ford started immediately, and he breathed a sigh of relief. They could get to the children as long as he was careful to watch for rubble that could damage their only means of getting away from the destruction. Mrs. Austin regained some confidence and looked admiringly at her husband.

"I'll help you look for things in the road," she said.

He looked at her, affectionately clasped her forearm, and kicked the clutch pedal to the floor. They were very close to the school and had a good chance of getting through the streets. He counted on his seven children having the good sense to be together and wait for them. The Carrs drove past collapsed houses and piles of lumber and household goods, occasionally looking away from dead neighbors who were crushed by mounds of rubble. He reached in his back pocket, checking to be sure his wallet was in place with the money they would need. It occurred to him that they were already fortunate, if their luck just held out with the children.

It seemed like hours to reach the fallen schoolhouse, but the mother and father immediately spotted their brood near maple spikes. The brothers and sisters ran to the old Model A, crying and extending their arms long before they reached the vehicle. After checking for injuries, Mrs. Carr realized they were short a child.

"Where's your little brother?" she asked.

The girls shook their heads and pouted hopelessly while looking at the lady who had always fixed fresh-baked bread so it would be hot out of the oven just as they came home in the afternoons. Mama was the lady who used a washboard to launder the best clothes they had and hung them in the sunlight to dry. The lady who worked with them at night on lessons that challenged their taxed brains. The lady who never gave up on them, long after they gave up on themselves.

It was clear that they were lost in the turmoil and were terrified of moving. Within a couple of minutes, the children were crowded together on the seats of the Model A, and their parents were walking slowly along the remains of school walls that barely stood above the fray of the storm's aftermath. The siblings saw mother leaning against father's chest for support. Then, Mr. Carr knelt to the ground and curved his strong arms underneath the ashen, still body of Howard. He carried him toward the family with the strength of the greatest father that ever lived.

Mrs. Carr took her seat beside the smallest daughter in the front of the auto. The father gently placed the little boy against her. In silence, Austin took his place behind the steering wheel and started the engine. It would be the longest drive ever for the Carrs. Mother cried softly as she held her beloved Howard close to her. The six siblings said nothing, not even asking for food. They were all together. That Wednesday night, the Carr family settled into the comfort of loved ones' arms in Nashville. Murphysboro and Howard's sweet days at the Longfellow School were far behind them.

24

Elena was dazed by the facts. So many people and so much heartache. She sat staring at the pages of information which the librarian had pulled from the shelves. The Sallie Logan Public Library was cool and inviting with light oak tables and neatly arranged books in towering rows of oak shelves. There was no hint of disorder anywhere. A lovely lady named Danielle had introduced herself and enthusiastically assisted the young reporter in locating every documented account of the Murphysboro Tornado.

Elena was detecting a tendency of individual towns to regard the Tri-State Tornado almost exclusively in terms of that community. In the case of Murphysboro, it was absolutely justified. More people died in the now-bucolic community than in any other town in the storm path. It made sense for citizens to see it as their tornado. Murphysboro became the hub for Red Cross relief efforts where volunteer doctors and nurses were rushed to southern Illinois in valiant efforts to ease suffering. On that tumultuous day of 1925, the National Guard was quickly mobilized to keep order and fend off looting. Elena had begun to log facts, but trying to enter all the data into the laptop was futile. She could be there for days and still not record everything. A copier and some time to reproduce the facts would be most useful.

Before she could bring herself to shift from note-taking to photocopying, she sat quietly and contemplated a town's destruction that was far beyond her experience and her imagination. Today was a sunny, windy day. It was impossible to think that life in this lovely community could be destroyed in three minutes, but history had absolutely proven the potential for such devastation. It was nothing to regard lightly.

Elena hardly noticed Danielle's presence. The librarian was beaming with willingness to assist today's guest. Elena was not the first researcher to scrutinize records that the librarian had meticulously organized, and she would not be the last.

"Are you finding everything you need?" Danielle asked.

"Oh yes, I'm doing well, thanks. Actually, I was wondering if I could copy these records and pay you for the copies. I'm afraid I cannot record all this information before I have to move on. These records are incredible!" Elena asserted.

"Thank you. I've worked really hard to put this file together. Researchers come from all over to study the storm. Have you seen the History Channel program?"

Elena sat up straight, curious to hear about a video narration detailing the very heart of horrific death and destruction. The History Channel had not popped up in the work she had done so far, and she hoped her writing would not be redundant or overshadowed by contributions of professionals with budgets much bigger than her personal savings account. Perhaps everything she had done up to this point was a mere repetition of work that had already been completed. How could she possibly compete with the History Channel?

Perhaps it was not a competition, but a cooperative gift for generations that could learn from the past. It was not the past that mattered so much as it was the future. Elena had some eye on a horizon where scientists, civic leaders, baseball coaches, teachers, and moms saw the potential for sparing children of the twenty-first century unspeakable suffering. If one child's life could be saved … just one … it would be a reward of sufficient proportions. One child. One life. It would be enough.

"It's so hard for me to understand this kind of danger, in a moment's notice," Elena said.

"Yes. We're in line with major storms moving east. But, we have so many opportunities that residents of 1925 never had. See that radio on the counter behind the desk? When the alarm goes off, I'm in charge of everyone's safety. Either people listen or they leave."

Elena nodded, understanding the full scope of one person whose responsibility it was to ensure safety of readers. Large glass windows were nearly everywhere. They clearly opened the way for natural light that flowed to many of the tables that were scattered throughout the one-story building. Although the fluorescent lights were turned on, Elena doubted the necessity of relying on them, at least for the moment. If the power went out, it would be a piece of cake to move about the stacks and tables. But the young reporter also recognized the risk of thousands of minute, glass bullets penetrating the bodies of patrons too foolish to get to a reinforced, windowless hallway.

She remembered talking to the new reporter at *The Sentinel* who left work one afternoon in Denver to drive straight toward a tornado he had seen from the 34th floor of the high-rise. Mike said it was a stupid thing to do, but he insisted that he was totally hypnotized by the distant tornado. He could not help himself. That was before he moved to West Virginia. There, he could only reflect on the power of the Shinnston Tornado and glean some sense of reality from its history. Usually, one or two weak F-0 or F-1 tornadoes touch down annually in the Little Mountain State, and most of them are in isolated rural areas, where no official record is kept. Despite the fact that the state is hailed as "Almost Heaven," he regarded its relative safety as a bit boring.

Elena had read about people who are drawn toward tornadoes rather than away from them. Of course, there were always those sensational storm-chasing videos on television that hyped encounters as though they represented nothing more than the equivalent of a rollercoaster ride. For these people, a hypnotic trance was inevitable, almost as though nature etched their name on the very clouds that beckoned them. After her close encounter near Fredericktown, Elena knew which kind of person she was. She was drawn to the subject matter, but terrified of the reality. She smiled as the library director pulled out a chair and sat down.

"I had a bad experience near Fredericktown, Missouri, day before yesterday. I'd hoped to make it to the Mississippi River before dark, but the farther I drove east, the darker the sky became. Next thing I knew, I was underneath a black-and-purple cloud that kept getting lower and lower. Sticks and leaves were flying through the air above my car. I don't get it. Cars with Missouri license plates kept driving into the dark, and there were blue skies behind us. My gut told me to get out of there. So, I pulled off the road and just started driving as fast as I could for blue skies. By the time I got back to town, there were radio reports of a tornado on the ground in Fredericktown!"

Danielle's jaw had dropped slightly. Her eyes widened like two raisin pies where all the filling had settled into the middle of the pastry. She nodded affirmatively and cleared her throat. She had something to say that obviously did not pertain to the Tri-State Tornado.

"You were driving into it. I know what you mean. I don't understand people sometimes. The afternoon you were near Fredericktown, the weather radio alarm went off here. I ordered everyone into the block hallway. Sure enough, there was a woman here at this very table who criticized everything I was doing. 'Oh, you people are always overreacting. I grew up in Oklahoma, and I'm not going to any hallway!' I just told her, you have two choices: either go with the rest of us to the hall or leave the library—now! You are not staying here. She left. What possesses people to act like that, I'll never know."

Elena smiled. Obviously, she and Danielle were operating on the same wavelength. The librarian was as sharp as a tack, and she was no one to cross when it came to safety. As Danielle related the details of the uncooperative patron, Elena had flashing memories of events at home just four weeks earlier. She spoke with a woman whose husband ordered her to settle down at a time when some little girls on a ball diamond were continuing to play as lightning flashed around them. The hair on the arms of the spectators was standing straight up. Ironically, most of the spectators were the kids' parents. Seemingly, the notion that the game must go on outweighed common sense. It mattered even less that the crowd of supporters was seated on aluminum bleachers. The coach had yelled for everyone to get inside their cars, but the woman cowered in a state of helplessness when her husband demanded that she shut up. The game continued.

Based on the sheer lunacy of that moment, Elena figured out why men are most often the victims of lightning strikes. They really were too stupid to get in out of the rain. She would have to be careful to keep that conclusion to herself. Half of her readership was male. She hated self-censorship for the sake of circulation, but sighed at the necessity of protecting egos of incompetents. She dreamed of a day when she could write whatever she damned well pleased, and the people who did not like it could sit on the top of metal flagpoles during thunderstorms. Unlike her vaguely discussed plans to assist with severe-storm education, the days of purely uncensored writing were not even a distant possibility. She knew that much.

It took her nearly two hours to Xerox the storm archives at the Sallie Logan Library. She felt self-conscious tying up the copy machine that long, but she appreciated the opportunity to use the librarian's key to override the coin activation mode. At mid-afternoon, she laid fifty dollars plus a twenty dollar contribution on the sleek counter near the front door. Another smiling lady had replaced Danielle at the front desk. She was eager to know if Elena would send the feature story to Murphysboro. Elena assured her that relaying the final report to them would be a high priority. Then she paused, thinking that the short, brown-haired lady might know something about the storm that was not obvious in news clippings.

"The destruction to the schools was, so—so terrible," she said.

"Oh, yes," the woman answered. "You know, they say that the voices of the children can be heard crying at night up there. A lot of our kids go up there to practice sports, and some of them say they can hear children's sobbing voices. I don't know. I have never heard them, but I've often thought I would go up there and see if—they would talk to me. I know that sounds crazy. It's just one of those things I've wondered. I would love for them to talk to me. Maybe I could comfort them some way … oh, I know that's crazy."

Elena was not sure just how crazy it was. She listened pensively, realizing how the trauma of the schools' implosions had carried all the way into the twenty-first century. She was trained to deal with facts, but she understood very well how the sadness of so many places in Murphysboro represented so much relentless despair. No ghosts had ever talked to her when she was on assignment, but the awfulness of the '25 storm had a presence in modern minds that was numbing and pervasive, both at the same time. She felt some unrealistic desire to be comforting as well. Her feelings were inexplicable, totally illogical, and all-consuming.

There was dreadful sadness here. There was grief today for people they did not know, and never would. There were tears that flowed like a peaceful current underneath plans for memorial services. There was emotion that underlay sweet, distant voices of dead children crying out for their mamas. There was reverence and hope for God's touch in the middle of all of it. Elena wondered where God was when it hit.

25

<u>7:30 a.m., May 19, 1925, Chicago, Illinois.</u> The wind outside the office of the Tribune Tower was chilly and brisk. Lights had been on all night as Henry Allison shuffled telegrams and telephone reports from sources in the Murphysboro area. It was an extraordinary night for the *Chicago Tribune* bureau chief. He was wrestling with facts that would constitute the story of a lifetime. It had been nine hours since one of his photographers had hopped the same train that carried Red Cross doctors and nurses into the tornado-ravaged, southern Illinois communities.

Henry filtered information via telephone calls from the field every few hours. Phrases such as "total devastation," "death toll," "unspeakable injuries," and "distraught families" circled through his brain like vultures moving insidiously close to odorous carrion. He grimaced to realize that the stench of dead people in Murphysboro would linger forever in the minds of rescuers and survivors. Although the lines of ethics were on his mind, the bitter rivalry between him and William Randolph Hearst was of far greater import. It drove him to the brink of madness when stories of this magnitude thrust themselves on the world. It also generated high levels of energy that would propel him through long hours of work on the next edition.

The photographer had been told to get the glass negatives delivered to the *Tribune* laboratory as soon as possible. The goal for beating Hearst's circulation was to print the first images of what history would one day determine to be the deadliest tornadic storm in the history of the world. Henry's gut told him that he had no time to waste, even though he could not have fully grasped the severity of the prior afternoon's Midwest calamity.

The last telegrammed communication he sent to his photographer had instructed the young man to deliver photographic negatives to the Murphysboro Western Union building. In all the distressing milieu, the office was still up and running and was a formidable hub for communication in and out of the disaster area. A courier would pick up the glass plates and transport them via plane to Chicago. For now, the *Tribune* morning edition blared front-page news about the deadly storm. The next addition would explode with full-page, pictorial coverage of devastated neighborhoods.

Henry was pacing the floor and studying hand-held telegrams when Henry Scheafer walked through the door at 8:00. Scheafer was a photographer with Pacific and Atlantic Photos, Inc. His office was just down the hall. The photography agency was owned by the *Tribune* and *The New York Daily News*, and it was understood that the highest priority of the office was to render the best pictures possible, particularly for major stories. Scheafer was a bright, industrious worker with enough experience under his belt to ensure the best layout of the next edition. In short order, he realized that today's photography and headlines would be among the most memorable in twentieth-century news media. This day was iconic.

"Scheafer! Get a hold of that young fella that's always flying stunts out in the country. Ah, that skinny guy—Slim!"

Scheafer was startled by the presence of Mr. Allison at 8:00 a.m. For a moment, his thoughts were jumbled as he considered the instructions. It was unusual to see the bureau chief working at an intense pace so early in the day. He understood that something big was coming down. Scheafer fiddled with the pencil stub in his shirt pocket, wondering if he could get to the pilot fast enough. He needed to react quickly in an effort to stay one step ahead of Hearst.

"I'll get right on it, Boss," he answered.

Within a matter of seconds Scheafer was galloping down the narrow hallway, knowing that every bit of time was invaluable. His heart was pounding fiercely as he flipped through files of telephone numbers. It was unusual for his hands to shake in anticipation of getting the right photographs to press in time for the next run. In this case, he knew that the credibility of the *Tribune* weighed heavily on everyone, but was particularly onerous in the hands of the photographers. Despite the finest writing the newspaper staff could muster, it was primarily pictures of disasters that beckoned readers to grab the latest publication. Only after scanning the pictorial representation of tragedy, did readers engross themselves in the story, and not before.

Finally, he found the tan folder that contained the names of pilots that the *Tribune* hired periodically for work at a moment's notice. The list of names highlighted the most reliable and fearless aviators that would abruptly drop everything to respond to an urgent job. By the time, he had returned to Allison's office, the bureau chief was engrossed in an intense telephone conversation with someone in the center of the destruction. Scheafer gleaned enough facts from the discourse to realize that schools had been in the path of the cyclone, and the results were nothing short of terrifying, even in the minds of strangers as far away as Chicago. The bureau chief was furiously scribbling notes in a report book on the oak desk in the corner. The photographer waved the folder in the air and looked determinedly at Allison.

"Got it!" Scheafer blared, looking at his boss.

The chief nodded and pointed to the corner desk where another telephone rested atop previous days' copies. Without hesitation, Scheafer dialed the switchboard, requesting a line to Gauthier's Flying Field. He was in luck. The twenty-three-year-old barnstormer was working on one of the planes parked at the forty-acre, grassy, flying center. He would be available to fly to Murphysboro within the hour. It would cost the *Tribune* a hundred dollars to rent the plane, plus a standard fee of $1.50 an hour for time and services. Allison was continuing to scribble details of the disaster in southern Illinois. He scrawled a note for Scheafer, and thrust it toward the photographer's left hand.

PILOT IS TO GO TO WESTERN UNION OFFICE IN MURPHYSBORO TO MEET TRIBUNE PHOTOGRAPHER AND PICK UP NEGATIVES. FLY BACK TO CHICAGO <u>IMMEDIATELY</u>. PAYMENT WILL BE MADE UPON DELIVERY OF NEGATIVES. HIRE BODYGUARDS TO MEET HIM AT AIRPORT.

It was almost an hour before Henry Scheafer arrived at the dirt-strip airport north of Chicago. He exhaled a loud huff of air, relieved to have made good time, and knowing that the skies were clear enough for a round-trip flight into the rural southern county. The steely eyed, young pilot was leaning against the biplane and swigging Coca-Cola from a small glass bottle. The meeting was short and to the point. The *Tribune* photographer would meet him at Western Union with the negatives, and he would fly back to Chicago where three bodyguards would escort him to the newspaper office. This story was too big to take any chances, and the chief needed a good pilot he could trust one hundred percent.

The two men shook hands. The deal was made. Within two minutes, the airplane was speeding down the dirt strip adjacent to the intersection of Palatine Road and Milwaukee Avenue. What a story. Henry shook his head, repeating to himself, "once in a lifetime—this is it." He stood almost motionless until he saw the plane clear the horizon. Then he drove back to the Tribune Tower, assured that the thick-trunked bodyguards who worked for Allison would handle any difficulties that might arise.

For the rest of the morning, he shuffled tasks with a roomful of reporters who laid out space for the best possible coverage of human tragedy in the towns and villages over three-hundred miles away. The office was buzzing as details of death, injury, and destruction poured into the *Tribune*. No one could recall having ever heard about such a violent, natural assault on so many people. Even the old-timers who covered the battlefields of Europe in The Great World War doubted that their field experience matched the current situation.

Henry Allison maintained his fierce efforts to outdo Hearst's *Chicago Herald Examiner* and *The American*, but he had to kick back for a couple of hours rest while waiting for the pictures. Most of his crew was well seasoned, and he had to be sharp for the final editing before putting it all to bed. The reporting staff and assistants could manage the work for several hours if necessary, but Allison was not about to turn over the final layout to anyone else.

When the door to his office was shut, it was understood that staff members were on their own. No one was to interrupt him, and his assistant would be sure to waken him after two hours. That was more than enough time to get him back into a sharp state of mind. In the meantime, Scheafer planned space for bold headlines and corresponding pictures. He was pacing like Allison, mulling over new angles to outmaneuver Hearst and his henchmen.

In the meantime, the Chicago-based biplane touched down in a field adjacent to the swath of destruction left behind by the storm in Murphysboro. Slim ambled out of the plane and asked a couple Boy Scouts for directions to Western Union. At first, the youthful volunteers insisted that no unauthorized persons were to enter the town. It took only a few words referring to the *Chicago Tribune* and the boys were complying with the request for directions. A fourteen-year-old named Roy volunteered to show Slim the location of the office.

Debris was strewn in every direction. Gray smoke towered over much of the town that had erupted in flames immediately after the storm. Murphysboro had burned all night. The pilot and boy had not walked far before hearing people discuss families that were burned alive even after believing they were safe from the tornado. Murphysboro was a nightmare of strangely intertwined black embers and charred boards. The Boy Scout and skinny flyer reached the telegraph office where other Scouts moved quickly in and out of the doorway. Some carried scraps of paper with reassuring messages to be sent to distant relatives. Others scurried through the rubble taking frantic inquiries to Red Cross headquarters. People were on the move. Some men were digging through piles of blocks and bricks, looking for intact bodies of those who had been buried alive or looking for the partial remains of those whose identities were perfectly clear two minutes before the cyclone swept through town.

The pilot approached a clearly exhausted, stooped man behind the counter. Two Scouts stepped aside, sensing some urgency from the stranger who had just landed his plane in the field to the north. The telegraph clerk looked up and momentarily stopped clicking a coded message. He looked relieved that he had a good excuse to rest his weary fingers and brain. The pilot dipped his head in a gesture of shyness and spoke.

"I'm here to pick up picture negatives for the *Chicago Tribune*."

Before the clerk had a second to respond, a pudgy, redheaded fellow bumped the pilot's arm with a rectangular object wrapped in brown paper. He knew exactly what to expect in the telegraph office and obviously was clued to the urgency of getting the negatives to Chicago as soon as possible.

"Here. Get these to the *Tribune*. Hurry!" It was that simple. Slim nodded his head in the general direction of the freckle-faced Scout and trekked back to the makeshift landing strip in the field. The boys paused in their work long enough to watch the pilot spin the propeller, climb into the cockpit, and take off for Chicago. The Scouts' long hours of work with the Red Cross resumed, and Slim was well on the way to completing his aerial assignment.

Back in Chicago, Henry Scheafer was working in high gear as was Henry Allison. Everything was coming together for an expanded special edition of the *Tribune* that would highlight the events of the previous twenty-four hours. Four extra pages would be added for pictures. The trick would be to narrow pictorial choices in an expeditious manner and then to pull it all together in time to run off five hundred extra papers. The news staff worked like a well-oiled machine. Allison had made perfect choices in staff members, and he knew it. They would be exhausted by the time the papers were on the street, but they would also be recognized as having the best news coverage in Chicago and beyond. No one would forget the *Tribune's* role in covering the story.

It was late afternoon when the bulky bodyguards escorted the freelance courier to the *Tribune*. Everyone waited with high expectations as Scheafer and an assistant wrestled with the photographic plates in the darkroom down the hall. The shy pilot waited patiently in a rickety wooden chair for a check to be cut for his services. It was a winning situation for everyone, until Scheafer returned to the editorial offices of Henry Allison. A bellow of consternation exploded from the chief's office, and the frenzied newspaper workers froze in their tracks. Reporters and clerks waited to hear the newest row between the two Henrys. Editorial negotiations were always touchy at the *Tribune*, and the general consensus was that he who yelled loudest won. No one dared to utter a word until the fracas ended. It did not last long.

By the time pilot Charles A. Lindbergh realized he had been duped by a carrot-headed Hearst confederate in Murphysboro, it was too late. In the telegraph office, he had been handed blank, glass-plate negatives. They had been switched for the ones he should have carried to Allison. No pictures of the storm would be printed in the next edition of the *Tribune*. On March 20, 1925, Hearst's *Chicago Herald-Examiner's* front-page, opening line read: **FIRST PICTURES OF STORM DISASTER - 1,000 DEAD, 3,000 HURT LATEST TOLL OF TORNADO. IN THE TWINKLING OF AN EYE, MURPHYSBORO WAS NO MORE.** William Randolph Hearst won the battle of the press. The people of Murphysboro forever lost life as they had known it.

26

Elena was hypnotized by the beauty of the stone-block, Northern Methodist Church on 15th and Pine. The brightly painted, red doors and the familiar red-and-white Methodist logo were both comforting and intimidating. A constant, snapping breeze blew her bangs over her eyes, and she squinted as she studied the towering edifice. By what strange miracle had this worship center with its sky-touching bell tower survived the tornado of '25?

A nearby church was holding a funeral service when the blast of winds brought the pious fortress down on top of mourners. No reverence had been evidenced by the monster that so quickly and efficiently snuffed out life and fueled a lifetime of fear. At the library, Danielle had indicated that only two remaining survivors of the storm would openly talk about the trauma, and they did so when the History Channel reporters descended on Murphysboro in 2007. Although other living survivors were nearby, they could never bring themselves to go through the pain of remembering the terrifying moments they had tried to bury in the past. Not even for the sake of history.

But this church held memories of its own that could never be tapped by interviewers, cameras, or wishful thinkers. Elena grimaced as she wondered what secrets these great walls would hold for eternity. She listened quietly, with some unrealistic expectation that she might hear the wailing of injured townsfolk who were carried here by the National Guard soldiers, neighbors, Boy Scouts, and volunteer doctors and nurses. This was the hospital. Better stated, it was one of many hospitals that answered the call to comfort helpless victims whose bodies were broken and torn by the horrific storm—a force so unrelenting it tore the clothes off some children. Among the shocked victims of the storm, there were those who were naked and unaware of it. Today, the Red Cross makeshift hospital of 1925 was a house of prayer, and a beautiful one. Elena took in the quiet. There were no voices to hear.

She looked at the street sign and then gazed at her feet when she realized that she was standing where Jack's sister had hurried to find the second grade boy who stood crying on top of a pile of bricks. Where had that seventeen-year-old girl found the courage to search for her father and brother with no help from anyone? Was there a mighty power that superseded fear for her? Was that power some gift that she openly received, but others could not muster? Or was it some attribute of personality or family genes that predisposed her to a response of bravery? Elena wanted facts for her series in the *Sentinel*. At the moment, she wanted also answers to questions that haunted her as she walked among beautiful neighborhoods.

The houses were surrounded by grassy lawns with yellow, red, and pink flowers. Every house was neatly maintained. Every lawn mowed. Occasional American flags along the streets incessantly furled in the erratic breeze of Murphysboro. Elena was fatigued and sighed with exasperation that there never seemed to be a break in the wind here. Plenty of wind awaited her at home in West Virginia, but wonderful calm days awaited her as well. She was missing calm, quiet air, but she was reconciled to pulling her ponytail through her Storm Stories ball cap every afternoon. Then something clicked loudly in her brain. Gestalt! A clear pattern of wind was kicking up every afternoon here. No wonder the 1925 kids on the lawns laughed and played without the slightest suspicion of death looming on the horizon. March 18, 1925, was a day just like any other in the spring. It was too easy for evil to take away these children.

She walked along North 15th Street knowing that the farther she walked, the more she was taking in the reconstructed area where flames towered into the sky destroying homes and businesses on the night of the storm. Elena had already uncovered eyewitness accounts of families who stood on distant porches, watching what was left of their town burn to the ground. They could do little to stop it. Tragically, the tornado had destroyed the local waterworks. Exhausted fire fighters had no water pressure to aid them in efforts to salvage the remains of the northeastern section of Murphysboro. More than one library record indicated that rescuers could hear survivors in post-tornado rubble plead for rescue, to no avail. Fire engulfed the helpless souls. 'Poor old souls,' Grandma Kiz would say. 'Poor old souls.'

Elena clinched her teeth, furious to believe that there was no way to save survivors under such horrific circumstances. Yet, objectively, she knew that if she had been there, she might well have been one of the dazed survivors who kicked away a child's hands that would have desperately clenched her ankles. She might have told a distraught mother that her son was dead when, in fact, he was alive. She might have stood with fire fighters who anguished helplessly as the screams of pinned neighbors' subsided in a furnace of injustice.

There was no loving God here. Perhaps there was no loving God. It tried her patience to imagine the brutal assault against hundreds who had suffered in Murphysboro and beyond. Here beneath whispering maples, she had uncovered the root of madness. It was no wonder that survivors did not talk about that day or that night. She shook her head defiantly. If she did not take a break, she would succumb to unrestrained cynicism. It would swallow her like a monster munching on the hearts of anyone who happened to be in the wrong place at the wrong time. Grandma Tom would be disappointed if that happened. Grandma Tom … whose chopped-off, third finger pushed darning needles through the heels of Dad's white socks that were stretched over jelly jar glasses. What a strong grandma she was. In some ways. She had more than her share of hard times. She never gave up. Elena winced to realize that her own life had been comparatively easy. Perhaps that was the heart of her consternation on this research trip.

A smile swept over Elena's face as she spotted two little girls playing Ring-Around-the-Rosie in their front yard on Elm Street. The little towheads giggled and rolled grass stains on shirts that Elena hoped were everyday apparel. The little voices sang the melody perfectly.

"Ring around the rosy, pocket full of posies, ashes, ashes, we all fall DOWN!"

It was moments like this that unexpectedly generated sheer exhilaration in Elena's head. These little girls were a picture of joy personified, and a much needed reminder to stay objective and optimistic in this place. It was heartbreaking to know that when the bricks fell down on the schoolmates of Murphysboro's schools, there was no singing … no laughter. These pretty, little blondes on Elm Street were too sweet to even imagine heartache for children who lived long ago. Inevitable joy encircled their play. When they fell down, it was fun. When their great-grandmothers fell down on this very spot, it was terrifying. Today there was nothing to worry about. Nothing to fear. It was a good day in Murphysboro.

Elena glanced in the general direction of the old Logan School building. Maybe there were voices there. Maybe not. It was not something she would pursue. Sensational talk about children's voices was too morbid and too ridiculous for a serious reporter to consider. There was another motive she could not own up to completely. Her emotional state was buckling from the research and reality of so much despair. She was truly amazed that people would take their recollections to their graves, but objectively she put it in the same box as overwhelming nightmares of traumatized war veterans. The memories were too much to bear.

Ten minutes later, Elena was buzzing through microfilm at the Jackson County Historical Society. She made a few notes, but believed that most of the material duplicated work she was doing at the Library, with one exception. Several publications were for sale. The one that caught her attention was titled Tornado, March 18, 1925. It was a compilation of photographic depictions of the town's destruction immediately following the storm and fire. No published work could be done without the benefit of this pictorial archive. As she dished out a twenty for the book and donation to the archive center, a blaring alarm sounded from the weather radio directly behind the old man. He groused.

"Ah! They have to send out these alarms, but you never know what will happen. It might touch down on the other side of the street or on this side! You don't know."

He slammed an arthritic right hand down on the alarm button as Elena gulped. She wondered if he had heard one too many tornado warnings. She thanked him for his assistance with her research and stepped outside the slanted-wall, steel building. The sky was clear as a bell with a few clouds coming together, but nothing close to what she had encountered near Fredericktown. She was a half-hour drive from the Marion Super 8. There was time to make it there. She was sure of that. Ire returned to her vocabulary as she debated whether to hit the road or scurry over to the library to crouch in the block hallway with Danielle and her patrons. This was nuts. She had no idea what to do. Obviously, no tornado was in sight. She would be safe at the hotel. Fifteen minutes later, she was barreling along the highway to Marion when it hit her.

"Shit!"

The little girls were probably still playing in their yard. As she strained to peer at gray clouds rolling together above the van, it never occurred to her to think about the Murphysboro children laughing and spinning around without so much as a clue of approaching danger. They were in the same place as their great-grandmas. Elena was senseless. She feared that she would lose her wits if the worst happened. She was getting exactly what she deserved. She had no reason to believe that she could do research about a killer tornado in the Midwest and not face tinge of fear attributable to unstable air masses. No one could find out about her trepidation. Her credibility as a fearless writer and journalist was at stake here. Never matter her life.

By the time she leaned against her hotel door from inside the room, she realized that the little girls would be fine. The National Weather Service was doing its job well, and any mother with half a brain would hear the town siren and get the playmates to safety. They would be fine. Elena was not so sure about herself.

27

4:00 a.m., May 19, 1925, Murphysboro, Illinois. The first group of
Boy Scouts of America arrived from Sparta as fire fighters struggled
to get the fires of Murphysboro under control. They had made the
forty-mile trip in the back of a truck with bandages, torches, blankets,
medicines, and canned food crammed against them. Not a half-inch
space was to be spared anywhere in the back of the truck. The young
volunteers were packed together tighter than canned peaches in a
Mason jar.

Roy and Benjamin were twelve years old and together had
enthusiastically studied first aid and rescue procedures for months. But
they had never seen anything like the mass of fire and wind destruction
that now pounced on their unsuspecting brains. Their innocent view
of life was abruptly and irreconcilably riddled with indelible images of
suffering that superseded everything they had gone through in their
friendship of seven years. This was just the beginning. They were in a
situation so surreal they thought they might be experiencing a heart-
stopping nightmare. It was not a night terror. In fact, one thing was
unmistakably clear. Their scout-master had brought them to Hell in
the name of humanity. They stared at people who stared back at them.
Gaunt Murphysboro faces winced pleadingly as the truck bed jostled
from side to side, moving carefully through debris along Walnut and up
20th.

At the first sight of people walking the streets in the dark, none of
the scouts said anything. The scene was as desperate as any battlefield
on any front. But the reality was that these boys had not been to war.
The conflict here was, thankfully, not between people. The war they were
about to wage was against the enemy of time. It was a battle to win lives
over death—a battle against surmounting odds of nature's crushing
blows upon the defenseless bodies of young and old alike.

Benjamin's eyes scanned the crumbled mound of bricks and blocks that only a few hours earlier had made up the walls of the Longfellow School. Cars were parked in a row as headlights beamed a warm glow on the pile of the worst area of collapse, the gymnasium. Fourteen hours had passed since the cyclone ripped the town apart. The boy had no idea that people would be digging frantically throughout the night for survivors. Even at the age of twelve, he realized immediately that it was far more likely that the fervent volunteers were searching for bodies than for breathing beings. Only a few blocks away, red bursts of flames shot through the black sky with no more regard for people's suffering than the Devil himself would employ.

Out of the corner of his eye, Benjamin thought he saw a little girl scurry past an overturned Model A. He vocalized a curious and seemingly inappropriate chuckle as he doubted that a small child would be stirring around through the darkness on a night like this. He looked deadpan at Roy.

"Did you see that?" he asked.

"What?" Roy replied.

"That girl. That little girl that just ran off over there."

"No. I didn't see nothin'. Would you look at this place! They didn't tell us it would be like this. Lord Almighty, what will we do here first? I didn't think it would be like this."

Benjamin shook his head in amazement with Roy and wondered the same thing. The two of them had talked about getting a little sleep once they hit Murphysboro, but now they knew without asking that they would not be allowed to sleep for several hours. They could hear the shouts of the volunteer firemen only a few blocks away, and they took in the ruins with baffled, twisting heads and curious eyes.

This was their first day at war, and it was the middle of the night. They were soldiers marching into Hell, and Benjamin believed that somewhere out there was a little girl wandering amidst terrifying heaps of rubble. But he shook his head defiantly. He must have been seeing things. No one in their right mind would let a little girl wander out at night in these awful circumstances. He convinced himself that he was just scared and, therefore, imagining things.

Police Chief Norman, Scout Executive E. H. Tyron, and two National Guard soldiers were huddled in consultation near the school when the wobbling truck came to a jarring stop. The men approached the truck, noting the neckerchiefs of the boys in the back. This brigade of unpaid workers was the first of over a thousand scouts who would descend on Murphysboro to aid in the rescue and recovery of tornado victims. The biggest battle at the moment was controlling and ultimately suffocating the fires that threatened more lives and the few remaining, undamaged buildings of the town.

The young men jumped out of the truck one at a time, saying nothing. Benjamin lined up with Roy and waited attentively for instructions. The Sparta leader was leaning on the hood of the truck, observing every action of his troop and secretly wondering if they could muster the courage to deal with devastation of such magnitude. Tyron stepped forward and gazed at the lanky boys.

"Thank you for being here to help us. As you can see, there is a lot of work to do, and we need your help to aid the Red Cross, the National Guard, the firemen, and the people here who've lost everything. We have to get food and blankets to folks who have no shelter, and we're run over with questions about where people are. Let me be clear. The wounded come first. We're still finding bodies, and we've set up morgues for people to come get their family members who didn't make it. That Presbyterian church building over there is where we're taking the dead right now. We're setting up relief headquarters at our Scout Council office, and I'm going to take you there in a minute. The large, stone, church tower over there is where the Red Cross is headquartered. It is being used as a hospital and has started giving out food and tents. But we can't set up tents until the fires are under control. The men up there say they've gotten water pressure again. Oh … if you hear any explosions, don't be scared. They're using dynamite to control the spread of the flames.

You'll take wounded to the stone-towered Methodist Church. You take the dead to the Presbyterian Church, and you'll run messages in and out of the scout headquarters. If you get in trouble, stop one of the soldiers, like these fellas, and ask for help. We'll need to shut off the roads to outside traffic. Keep your kerchiefs around your neck at all times. Your kerchief will get you past soldier lines and into the hospitals and morgues. Don't take your kerchiefs off! And watch out for looters! When things like this happen, some sorry sons of bitches will steal anything they can get their hands on. If you see anyone taking property, report it to the soldiers or police right away. We already had a looter killed by police today. We're not putting up with no thieves when so many people are sufferin'."

Benjamin could barely take it all in. Hospitals. Morgues. Wounded. Red Cross. Police. Soldiers. Thieves, here of all places? That didn't make any sense in his mind as he wondered what kind of animals would think to steal from people hurting so badly.

"Sir," Benjamin asked, "did I understand that we might see someone stealing … did you mean from dead people, too? I'm not sure I understood …."

Tyron lowered his chin, and his face darkened with some combination of anger and overwhelming despair. He stared straight at Benjamin, then at Roy, and then at the others. His chin quivered, and he looked as if he would cry right there in the middle of Murphysboro as it burned to the ground. Ben gulped and felt a tremor of doubt shake his body. That was not the best question to ask here. It was just so confusing.

"Boys," Tyron began, "you're gonna see things here you've never seen before. It's gonna be hard work, and you need to be courageous. We're not puttin' up with people who come here to stare at our hurtin' people, and we're not puttin' up with no one who thinks they can get away with stealin' from anyone in Murphysboro, dead or alive."

Chief Norman stepped forward, nodding. It was his responsibility to keep order and to coordinate his men's efforts with the contribution of the National Guard men. These brave boys were greener than saplings.

But, as he stared at their earnest eyes, he sensed great determination and bravery, even as he saw the skinniest one shaking in the new surroundings.

"Boys, Mr. Tyron is right. Take care of the injured first. Your response will be the difference between life and death for a lot of people. Doctors have already had to amputate arms and legs, sometimes out in the open fields—wherever needed. One doctor we know about is at a house over yonder. He's been doin' surgery on a little girl's head since he got here ten hours ago. Just do the best you can, and plan on workin' hard. I'm sorry to tell you that one of my men found a man takin' rings off a dead woman's fingers today. My officer picked up a board and hit him in the back of the head. It killed him, and we got the woman and her rings delivered to the morgue over there. Let the soldiers and police deal with vultures … just let us know where there is a problem. Most of the people you'll see will help care for others any way they can. Some people are in shock and are wanderin' around the streets. Try to direct dazed people to Red Cross nurses and shelters. Look for the Red Cross signs and banners. Do the best you can. Ask for help if you need it."

Tyron nodded and added, "You boys are heroes, and there may not be time to thank you individually. Just know how much we appreciate your being here. The help you give here will not be forgotten. People may not know your names, but, they'll know what you do here. Let's head over to headquarters. We'll set up assignments for you to work right now as messengers. We've got to get nurses, doctors, and rescuers workin' together to do the best that can be done. Any more questions?"

Benjamin was afraid to open his mouth, and he stared at his toes for answers that were not there. Would he ask about that little girl? It could have been a shadow. He was probably wrong. Roy saw his buddy squirming and raised his right hand straight into the air.

"Sir, we thought we saw a little girl over there by that upset car. Is there any kids out here this time of night?"

Tyron's mouth fell slightly open, and he turned his eyes toward the pile of debris near the curb. There had not been any reports of wandering children after dark, but they had all been so busy that he knew it was not an impossibility. The boys would learn in a few hours that they would also be in charge of canvassing the town for missing people, hooking up family members with loved ones who were separated in the mass confusion. A small child could get into trouble too easily this night. He sighed and pointed to two older volunteers.

"Sam, you and Kenneth take a look over there! Boys, we don't know who's out there. People are in shock. They need first aid, just like people you see who are bleeding. If you see any children, get them to the Red Cross immediately. All right, let's head out."

The band of scouts walked behind the new leader-in-charge as their scoutmaster trailed behind them. Each boy held armfuls of supplies against his chest. The food, medicine, and blankets would be stocked at the council office. Volunteers would avail themselves of needed sustenance, and caregivers in homes blocks away from the heart of destruction would obtain blankets, more to comfort the survivors than to warm them. Some of the houses on the west end of town were overrun with strangers who hugged each other throughout the night.

Roy and Benjamin said nothing but continued to look in every which direction for signs of the lost child. Some areas were so foreboding that it was impossible to detect anything beyond unrestrained blackness. Daylight would offer a better opportunity to find lost souls in the rubble. Benjamin hoped that he would have enough time to save a few more people, especially the children who leaned heavily on adults for care and comfort. By the time they reached council headquarters, Benjamin was feeling more like a man than a boy. He would be fine. He would do all that he could to turn a horrible moment in time into an occasion of hope and compassion. That he knew.

In long hours ahead, the Boy Scouts of America quietly and obediently gave all their strength and skill to the people of Murphysboro. The scouts from Herrin unearthed ten dead children at the Longfellow School. Dedicated boys were the first to administer first aid to people who never knew their names. Scouts dug through the rubble in search of survivors. One child who had been buried for two days was pulled out from underneath a collapsed wall, alive and able to make a full recovery. The Boy Scouts carried supplies, worked as messengers, prepared meals for the newly homeless, blockaded roads, served as hospital orderlies, carried injured on stretchers to makeshift hospitals, aided the Red Cross, delivered cloth and clothing to undertakers, collected sheets throughout town for use as bandages, coordinated telegram deliveries, burned used bandages to prevent the spread of disease, escorted a would-be famous, young pilot to the telegram office, and collected food. It was the tireless efforts of the scouts who piled two, large, store buildings full of food, which was distributed to shock-filled townsfolk. By Thursday afternoon, the scouts, under the supervision of the Red Cross, began compiling a list of missing people and cross-checked the names with the morgues and hospitals.

Roy and Benjamin found strength they hardly knew they had. It was 7:30 a.m. on Thursday when the two lads rounded a corner just above the Methodist Church and spotted stringy, brown hair flickering in the morning sunlight. They moved close to the remains of a stone cellar where the strands of thin hair billowed just above a broken cobblestone wall. They silently hoped it was just someone's old rag doll with russet threads for hair. They had already found two bodies and moved them to the Presbyterian Church, but they hoped anyone else they found would be alive.

They paced themselves confidently toward the beckoning fine strands and peered through a maze of boards, shattered glass, and rocks. Crouched down in the corner of what remained of the small cellar room was a little girl. She looked up with tear-filled eyes as she hugged her knees close to her chest. Her body contorted tighter and tighter as the two young men moved gently toward her. Benjamin smiled for the first time in this godforsaken town. He knew who she was, and he had found her.

"Hello, little girl," he whispered. "I saw you last night when it was dark. We came here to help you find your Mommy. Come on, Honey, we'll help you find your Mommy."

A dirty tear streaked down her puffy cheeks, and she reached her hand to her new best friend. As she edged closer to the scouts, her shoulders shook. She looked up again at the boys, and then burst into tears. Benjamin choked back his own tears and knelt in the middle of the collapsed room. Gently, he wrapped his right arm around her muddy shoulder, and emulated his mother's comforting gestures as best he could.

"Shhhh," he whispered, "Everything'll be all right. There is a nice lady over there at the church who will help take care of you. We'll take you there."

The ragdoll-like figure was weak with fear and unable to respond. Except for gentle crying, she barely whimpered a response. Benjamin knew she had to be exhausted. She had probably been without water for several hours. Possibly she had injured herself as she jostled along the junk-filled streets. He looked at Roy and, without so much as a word, Roy picked up the fragile, live doll. He laid her rounded body in Benjamin's arms. They walked carefully toward the Methodist Church, eyes fixed on the huge Red Cross banner beneath the bell tower. The little girl hugged his skinny neck and uttered her first words.

"I go there with my Mama on Sundays."

Benjamin held on tight to his little friend. For the first time since his arrival in Murphysboro, huge tears rolled down his cheeks. He did not care a whit that he was crying. Silently and modestly, he knew he was a hero. History would not recall his name, and he would have no special accolades bestowed on him. But he was not there for awards and meritorious service recognition. He was there for that little girl. In the years ahead, he would care for many more children as a small town doctor, and he would always hold a special place in his heart for some unnamed, sweet, brokenhearted girl in a Murphysboro cellar.

28

Elena rested well in the Marion Super Eight, once the storm passed. She had watched the night sky with caution and then took a break in work long enough to see *Ratatouille* at the theater across the road. It was a silly break in the middle of a serious research trip, but she needed it. Much of her fatigue was related to the sheer stress of hoping she could successfully outmaneuver one tornadic system after another. Her back ached so badly that she was sure it would be less painful to be hit with a thousand sledge hammers. Better that than tornado debris. Most exasperating of all was the enormous tragedy of the Tri-State Tornado that permeated each waking minute of the day. Images of horrified victims crept into her every thought until she could bear no more. Only pictures of a rodent chef on the big screen could offer laughter and downtime that would be a respite in the middle of her strange and demanding quest.

By morning, she was on the road again. She backtracked to Carbondale and debated whether to stop at the University for more archive study. Time was pressing, and she needed a good sense of the land and community as she constructed her view of the 1925 storm. The plastic crate behind the driver's seat was filling quickly with historic records of the region. Secretly, she wanted to spend the entire summer in southern Illinois, but she could not afford it. She had a responsibility to get back to the *Sentinel* with the best research possible in a reasonable amount of time.

Reluctantly, she steered the red minivan north on 51. There was an enormous power drawing her to the one town where the school held an unmatched ghostly record. Elena had tried to rest her mind from the repeated accounts of schoolchildren suffering in Murphysboro. But here she was, driving straight into another site of unspeakable trauma. The Desoto School had the greatest number of children die in a tornado in all recorded history. She had hoped to veer away from family tragedy stories at this point, but she understood it was not an option. So far, Murphysboro had the most comprehensive documentation. Even in 1925, the town was the focus of attention from the media, and for good reason. More people died in Murphysboro than in any other town in the cyclone's path through three states. Elena thought back to Annapolis, and wondered how in the world it could have been wiped off the face of the earth leaving almost everyone stunned, still living with bruises, cuts, and a lifetime of nightmares. It was unimaginable that some people could have survived an assault of such magnitude while so many residents of Murphysboro fell victim to savage, life-crushing forces of nature.

Today's drive was perfect. It was sunny and warm, and the sky was as blue and as inviting as Caribbean water. Many times in the last couple of days, Elena wished she had elected to take a trip to the Bahamas. Maybe that was an option after she put this baby to bed. The whole experience was simultaneously exhilarating and exhausting. On one hand, she had been impressed with the cordiality of the people along the path, but there was an undercurrent of tragedy that was pulling her down. The monster was still in the air, after all these years. She was not a crier and was disappointed that she wiped tears from her cheeks more than once. As she had noted so many days before, it was impossible for her to imagine that at one minute life could be perfect, and then a violent turn of events could wipe life away in a heartbeat. A lesson was to be learned in this madness. Live each day as if it is your last. Tim McGraw's lyrics came to mind: "Live like you were dying." The words were spinning around her heart and she smiled, realizing how extremely fortunate she was to be pursuing the one thing she loved to do.

In short order, the Desoto town sign caught her attention. It was time to brace for the roller coaster. But, as quickly as anxiety rippled through her, it dissipated. There was little evidence of vulnerability in the community of 1,700. Interestingly, here was one town that had more than twice as many people today as it had in 1925. Elena marveled at a people whose resilience assured humanity that life did, in fact, go on. She knew she would be frightened to live here. She wondered if a matter of denial gave people a sense of confidence. On the other hand, perhaps she was overreacting. She had to remind herself constantly that these families get up every day, go to work and school, and understand how to take care of each other in severe weather.

At home, she had spoken with tornado survivors who had packed their bags and moved far away from Tornado Alley. One military wife had crawled into her closet with her children so many times that she gave her husband an ultimatum: he was to resign his commission or sign divorce papers. He chose the Air Force and tornadoes over his family. She moved on with no regret. She and the children were safe.

Another *Sentinel* subscriber had lived through twelve Illinois tornadoes in five years and did not miss the sheer terror of nature's violence. She and her family had moved and adjusted well to Appalachia's temperate climate. Elena did not have the heart to tell her that the fourteenth deadliest tornado in history had devastated Shinnston in 1944. It was a town just thirty miles south of her new West Virginia home.

Then, here was Elena. She was drawn to risky encounters but content to sleep well at night. It could not be both ways in Tornado Alley. Most frustrating of all was the fact that the NOAA radio was worse than worthless. It had afforded a false sense of security in the Ozarks, but not anymore. It was becoming clear that local spotters and local radio DJs had the best news for the area where storm watches and warnings were concerned. She kept a keen eye on the sky, but everything looked clear. Nothing to worry about here in this quiet, historic place. It looked like home. She murmured.

"It doesn't feel like home …."

Then, as soon as it began, it ended. The drive through Desoto took less than two minutes. It was a neat town with middle-class ranch homes and a long, one-story, grade school that stood out as a neat, modern building. Surrounded by a well-kept lawn, the red-and-beige-brick school was very quiet. The summer sun cast the building in a warm light. Elena hoped that the children who studied there were confident that they were safe. She hoped also that they knew nothing about the storm of 1925, and that the teachers knew everything about it. Here was one more beautiful town settled between fields of corn on a perfectly level horizon. The reality was a heavy memory for everyone who looked back at 2:36 p.m. on March 18, 1925.

Elena jotted a few notes in the spiral binder and continued toward Hurst. She saw no sign of a library here and was not comfortable knocking on people's doors in pursuit of stories. It simply was not appropriate, and it was absolutely not necessary. Her eyes were fixed steadily on the road ahead of her, but the images she had seen in the Jackson County Historical Society documents were ones she could not forget. The old Desoto school was a strong fortress in 1925. With steep-gabled roofs, two chimneys with fireplaces on each of the two floors, and distinct, arched windows and doorway, it was a towering structure overlooking the village. The bell tower two stories above the main entrance was the striking feature that held the bell that tolled gentle rings when classes were called together. Elena had studied the old picture, reflecting on her own red brick grade school and knowing that old Doc Price would protect them if the occasion had called for it.

She remembered silently lining up single file for regular fire drills as she and her classmates marched quickly through the downstairs hallway into the cafeteria and up the stone steps to the sloped walk beside Doc's "smoke house." The skinny principal at Wadestown was a masterful school administrator, except for the time he broke the wooden paddle over Jeremiah's hind end. Elena could still see the two-inch strip of wood flying through the air as though it happened yesterday. Flickers of imagined wood planks flying through the Desoto air crisscrossed her brain. School thoughts leapfrogged in her mind. First Desoto. Then Wadestown. From Jeremiah's day on, she knew beyond the shadow of a doubt that people who resort to violence to change behavior only reinforce violence in the offender.

As a shy, ugly little girl in fourth-period, geography class, she wanted to run up to the desk and order the mean-spirited principal to stop hitting Jeremiah. It was wrong. She knew it then. She knew it now. She had sat quietly in her seat unable to look at the boy's anguished face. It was an old memory she wanted to erase, but could not. If Grandma Kiz were with her in the passenger seat, she would sum it all up by saying, 'Jeremiah never amounted to nothin' anyway.'

Elena whispered, "When we let people hit others, we are guilty of the violence. We are violent by default. Poor Jeremiah. Why didn't I speak up? Because I would have been slugged. Nah. Because I felt helpless and terrified at the same time. I was just a kid."

Elena looked out the passenger window and then out the driver's side window. She knew damn well everybody talked to themselves while driving. She was just not interested in being seen doing it. Her thoughts drifted somewhere between her own school years and her research of the Desoto school. She could not shake the feeling that some extraordinary force was driving her through this storm-stricken region. It was as though she were responsible for all the children who died here. Of course that was not the case at all. What a stupid thought.

Elena was energized as if an electric magnet were pulling her through the towns. She was exhilarated by the pursuit of storm history but humbled by the tornado's pillaging power. She wished she had known the children of the Desoto school. She would have played hopscotch with them. Their laughter in the school yard would have been sweet music before the evil wind descended. A dreadful way to die.

Elena hated the fact that their lives were so brief, and she was guilt-ridden that hers was not. Survivors' guilt was creeping into her thoughts and sabotaging her objectivity. What human being would not feel moved? The children of Desoto had deserved sweet laughter and full lives. As quickly as a preschooler's puff could blow away dandelion seeds, the cyclone whisked laughter in the Desoto school from the face of the earth. The village children had been truly helpless.

29

<u>2:20 p.m., May 18, 1925, Desoto, Illinois.</u> The eighth grade class had been working on their writing skills when the first signs of a storm appeared on the horizon. It had been breezy all through the early afternoon, but that was not out of the ordinary for the town of 700. It was a typical March day, except for the stifling humidity. The choking air was earlier this spring than it had been in the recent past. At least that was how Garrett Crews remembered it.

Recess was supposed to last until 2:30, but the principal had rung the bell earlier than usual. Garrett thought he had heard thunder while scurrying around the small basketball court below the second-story classroom. But he questioned the need to end the shooting challenge between the other boys and him. He saw no imminent threat from where he stood and quashed a fume of frustration upon realizing that they would not be finishing the game. The lanky Desoto boys of northern Jackson County were tied 22-22. One more shot by Carl would show the Skins who the best shooters were under pressure. Garrett was as competitive as any of the fighting athletes. He relished a fiercely obtained basketball victory like a half-starved farmhand licking a chicken bone clean. There was nothing like it. In reality, the two opposing squads were well matched. That made for great competition every day they played ball in the school yard.

He had reluctantly lumbered toward the arched doorway of the main entrance and, for some peculiar reason, noticed a lone student heading down the path toward the girls' outhouse. He was amused by her desperation to take a leak after the third-story bell tower sounded the call to break from recess. He shook his head and silently considered the humiliating consequences of her likely tardiness. From his experience, none of the girls he had ever known could piss expeditiously. They were always holding up the lines, lollygagging, giggling, and taking way too much time for what Miss Andersen referred to as personal hygiene. Garrett mumbled an inaudible assessment of the situation.

"You better hurry up or your name will be in the detention box on the blackboard. You'll be wishing you had played a little less time with your dollies and made a little more time for taking a leak before the bell."

His face blushed as he heard his sarcastic tone. His lack of concern was suddenly replaced by a little bit of shame and a lot of compassion. He never liked to see any of his friends get into trouble. Standing in front of the class with his nose stuck in a chalk circle on the board was far from the fun he had when it was time to play on the ball court. He was content to do his work and see that others did their work as well. It was unsettling to see fellow students ridiculed for the slightest infraction. Even though it was hard work to keep his mouth shut and do what he was told, he did it. The Shirts could not afford to lose one of their tallest players just because he took a hankerin' to break the rules. He had concluded that the teachers and principal were lost in some autocratic warp where even urination was an imposition on the school day. Autocratic. It was one of their vocabulary words this week. He had all kinds of sentences in his head he could compose using the word autocratic. Nevertheless, he was careful to create his sentences with his self-confidence and his backside in mind. The shortened recess was just another example of school administrators trying to ruin his life.

"Girl, you better get to movin' back up that path," he earnestly articulated.

As he sat at his desk, he briefly focused on his recollection of the playground scene at the end of recess. He recalled that the outhouse door was closed when he stepped underneath the stone archway. Heavy oak doors made up the front entrance leading to the main hallway. He left the whipping breeze behind him and shuffled through the crowded hallway toward the side stairwell. Within two minutes, he was marching into his classroom. Garrett was an optimist and a dreamer. He liked to think that taking time away from recess was unnecessary. They could just finish out recess indoors until the official class time began. He hoped the day would come when the students could play longer at recess and study a little shorter time.

It was not looking good for the girl in the double-seat, oak toilet. He stuck his lips out in a demonstrable pout and dreaded her inevitable confrontation with the Rule Rigid Dictator at the front of the room. He hoped the teacher would have a change of heart and not start the ear-piercing bellyaching when the lone classmate made it to her seat by the window.

Recess was too short anyway. No sense could be made of too much formality where a person's bodily needs were concerned. Amidst thoughts of pissing and screeching, the sweaty ball player contemplated becoming a senator one day. He would enact a law to laugh first, make lessons fun, and worry about rules way down the ladder. Garrett had all kinds of great ideas for the perfect school and the perfect teacher. Maybe he would just do away with rules altogether. The hickory stick would be the first thing to fly out every classroom window. Except for being safe and learning lessons, too much fuss was aimed at making students' lives miserable. He was sure of that. Safety was the last thing on his mind when he opened his speller. The class began scrawling sentences on yellow papers.

The five, side-by-side windows on each end of the Desoto school were raised as high as they would go. Cross ventilation of erratic air currents made the upper classrooms tolerable and kept the students alert. Afternoons were the hardest times for teachers to hold students' attention. By 2:00, the scallywags were nodding off or staring through the wavy glass panes in anticipation of running home to their families.

Many of them regularly looked forward to afternoon snacks of canned apple butter and fresh, homemade butter melting on thick slices of just-baked bread. Garrett's Mama always saved some dough, and rolled it up with butter, cinnamon, and brown sugar to make the best cinnamon bread rolls in the county. Some days, he was so starved he ate the whole pan of cinnamon bread by himself. Mama would smile as he licked his fingers clean on those days. Wednesday was Mama's baking day. Today was Garrett's favorite day of the week.

He had just opened his speller when a gust of wind blew the graded papers off the teacher's desk. They were skipping along the floor in complete disarray. The eighth graders had learned long ago not to laugh at these mishaps, and Garrett clenched his jaw to hold in the chuckle that sprang into his mouth from nowhere. At the same time, he noticed the kids gathering near the open windows on the west side of the classroom. Curious to see what they were watching, he slammed the speller shut and tucked it on the cubbyhole shelf underneath the inkwell of his desk. He jammed his stubby pencil behind the book so it would not roll away and be claimed by one boy with an even smaller pencil.

Garrett's face took on a glum expression when he saw the rolling, black cloud in the distance. A life-threatening tower of wind reached all the way to the ground and was obviously the force behind the gusts cutting through the open window. Then he remembered the girl on the outhouse path. His heart quickened and a feeling of helplessness rippled through him like a sheet waving on a clothesline. His knees buckled slightly, and he raised his hand to tell the teacher about the classmate. Someone needed to get to her quickly.

Just at that moment, the teacher barked orders to close all the windows. Her eyes were filled with anguish and heartfelt concern for her students. Garrett slouched in his seat as he watched five other boys slam the wooden window frames against each casing. Each boy twisted the metal, clasp lock sideways at the top of the lowered panes. The girls had already begun to move back from the glass-covered wall.

Garrett's jaw dropped slightly, and he froze in place. He stared at the outhouse door. He prayed like he had never prayed before. It was all he knew to do. What was her name? He knew she should have hurried along with the class when the bell rang. He knew it! Now there was only silence and prayers between them. The wind carried death in its grasp.

"Oh please, God. Help her. Please help her," he begged.

It never occurred to him or the others that they were in the path of a killer storm. The bell tower was three stories high, and the school walls made up a powerful brick fortress that had always been a reliable shelter from the elements. They were fine. But she was outside and alone. She was not safe, and Garrett was helpless. He watched the two wooden goalposts on the basketball court weave violently in the wind. In a heartbeat, they snapped in two, like dried twigs severed in the mouth of a rabid dog.

Then, the worst happened. The outhouse door was flung open, and the girl stepped onto the path. She was standing in the northwest corner of the school yard alone with nothing but a prayer between her and her schoolmates on the second floor. Garrett prayed again as he watched her frantic eyes look toward the front doors of the school. Her arms flailed wildly as the wind picked her up five feet into the air. Garrett watched the fragile body being tormented by unmerciful wind. It carried her straight as an arrow into the fence on the building's north side.

"Children! Get out of the room now!" the teacher bellowed. "Get downstairs! Go!"

Garrett stood numb, watching an entire house pierce the air as though it were nothing more than a waxed-paper kite. Boards, trees, furniture, and pieces of everything were moving crazily through a sickening, green sky. The billow of the black, mile-wide vortex racing toward the children and teachers was ferocious and lethal. He looked at the teacher who waved her arm furiously as she motioned the students through the doorway toward the staircase. Her face was filled with a genuine regard for him and his friends. In a flicker, he realized that underneath her braying manner was a good-hearted caregiver who put her students first.

Carl grabbed Garrett's elbow and tugged him in the direction of the door as shards of glass filled the classroom in a fearsome explosion. Garrett lost his breath and moved as best as he could toward the doorway. He felt what seemed to be a thousand needles penetrating his neck and arms. It was as if he were in the midst of a terrible nightmare.

His brain shut down, and he could not make sense of anything that had happened in the few minutes since the bell had rung.

The wind tore through the room. Then, it inexplicably and abruptly changed directions as he made it to the classroom door. What had been a powerful force hurling him toward the hallway was now an exploding blast, bowing his gut in an effort to catapult him backward across the desks and through the windows that had been blown out. He prayed again. He was tall and strong. Garrett reached toward the ceiling and grabbed the upper door frame with both hands. He held on for dear life. That was the last thing he remembered.

30

2:47 p.m., May 18, 1925, Desoto, Illinois. The former state senator struggled to lie prone on the ground. He felt strangely embarrassed as he fiercely clung to the fence post that kept him from blowing away with the rest of Desoto. Entire houses, pans, glass shards, Fords, boards, and bloody bodies soared above him. He need not have felt embarrassed. It was impossible for anyone of repute to witness his desperate stranglehold on the post. They were too busy saving themselves.

F. M. Hewitt resided in Carbondale and had headed north to conduct business in Desoto. T. L. Cherry was accompanying him as he approached the side door of a two-story, white house on Hickory Street. The wind whipped the coattail of Hewitt like a stinging bullwhip cracking against his thigh. He held his small, brown, leather satchel close to his chest. Hewitt's head was bowed, and his eyes squinted in an effort to fend off small grains of dust that were piercing the air. Just after knocking on the screen door, Cherry excused himself and walked back toward the auto.

In the meantime, Hewitt was greeted by the lady of the house, and the two began discussing her farm just east of Desoto. It had been the only asset left to her by her grandfather. It was a nice piece of ground that would come into demand, and Hewitt was always interested in a good, real-estate investment. He owned and operated the Hewitt Drug Store on South Illinois Street in Carbondale, but he always had an eye open for ways to stretch a dollar. He smiled at the young woman as she welcomed him into the kitchen.

She caressed the smaller of her six-week-old twins and glanced intermittently at the other cradled in a small oaken bed nearby. Hewitt looked down at the little people and smiled the requisite smile. Most newborns were ugly little creatures from Hewitt's experience, but his compliment to her on the angelic babes was filled with genuine warmth and regard. Their filled bellies extended smooth, round abdomens that moved slowly up and down as they breathed rhythmically in cherubic sleep.

"What beautiful children," he spoke softly to the mother.

"We think so," she responded.

The slender mother looked weary. Her eyes were wide open, but dark circles gave away her fatigue. Her narrow shoulders drooped slightly, making her assume the posture of a little old lady with weak bones, rather than a vibrant woman in her early twenties. She was exhausted. Hewitt surmised that the cause was most likely long nights of tending to angels who slept so sweetly in the daytime. Frank Hewitt would need to be brief in his inquiries. Otherwise, he would alienate the lady and her family. He had no intention of adding to her burden.

As soon as he had diverted his eyes from the cradle to the frail woman looking over the twins, a loud, rolling bellow welled from the southwest sky. The mother picked up her babies and stood by the doorway with the businessman. Hewitt had already scurried down the steps from the small wooden porch as the infants stirred sleepily in their mother's arms. His mood turned from sweet reflection at the sight of gentle new lives to stunned amazement as the rolling, black cloud was destroying everything that touched the earth. The approaching cloud was nothing less than ferocious, ingesting jaws of a ravaging beast.

"Inside! Inside!" the mother called as she turned toward the screen door.

"No," Hewitt insisted, "I believe it's a tornado. We ...."

Then he looked away from the churning, dark funnel and lightning. Another young woman stood on the cobblestone walk in front of her house directly across the street. She too had a small baby in her arms. Hewitt realized he was in a precarious position between dear mothers and sweet infants with no place to go. He had lost track of T. L. Danger had been thrust upon them so quickly, Hewitt could hardly think straight. He looked around for a cellar or a low place where they could take shelter. No place was safe. Hewitt knew that the houses would not withstand the impact of the torrent speeding toward them. The boiling vat of clouds was as wide as the town. His hands shook as he found himself following behind the mother whose twins were wrapped in snow-white, knit blankets.

"Come on! Get in here!" the neighbor yelled.

Hewitt insisted that going inside the house was not safe, but the two mothers were inside the hallway off the kitchen before he could persuade them otherwise. He looked over his shoulder as he passed under the door frame. The giant cloud had a mesmerizing effect. Hewitt stared as if entranced by the vortex. He feared that the strength of the tornado would overpower everything and everyone. No one would be spared.

He moved close to the ladies and their babies. The sextet crouched along the white baseboard, and Hewitt studied the small children curled in their mothers' embrace. They were surprisingly calm. He felt the energy drain out of him as he realized that the little ones could not possibly understand the power that was descending upon them. God gave them good mothers to watch over them. Indeed, the two mothers responded instinctively as they curled their own bodies around the babes. They were human shields to take the blows so the children would be spared. Or so they thought.

Hewitt later would report that the encompassing howl that engulfed them at that moment sounded like a huge lumber wagon coming down the street. His ears ached with maddening pressure and pain. The small whimpers that surged from the lips of the smallest woman were quickly overpowered by the roar of death reaching from the sky. The muscles in Hewitt's neck tightened like wet rope twisted into strong baling twine. He anticipated a gruesome death. It was sure to take him. He did not pray not to die, but he did pray for God to take him quickly. He prayed that the youngest people here would miraculously live through the assault. Then he relaxed and let fate have its way with him and with every other person unlucky enough to be in Desoto, Illinois, at 2:36 p.m.

Suddenly, he felt his stomach rise into his throat, and a paradoxical, wispy exhilaration embraced him. It felt like the floating movement of the Ferris wheel he had ridden at the state fair last year. It was identical to the thrust in the pit of his stomach when the carnie had revved up the gasoline engine and flew the passengers at full speed above the carnival tents. It was the moment just as he sailed below the crest of the arc—the moment when gravity had no effect on anyone who floated in the updraft underneath the wooden seat spinner. That was a carnival ride. This was not.

Here he was with five strangers in a little house in Desoto. They were floating. The whole damned house was floating.

"Jesus …," he whispered amidst the gentle rocking motion.

Were these the arms of God carrying them from earth to afterlife? Was Heaven one big carnival ride, or were they still alive? Hewitt thought he was going crazy and, at the same time, believed he was being killed. It must be his time. He and Cherry did not start out on a business trip with the intention of dying. But death does not come with intention. It comes when it comes. Where the hell was Cherry anyway? He was lost somewhere in this wretched assault. Hewitt thought of his family, but his focus did not stray far from the moment. He was not sure how to respond but, for the duration of the Desoto ride, he could do little. The six of them were at the mercy of nature's wrath. Cherry was on his own.

The white house of Hickory Street was carried eastward, then gently set down on a patch of ground that had been brushed flat to the dirt floor where a lawn had been. Every blade of grass had been torn out by the root. Once the house landed, Hewitt scrambled outside with the mothers. They all knew that the clapboard structure would afford them no real protection, and that is when the friends parted ways. Not of their own volition. The cloud was not done with them. Hell had just opened its door a little wider.

Frank Hewitt felt his body being pulled upward, and once again gravity was failing him. That was when he saw the fence post. He dropped flat to the ground and began crawling toward the post. If he could just hold on, he might not be carried away as people often were in these situations. He wrapped his right arm around the post at the elbow while clasping the base of the gray post with his left hand. As he struggled for his life, he knew the worst. The others were gone. Only Satan and Frank himself remained in the fight for life. Hewitt closed his eyes tight and held on, hoping the local dignitaries would not be watching him from a sidewalk beyond the tornado's grasp. In some foggy state of mind, he blushed to think of the jesting that would inevitably go on for years when customers came to the Hewitt Drug Store. Fortunately, it would be a small price to pay for saving his own life.

Then, as quickly as it started, it stopped. Total silence replaced the roar. Hewitt eased his grip, but kept touching the post with torn fingertips. He was terrified to move, lest the beast circle back and devour him. It was over. He was alone. The babies were gone. An old woman's crumpled body lay just feet from him. Her clothes were gone, torn from her by death.

31

2:58 p.m., May 18, 1925, Desoto, Illinois. By the time Frank Hewitt got to his feet, he knew that he was alive because of some inexplicable miracle. Bloody bodies were everywhere. The first sounds he heard were the cries of babies. Most of the dead people he could see were either children or old people. His hands were bruised and bleeding from tiny lacerations, but his legs were strong enough to walk. Dulled by the awfulness that stunned or slaughtered everyone around him, he contemplated what to do. It was difficult to imagine what one person could do.

Frantic mothers were screaming the names of children who had been pulled away from them in the turmoil. He heard the cries, but he could not see the desperate women. It was as much as he could bear to hear the piercing wails pounding inside his head. Injured townsfolk cried out for help. Many were in agony from broken limbs that were crushed underneath buildings, furniture, bricks, collapsed stone walls, and mangled automobiles. Everything was out of place. Desoto was gone. Only debris and broken bodies remained.

Hewitt found his wits and moved toward one man who was moaning from underneath a would-be sarcophagus of rocks and bricks. The drugstore proprietor began throwing red blocks sideways from the man's head. He was able to uncover the broken body, only to be drawn to another victim who cried louder from more serious injuries. A third plea for help drew him away from the latest victim and forced him to render aid to a lady whose legs were pinned underneath beams. Even with all the might he could muster, he could not budge the oak ceiling that now held her captive. These people were next to Death's door. Nothing he did would matter if they were going to die anyway.

Hewitt kept trying to uncover stunned, buried men, women, and children, but somehow his brain shut down and he understood some inconsolable truth: he was the only person alive. Now his breath was gone too. He could not move. A shroud of blackness strangled him, and in despair he realized that he had escaped the tornado but that he might die now of suffocation.

Then he saw someone else—walking. One of the neighbors on Hickory Street was lumbering through what probably had been a side street ten minutes earlier. Hewitt took in a slow, deep breath which helped him recover from the shock of so much death and suffering around him. A burst of energy surged through his legs, and he half-ran toward the man. His brain was still shuffling strange messages, but he was certain now that the two of them were the last people alive. In a later newspaper interview, Hewitt would note that this man was the "only friend I had in the world, and I did not want to lose sight of him." They pulled themselves together and found incredible strength to do what they could to answer the violent assault on the little Illinois town. They became a two-man team, helping injured people out of the ruins of a community that would suffer for years from just five minutes of nature's unmerciful wrath.

While the men provided comfort and assistance to what seemed to be hundreds of people, a young man ambled through the debris-strewn roads. He was a schoolboy. His face was dazed, his shoulders were slouched, and his posture cried out for understanding. The lad's eyes were fixed on a distant point, but Hewitt and Friend were distracted by efforts to unbury helpless victims. Thoughts of enlisting the boy's assistance were fleeting and erratic. Death all around them tore at the very souls of the two people who were able to render aid. It was a town filled with numbed brains, dismembered bodies, and shocked, frantic hearts that beat strong against all odds. The men watched the boy pass by the remains of a Model T. The farm truck was crushed as sure as it would have been if a boulder had fallen from the sky. No one spoke. There was nothing to say.

Garrett had been dazed when he pushed his way out of the schoolhouse ruins. He had seen a twisted, bloody arm that fixed in his brain an image he could not erase. It was important to get as far away from the remains of the assault as he possibly could. The young man knew only one thing to do. Go home. The Crews' house was five blocks west of the school, but as he approached the site of Redd's Store building, the familiar path he had walked so many times turned into a dead end.

The once stalwart store building had failed to protect Mr. and Mrs. Redd from the killing wind. All four walls had collapsed, and the couple was trapped beneath a weight so burdensome, no one could have saved them. A fire had broken out amidst the inventory of dry goods and farm supplies. Nobody would ever know if it were the injuries that killed them or the fire that broke out within minutes of the storm's passing. Only God knew.

Garrett's pace slowed as exploding flames threatened to spread a second wave of death in his general direction. But he had to get home. He would be all right, if he could just make it to Mother. She would know what to do now. He would probably be needed there to help with recovery and repairs to whatever extent possible. He was ready to fight on. He was strong, and he was able to do whatever was necessary for his family. That was his first responsibility. It was also his first need.

As he moved closer to the store building, his pace was slowed by jumbled piles of debris. He carefully placed his feet in each successive step, so as to prevent injury that he had already managed to avoid. His grip on the door frame of the classroom must have saved him from dying with the others. Like Frank Hewitt, Garrett Crews' thoughts were a jumbled mess of questions, fragmented, short-term memories, blocked-out periods of time, and pain. He was helpless, except for the power to press on to a safe place.

He raised his right arm in front of his face to fend off the emanating heat from flames that reached higher than the store itself had been. Garrett's breath was displaced by smoke and noxious gases that poured out in every direction. The old store had been transformed from a center of consumerism and social gatherings into a giant, debris-fired furnace. As his arms and face grew hotter and hotter with each step, he realized his attempts to get beyond the store were futile. The fiery blast drove him back. He prayed that Mr. and Mrs. Redd had escaped. They must have escaped.

The boy turned north and circled around erratically strewn piles of rubble and then made a turn toward the southwest part of town. As he walked by the remains of one house, he saw a man and woman standing helplessly in the spot where their home had been. The man's eyes were crimson, his face blackened with soot and mud, and his shoulders shaking in pain. Caressed in his arms was the limp body of a small child who breathed a last breath in front of Garrett and the child's mother. The little one died, and Garrett did not. For a moment, he watched the woman as she stood staring at the splintered, hickory tree trunk that jabbed the gray air a few feet in front of her. Her eyes were glazed with disbelief and somber reflection. Unlike the other women of Desoto who Garrett heard screaming for their children, this mother merely stood frozen in place. As the Logan schoolboy walked by, the woman's strength evaporated, and she slithered to the ground, limp and lifeless. Garrett kept walking.

Before he could reach the southwest corner of what was left of Desoto, he knew on some level that the outcome was probably not a hopeful one. But hope is a formidable ally in times of tragedy. Hope builds on the hearts of those who believe in some greater good in the midst of desolation. Belief in something good was the driving force of each step Garrett took. God had a plan here. He would find it as soon as he got home.

Slowly, the schoolboy gained a shaky awareness of people around him. Some dead. Some not. His eyes dropped toward the ground, and he watched his booted feet slog through contents of households strewn in places where they should not be. If he refrained from looking at the people and parts of them that remained in the storm's aftermath, he guessed he would not go crazy. Otherwise, there would be no recourse except to succumb to total madness. He thought he heard himself screaming, but he was not sure. It was too much to bear. Mama would wrap her arms around his shoulders, and the two of them could figure out what to do next. He was almost there.

Some houses had been lifted from the earth's floor only to have exploded in midair above the streets and neighborhoods of Desoto. With few remains of familiar landmarks in view, Garrett had to pause frequently to get his bearings. He was a drunken slug, disoriented and mute. A few walls remained intact, held together by interlocked corners. But the fractured houses lacked roofs, window panes, and in too many cases, life in any form. He prayed that it was all a terrible dream and that he would awaken to the sound of Mama humming "In the Sweet By and By" as she did every morning when she fried bread and eggs for her family's breakfast.

At one point, Garrett passed a small brown house where the roof had collapsed toward the back end of the building. It was a ghostly sight and simply more of the wreckage he could not remedy. He could see angled beams extending from the back rooms and thought that the support system should have blown away with the other houses. Little good it did now, for all he could tell. Garrett had no hope that anything survived the storm. He saw no shelter anywhere. The view held nothing close to sanctuary. Not a single home remained intact on any street, and yet, he hoped that a miracle had touched the house where he had spent his first fourteen years of life in Desoto. He would know soon.

Garrett was passing by the farthest corner of the small brown house when he thought he heard a whimpering cry of a baby. In a sharp reflex, he jerked his knobby head in the direction of the space where a front door once opened into a little parlor. He must have been mistaken. There was no stir of life and no sign that anyone could possibly have survived beneath the jumbled piles of wood. He did see what appeared to be a moonshine still, and he marveled that a private brewery had probably been concealed from prim and proper neighbors for who knows how long. Little did he realize, many home-devised whiskey factories would be detected as houses and cellars far and wide were opened for the world to see.

But as quickly as his eyes had focused on the coils and metal tanks, his ears alerted him once more to listen for life, anywhere. A baby cried. He thought. He was not sure. As weeks would pass after that fateful afternoon, he would learn that a new mother had been found inside her bedroom where she and her newborn were saved by beams that fell at angles across the bed. When she heard the roar of the ravaging cloud, the whimpering mother crawled between the warm covers with her baby. There, she begged God to spare their lives.

After the storm, the two were fine, saved by a house that refused to yield completely to the slaughtering cyclone. But no one would ever have known she and her smallest child were alive, based on the experience of the half-witted, dazed, schoolboy who had uncovered himself amidst bodies of fellow classmates. He was frantically compelled to reach his own mother. So he walked. Mama would know what to do. He was lost smack-dab in the middle of his own neighborhood. Garrett was surrounded by bodies, and he was being thrown into a state of absolute despair and terrifying solitude. He understood very little about what had happened in the past half-hour. The weight of it all was pushing against him with the force of the storm itself. Something helped to lift his increasingly heavy feet. Some extraordinary power moved him from step to step. Perhaps it was the strength of his mother's love reaching out to him through a misty haze.

Something happened to the time between the crying baby's house and Garrett's destination. Somewhere on the jagged course, he lost memory of where exactly he had been and what he had seen. But he snapped back to the present when he found the narrow, stone steps that led up to the cobblestone walkway between the Crews' front porch and the street. The curved, uneven, walk stones were all in place, but there was no porch. So too, the house had vanished. The only remaining signs of its existence were a few whitewashed boards that had been tossed haphazardly across the space where the back porch steps should have been. He had just painted that wall last week. Garrett shook. Then he took in a long, deep breath, realizing that this was not a complete surprise. He knew before he got there that his home had been carried away with the rest of the town.

His childlike hope ebbed slightly, but did not abate altogether. He was smart enough to figure out his next move. As the wheels of problem-solving ideas spun wildly in his skull, the part of hope that had propelled him to this place encircled him with perfect love. A gentle touch on his right shoulder showered him with warmth as dear as life itself. He looked to his left and stared at the angel who had taken her place beside him. Amidst cascading tears, he cried out his first word since he was blown from the second floor of the Desoto School.

"Mother!"

32

Elena was exhausted. She could hardly concentrate on the trek eastward. As she drove across Little Muddy River, it occurred to her that the children of 1925 may have gone swimming in the very stream that flowed gently here for decades before and after the storm. In all probability, a hundred years from this very moment, it would be flowing with the inconsequential meandering that rivers inevitably pursue.

She glanced to the left at thousands of Queen Anne's lace blossoms. The fields were spread out like a huge pancake. This was the flattest terrain on God's good, green earth. It made sense to her that a tornado had made a clean sweep of this village. The terrifying reality was that tornadoes are equally lethal in mountainous terrain. She would be sure that her feature article admonished readers to be on guard in the mountains as well as in the openness of Tornado Alley ... wherever they were. Unfortunately, thick tree lines and rolling hills allowed for little warning. Sam barely had a moment to roll into a ravine, and it failed him in his last moments. Yet, a good view did not save the people here either.

Desoto was an easy mark for a ravenous cyclone. The fields were remarkably easy to plow for acres upon acres of crops. Farming made sense here. But the rich soil and open land made a facile pathway for killer wind. Mobile homes were too common. Elena was furious. She trembled to realize how affordable the flimsy housing was, but how open to devastation it would be, if the conditions were right. Surely families with modest incomes had options for acquiring homes that were stronger than cheap, tin cans. If she lived on this turbulent terrain, she would build an energy-efficient, underground home, like the one Dennis Weaver built. She would crawl into it like a groundhog, and on sunny days, she would tend the flower garden and white gazebo on top of her woodchuck-hole home. But she did not live here. People had to go to work, go to school, shop for groceries, go to church, and live with nature's bouts of mania.

Elena's eyes flickered back and forth between the road ahead and the lush fields. She wondered where they found the Bratcher twins and their loving mother. The records she had uncovered at the Jackson County Historical Society had not noted the babies' names. She supposed it was enough to account for their existence. "Female Bratcher, w/o John" (female Bratcher, wife of John). "Infant Bratcher, c/o John, Infant Bratcher, c/o John" (children of John). That was all. Crushed skulls. It was no way to die. Even if it had been their time to die in "that way," they should never be forgotten. Never.

Anger and torment rushed through Elena's mind once more, and she wrestled with the absolute futility of a brief existence. There had to be a higher answer. A higher power. A greater good. Her tiny feature story would matter little, given the limited circulation of *The Sentinel*. But if it saved one life, her job would be done. Her quest would have purpose.

She had told Greg that she dreamed of a Tornado Chase vacation, but the reality of the life and death in Tornado Alley now wrenched her stomach and instilled a healthy respect for nature and its lethal moments. Shelter and tornado warnings had a new meaning that would never be shaken again by the need for exhilaration—the rush of the chase. At the same time, she had the utmost regard for scientists who spend their lives analyzing fronts, so as to issue storm warnings with expeditious timing.

As much as she respected nature, she idolized scientists whose motives and gifts saved lives every day. There is nobility in the study of meteorology. Life was safer now. It was astonishing that even the word "tornado" was banned in 1925. Banned. So that people would not panic. The economy would have suffered too much if the masses were taking shelter from storms. A burning fluid as acidic as lye welled in Elena's throat. This sounded too familiar.

Elena was not a drinker, but the depth of the Tri-State Tornado research was taking a toll. Maybe there would be a nice bar in the next town. Nice bar. She shook her head and smirked. That was an oxymoron, if she ever heard one. It had been only three years since her niece Clarine had been killed by a drunk driver on Route 250. A bitter taste had welled from deep within, and she grimaced at even the most innocent discussions by friends who were hell-bent on "tying one on." Behavior so self-destructive paled in comparison to the large number of highway fatalities attributed to drunk driving. She had covered a story on drunk driving a few months after the crash. Fury and absolute despair reared its ugly head in the writing, and Charles toned down the story before he would agree to print it. Every year. Five times the number of people killed in the World Trade Center. Five times. Drunks. Worthless souls imposing homegrown terror on innocents like Clarine. Elena was not sure if she was angrier about the loss of children in 1925 or the loss of one little girl in 2004. Perhaps it did not matter.

Rage could be a compelling ally for a writer. Here she was losing herself in a story once again and beginning to believe a strong drink would temporarily ease the pain. On one level, she did not believe solace is found in a bottle. On a more desperate level, she craved a time to black out the archives of suffering that were piling up in the box behind the passenger seat. A few drinks in a nice bar could drown her despair. Is that not the claim of old movies and mindless alcoholics? Drown your sorrows. One thing she knew. She hated beer. Although she had not tried it since the day she turned twenty-one, she was not going to "try" it again. The rambling reporter would rather drink water from an unflushed toilet bowl.

A picture of a high-calorie pina colada emanated from nowhere. Aaah, yes, a little rum and a lot of sweet coconut in a frosty, tall glass. She could settle into a nice hotel that had a bar on site and get smashed so she would not have to think about Desoto children or dear farmers who foolishly crouched for safety that eluded them in lonely ravines. Maybe another movie would sufficiently distract her. She definitely needed a diversion but loathed the thought of adding a single penny of revenue to any brewery's profits. She would die first. As the drive continued, she almost missed the sign welcoming her to Hurst.

"Oh, Hurst," she mumbled.

What was in her notes about this place? Something. The towns and their details were starting to run together. Weary from driving and running from tornadoes herself, Elena was losing track of all the stories along the storm path. At least, photocopiers and microfilm printers would supplement her faulty memory. She had accumulated so many records, she had begun carrying the crate of files into her hotel room at the end of the day. She could not take a chance on roaming, teenage vandals destroying all the work she had done thus far. She would never be able to retrace her path to regain her losses.

On the other hand, she did not recall having seen a single teenage vandal anywhere on the journey. How tiresome. One minute she was thinking about getting drunk, and the next she was fending off imaginary gangs of thieves who were hell-bent on stealing her work. Time for a break.

Elena pulled to the berm, shut off the engine, and closed her eyes. She despised the opportunity to look at bucolic countryside that screamed with a maddening history. It was possible that this whole trip was some strange quest that would end in nothing more than despair over events that could never be changed. She began to doubt that there would be any interest in yet another tornado story. The media's fascination with gun violence and America's general obsession with terror from foreigners filled the bill rather nicely, she thought. Readers and TV addicts were desensitized from too much exposure to disaster reports from New Orleans to Greensburg, Kansas, and back again. This story could be just a sad series of tales that held little value for her contemporaries. She did not believe that. At the moment, a lull in energy was distorting her perception. Rest was more important than driving.

She drifted to sleep and fell into a dream about this small village and its townsfolk. Elena was on the floor of the Hurst School, looking around at wide-eyed children who whimpered like thin, beaten, baby animals. A little brown-eyed girl a few feet in front of her stared at her, unable to speak. Her eyes burned an impenetrable image on Elena's brain, as she clutched the curved, wrought-iron, school-desk support with one hand while extending her left hand toward Elena. Something kept Elena from moving. A force greater than her own strength pushed her backside onto the floorboards, holding her just a hand's grasp away from the brown-eyed child.

A skinny, farm boy to her right wailed a scream in the general direction of the door of the one-room building. Elena shivered in complete terror as his words pierced through the howling air and into her heart. She tried to scream with him, but the words choked in her chest. A wave of fear washed over her. The little brown-eyed girl lowered her eyes into a blank stare as she realized that Elena was not there to help her. The boy bellowed an ungodly plead.

"Let us out of here! Let us go!" he screamed.

As immediately as the unseen force had planted Elena in the middle of the classroom, an opposing force lifted her above the children. She floated around the room, studying every innocent, anguished face. The little ones held to their desks that were bolted to the floor. The older children had begun crawling toward the one-armed man who stood plastered against the lone exit. Having a one-armed teacher yelling at them every day was frightening enough. Today, his demeanor was mild in comparison to the monster that raised the school from its foundation. The children cried in a chorus of woeful pleas. But the teacher scowled and snapped orders to them. His exploding voice overpowered the very wind that moaned an evil dirge.

"Stay where you are! No one is going anywhere! Do you hear me?"

Elena was losing hold of her breath and feeling faint. Of course, everyone heard the sour old coot. A person would have to be dead or stone-deaf not to have heard him. All she saw were the children sprawled like lambs to be slaughtered for mutton sandwiches for the county fair. She wanted to help someone … anyone, but she was out of arm's reach of the children in the schoolhouse. She bore no scar, suffered no blows, and cried no tears. She rested her mind in the serenity of elevated suspension. Would that it were the same for the students at the Hurst School. They whimpered and cried for their mothers, who were no place near when the building became airborne at 2:57 p.m. The grimacing old teacher had held them prisoners in the death trap of a building. He would burn in Hell for his callous disregard for students whose lives he held in his grasp.

Then the schoolhouse smacked down on the ground, soundly jarring its occupants, but remaining miraculously intact. With the thud of descent, Elena awakened, panting frantically and clutching the tilted steering wheel of the Windstar. The children of the Hurst School lived. The tyrant with a hickory stick mounted over the door casing probably had saved their lives. But, as Elena's heart pounded furiously against her chest wall, she felt little consolation knowing the truth. And she felt a distressing sense of guilt that her life had been so easy, so full, and so relatively happy. Survivor's guilt. More than eighty years after the storm.

The fatigued writer was losing her mind. She glanced around the van, hoping a local cop was not circling her vehicle like a vulture ready to pounce. If he were calling in her plates, it would be her just desert. This was no place to catch a nap. She looked very suspicious. As she strained to see through the backseat window, a snapping series of thuds on her driver's window scared the wits out of her. She rolled down the window.

"Ma'am, you all right?"

"Oh … oh … yes, officer, I'm fine. I am traveling the path of the 1925 tornado and pulled off here to rest. I was getting drowsy."

"License and registration, please," he replied without an ounce of regard for the alarm she had just experienced.

He studied the cardboard documents and then feigned a youthful smile in her direction. Elena knew she had needed to take a break, but she recognized the impropriety of parking so close to the highway. If she got a ticket, she had it coming to her.

"Ma'am, glad you're taking a break, but you might want to go on out the road apiece. There's a park off to the right. It's close to a little gas station. You can rest there and get your car a little farther off the road. Okay?"

"Yes, thanks," she sighed. "About a mile or so?"

"Actually, it's not a mile. Just drive safe," he ordered.

"I will," she smiled.

She saw the cruiser door was open in her rearview mirror as she drove back onto the road. Suddenly, her brain was in focus, and the memory of the Hurst kids who actually had floated inside their schoolhouse was secondary to her desire to get as far away from the sheriff as possible. She had wiggled out of that ticket, but she had some self-righteous notion that she had done nothing wrong, except for the fact that she had parked illegally on some quiet Illinois road. Her vision was sharp, and at the moment, she had one thing on her mind: little park on the right. She would rest a while longer, relying on the blue alarm clock to waken her. After a short respite and a quick walk around the picnic tables, it would be time to move on.

Elena drove eastward and tried to rid herself of the last image of Desoto she could bear. Grave diggers are the saddest people on earth. In 1925, they had the miserable task of preparing resting places for the broken bodies of so many good people in the little town. Caskets were shipped by rail and truck into the deadly farmlands of Illinois. Sadness danced like devils stomping the hearts of all who survived. They were neighbors, sisters, brothers, parents, and grandparents who stood by helplessly as coffins, big and small, were lowered into the cold earth. Loose, crisscrossed boards, held together by bent nails, marked each grave. Penciled names on the crosspiece of each marker identified every soul. Elena wondered how many families were able to replace the temporary markers with permanent, granite slabs of honor and dignity. Over time, the weather would have done away with the pathetic wooden crosses that marked the lives snuffed out by the storm.

Elena clutched the steering wheel with vice grip force. She was not far from West Frankfort. It was not a big town, but probably it would be a good place for her to unwind and freshen up. A hot shower would feel great. She was wide awake now. She stared down the double yellow line, popped *Chicago's Greatest Hits* into the tape player, and pursed her lips.

She still had a lot of work to do. It was too soon to stop the research. The storm had not ended here. Why should she stop here? Yet she was tired, and she needed a break. Elena mumbled.

"Crap, there must be a bar around here someplace."

33

West Frankfort was a nice surprise. It was definitely bigger than Ellington and De Soto, and it had the same cordial atmosphere of Murphysboro. As Elena passed the town sign, she had the distinct notion that this was a good place to be. Once again, Tornado Alley was exuding the calm and reassuring atmosphere that she loved. It was not home. But it could be. Being here felt like the gentle sway of a wooden swing on a cool autumn day. It fit with her sense of place and peace. Except for the silent clash with the one, overzealous, town cop in Annapolis, the trip was a strange blend of excitement, restfulness, cordiality, and a generous dose of melancholy. Elena headed for the library on East Poplar, determined to retrieve the best historic materials possible. She knew that the neatly groomed blocks of the town and the well-manicured lawn in front of the brick and stone library were good signs for work. Thoughts of unwinding in some hole-in-the-wall, dingy bar mingled with the practical side of her brain. Work first. Then play. All work and no play … yadda … yadda … yadda….

A maple tree in the corner of the parking lot invited her to rest in the shade before pulling her notebooks and pens together for more research. This would prove to be her most excellent writing trip, and she knew, before going through the double, glass doors, it was a good place to work. She lowered the laptop into the Coleman cooler, having decided to come back for it later if necessary.

So far, the pattern was becoming one of microfilm reels and piecemeal printouts that she would tape together later. Elena did not have enough time to take notes the old-fashioned way. She could organize everything back in the *Sentinel* office. Charles would want to get out the first part of the story in short order, but she knew it would be a huge task to piece together all the news stories. It was practical to write chronologically. At least she could make sense out of the storm's path and what happened throughout the entire length of the cyclonic sweep.

Elena had gotten her second wind. Energy was easing back into her thinking. The sheriff outside Desoto had been pretty understanding. She had no need to feel frazzled now. She was sharper, rested, and ready to put in some more time tackling the monster that had sucked life and breath out of so many good towns like West Frankfort. It was as though she were fighting for people she never knew and for many people she would never even imagine in the future. Writing was the best job in the world. Elena loved nothing more than putting the final touches on a feature story and heading it to press for 50,000 people in northern West Virginia. This one would knock their socks off. At least she hoped it would.

As she stepped out of the van, a classy, white, '53 Corvette convertible rolled into the shaded space beside her. She was inclined to look the other way, but the vehicle was gorgeous. Who could help staring? The guy driving it was not too bad either. He was a lean, coarse-haired facsimile of a young Harrison Ford. She grimaced to hold back a smile that welled at the sight of him and his car. She was not sure if she were more taken with the convertible or its driver. In either case, her distress with tornado-victim stories evaporated right there in the middle of the West Frankfort Public Library parking lot.

"Nice day, isn't it?" he asked, rising from the ground-level seat of his prized possession.

Elena was caught off guard. This was one of the few times she had not initiated a conversation. In fact, she did not think she had had a real conversation since she left West Virginia. Every inquiry, every comment, and every thought was linked to the Storm of '25. She was not in the mood for flirting, but could not resist the draw to the exquisite car and driver that had landed right in her lap. A real conversation now would be a treat.

"Oh, hi," she said. "Sorry—I was admiring your car. Wow, what a beauty. It's a '53 isn't it?"

The Harrison Ford clone raised his eyebrows and smiled a crooked grin.

"Not many people know the year at a glance. I'm impressed."

"Ah, my Grandad was a Chevy dealer. I grew up with Vette posters every place I could put 'em," she replied.

She sighed, and finally the smile that had welled inside her chest burst onto her face. She shook her head back and forth, admiring the two-seater and its driver. What in the world was a guy like this doing in a little town like West Frankfort? He was as out of place as Elena's West Virginia tags. She walked around the back of the Vette, eyeing every detail and thinking she could handle a convertible like this. The Kentucky license plates jumped out, which added to the confusion about this interesting stranger. And she reminded herself that he was indeed a stranger.

For all she knew, she was in the presence of a serial killer. On the other hand, it did not seem probable that he could whisk her away to her killing in a small convertible without arousing suspicion. Her radar went up as she studied the Vette's leather seats and chrome dashboard instruments. A guy back home was waiting for her to marry him, once she climbed a little farther up the career ladder. This Kentucky dude was cute, and he had impeccable taste in automobiles. He was just a nice fellow she met at a library, for crying out loud. Paranoia and romance were not requisites for each new encounter.

"My name's Will," he said.

"Hi, Will. I'm Elena. Just stopping here to do some research on a feature story I'm writing," she nervously replied.

He extended his right arm and smiled as she shook hands with a confidential grip that took him off balance. For the first time, she looked him square in the eye, searching for some evidence of an ulterior motive. She had no time for a tryst. What she did have were several hours of time to unwind with a good conversationalist. The fact that he was in a library parking lot was a good sign. Chances are that he was not here to fix the computer monitors in the archive lab, if there were such a thing. Nothing ventured. Nothing gained—or lost.

"What a coincidence. I'm doing the same thing," he beamed. "What are you working on?"

"Actually, I'm gathering historic files about the Tri-State Tornado that hit this area in 1925. I'm retracing the path of the storm, and putting together a feature article based on the aftermath," she replied.

"You're kidding!" he said, "I'm from NOAA in Paducah. We've been hashing through old files for months trying to construct a computer model of meteorological variables that indicate causality in such a violent outbreak! Can you believe the power of that storm?"

"No," was all Elena could say as sadness pulled her temporarily away from the obvious attraction she was experiencing. Here was one of the guys she idolized, and he had a '53 Vette to boot. This could be as good as it gets. Here, also, was an opportunity to carry on a relatively sophisticated conversation with someone who could expound on the movement of the storm system and its overwhelming force. She had hit pay dirt under the maple trees of West Frankfort, Illinois.

In a matter of minutes, the two researchers had pulled every reel available from March 18, 1925, through January 1926. Elena had already figured out that many long stories were published well after the day the storm system combed the farmlands and towns of several states. The Tri-State Tornado was only one facet of the gargantuan system of multiple cyclones. It was, nonetheless, the ferocious heart of the storm. Kentucky, Tennessee, Alabama, Ohio, and her beloved West Virginia were assaulted by spin-offs that were as lethal to a few as the main vortex was to so many. It was Missouri, Illinois, and Indiana that harvested the most notorious headlines. Well they should. That was absolutely clear to the young, feature-story journalist.

Will and Elena huddled like football players in the last three minutes of a tied fourth quarter. He enthusiastically shoved the human interest stories her way, and she shared with him matters of record-setting barometric pressure, physical descriptions of multicolored storm clouds, and the eyewitness testimony about the day that instantaneously turned into night. The duo worked like a fine-tuned instrument set on the same end, getting the facts and building on them. She wanted the world to know the names and places that were beginning to fade in some local files. He wanted to discover new truths and theories of storm development. Together, they hoped to save lives. Everything between them was clicking perfectly.

Minutes turned into a few hours as the research pair scoured every file, newspaper article, and photograph on record. It was late afternoon well before the two imagined it could be. Elena's enthusiasm was back as strong as ever. Finally, she had a real, live person with whom to share her quest. The dead people had been pulling her toward their graves, and she still had plenty of life in her for this project. Will was a dynamic researcher, sifting through innuendos on which to build new hypotheses about the weather factors leading up to the deadliest tornado on record. His was a typical left-brain quest to summarize, analyze, and hypothesize his way to the next paper for the American Meteorological Society. A formidable force was at work within and between them. The heat of their arms emanated against the other, and whispers of discoveries were filled with celebrated inquisitiveness. Each stranger understood the other's tone and observations. They shared an incessant passion for violent weather. It occurred to Elena that it could be the passion that could underlie a lifelong friendship, or more. They were clicking.

Will glanced at the clock on the east wall, noting how much time had lapsed. Although he had planned to head back down the road that night, it was a rare moment when he encountered a new person with the interest and dedication he had to resurrect the storm of '25.

Here was an opportunity to unwind and share facts that his weekly golf buddies found tiresome. Here was an ear, willing to listen and, more importantly, to understand the force that drove him to work long hours on his own dime. It was as though a whirlpool of inquisitiveness whirled inside his brain, and he had to put it to rest.

"Oh, look at the time," Elena whispered.

"Yeah, I just noticed. We got a lot done here. Not sure there's much more to unravel in these files. What do you think?" he asked.

"You're absolutely right. Man, I have more than I can use for West

Frankfort's part of the storm. But it's great information. I always want more than less. It's easier to edit down than it is to write up," Elena said.

The two smiled and collected their files from the afternoon's work. Elena did not want to simply jump in the Windstar and take off to Anywhereville. But she was an old-fashioned girl who had no intention of breaking with tradition by asking a perfect stranger to go get a drink with her. It was unseemly and unprofessional, at least from her perspective. Will was as cute as a little puppy dog. Crossing the line into social discourse would be easy, just not appropriate. His good looks were a distraction that sat well with Elena. Looking at faded newspaper articles, outdated photographs, tombstones, and ghost-filled schoolhouses had drained her emotionally. Now, here she was, working with a real, live hero in the middle of Tornado Alley. The turn of events was a breath of fresh air at a time when she feared absolute suffocation.

"Hey, there's a Mom and Pop café up the road a couple miles. It's not much to look at, but the food is great. Wanna tag along with me?"

Will's invitation was not entirely a surprise. Elena thought she had seen him watching her a couple of times when his gaze did not correlate with one of scientific inquiry. She pretended not to notice and buried herself in the news stories they were cranking out of the microfilm printer. He had been checking her out while getting up the nerve to extend their meeting beyond the safe walls of the library. That was clear now. She was flattered and more than happy to take a break from the loneliness of travel for such a long time on one assignment. She would be careful not to get herself into a compromising situation. Alcohol was most definitely not in the arena of appropriate conduct with a stranger. That dilemma was solved, and a new one was facing her.

"Sure. That sounds great. I'm famished," she answered.

The red Windstar trailed behind the small white convertible as the new friends headed toward Joe's Burger Barn. Elena was relieved to have a new ally on the road, but wary as she followed the Vette. It occurred to her that, at its worst, this situation could be as much trouble for her as the tornado had been for the people of south central Illinois.

What would happen next was a surprise she could never have imagined.

Elena squeezed the lemon slice above the Mason jar of iced tea. Joe's Burger Barn was clean and pleasant. The wide windows facing Deering Road opened to warm sunshine that beamed through multiple, crystal, clear panes. Fresh, white paint added to the light atmosphere and red, checkered tablecloths were classic accents for a small-town restaurant. It was a perfect respite from fast-food booths and drive-thru, paper-wrapped burgers on the road.

"This is great," she said.

"Yeah, I like it. It's a little out of the way, but a nice stop when I'm passing through the area," Will replied.

"You do a lot of work on the road?" Elena asked.

"Well, there's plenty of work in the office, but I spend a lot of time compiling data and making firsthand observations through this part of Tornado Alley. Sometimes I'm just out here cruisin' the back roads, and takin' in the easy lifestyle of the country. It's a nice break from traffic congestion and deadlines of day-to-day livin'. Nothin' like the open road."

"I know what you mean. This trip has been a breath of fresh air. A real eye opener. I don't think I've ever been so challenged by any story."

"Oh?" Will asked.

Elena smiled and ducked her head sideways in some simultaneous moment of shyness and warmth. It was refreshing to have a bona fide scientist sitting in front of her talking about the storm. She had hit the mother lode of meteorology. Only Jim Cantore could match this meeting. It occurred to her that this young weatherman might need a break, though. He obviously had a penchant for Corvettes, and she could quickly steer the conversation in that direction. But she stayed on track.

"Uh, knowing the scientific reasons for a force of such magnitude is one thing. Studying the personal tragedies of so many people is another. I read as much as I can, and then stop. Sometimes I think if I read about one more dismembered baby in the pile of humanity that was strewn through here, I'll quit. It's unbelievably sad. And, I wonder if it's exploitive. In my heart, I want to warn people in every state to be on guard for the Big One, and … I think there may be honor in that. But I don't know. Maybe I'm just sensationalizing the horror of death for a new generation to read. Actually, I don't drink, but I was giving some serious thought to the possibility of getting drunk out of my mind. These awful images are as real in my brain as you are here in this restaurant."

Will smiled and leaned forward across the small table. He pursed his lips in a pensive moment and looked Elena straight in the eye. After staring for a few seconds, he spoke.

"They don't serve liquor here, lady" he joked. "Hey, I always say, 'If I save one life,' I've done my job.' There's no way to know if I'm doing that, but we're working as hard as we can to improve warning times and educate the public."

"Oh, no doubt about that," Elena answered. "You're doing a helluva job."

It was the first expletive that had come out of her mouth in his company. She winced. She sounded more like a drunken sailor than a Phi Beta Kappa on a mission to tell a great story. Not a good story. A great one. She flinched as she silently reminded herself to be polite and cordial with her words. Will sat quietly waiting for more information from the Appalachian reporter. Elena stared out the window as maple limbs bowed up and down in a stiff breeze.

"You know. We're right in the middle of the path. It was here. It could come again. A little three-month-old baby was found here in a field by a farmer. They say he came upon the baby about an hour after the tornado passed. The little one was forty miles away from home. Poor thing had no clothes left on it, but, by some strange circumstance, didn't have a single scratch on its body. Whoever the farmer was, he was in the right place at the right time. So many questions. So many unanswered prayers. I don't get it."

"Umm," Will murmured, "prayers, I don't know. Guess I don't

think too much about it that way. What is … is. I do know we can do better. If you look at the statistics on deaths through the twentieth century, you can see we're doin' a better job than ever. Greensburg's a good example. Leveled with eleven people in 12,000 losing their lives. I'm not sure their storm was any less violent than the Tri State. Some climatologists say the '25 tornado was an F-6, but that's not official. Doesn't matter. They just didn't have any warning. Never saw it comin'. But Greensburg's alarms went off, and the people took cover. That's my goal, and it definitely sounds like it's yours. Maybe we have to put this stuff on the table to make the point for people to get underground or suffer the consequences. I think people need to know how other people have died. That's not my job. It's yours."

Elena smiled. This guy was good. He was sharp, compassionate, and well informed. His arguments were well founded on irrefutable, ethical principles. The hero sounded good. Will was also a great flirt. Said all the right things. He was either a slick con or a very decent researcher out to help the everyday folks in West Frankfort and the region. She had no way to know who he was. She would proceed with caution. Feelings of trust smacked against what she believed was healthy skepticism. She had done enough professional work on scams and extortion to have a reasonable amount of suspicion when it came to strangers' testimonials and self-disclosure.

Back home was Greg. He was waiting patiently for her to move into an editorial slot at the paper before walking down the aisle. He managed the local branch of Appalachian Community Bank. Both he and Elena had worked diligently building their individual savings accounts. She would have a lovely wedding and pay for it herself. The two of them would pool savings for a down payment on a little house in the country. They had a future.

But Elena was not home. Her assessment of the 1925 tornado now reminded her how easily tomorrow could be whisked away. The moment was all she had. Even that was suspect in this eerie, beautiful town. At the moment she had the extraordinary opportunity to network with a

NOAA researcher. She was not going to let it pass. Work? Play? An intelligent ally had a legitimate place in her professional repertoire. So she would take in Will's comments with an open mind and a touch of caution.

"So the baby was a positive part of the storm scene. You must have come across some other good stories. Any funny ones?" Will probed.

"Oh, sure. There were all kinds of strange happenings. I know it sounds awful to laugh about this, but every time I think of this one guy, I can't help it. His name was Stanley Reed, and he was unloading powder from a dump cart when the storm hit. I know you've read about weird things falling out of the sky, and this poor fella … oh … talk about being in the wrong place at the wrong time. Before he knew the danger heading at him, he was knocked to the ground by a mule that fell out of the sky! Oh, my gosh! There is nothing in my experience that comes close to being hit by a mule falling out of the sky!"

Will's shoulders shook at this new story. What were the odds that anyone would be hit, in a relatively rural setting in the middle of southern Illinois, by no less than a mule? It was hysterical. Of course, all kinds of debris could fall in an F-5, but a mule? He had to admit, it was pretty funny, assuming the guy lived. That would be something to tell your grandchildren.

"Cuuuhhhh …," Will chuckled, "are you serious? A mule? Tell me the guy lived."

Elena giggled uncontrollably and replied, "Yeah! He lived! Broken skull, ribs and arm. If it's the same guy, I think he went on to have a healthy family and still has descendants in West Frankfort and nearby communities. What would ya think if you were hit out of the blue with a mule! I'm truly sorry he was hurt, but it sounds like something out of a Three Stooges episode. It's actually funnier than anything I've seen in slapstick comedy. Somehow, that story is stuck indelibly in my brain too! Oh man!"

The rosy-cheeked waitress placed the porcelain plates of burgers and slaw in front of the two laughing friends, and they calmed down long enough to thank her for the food. It was piping hot, and Elena would later swear that it was the best burger she had ever had any time, any place. She tried to watch her manners, but felt herself gnawing on the thick, stuffed bun as though it were the last plate of food on earth. It had been a long workday, and the reward here with Will and a good meal was the perfect payoff.

"So, where's your next stop?" Will asked.

"Actually, I'm going to stay over at a little bed and breakfast up the road, and then on to Parrish and McLeansboro tomorrow. I'm hoping that I can hit the files hard and then make it to the Wabash River. Money's getting a little low. Besides that, I'm getting worn down with the tragedy of these towns. I love it here. But I hate the history. How 'bout you? What's next on your trail?"

"Well, seems like our paths have intersected. I'm set up to do some work down in Murphysboro the next couple of days. I'll circle back around to Paducah in a day or two. Tell you what. There's a severe storm seminar coming up in Natchez, Mississippi in September. If you get a chance, why don't you come down? I think you'd get some interesting insight from the seminar. Not that I think you need it. Obviously, you have your stuff together. I'm impressed."

Elena gushed, thinking that if anyone at the table had their stuff together it was Will. True, she had rolled up her sleeves and tackled this project with the ferocity of a rabid wolf. She just had not reached a point in her mind where she equated her work with his. Maybe it was time to accept that possibility.

"Uh … thanks. That's great feedback to get on the road, especially from someone of your caliber. Very sweet of you to say so—"

"Sweet, my ass," he whispered. "You're breaking ground other people just thinking about doing. You're doin' it! Here's my card. Please let me know when your story is run. Promise me. I want a copy to frame for the wall over my desk."

Elena winced a crooked grin. Nothing had prepared her for a compliment so flattering. There was an air of excitement in the townsfolk with whom she discussed her research. But, this dialogue was on another level. High praise indeed. Deserved? She was not sure.

"Thanks," she whispered.

"This has been a great meeting. I'm not superstitious, but it almost feels like our paths were supposed to cross. It's been fun talking with you. I'm ready to do some work!"

"Me too," she agreed.

The two polished off the burgers and slid generous tips underneath the cola glasses. They walked through the parking lot toward their vehicles. Nothing needed to be said.

At the Corvette, Elena extended her right hand and a warm smile. She squinted as her eyes focused intently on Will. Her energy level was soaring to its highest point. This had been a great meeting, and new ideas for adapting scientific concepts to her writing were coming together nicely. Kudos from a credible stranger was the shot in the arm she needed. But money constraints were pressing her to shorten her trip. A quick review of Indiana news stories would not be adequate. Princeton and other Indiana towns deserved at least as much regard as the Illinois towns. Hours of hard work still lay ahead. Charles would have to wait a little longer for his best writer to come back to the hills.

"Take care of your wheels," she smiled. "I'll take a look at my calendar for the storm conference. Sounds interesting. But, I'm guessing I'll be rolling this story off the press before I have a chance to get to Natchez. Anyway, I'll give it some thought. Sounds fascinating. So nice to meet you."

"Me too," Will responded. "Hang onto my card. We could get together down the road and talk storms. Most of my friends are tired of my stories. I can always use a new ear and a new perspective. Take care. Watch out for the wind."

The meteorologist drove slowly out of the lot, and Elena waved in the general direction of the white convertible. She turned toward the maple trees that ran along the side street. The boughs were still waving up and down, and she became conscious of whisks of hair strands fluttering in front of her eyes. The boughs held her in some hypnotic trance. It was as if they were reminding her to stay on task. Elena was getting used to the high breezes of the Midwest. She loved brushing out her tangled hair every time she got back into the Windstar. She looked down at the ground and moved her feet in the direction of the red van. She tucked the longest hair behind her ears and slid into the gray, saucer-shaped seat. The words Will had spoken echoed all around her. People need to know how they died. That's your job. She nodded, took one more look at the side street, and silently said good-bye to the West Frankfort maples. The mystery of the baby was near here. Stan Reed was here. So was the mule. The miners. The mothers. And, on this day, she would leave part of her heart at a window seat in Joe's Burger Barn. Work awaited.

35

3:05 p.m. May 18, 1925, West Frankfort, Illinois. The morning had been normal. Men had donned carbide-lamped, hard hats and lumbered steadily toward Orient Mine No. 2. Gray silhouettes of round-shouldered fathers, sons, and brothers had carried tin buckets of sandwiches, resigning themselves to put in another day of hard work. When they kissed their children and sweethearts good-bye, none imagined the horror that awaited every single one of them. Mining coal was a good day's work for a good day's pay. The most they had on their minds were their two everyday dangers. Carbon monoxide was a silent killer that lurked within pitch-colored corridors 600 feet below the surface. And odorless methane kept its silence in pockets of the same ebon caverns, waiting to explode with the slightest spark. These were the enemies.

All the men knew the dangers below ground, but it was a risk worth taking. The money was good, but this day would be different. They were not prepared for the darkest monster of all. They were not prepared to learn about killing, black winds that would quash life while they toiled in the chambers of darkest earth. They could never have imagined that from within the very bowels of the earth, they would know when the tornado hit, and that it would be too late to mitigate the howling force that breathed the stench of death along its path.

Charles Hartley was loading a coal car when an exploding force hit him and his fellow miners. The dreaded explosion they had often spoken of in hushed conversations was happening. Their lives were on the line. Charles gasped for breath and looked toward the shaft opening that led to the surface. He shivered, realizing that he was still alive, in spite of the blast that weakened his knobby knees. His heart pounded violently, and he hurled his shovel against the foreboding black wall. Flashes of light streaked through the tunnel, and he braced for the final blast that would blow him to bits. Someone ran past him at full speed as another man was coming into his peripheral vision.

"Run!" a voice bellowed, "Let's get outta here!"

A memory flash of his wife's smile and his three children giggling in a game of tag became a vision for Charles as sharp as a razor's edge. Family. He had to get to his family. Within a terrifying second his legs were bending and extending at full speed toward the electric cages in the distance. He could hear the thumping pace of men behind him and realized a terrible truth: this could be his last day on earth. But the will to live was as strong as granite in his very core. He would have another day with his family, as long as his heart did not give out in this race to get to light on the earth's surface.

The yellow light bulbs strung through the bituminous tunnel flickered briefly and then were extinguished suddenly by an invisible force. Bobbing heads with streams of gas-powered lights emitted soft, bouncing glows from all who were headed toward the cages. But the power that failed the electric bulbs failed the men again. The electric cages were knocked out, and in the melee, the foreman was trying to make sense of it all. The escape shaft was the men's one hope for survival.

"Stay calm, men! Stay calm! We're gonna git outta here. Let me see what's goin' on! Quiet, everyone!"

The miners obediently stood at attention, but their eyes rolled in the general direction of the mine opening above their heads. Mothers and children were waiting to hear word of their survival. Life itself held a precarious sense of desperation and gratitude with every breath the men took. They were comrades in work. They were friends in need of help. Yet, at this moment, each one was alone with his own mortality. It was precious life that would propel them toward the escape shaft, and each man sensed his own aloneness in the middle of all of it.

The passing minutes seemed long as the miners grew steadily uneasy. They held their tongues but squirmed with shaken nerves that quivered their blackened bodies. Finally, the skinny foreman ordered the crew one by one to climb the 600-foot ladder that zigzagged to the surface. So the escape began. Charles was near the front of the line, and with the discipline of a war hero, he waited calmly for his turn at the ladder. He was not certain what had happened. Roof props had given way to the explosive force, and the door to the mine entrance had been blown off its hinges. This had not been a gas explosion. It was something else. Charles knew only that the workers had to get to solid ground above these coal-lined walls where wind had never blown in all his years of mining ... until today. He climbed with strength and remarkable agility. For forty minutes, he climbed.

Once on the surface, he was stunned. What he believed had been a mine disaster hit his eyes with such repulsive urgency that he stepped backward with alarm. He stared at spaces where homes had stood only a few hours earlier when he had walked to work. Boards, mangled automobiles, clothing, household goods, and bodies lay on the earth that for years had given sustenance to the good people of West Frankfort. Charles was a mile from home, but he felt strength surge into his legs. He began the longest run of his life. Years later, he would marvel at the strength that found its place in his body at that moment. He was scarcely aware of breathing, and he felt no fatigue. In fact, his legs moved faster with each stride.

His thoughts raced and his brain registered fear as he had never known it. A crumpled body in the road, from which an arm had been twisted free, barely registered with the terrified miner. Dazed neighbors were wandering through the streets, but he could not stop to inquire about them. No time. He thought he heard a child whimper, but he was not sure. He had to get to his family. Some part of Charles Hartley knew his story had already been told a hundred times over. Within days, it would be clear that the story would be told 15,000 times over. His house had been completely demolished. Nothing was left but fragments of personal belongings strewn haphazardly every which way. It was a small price to pay for the reward waiting for him. His wife had escaped injury, and the three children survived with only a few scratches. They huddled, cried, and clutched each other as though it were all too much to believe.

The Hartley family began the walk toward the southwestern part of town which stood intact. Mrs. Hartley covered the children's heads and eyes with her arms when the tortured body of a neighbor lay torn and ravaged in their path. There was an eerie silence in West Frankfort until someone cried an unmerciful scream for help. Within minutes, people came running from all directions offering aid to moaning victims of the storm.

Charles sent his family on to the Parkinsons' home in the southern part of town, and he joined the rescue effort. He had regained his wits, assured that his loved ones would be all right. As he looked around, he realized that the blackened coworkers were doing the same thing he had done. They combed frantically through the wreckage, praying for life. Too often they found death and grief of such magnitude that many broke down in fits of temporary madness. Women screamed for their children, and as it turned out, most of the fatalities of West Frankfort were women and children, the ones above ground when the storm hit.

A sooty miner in his pit clothes emerged from a wrecked house, and Charles called out.

"Is the boy alive? Is he …?"

The miner was carrying little five-year-old Leroy Roberts. He cradled the child in his arms like a small baby. Streaks of tear tracks appeared on his coal-blackened face, as he moved the child toward a safer area. Dangling, limp, sock-clad feet painted an indelible picture in Charles' mind as he intently studied the still boy.

"He's alive! I got him. He's alive," the miner replied.

Inside the broken house, the severely injured bodies of Mr. and Mrs. Porter were pinned, until additional rescuers pried beams and rubble from atop them. The Porters were taken to the Miner's Hospital as the streets filled with hundreds of caring neighbors who were hell-bent on saving all who could be saved. In one house, a tiny infant was found alive. She was crawling across her mother's ashen body, trying fervently to nurse from the breast of the angel that had been called to Heaven. Rescuers wrapped the babe in a white curtain that had served to keep privacy in the parlor only an hour earlier. They carried her to a shelter that had been quickly set up by West Frankfort's Salvation Army office.

Charles continued digging and calling out to trapped victims. One dead woman lay on her porch, her head split open from the impact of 200-mile-an-hour, hurled debris. A foreign woman lay pinned beneath the weight of her house. She screamed words the rescuers could not understand. Her bony fingers pointed frantically toward a collapsed room, and she screamed nonstop. Beneath the beams and collapsed walls, rescuers found a five-day-old baby inside its carriage. The little one was unharmed, protected by some miraculous chain of events. Another woman was found whose skull had been pierced all the way through by a piece of wood. A young mother and her newborn both perished in bed. She had held the babe tightly to her, but to no avail. They both succumbed to the mighty blows of death. It was their time. Hundreds of automobiles were lifted, rolled, twisted, and carried to places where they should not have been. The miners and rescuers from the southern part of town dug frantically for life. And they prayed.

The No. 2 was not the only mine affected by voracious wind. The Orient No. 18 survivors reported similar accounts of wind blowing the wrong way through the mine shaft. Miners were a mile-and-a-half away from the 512-foot-deep shaft, when the gust of wind washed through the dark, work area. The lights went out, and the exodus soon began, as 800 strong, level-headed men began climbing up the steel escape ladder to safety. The roundhouse was destroyed, and three men inside died in the havoc. Charles' experience was repeated 1,500 times over. The men of West Frankfort were safe from the tornado. Their families were not.

At No. 18, Jack Burboge was inside the washhouse when it was blown down. Although he and others were buried beneath bricks and mortar, he was dug out within a half-hour, suffering only a few scratches. One of the first men to climb out of No. 18 was Edward Joicey. He took shelter inside the washhouse as the heart of the storm descended on West Frankfort. From a crouched position, he caught a glimmer of two small children running into the washhouse for safety.

Although Burboge tried to reach them, his ribs were crushed when the walls collapsed. He never made it to the little ones. They were buried beneath the rubble with the men.

Tales of horror reared ugly heads throughout the afternoon and night. The family of Ike Karnes had survived the 1912 Tornado, but in this assault, they gave up eleven loved ones to God. Three of the Karnes children were found in the mine pond. They were three of many. The suffering of the children and women who had dutifully gone about the day's business above ground created an overwhelming blanket of despair for the fathers, sons, and brothers. Their broken spirits wailed ungodly screams, as bowed men stirred inconsolably through domestic debris and human remains.

Inverted CB&O boxcars had been lifted into the air and smashed down atop automobiles in the mine parking lot. The roundhouse of No. 18 was destroyed; inside three men died. Almost forty deaths in West Frankfort were babies. The legacy of the town of 20,000 people would be a haunting presence in the hearts of neighbors for the rest of their lives … and beyond.

Although the Red Cross, Salvation Army, National Guard, and a host of unnamed volunteers, doctors, and nurses converged on the devastated area, unbearable grief loaded down the gentle hearts of good people. As in Murphysboro, accounts were told of looters who pilfered through precious remnants of homes and lives that would never be the same again. The cries of so many would be hushed by time, but the sorrow of all would be an indelible memory for generations to come. There was grief in the moment. There was terror that lingered in the hearts of all who trembled with each new storm thereafter. Memories of the monster gnarled evil laughter, as orphaned children hunkered underneath covers of makeshift beds in hastily organized hospitals that were ordinarily lodge halls, churches, and homes.

One little boy with a broken arm in a sling was unable to pronounce his name clearly when caregiving strangers asked about his family. With the strength and surety of a child who had been always loved unconditionally, he assured the nurses that his mommy and daddy would come to get him soon. The gentle women turned away, so that he would not see their tears in the midst of Hell itself.

The little fellow had no way to understand the number of mommies and daddies whose shattered bodies lay in temporarily established morgues of West Frankfort. There was no way for him to comprehend the finality of the moment for over 120 lifeless victims, whose families waited for them. He would wait for his mommy and daddy.

Life would go on in the days and weeks ahead. Volunteers would come from miles around to flail shovels of earth as they opened cold tombs in which to lay remnants of lives torn forever from the earth.

Terror would accompany the children's days for the rest of their time on earth. Every slight gust of wind on a spring afternoon would pose an exaggerated threat for the small survivors. On March 18, 1925, they embraced more heartache than most people could ever imagine. The storm was over. The suffering would linger a lifetime.

36

Elena slowed the red Windstar as she glanced from side to side. Miles of fields and trees stretched serenely from horizon to horizon, but she saw no sign of the little town of Parrish. An occasional distant house, a grazing cow, or a side road hinted of a few residents in the area, but there was nothing of a town she could see. She blinked and considered the possibility she had turned onto the wrong road. Somewhere, amidst the neat rows of crops, were the remnants of a small town that had been wiped from the face of the earth in 1925. But where?

It was perplexing to know that there was a dot on the state road map which stood for Parrish, but no such community seemed to exist. Tiny hamlets in West Virginia often gave the same impression. Some little mining town, just like Parrish, had once thrived with coal diggers and their families, but had long since been replaced by crops, grass, small herds of cattle, and intermittent, modest houses. Somewhere in her notes, she had read that the Illinois town of 500 was never rebuilt after the storm. And, so it was. She was driving through an invisible town called Parrish.

Annihilated was the word that popped up in newspaper accounts. Without notice, people and their homes were swept away as casually as a cow swallowing its cud for the fourth or fifth time. In Parrish, jaws of evil had devoured everything, leaving all but a few of the town's residents dead or injured. Dead or injured. In less than three minutes. Elena could hardly imagine it. Of more than one hundred houses, only two had stood in place after the storm. How curious it was to realize that by some quirky circumstance, school, a church, and two houses remained intact, while everything around them was savagely eradicated.

Elena sighed. The stories were beginning to run together. Every town felt alone with its recollections of the tragedy. But, every town was much the same. The wind came. It blew destruction through the very hearts of the people. And, in moments, it was all gone. The roving reporter thought it would suffice to write, "and what happened in the last town, happened here, and in the next … ditto." But that was not good enough for the young researcher. No two experiences were truly alike. Heartache of one person could never be duplicated by another. Each place had its own story. Elena was firm in her belief that justice rested in telling a story well, completely, and with respect to everyone along the way. Those who lived. And those who died. She was fatigued, but she found each point of her journey alluring and poignant.

This stop had an eerie presence. It was nearly indescribable. Elena studied the rich, green hues of open fields. Unlike Gorham, Murphysboro, Desoto, West Frankfort, and the other towns, this place was empty. It had been gutted by destiny. Annihilated. Perhaps the stories here were greater because of the conspicuous absence of Parrish. No general store. No post office. No gas station. Nothing left. A somber history was pervasive, nonetheless. There was simply nothing tangible with which it could be connected. Corn and soy. Rows of rich soil. And memories. Elena loved it here.

She wondered where Clarence Lowman's general store had stood. In her mind, she imagined the sight of the thirty-year-old running along this very road. He had left his store and tried to make it to his home, which was only two blocks away. As foreboding, black winds descended upon him, he grabbed the railroad track and held on for dear life. Dear life, indeed. With fierce strength and determination, he sustained his grip on the rail, but his body was lifted into the air and batted back and forth as if he were a laundered shirt whipping upward from the Almighty's clothesline. When the lashing winds subsided, Clarence's injuries included a broken shoulder, a broken arm, broken ribs, and a fractured spine. He was transported to the hospital in Benton, but not before learning that his house was still standing. It was one of only two domiciles left untouched by the tornado.

Elena wondered if she would have had the presence of mind or the physical strength to hold onto a railroad track if her bones snapped like dried kindling, and soft tissue tore like Kleenex in the hands of a child.

She doubted that she had the upper-body strength for such an ordeal. She had the discomforting notion that she would panic and do nothing.

She drove slowly along the quiet road. On the distant horizon, Elena imagined seeing a brewing cyclone. She wondered whether she would have time to make lifesaving decisions, and she hoped she would not be confronted with choices of such magnitude. Parrish land was so flat, it would be virtually impossible to "lie down in a low place," as recommended by NOAA. The problem was that Parrish had no special, low places. The entire place was low. She had read conflicting reports about trying to outrun tornadoes as a dangerous option. Traditionally, most reputable material indicated that trying to outpace a storm proportionate to the one of 1925 was foolhardy. On the other hand, she had also read recommendations to drive at a right angle to a storm's path in order to avoid impact.

Something was horrifically alarming about the prospects of lying down in a ditch for safety. You never know when a mule might fall on you. But knowing that the storm of 1925 traveled through this very area at a speed of sixty miles per hour, she understood on some level that trying to drive to safety was inherently dangerous. If there were the shelter of a permanent building or a ditch in which to lie at a moment's notice, she would be smarter than she had been in her Fredericktown retreat. At least that was what she hoped.

It struck her as curious that, in some respects, people's reactions were strikingly similar when the Tri-State Tornado hit. They tried to get to low levels, they held onto solid bases when possible, and they ran invariably and desperately in search of family and homes when it all passed. It was extraordinarily difficult to imagine the events that happened here. It was accordingly difficult for survivors to articulate the horror. Some took the storm to their graves. One way or another, the tornado killed some part of everyone's life. Part of the spirit of people who survived the storm was snatched away forever. Nightmares filled the void.

Elena pulled the Windstar to the side of the road and jotted down notes about her surroundings. "Drove on to look for Parrish but never found it. May have been off side road near Logan …" Her work in the West Frankfort library had already revealed the tornadic events of this area. She had mapped out libraries and historical societies before leaving West Virginia, so it was no surprise that only a breeze in this part of Franklin County carried whispers of its past.

As she closed the spiral notebook, she once more scanned the fields beside the van. No black clouds today. No hint of discord between Heaven and Earth. But Elena knew what had happened here, and she wrestled with the ethics of journalism that might shield the public from the whole truth. Some details were too horrible to contemplate, let alone articulate in a *Sentinel* feature story. Her old journalism professor, Syd Brach, would caution her to regard very carefully the severity of suffering when penning the final copy for print. How much should she tell?

Some stories were simple and wondrous. Five-year-old Margaret Parks had done her best to tell hospital workers what had happened. Their home was just a half-mile from Parrish, and they had no time to take shelter. Six-month-old Imogene was lying on a cot beside Mama when Margaret told about the big black cloud that picked them up. Imogene's face was cut and bruised. Her brother D.C., was only four years old and had been taken to a home in Benton to recover from minor injuries. Her Daddy, Everett Parks, survived the storm as well. Margaret said that they were all blown away before they knew what was happening. When she woke up in a field, maybe the very field Elena was surveying, her mother was beside her, holding her tightly in her arms. She reported that a big plank was on top of her, and her dress was gone. She thought a nail or something had torn her underwear. Her Daddy picked up both of them and took them to Parrish where they boarded the train for Benton.

His description of the experience was memorably poignant. He and his family were carried by the wind about a quarter of a mile from their home. His last memory was one of him holding on to a fence post when he saw his little boy flying through the air a few feet above the ground.

He reached for D.C. and successfully pulled him down to his chest. Once again human strength triumphed as he held the four-year-old tightly against his chest until the storm passed.

Elena rubbed goose bumps on her arms, trying to fathom the enormity of strength that welled within the soul of fathers and mothers who were embraced by abject terror. To survive in a field under the strain of 300-mile-an-hour winds was astonishing. It was good to know these facts. Spoiled people who complain about their newspaper being delivered late two mornings a year might want to think twice about things that genuinely warrant protest. A late paper certainly did not match the suffering people experience in natural disasters. Her story would most certainly include the survival of the Parks family.

Elena skimmed her notes from the previous day's work, and she smiled as she envisioned seventeen-year-old Mary Melvin lying on a cot beside Mrs. Parks in the hospital. She, her mother, and five brothers and sisters had held on to doors and windows of their house as the winds lifted their home off its foundation. They were carried several hundred feet away; the home went with them. Suddenly, they were dropped to the ground, and Mary remembered nothing until she woke up on the porch of a neighbor's house.

Elena pondered the role the mind plays on traumatized people. Were these people unconscious, or was the memory too painful to retrieve? There was no way to know. But another pattern was emerging in her research about amnesia. People can bear just so much pain before the mind yields the peace of forgetfulness. But head injuries were common too. Many survivors suffered concussions from flying debris. It was just as plausible that many were, in fact, unconscious for untold bouts of time. There was no way to know. The assimilation of facts and speculation was part of an enormously complex tapestry that the journalist was weaving. She was changing with each story. The tapestry of Tornado Alley was embracing her with a new perspective, even when it came to her own pain.

A great inspiration from Parrish came in the form of Dr. W. J.

Partington, a physician and surgeon from Cedar Rapids, Iowa. He was traveling to Paducah, Kentucky, when the tornado obliterated Parrish. A relief train was backing toward Parrish just as the surgeon arrived in Thompsonville. He ran to the Thompsonville Drug Store, where he took possession of all the surgical bandages and supplies available. He boarded the train and traveled with relief volunteers to the ravaged town. It was Dr. Partington who organized the first relief team in Parrish where he loaded a group of fifteen injured people on the train to Benton. When the train pulled out, he dug through the rubble, helping volunteers retrieve thirty more injured and dead citizens from bricks, boards, mortar, and every other imaginable object that could weigh victims down after America's most violent tornadic storm. Not only did he administer first aid to survivors, but he also traveled with the next train loaded with the injured to Benton, where he cared for strangers who were his new patients. Patients he had not planned to treat at the time he left Cedar Rapids. He was one hero cited among records and newspaper reports in March 1925. Elena knew that thousands of unnamed, unnoticed volunteers saved lives that day and thereafter. They were gone. There was no way to honor them in the year 2007, except to tell their story through the actions of Dr. W. J. Partington, Everett Parks, the American Red Cross, the Salvation Army of West Frankfort, the National Guard, and others. She understood. Greatness comes in the gentle hands of anonymous souls who act with valor.

Elena must contend with death in her writing. It completed the story. Published descriptions from 1925 were frequently horrifying. Clamoring about heroism, strength, unselfishness, miracles, and courage was only one part of the awful aftermath. There was so much more. Every day, it seemed she found more details than she could address. But for all the time and expense required to trace the storm path, Elena was determined to leave no stone unturned. She was committed to accumulating stacks of archives from which to elucidate all the good and all the bad of that one day.

She could not do justice if she did not balance the narration with accounts of looting, pilfering, greed, and vulturous conduct. It was the side of war within society that necessitated written laws, punishment, and incarceration. Death was another matter. It was a natural part of life's inevitable end; it always weighed on the hearts of decent people like an iron shroud loaded on the shoulders of those left behind to live. Death was hanging in the air above the fields of Parrish. Children's lives were shortened through no fault of their own. The living were left with the question of "Why?"

One body carried by the storm over Parrish was so dreadfully mutilated that the family could identify the victim only by her red hair. During the storm, most of the men of Parrish were working at the Black Star Mine near Logan. But William Rainey was at home on his farm at the edge of town. His life was quashed by the storm, and his broken remains were found more than a mile away from his home. His neck had been broken, his right arm had been torn off, both legs were broken, and he had a hole in his head. Surely sweet words were spoken at the funerals in the days to come, but the calamity of March 18, 1925, was documented arguably too well.

Newspaper records were sketchy as to the number of wounded and dead in any of the towns hit by the storm. *The New York Times* published contradictory numbers, and the consensus among the analysts was that there was no absolutely clear way to know the precise number of people who died. Volunteers were so strained to provide comfort and first aid to those who were suffering, that an exact count of missing and dead was a waste of resources and unequivocally, impossible to ascertain. It reminded Elena of the tours at Gettysburg where the numbers of dead, injured, and AWOL soldiers were still being debated 144 years after the battle. No one could ever obtain the precise count. Did we ever know the final death count of Katrina? The Iraq War? The Great Sunami? We would never know.

So, it was in Parrish. Some reports said 36 died and 60 were injured. Other reports asserted that 65 died, while yet another newspaper printed the death count at 20 with 100 injured. One source indicated that only a handful of Parrish's citizens escaped death or injury. Elena's notes also included references to 80 dead and 300 injured, 75 dead and 422 injured, and still another reported that only 3 people out of 500 escaped injury.

One thing was certain. In 2007, there was no town of Parrish with 100 homes and 250 citizens, 300 citizens, or 500 citizens. The storm had flattened the town and scattered the people who took shelter in other parts.

Elena did not believe in ghosts. It railed against her professional training as a true journalist, and it violated her ethics as a reporter. But she felt a somber sense of loss for children she could never have known, even if they had lived. Why they died was an undercurrent for curiosity that made her quest all the more worthwhile. The NOAA radio scratched an indiscernible screech on the seat beside her as she turned the black dial until it clicked. Silence reigned by the side of a field in the general vicinity of Parrish. Her final thoughts as she drove away were for the little ones who perished:

> Wilma Braden, 5
> Billie J. Cunningham, 3
> Royal Eugene Galloway, 14
> Bertha Kerley, 3
> Homer Kerley, 12
> Kenneth Taylor, 3
> Merl Taylor, 4
> Jackie Jean Price, 1
> Baby Price
> Unidentified Negro

37

<u>3:47 p.m., May 18, 1925, Hamilton and White Counties, Illinois.</u>
The storm barreled onward through the farmlands of eastern Illinois,
devastating families whose lives were sprinkled across the rich, brown
foundation of life: fertile earth. Small villages were few and far between,
so the mile-wide swath did most of its damage to trees, fences, animals,
and crops. In retrospect, the people of Illinois would focus so much
attention on the towns that served as major targets for the storm's
impact that the rural areas near McLeansboro and Dahlgren were
almost a side commentary. But the anguish of individual families
would be every bit as bitter as that of hundreds of fellow Illinoisians
living in close-quartered neighborhoods of Desoto, West Frankfort,
Murphysboro, and Gorham. Masses of sufferers were appropriately
deserving of sympathy, but so too were the individual, farm families of
Hamilton and White Counties who were destined to lose life as they
had known it—in seconds.

Even greater would be the concern for schoolchildren who were
either dismissed before the tornado hit, or who were finishing their
last lessons of the day. Like all children, the boys and girls looked out
wavy window panes of the one-room school, anticipating the run home
with warm breezes carrying their laughter through the fields. Waiting
for them would be freshly baked bread, cold milk from the icebox, and
mouth-watering cinnamon buns lined up on metal sideboards. Best
of all would be the warm hugs from doting mothers. Mothers who
dreamed of life's best for their children. It was a community of love,
hard work, rewarding moments of play and faith. Today, the faith of
every person would be tested to the breaking point.

Many of the farmers observed dark skies over the countryside, and
some children pointed out to their teachers that the sky was the color
of grass. It was beautiful in its own way. Unique, but not necessarily
foreboding. After March 18, the ones who survived the Great Storm

would see green skies from an entirely different perspective. The very color of green would become an unrelenting spark for infernal night terrors, crying, and trembling among the young and old alike. It was a day that would never be matched in the lifetime of the farmers and their children. Truly, it was a once-in-a-lifetime experience.

Cows had been turned out to pasture and were chewing their cuds as on any other afternoon in rural Illinois. Although the thick beasts could trot a good ways when slapped with the crack of a hickory switch, they were no match for 300-mile-per-hour rotating air that engulfed the meadows near McLeansboro. No one paid particular attention to the bawls of the bulging bovines. The poor animals that were in the wrong place were plucked off the earth as clean as a broom whisking away a spider from a family's back porch.

The horses were another matter. They had speed on their side. Savvy and attuned with nature in a profoundly perceptive way, some hurled their lean, fast bodies through the wind, away from the tumbling black assailant that swept toward them at sixty-miles-an-hour or more. Their hooves dug furiously into the earth as taut, rippling muscles propelled them in the general direction of blue skies. But they too were as much victims of chance as anything. The wind was faster than they.

The livestock of the plain people of rural Illinois was the equivalent of fine silk wares in an Asian market, or gold buillon in the guarded vaults of Fort Knox. Each family's life savings were invested in the animals that kept them alive. These beasts of burden gave each household milk, meat, and the power to turn the soil behind heavy, wooden plows.

Saddled roans and stoic Arabians were the pride of every young man who rode to town for supplies or courted a lovely young lady on Saturday nights. Bulky, dapple-gray workhorses took highest honors when care was needed. They were well fed and sheltered from the elements when necessary. This day's tragedy would occur too abruptly to address the animals' need for shelter. It would have been to no avail. No barn in the path of the tornado was strong enough to withstand its hellish power.

Neither could the wooded shelters forestall the thrust of piercing blades and makeshift epees that were thrust randomly toward all living things.

Much was lost. A good horse was worth more than money in the bank. An amply producing cow was sustenance that yielded not only milk, but also cheese, cream, cottage cheese, and sweet, churned butter that melted in the salivating mouths of farmhands, families, and visitors who stopped by from time to time. Both cattle and horses brought fair prices at auctions where new owners made plans for farming with their acquired prize, and old owners pocketed cash for grain, seed, household supplies, and small sticks of candy for sweet loved ones.

On the afternoon of March 18, one horse with the unlikely name of Cyclone broke into a ferocious stride as the cauldron of death raced in a northeastward path. Cyclone's white-stockinged legs chipped heaves of dirt against his belly and rear flanks as his remarkable body streaked through the pasture near the two-story farmhouse southwest of McLeansboro. The straining horse lunged into the air above the creek that fed cool water into a cistern near the garden. At top speed, he hurdled the wooden fence, catching his rear hoof on the top board with such power that it was flung twenty feet through the air. The prize-winning steed's neck stretched forward with all the power he could muster. With the might of a great Bluegrass racer, he fought for his life. To no avail. When the tornado picked him up, he whinnied a final shriek, twisted his sweaty neck crazily from side to side, and disappeared into the roaring billow of death.

Farmer after farmer who survived the storm, inevitably lost part of his working animals. Cattle farmers John, Thomas, and Charles Dunn were at home with their mother, Anna, and two sisters, Maggie and Mamie. They spotted the tornado in the distance and took heed as the storm tumbled across the fields toward the house. Maggie was scurrying around the kitchen, grabbing cherished pieces of her grandmother's glassware, when her mother clutched her arm and pulled her toward the parlor. The six Dunns huddled low on the board floor as the deafening monster bellowed its ungodly message of approach. Anna covered the girls' heads with outstretched arms, and they braced for the worst. Low-pitched sobs of the younger ladies were inaudible in the last few seconds before the tornado hit. The noise of exploding thunder and the fiendish bawl of 300-mile-an-hour winds overwhelmed the family.

Then it happened. The roof was torn from its struts, and Mamie trembled as the walls in the adjacent rooms snapped like dry twigs underfoot. Anna held fast to her beloved girls and prayed that whatever happened to the boys would be pain they could bear in their last moments on earth. They had worked the farm together, and this was the day they would die together if it were God's will. And his will would be done. Nevertheless, Anna prayed to live. She prayed this was not their time at all. The girls shook, and Thomas opened his eyes to look one last time at his mother. It was her face he wanted to hold as his final memory before the fatal blow was laid. She had cared so well for them, and they had prospered with the herd of cattle, crops, and other farm animals. Life was abundant, and he knew it. What would he do without dear mother? What would she do without him? There were no answers as the upstairs of the farmhouse lifted as a thousand pieces of wood yielding to the almighty force.

For what seemed like the longest two minutes on earth, the Dunn family pressed themselves low on the parlor floor anticipating the darkness of death that would settle upon them when the final surge thrust lethal timbers into their defenseless bodies. Then it ended. The air was silent. The wide-eyed siblings and mother slowly raised from cowered positions in the center of the house. They checked for injuries, bruises, broken limbs, but they were unscathed. Some miraculous shield had settled over the sole room in the house that was left untouched by the tornado. So too, were the Dunn family's bodies sheltered from what seemingly had been inevitable death. All the rooms around and above them had crumpled, broken apart, and disappeared on the arms of an evil, black cloud. Anna bowed in a prayer of thanks. But all six knew that a violent truth underlay the brevity of their experience. They sensed great heartache for other families in the countryside. The storm must have strafed every life, every school, and every home in the area. They could never have imagined the horror of human suffering that stretched for 219 miles through three states. Neither could they fathom spin-off cyclones that moved farther east, crippling community after community, farm after farm.

In farm country, lives hung on the strength of the land. The Dunn matriarch stood where the kitchen door had been. She stared at an empty space down the dirt drive. Their new barn had vanished. It was clear. The farm was gone. The herd of sheep had been strewn like cotton-sock dolls across the meadow. Dead. The hogs that should have been in the pen behind the barn were impaled and broken in the same field. Feathers of the flock of 200 chickens dotted the ground. Half-skinned carcasses of her best hens lay mud-covered and haphazardly plunked onto the ground as far as she could see. The Dunns had lost everything, except each other. Their livelihood was ended at the whim of the Devil himself. How would they live?

The Dunns were not alone. William Seitz's home and outbuildings evaporated into thin air. Chris Seitz's barn was blown away. Herman Frymire's home and barn vanished from earth. He, his wife, and his father saw the storm coming and went into the yard, lay down, and held onto the base of fence posts for dear life. The elder Frymire's grasp was too weak for the savage beast. He was blown loose and into another post, sustaining injuries that resulted in his death the following night. Two horses were killed. A mule was killed. Three hogs, three sheep, and two lambs died in the fiendish slaughter.

Joe Dunn's two boys crawled underneath their barn when the tornado rolled over them. Their house evaporated like fine droplets of steam whirling into the air above a teakettle spout. The smokehouse was demolished. Three sheds were broken to bits. The big barn was completely destroyed. Two horses and three cows were killed. The granary was carried in pieces to the northeast field. A shed was snapped into bits as easily as a child could snap a cracker biscuit. But the barn that covered the brothers was moved only four inches. Something was salvaged: thirty hogs were later located in a small glen nearby. Somehow, they lived. No one knew how.

John Fields' barn was destroyed. He lost two sheep and three lambs. At the Trousdale place, the large barn and silo vanished into black air. Trousdale, unwillingly, surrendered a horse, a cow, eight hogs, and untold numbers of chickens to the storm. Old man Wilson died as his home was torn apart. His wife and daughters had held tight to a hallway door which finally yielded to the strength of the twister. They ended up in the yard after the porch was lifted above them. Remains of the house exploded into flames, but the women succeeded in pulling the body of the dear patriarch from the flames. John H. Wilson died instantly. He had sustained a broken neck, broken legs, and a broken shoulder. He departed from the world along with a mule and two horses.

The houses and barn of George Speck were destroyed. Ralph Miller's barn was shred like cabbage on a plate of sauerkraut. All of John and Tom Finney's outbuildings were demolished. Marion Bleeks' house, barn, and eighteen head of cattle vanished. His neighbor Luther Lee lost his house, barn, a horse, some cattle, and five head of hogs. The home and barn of Mr. and Mrs. George Akers were strewn into the erupting sky. Mrs. Akers would die of her injuries the day after the storm. John Powers' barn was smashed and carried away. Frank Wagner's barn was totally wrecked. One of Homer Dickey's two barns was ruined in seconds. When William Hanagan looked for his house and barn after the storm, he saw not so much as a hint that the two structures ever existed.

Charles Leisure's home and barn were obliterated. Max Nibbling lost his barn. So did Walter Warthen. Jake Burkhardt's barn … gone. Clarence Hubele's home, tenant house, and barn were swept to oblivion. Gone. Jacob Mauer, Sr.'s home and barn disappeared. John Green's house and barn: vanquished from their very foundations. Henry Frieberger's house and barn … gone too. Two barns blew down on the William Burkhardt place. The silo, large barn, and tenant house of Clarence Hubele were whisked away like dandelion seeds carried on the breath of a playful child. One of the children of Charles Mays was hurled through a window when their home exploded in the middle of the wind.

The list was endless. The suffering, interminable. Long after broken bodies were buried and broken limbs and cracked skulls healed, a shadow of fear and bizarre wonderment would hang over the flat roads of southeastern Illinois. The world would know of the unforeseen power that took children, parents, and even cows, horses, and chickens from the sweet sanctuary of homes and pastures. Newspapers would detail every account and document the sheer terror for future generations to peruse. Editors of two papers would join together to publish one newspaper, so that the men could leave the office and render aid to those who suffered.

Lives of children, cattlemen, farm women, and domesticated creatures were snuffed out, but not without purpose. In the blink of an eye, life seemed to be casually expendable. But such was not the case. At the time of the storm, precious breaths were as fragile as a flame of a candle lit for guidance through a dark and drafty hallway. Would that they had known. The life and death of the people and animals would not be forgotten. From the earliest hours of rescue and recovery, exacting goodness from such overwhelming tragedy was futile. Too much pain. Too many tears. Too much despair. Souls racked with grief. If only they had understood. It was impossible for those who died and for those who survived to realize that their story would be a great legacy for so many people to contemplate in decades to come. Their lives and deaths were not incidental. They were precious flames that would guide countless others to safety … when skies turn green.

38

<u>3:40 p.m., May 18, 1925, Trousdale School, Southeastern Illinois.</u>
It was the same story. Every town, every community, every farm, and every school. Children in the tornado path shared a common bond. The fortunate ones who skirted the edge of the great storm marveled at the miracle of their own lives. Many in the midst of the furious winds died. More survived. Most who lived through it held the story deep inside in a fervent plea for peace in the life that lay ahead of them. Terrifying recollections were hoarded like precious gold coins to be cashed in at Heaven's Gate. God would know that they had already been through Hell.

Miss Pauline McMurty brushed chalk dust from the skirt of her powder-blue dress. She loved the children under her care in the Trousdale School. She knew that some were destined to be farmers, and that was a worthy endeavor. She always used care to praise the hard workers in the rural landscape, but she fought against the odds, encouraging each student to strive for excellence in all walks of life. She prayed for full lives of great gifts for each child, regardless of his or her background. Not one gifted child was in her school. All of her students carried a gift when they slid into the wrought-iron desk seats and placed the McGuffy Readers on the golden slabs of wood. Illinois children were absolute heirs of the great Lincoln legacy, and the pride of patriotism was mixed with the ethic of hard work in Miss McMurty's room. No one shirked math, spelling, geography, reading, or writing. Not at Trousdale.

Magnanimously framed portraits of George Washington and Abraham Lincoln looked down on every student from behind the teacher's desk. Each day was a reminder that greatness comes not from wealth but from duty, respect, and determination. The gas heater in the corner was not the only source of classroom warmth. As soon as the teacher smiled at each sweet child who answered, "Here!" during roll call, the room filled with appreciation, cordiality, confidence, and great aspirations. Today was no exception.

Miss McMurty walked past the students' desks and stopped when necessary to correct spelling or grammar on each child's paper. The students were writing stories about their favorite time with family in the previous year. Twelve-year-old Vernon Miller had completed his assignment and was working hard at the blackboard. He had soaked the cotton rag in cool water from the well and stood tall while swiping long strokes across the gray dusty slate. He dipped the cotton rag into the bucket and loosely wrung it out for a fresh start on the next piece of board to be cleaned. Vernon thought he was Miss McMurty's favorite. Little did he realize that every child behind him felt the same way. He had shot up a good five inches from last year, and he was one of the students tall enough to reach the top of the board. Only Miss McMurty had a knack for making blackboard washing a source of pride. It was a reward. Everything was a reward in Miss Pauline's world.

A sudden gust of wind cracked against the southwest wall of the school, but no one took much notice. The winds whipped the trees and bushes outside Trousdale every day. The slightly warped boards of the one-room schoolhouse creaked in irregular rhythms as the open fields invited westerly winds to brush the countryside with cool air. Many of the girls boasted braided hair in an attempt to ward off tangles that required many minutes of hard combing to unsnarl. The day had too many chores and wonderful play hours to spend time brushing through long, intertwined streaks of blonde, brown, auburn, and black hair. A few of the girls in the class had opted for the latest bobs and felt very stylish flaunting the wedged, straight hair on days they showed up nearly sheared like blue-ribbon sheep. The boys' bowl cuts and sheared heads posed few problems in a day's affairs. A few of the better off young men streaked their locks with lard in efforts to emulate the sleek styles of tweed-jacketed men in the Sears Roebuck catalog.

Miss McMurty restrained a chuckle as she perused Reba Jordan's account of her chase after the sow that escaped from the rickety sty on

Christmas afternoon. The slim teacher pointed to the misspelled word, *rickkuty*, as Reba ducked her head in slight embarrassment. The teacher smiled and spoke softly.

"That's a wonderful story. I've never chased a pig on Christmas Day. Nice writing, Reba."

The girl scrunched her chin and twisted her lips, trying not to appear to be too smug. After all, she had just misspelled a very important word in her story. She picked up the gum eraser and methodically rubbed it back and forth over the neat, carbon, cursive writing. Slender, white fingers flicked tan, rubber chunks from the yellow tablet paper. The self-conscious student listened carefully as Miss Pauline slowly spelled r-i-c-k-e-t-y.

"Thank you, ma'am," she whispered.

"I'm happy to help you, Reba. Just raise your hand if you have any questions about your writing."

"Thank you ma'am. I will," came the gentle reply.

"I *shall*," the teacher whispered, so low that no one else could hear.

The porcelain cheeks of the girl grew into a sweet, pink glow as she realized she had made yet another mistake. But it was all right. She was learning, and she felt encouraged by a teacher as sweet as Miss McMurty. Just then, the schoolmarm lightly patted her right shoulder, and Reba sat a little taller in her desk.

"Miss McMurty! Miss McMurty!" a squeaky, male adolescent's voice bellowed.

Charles Williams was flailing his right hand, more or less in accordance with the rules of seeking permission before speaking. His screeching and his erratic, hand waving were disconcerting for the teacher. Either she had failed to communicate the rules adequately, or something was amiss. Charles would not take a chance on missing softball at recess for speaking out of turn. The boy's wild eyes were staring out the back left window. He did not attempt to look at the teacher. He just continued to thrash about in his seat with his fingers spread wide as he struggled for attention.

The teacher brushed past the other children's seats as she whispered a call that was more filled with concern than impatience for the outburst. She could not reach his desk fast enough, and she knew, before she got there, that this was not behavior typical of the Williams boy. She froze in her steps and stared out the window beside the plaid-shirted student. There was not a minute to waste.

"Charles…," she uttered, "Children, listen and do exactly as I say!"

Now her voice was strident and authoritative. Everyone's eyes fixed on her face, and silence fell over the classroom as sixteen pupils awaited the next pronouncement. Johnnie Fields frowned a little, wondering why Charles always seemed to get more attention than he did. He was sweet on Miss Pauline and hoped she would marry him someday, but he did not have a chance if Charles kept getting all her interest. Not only was Charles an attention-getter, from Johnnie's point of view, but he got away with more rule infractions, too. He was certain of that. He wanted to blubber a "What now?" in the middle of the silence, but he knew better. Miss McMurty's eyes widened in unmistakable terror. Now it was her hands that waved demonstrably above the heads of her sweet protégés.

"Children, get down! The floor! Cover your heads! Down!"

As eyes stared perplexedly at the kind teacher, a distant howl welled into a deafening explosion. Thunder crashed and a streak of shimmering redness darted beyond the window pane next to Charles' desk. If the children cried, Miss McMurty never heard them. She screamed one final "DOWN!" before falling flat in the aisle. Her gentle, skinny arms curled over Fern Lee and Florence Malone who had stretched out their arms to her when the west wall began buckling inward. Shards of glass bulleted through the air in front of Honest Abe, and his portrait was the first one dislodged in the melee. No sooner had the wall slammed atop the terrified students than its position reversed; the wind sucked it toward the west from where the monster originated. The children were uncovered from the crushing weight of the wallboards, but missiles of trees, glass, nails, wrought-iron desks, books, and slate smashed into the skinny bodies. Silent screams went up into the bowels of tumultuous wind. The tornado bellowed with a wicked ferocity so intense that the crying mouths of Miss Pauline's pupils appeared to be doing nothing more than mimicking sock puppets as they were hurled into a merciless void.

Harry Erkman had curled underneath his desk, and he felt its scrolled, black legs brush against his pants. The wind had plucked the mounting bolts from the oak floor with the ease of a grandmother plucking early peas on a sunny day. But no sun shone for the children of the Trousdale School. Black air was spinning maniacally through the country school, leaving no sense of goodness where only goodness had prevailed minutes before. Miss McMurty raised her head to check on the children just as Harry's desk catapulted into her legs and left hip. She fell upon the two girls whose bony frames were still huddled in place where she had extended her arms only moments earlier. She lifted herself again in an earnest effort to reach children who were being tossed like rag dolls through the ebon cloud. Lanky Vernon Miller was whipped erratically above the room before Miss McMurty could react. His string-bean arms and legs jerked spasmodically as forces far greater than he jolted every inch of his body until he was out of sight of his beloved teacher.

Once more, Miss Pauline lifted herself into the bellowing air. Her strength was monumental in the heart of the room. She was the children's guardian in this place, and she had to do everything humanly possible to help them. Years after the powerful storm, she would be hailed, not merely as a guardian, but as the children's guardian angel who selflessly responded with superhuman ferocity. She was just a woman who scratched letters and numbers on a chalkboard, but on that day she was the salvation for little ones who were fraught with helplessness.

Vernon was not the only student carried away. There was sweet little Reba. Just a minute earlier she had blushed with a mixture of pride and embarrassment as she relayed her Christmas pig-chasing tale. Now she was flying past the head of Miss McMurty. The teacher reached frantically for Reba's laced shoe, but the delicate foot was snatched violently away from her, leaving the shoe in close chase of its wearer. Rage welled within the young schoolmarm as she leaned into the twisting cloud. She would fight to the death, if necessary, but she would give her best, fighting with all her might to save the children.

The portrait of President Lincoln had been momentarily carried northeastward, but in the contortions of the wicked winds, it somehow hurled its way back toward the face of Miss Pauline. The glass had shattered a moment earlier, but the frame remained intact, and it landed a mighty blow against the teacher's face and left eye. She fell once more under the commanding blows of the tornado. She was stunned, but she staggered to her feet and looked toward the heater that had been become detached from its fittings, causing natural gas to hiss beneath the torment of yet blasting winds. Harry Erkman was obediently hunkered down by his desk when the stove crashed down on him. He was the first child Miss Pauline reached. She tugged furiously at the young man's legs, rescuing him from his pinned position beneath the gray gas heater.

Time had slowed dramatically, and terror reigned in the hearts of the seventeen occupants at Trousdale. Would the violence never stop? It had to stop. The children needed help. With no regard for her own injuries, the teacher found herself stirring through boards and wreckage, determined to save every life possible. As the tornado passed on, the extent of the destruction and injuries became clearer. Miss McMurty was blown down two more times as she searched desperately for every precious child.

Harry was shaken but unhurt from his encounter with the school stove. He listened attentively as his teacher directed him to uncover children who were buried or nearly buried under the strewn remains of the school. Fern and Florence, who had sought shelter in the arms of the teacher, stood shakily among ruins, looking fervently for guidance from the classroom leader.

"Girls, help uncover the children. Call out when you need help."

In the most horrible moments of their lives, Miss Pauline McMurty, Fern Lee, Florence Malone, and Harry Erkman dug through the worst imaginable circumstances to save young neighbors and friends. This was no time to cry. This was no time to take in any other concerns except to help the others. In the school yard, Miss McMurty retrieved a muddy Reba Jordan from a hole where a tree had been. The genteel pig-chaser had been hurled head-first down into the water-filled cavern. The fast action of her loving instructor had saved her life. She would chase a pig another day.

Another girl, named Reba Hollister, was unconscious but breathing when Harry aided Miss McMurty in lifting part of the porch floor off the young lady's head. She had been rendered nearly lifeless by a blow to the side of her now-swollen cranium. As the sky broke open to a drizzling rain, Miss Pauline caught sight of a waving, checkered sleeve in the field to her north. It was Charles. She ran toward him with the speed of a gazelle, hoping he could sustain consciousness long enough to continue to signal his whereabouts. He had been blown a hundred feet from the schoolroom. His face was bruised, he had a cut above his eye, and he could not walk. His kneecap had been shattered by some forgettable blow when he crashed to earth. Pauline lifted the red-shirted, young man as gently as she could and carried him back toward the oak floor where a building had once stood.

Edmond Fields' head and face were badly bruised and something had sliced open his pant leg and ripped apart the skin on his right hip. Johnnie Fields was immobile as one of his legs had been visibly broken in two places. Roy Erkman was conscious and showed no outward signs of injury, although he clutched his belly and screamed in sheer anguish about pain which would later be linked to internal injuries. Lucille Lee whimpered and clutched her shoulder as sharp pain from a snapped collarbone pierced through her with every breath. Miss McMurty tore her petticoat into strips to bind the cuts on Lee Jordan's head and legs. Just as the sweet teacher had begun to hope for the survival of all her students, she spotted the body of Vernon Miller lying gray and still beside the jagged spires of nearby scathed woods. Dear Vernon had always done his school chores competently and with amiable compliance. He would not be forgotten. Neighbors soon arrived to aid the survivors of the Trousdale School. As each child was lifted soothingly onto buckboards and buggies, Miss McMurty knelt quietly beside Vernon. She brushed leaves and dirt from his wavy hair and, only then, took a brief time to cry for the one child she could not save from the storm.

Within a half-hour, she accompanied the children and the rescuers to the home of Willie Jordan. Scurrying neighbors administered medical aid to each weeping and moaning victim. Warm water and peroxide were gently dabbed on open wounds. Muddy clothing was replaced with oversized pants and shirts from the Jordans' chests of drawers. Sheets were torn into bandages. Sassafras tea was brewed on the gas stove. Miss McMurty worked diligently to comfort every child, continuing to slough off her own discomfort. On the soft, quilt-covered bed in the back bedroom, Vernon Miller lay still, his name lingering on the hearts of everyone who had survived the storm.

39

By the time Elena approached the Wabash River, her head was spinning. Having a brief reprieve visiting with a stranger named Will had boosted her enthusiasm for pressing on. But dredging through the archived mayhem of Hamilton and White Counties had showered her research with yet more tragic reflection and sadness. For the first time, she understood why some people believe they can drink away their problems. Objectively, she knew alcohol is never an answer, but she was shaking. Some numbing experience might put everything back into a positive perspective. Research was taking a toll in a peculiar, unforeseen way.

She wondered about adults who survived the storm. They had surely suffered post-traumatic stress. Probably many poured liquor on top of the pain. Iraq veterans were doing as much. Some 1925 rescuers had indicated that the tragedy was worse than that of a war zone. Here were babies, children, neighbors, friends, family, or part of their remains. No one was spared. Would Elena have known how to respond in the appalling circumstances, or would she have frozen? She had a nagging suspicion that she would not have been a leader in the midst of hellish torment. What good came from what must have seemed to be unbearable suffering? It was too much for those poor people. Simply unbearable.

In addition to her personal moments of doubt, Elena wondered about the purpose of her *Sentinel* work. In some cases, the people of 1925 did everything right and still died. Maybe dumb luck was a bigger factor than anyone cared to admit. Sam Flowers' retreat to a low-lying hollow should have sheltered him, but some flying limb, rock, or board had found him in spite of his best efforts. The Trousdale School was filled with injuries, notwithstanding the heroism of Pauline McMurty. At the Graves School, Scigal Martin sent his students into the school yard where he ordered them to lie flat on the ground. Their school was obliterated in less than a minute. But every child on the ground escaped without injury. Percy Rawlinson dismissed his Bell School students early. The building was blown to smithereens with no one inside. In the storm's aftermath, not a single sign of the school remained. At the Hadden School, Herman Bingman died from injuries incurred in the building's tornadic explosion. Almost all the children were injured in the Newman School where their teacher, Jasper Mossberger, was critically injured.

At the Murdach School, Snowden Biggerstaff dismissed school early when he saw the sky changing. But, as he rode away on his horse, the tornado changed direction, and he was riding directly into its path. After the twister finished with him, his horse had a broken leg but stood faithfully above his injured master. In the hours that followed, Biggerstaff's broken leg was amputated. Both of his arms had been broken by the furious impact of debris. Yet, with all the efforts to preserve his life, he died a couple days after the storm. Nine-year-old Wilburn Felty died instantly at the Freiberger School. Lena Young was a pupil at the Newman School where the tornado drove a board through her leg. She later developed tetanus at the County Infirmary in Carmi. A bachelor by the name of George Randolph vanished in the tumult. He was never found. Mr. and Mrs. Fred Speck's baby was found alive by the side of a road. Mud was packed inside the infant's mouth. The list went on and on. It was sickening. Elena needed a break.

She spied the cornfield and the shiny, yellow sign of the Super 8. Finally, she smiled in relief. The reporter blew out a long sigh. She was due for a rest, a phone call to Charles, a quick email to Greg, and any healthful diversion she could devise. Her back ached from tension and her right shoulder cracked like a broken twig as she shoved the gearshift handle into PARK. The journey was almost over, and what a journey it had been. She was exhilarated by the opportunity to retrace the storm path, but she was overwhelmed by the task of conveying the right message to *Sentinel* readers. This was not Pulitzer-worthy material, but in the simple words of Charles, it was "good stuff." The research trip was Elena's biggest undertaking to date, and she would make the story as meaningful and memorable as possible. Something was happening to her, and it was puzzling. Objectivity came to the forefront of intent, but questions about her own values and responses to crises were looming within her thoughts. What would she have done?

She pulled the red van into the parking lot and smiled, knowing she was going to get a good night's sleep. The Illinois map indicated that she was just off I-64 in the Grayville vicinity, but there was no town to be seen. Open fields were visible in all directions. A Super 8 and a restaurant stood across the road. Was this the site of an early twentieth-century town that had once prospered but gone under with one storm too many? One drought too many? Super 8s at home were close to McDonald's, Walmarts, and small businesses. Why was this motel in a field? True, it was adjacent to the interstate. Perhaps that was enough. The neatly rowed box of rooms with the familiar yellow-and-black sign was smack-dab in the middle of a magnificent field with perfect rows of corn. It was pleasant. It was better than that.

Once she checked in, she really should call Greg. But thoughts about him were slipping away like a distant face in a faded, color photograph. Another force of concern was taking his place. It was not what she imagined would happen on this trip. For the first time in her relationship with the handsome young man, she wondered where their relationship was going. Here in eastern Illinois, something bigger was looming in her heart. She seemed to have little room for a boyfriend three states away. She was surprised that this new perspective did not shake her. She was fine with it. Time would tell how it would play out for the duo.

In the meantime, she needed a hot meal, a cup of tea, and a little conversation with the locals. Maybe she would find a movie theatre down the interstate a ways, and she could once more escape the ghosts of the Tri-State Tornado. A movie sounded great. Could she be lucky enough to find a concert in a local auditorium or a play by a community theatre troupe? Either would be a perfect diversion.

"Honey, you're in the middle of nowhere," the sweet desk clerk asserted as she nudged the credit card slip across the counter. "You need one key or two?"

"Just one," Elena replied. "What's the food like across the road?"

"Pretty good. American fare. Nice staff. You'll have a good supper over there."

The reporter smiled again. Something as seemingly minor as small talk with a motel clerk was already easing tension in her taut body. A hot shower before dinner would complete the therapy needed to ease her into a restful night's sleep. A skinny truck driver strode into the lobby as Elena remembered the words from Charles Kuralt's *On the Road*.

"Oh, down and out, up front, please," she requested, which translated to ground level, door opening to parking area, and toward the front of the motel where truck fumes and loud engines were least bothersome. Then she realized the blunder she had just made. All the room doors opened into the hallways. Only the main doors opened into the parking lot. But she kept her silence and the clerk nodded. Elena was handed a plastic-card key for her room which was just down the hall from the desk. If she needed anything, she was close to motel personnel. This was a good stop. She could tell. Already, she felt relaxed.

Within a half-hour, she had ordered fried shrimp, mashed potatoes, cole slaw, and a huge piece of apple pie with ice cream for dessert. A middle-aged couple chatted affectionately with their teenage girl, and a juke box robotic arm flipped randomly through CDs beneath a curved, glass dome. George Jones and Johnny Cash classic vocals were tossed gently through the aromatic restaurant. Elena salivated as she munched on homemade biscuits, waiting for the biggest plate of shrimp she would ever devour. One more state, and only two major towns to cover, and then she could boogie back home.

Even though she had momentarily disconnected from the details of each mighty blow along the violent storm path, the nagging question of intent relentlessly pounded her skull. She wondered if the waitress had been through a tornado, or if the couple with the daughter stirring through her salad bowl had experienced any close calls. Her gut told her that everybody in Tornado Alley had a story. But she would not approach these strangers to gain their perspective. This was a nice evening out for all of them, and it was not a good time to interview locals about their experiences. Besides, Elena was exhausted. She needed to rest. Tomorrow she would cross the Wabash, wrapping up the 219-mile drive along the path of the single most destructive tornado in the history of meteorology.

Elena wished she could go down to Tennessee to track some of the other spin-offs of the monstrous 1925 system, but already she had more notes than she could ever use. Sadly, many other people died outside of the Tri-State area, but because the one funnel cloud had been so vast and so lethal, deaths beyond Missouri, Illinois, and Indiana were almost a side thought. Maybe Liberty, Tennessee, would make her list in the future, but for now, she had to wrap up this work. Sifting through a pile of files in the plastic crate behind the Windstar passenger seat would probably prove to be as arduous as all the hours of work to date.

It was not just the story that mattered. That was only part of the quest. Elena wriggled in the red-cushioned booth. She shuddered to think of the possibility that she would ever be confronted by such horror. It was warm and cozy in this restaurant. Food was sizzling in the kitchen. She was resting from the mental blow this work had laid on her heart. Elena had never been through any situation close to the one she was documenting. An F-5. F-5! One noted climatologist theorized that the tornado was in fact an F-6.

If she were a teacher, how would she protect the children entrusted to her? If she were driving down the road, how would she respond to a funnel cloud barreling toward her? She was not sure she had enough sense to get out of the vehicle and lie in a ditch. Something was terrifying about making a choice to be completely exposed to the elements as the best line of defense.

But then there was the quick-thinking Scigal Martin. What authority he exerted to send children outside a schoolhouse to lie vulnerably on the ground while their school was given up to such evil power. Elena winced. Then she curved the side of her mouth and

squinted her eyes in contemplation. The newspaper cartoon she had
Xeroxed was a depiction of a rotund, black coated Martin holding
hands with little ones as he led them "safely home." The paper had
declared him the "Man of the Hour." What experience had prepared
him for such quick action? Or was he just lucky in the choice he made?
Contemporary storm aficionados encourage people to seek shelter in
the lowest level of a strong, permanent building. It was dumb luck for
Martin and his students. Maybe.

What about advice to drive at a right angle to the tornado path?
What about the repeated cautionary to abandon mobile homes and
vehicles? Outrunning a violent cloud hurled from Hell is futile. Get out.
Get out. She repeated the words in her head, but she felt some instinct
to control a threat that far exceeded human strength or vehicular speed.
Trucks, cars, vans, and tractors were lethal missiles that too often carried
death for occupants and to those unfortunate enough to be in the path.

The path. That was the mystery. Where did a funnel cloud go? How
could one anticipate a change in direction? Was anticipation even a
possibility? When Elena had reviewed her county school disaster plans,
she marveled at instructions for a designated teacher to watch the
southwest sky in anticipation of sounding a warning of an approaching
funnel. The movement of the Tri-State Tornado seemed to validate the
advice. Seemed to.

Anybody with half a brain knew better than to put such instructions
into print. Not all deadly funnels hail from the southwest. Elena shook
her head and crunched on the fried shrimp as though it were her last
meal on earth. Fatigue had boosted her appetite to a ravenous plateau.
She would have to work off the calories, but she had a good notion she
could do it. She ducked her head to hide the smile of irony, imagining
some idiot watching the southwest sky as a tornado came in from the
northeast. It was not typical, but it did happen. A little research goes a
long way in a disaster.

Elena was more than hungry. She was giddy with fatigue and
imagining senseless scenarios where people with dunce caps were

watching out for children. It was easy to be sarcastic when critiquing other people's work. A fine line existed between investigative work and sensationalism. Too many of her competitors were stirring up trouble where no trouble existed. She refused to stoop to that level. If she were not careful, her good intentions could backfire and alienate the very people she hoped to inspire. Genius or moron. It was all a matter of perception.

That was it. That was what was changing. Her view of tragedy was taking on a ring of radicalism. Nobody in West Virginia cared about relative risk. Not in a rural state that averaged two small funnel clouds a year. Convince people to be a little more cautious and lot more well informed on every front would be a hard sell. That was her professional goal.

Then Elena gasped as she uncovered another perspective. It slammed into her conscious thoughts with the power of a sledgehammer blow. The truth was, she was not brave. She would not know what to do, if it happened to her. She would not act responsibly. Beneath the compelling moment of self-awareness, she now knew the whole truth. When a storm of this magnitude would find its way into her life, she would cower like a frozen idiot who would watch only the southwest sky—not knowing she would be hit from behind. It was a clear revelation of the timeless admonition: watch your back.

40

"Listen to the jingle ... the rumble and the roar ...."

Elena half-sang, half-hummed what she thought were lyrics of "The Wabash Cannonball." It had been a few years since she had bellowed the old song. Some of the words had slipped away, and she wondered about the historic significance of the tune as she crossed the Wabash River. She was nearing the end of the trail and feeling relief lift off her like a rain-soaked cloak being pulled from her shoulders. Only a few more hours of work, and she could go home. The skies over Indiana were clear and blue. The local radio stations and the NOAA radio had not so much as a peep about anything but sunny skies. Part of her relaxed state was wrapped up in the fact that she did not have to keep looking over her shoulder for violent funnel clouds sneaking up on her. Modern meteorology was a gift she had never fully appreciated until now. It was a good time to be alive.

However, it was not a foolproof era to evade tornadoes. Only last year, sixty-seven tornado fatalities had been reported in ten states. Although mobile homes were generally considered death traps, more people died in permanent structures in 2007. Besides those fatalities, seven people died in their cars and trucks. Elena wondered if the unfortunate drivers were trying to outrun the storms when they involuntarily ceded control to killing winds, flying debris, and irrevocably mangled vehicles. She was always amazed to watch frequently televised programs of tornadoes which showed cars and trucks traveling along highways as if drivers and passengers were immune to catastrophe.

She rubbed her lower lip, realizing that if anyone had photographed her driving into the black Missouri horizon, their conclusion would probably have been the same. She shivered to think that she may have made a foolish decision to do a 180-degree pivot in her flight from the black-skied horizon. She would forever remember the eyes of the young waitress in the restaurant who alerted her to the tornado on the ground in Fredericktown. How close had she come? She did not want to know.

At the moment, Griffin, Indiana, was high on her list. Here was compelling truth that moved her in a way that was markedly different from any wrecked, Illinois town. Griffin staked a claim on survival that was distinct. Elena knew a historic marker had been placed in the community in remembrance of the tragedy. It was something tangible to see, to photograph, and it represented some concrete effort on the part of the people of Indiana to further the memory of dear residents who did not deserve their horrific suffering before yielding to death's embrace. The 1925 tornadic destruction and subsequent isolation along the Wabash weighed on her heart in a unique way. One file she had already retrieved in Illinois referred to the power of the storm as being so strong that it literally carried Griffin away. Carried away.

The land was flat. It was mesmerizing. Having grown up in Appalachia, Elena's tendency to brace for turns in hills and valleys threw her out of kilter in the flatland. It was as though she were plowing through the Twilight Zone. The only thing missing was Rod Serling. It felt as if the van were hardly moving. She recalled this sensation from a trip many years before—a trip where she told Gram Kizzie that she would be happy if she could see one anthill. The protestation always brought laughs, no matter how many times she told it. Ten years earlier, a friend's little girl who was visiting from Iowa announced to Elena that a mountain was outside her window. It was not really a mountain, just a nice hill. Elena smiled. Neither hills nor mountains were part of this easy land of Indiana, but the land had an omnipresent quality of goodness.

Flat terrain was an inviting path for the brutal storms that swept through here, years ago and days ago. Any day could be the last day here. The fields were destined for assault by unbridled winds and ensuing savage destruction. On a beautiful day like this one though, it was genuinely hard to imagine that such destruction found its root in lethal rage pummeled from Heaven. She thought again. The storm had not been Heaven-sent. It was from Hell. That was clear.

Elena smiled as she moved over the railroad tracks. The old depot was now a gas station and small store. The houses of Griffin were one-storied bungalows, modest edifices casually updated since the first nail was hammered within a year of the Tri-State Tornado. Today, trees arched over the narrow streets like lace-trimmed umbrellas blocking out direct sunlight. Elena opened the driver-side window to take in the crisp air and cool shade of this pleasant village. In 1925, every home had been destroyed. Today, perfectly flat terrain encircled the hamlet, where not a single car moved. All was quiet. How peaceful it was. Only Elena's Windstar hummed its way along North Main Street. This was middle-class America at its finest.

Then she saw it. The reporter's heart thumped against her ribs, and her smile waned as she stared at the distinct historic marker that had been mounted on a metal post. It was what she expected, much like the markers in West Virginia. But here was a presence like none she had felt so far. Embedded in a gray, granite boulder was a bronze, memorial plaque. Without getting out of the van, she knew exactly what was on the plaque. The display was only a few inches above the ground where Wabash floodwaters had surged days after the cyclone. Where else could the water have gone, if not onto the tortured town plots where bodies were scattered? A newspaper article Elena had uncovered in Carmi stated that forty bodies lay in the streets of Griffin immediately after the tornado. In this sweet town, such anguish was unimaginable.

Elena continued driving, and as she approached the intersection at First Street, a familiar scene rolled into view. They were strangers, but at one time they could have been Elena, Billy, Sherry, Caroline, and Kevin spinning their bikes through Wadestown. Today was a perfect balmy day in Griffin. Elena wished she had packed her bike. The local Indiana gang was popping wheelies and weaving in S-shaped maneuvers under the maples. Elena wished every kid could ride safely along streets as pleasant as First and Railroad. Their memories would warm them on cold days down the road. With any kind of luck, these kids would never come close to the destruction the former residents of Griffin experienced on March 18, 1925.

Two of the girls glanced at the stranger's van that had pulled into town. Elena smiled and nodded, giving her best effort to assure them that she was a friendly visitor. She wanted to interview the kids. It would be fascinating to find out if the current generation had some realistic perspective of the deadly storm. Or, was every day just another one to spin around the block on the Huffys? Elena hesitated. The reporter would not cross a line of intrusion, especially in small-town America. This village of fewer than 200 people showed no signs of a Town Hall like the one in Annapolis, Missouri. She had no open invitation to approach anyone here about the tornado. She would hold back. It was enough to get a sense of place, then and now.

Facts of Griffin's disaster were sketchy. Every newspaper report referred to the annihilated town of Griffin, where children died as they walked home from school. But the facts were jumbled with questionable stories about behavior that ranged from compassion to inhumanity. Some people ran to the café for shelter when the black cloud boiled down on them. Stable buildings were always recommended in storms, but no edifice was strong enough for the F-5 in 1925. It happened too fast to take sanctuary in shelters that were decidedly lacking in reinforcement. Like so many other townsfolk, Griffin's victims who suffered the most were simply in the wrong place at the wrong time. Nine dear friends had huddled around a café coal stove when the blast of debris and black air hit them. On any other day, it was a place where home-style meals melted on the palates of chatty diners. On March 18th, it was a fatal trap as walls were flung atop startled neighbors.

Within minutes, those who had survived the tornado heard the screams of people buried inside the café. Bleeding hands of fervent rescuers were unable to free distraught souls from the wreckage. Fire replaced wind too hastily for the strongest men, and desperate voices fell silent beneath smoke and broken, charred debris. Crying, unseen angels lifted the spirits of good Griffin people into Heaven. All that remained were heaps of human ashes. Unmercifully, torturous flames had devoured what once were laughing comrades. They were burned beyond recognition. Elena choked as she stared at laughing bikers in her rearview mirror. The Wheel Popping Gang had rounded the corner onto First. Today was not the day to talk about tragedy.

Elena drove carefully, keeping an eye out for straggling bicyclists who might be reckless in their haste to catch up with the quintet of pedalers. The bicyclists were now a half-block behind the Windstar. It was good to see kids happy. She whispered a prayer that their lives would be long, happy, and purposeful. She prayed that they would never come close to knowing, firsthand, the likeness of the history that haunted this place. Between thoughts of good wishes, she glanced around, wondering if any sign were left of where the café might have been. Most likely, her tires were rolling over the very places where helpless wretches breathed their last sighs in this world. It was haunting. This was hallowed ground.

The town was small, consisting of no more than four blocks in the heart of the sleepy farmland. Elena turned the steering wheel to the right and coasted onto Price Street. An oil pumper in the field caught her eye. She thought she remembered something about this area being an affluent community at the height of the oil boom. She was momentarily distracted by thoughts of wildcatters and wealth to be had when natural resources presented themselves to lucky explorers in every state. Whether it was the imported Chanel No. 5 perfume in the company stores of southern West Virginia coalfields during the nineteenth century, or fine tapestries in the stores of gold towns of the Wild West, wealth had a way of transcending the quietest areas on earth.

Here in Griffin was no great wealth. Even in 1925, Griffin had only one restaurant owned by Dr. and Mrs. Kokomoor. About four hundred folks patronized a general store, garage, and bank. After the destruction of the town, many citizens moved away, never to return. The day haunted them until their death. Today, Griffin was much smaller, with no sign of a restaurant or a bank. No visible clues of its annihilation remained after so many years, but one street in the heart of town bore a haunting message. Tornado Street was on Elena's right. When had this street been named? Elena shivered. She continued on East Street, which had curved off Price, and circled toward the small green park where the historical marker had been celebrated only a few years before. TRI-STATE TORNADO headed the pole-mounted plaque.

Elena eased the Windstar to the right and grabbed the camera. A white gazebo headed up the straight, concrete walk that separated neatly trimmed, tracts of green grass. Small, curved benches rested on a lawn, flat by Omniscient design, and beautifully maintained by the loving hands of some groundskeeper she could not see. Someone was doing a lovely job maintaining the dignity of a site designated as a memorial to people who may have felt their lives were too insignificant to have been lost in such despair. They were not forgotten.

Elena read through the list of names: Ruby Cleveland … Winfred Fisher … Virgil Simmons…. Giving names to this place distinguished it in a fitting way. Real names. Real people. They were more than statistics. They were living, breathing, laughing, loving, human beings. Again, Elena felt a sense of regard that was indefinable. Some perspective she had on the world was shifting along this storm path. Everything she had taken for granted was brazenly magnified in her mind. Her research was quickly becoming more than a means to a paycheck. Storm researchers were her heroes now. Material possessions were fading behind her. She did not know where this storm path was leading her philosophically, but it was a new domain like none she had ever experienced. Her work would be cut out for her once she landed back at her *Sentinel* desk. That was all right. What was it about this story?

A beat-up, Ford pickup stopped across the road in front of a boxy, red, two-story building. A skinny guy in jeans and tan tee shirt eyed her suspiciously as his feet hit the gravel berm. Elena's defenses went up, and she went into tourist mode, pointing her camera toward the TRI STATE TORNADO marker. She retrieved her tripod from the back seat of the van, and set it up for a self-portrait in front of the marker. By then, the guy had ambled into the building and disappeared. Apparently, she had satisfied his curiosity and adequately painted a picture of yet another sightseer who had meandered into town to gawk at the marker.

Normally, Elena would have approached him directly and asked about his knowledge of the storm. But, today she was not so inclined. It had been a tiring trip, and she had more than enough files stacked high in the back of the van. The marker and memorial plaque would absolutely suffice for writing purposes. Chances are she would be overwhelmed as she whittled away at the final work for the paper. At the moment, some force of intent was whittling away at her psyche. Maybe it was nothing more than homesickness and fatigue. Everything looked different after research treks. On evenings after a trip, she would snuggle in front of her bedroom fireplace and sip herbal tea. Then she felt truly home. She could rest under her down-filled comforter in a way that defied hotel beds and naps in the Windstar. A nice shower in her own digs was beckoning her. As was some good conversation with Greg and Charles. She was missing her old editor, like a doting cat-lover misses a tabby. For some unexpected reason, Greg was another matter. It was like the old saying, absence makes the heart … someone else ….

Suddenly, the Bicycle Gang came barreling around the corner. Elena looked up and waved spontaneously. A toothy smile spread across her face, and she momentarily pondered the possibility of borrowing one of the bikes for a quick ride around the town. Clearly, that would be crossing the line. She had no intention of startling anyone, in this town or anyplace else. The kids waved back. Elena walked slowly toward the gazebo, reflecting on some powerful, invisible presence of other children who once laughed here.

They had boarded the town's one school bus and were almost home, when the driver stopped in front of the McVay house. The cyclone slipped up on him and the students with the stealth of a flesh-slaughtering maniac. Before the driver and children understood what was happening, the bus had been flipped on its side, lifted into the air, and smashed to the ground in a field outside of town. Two children and the driver died when the vehicle was slammed to earth. Dazed students scrambled to safety and wandered through the pasture like lost animals.

In the meantime, Oth Shaw, principal of the Bethel Township
School, awaited the return of the bus for its final run. Most of the
250 children had departed the building. When its bricks and mortar
crumbled under the impact of the tornado, the children were spared
death, but not some injuries, shock, and unrelenting terror. Other
children were not so fortunate. One boy was identified by a few marbles
in his pockets—another by his penknife.

Within minutes, the streets of Griffin were littered with bodies.
Boards, galvanized washpans, bricks, and boards buried others. Debris
was everywhere, consisting of mounds of personal property as seemingly
innocuous as a perfectly stitched, "Hen and Chicks" quilt rumpled atop
a striped mattress and twisted coil springs. Injured people lumbered
through rubble, unsure of their own whereabouts or the whereabouts of
their homes. It was not long until vultures began scavenging through
the rubble, retrieving relics and treasures that never would have belonged
to them otherwise. Looting found an evil foothold in the village
even while entrapped neighbors lay crying out for help. However, the
goodness of fierce, bleeding rescuers prevailed alongside vile animals
who tucked gold wedding bands into deep, dirty pockets.

Victims in shock ambled mindlessly along paths strewn with rubble;
their arms, hands, legs, and faces were embedded with mud hurled from
the Wabash River. They stepped over broken, limbless bodies on their way
to nowhere in particular. The town doctor organized medical relief and
recovery efforts while many survivors lost their minds in the midst of all
of it. One minute, the town was intact, and the next, not a single home
was inhabitable. Within hours, the Wabash River would creep over its
banks and surround the village. Only train cars carrying relief workers
could access the town. Through the efforts of the American Red Cross
and the 139th Indiana Field Artillery, lives were saved, and the roads were
cordoned off from conscienceless sightseers and looters. Evil had found its
hold on the hearts of people who found no interest in saving others. But
strength reigned in the end. Griffin was rebuilt within a year.

Elena watched the Bicycle Gang disappear along Second Street. The man in the Ford pickup rolled a crunchy retreat across the gravel berm. Once again the little town was quiet. Elena leaned on the white railing of the gazebo one last time, said a prayer for all who braved the wide plains of the Midwest, and began her own retreat toward the red van. She wanted nothing more than to be away from the little Indiana town that had impressed her with its honor to those who had died there. Between here and Princeton, eighty-five farms were destroyed. The monster had not finished by 4:00 p.m. Eighteen minutes later, it crashed into the south side of Princeton. No one there imagined their fate that afternoon. Elena had one last library stop. Princeton was the end of the Tri-State Tornado's path. But it was not the end of the storm.

41

Ditto. It was the only word Elena could think about as she reviewed the newspaper files at the Princeton Public Library. The staff was gracious and accommodating, but the same stories she had uncovered in the other towns were popping up here. Victims and streets simply had different names. Roofs were torn away. School building walls collapsed. Terrified children were assailed by flying debris as they walked home from school. Some were carried away by the black cloud that came out of nowhere. Killing fires were started by overturned coal-fueled cookstoves. The stories were running together. The towns all looked alike. Yet, each community claimed the tornado as its own. The *Princeton Clarion-News* was no exception. Reporters listed every heart-wrenching detail of death and destruction. It was personal.

The Princeton Public Library was a sturdy, brick building with tall, white columns. Its history was an old one, dating back to the nineteenth century. It felt like an old school building somewhere in Elena's past. Tables were sturdy and well worn. File cabinets containing cherished archives were predictably gray metal, and a distinct musty smell of age was in the air. A young lady named Franny bubbled around Elena, pulling treasured newspaper copies from drawers and stacked, manila file folders. Everything was laid out beautifully for the West Virginia reporter, saving her hours of microfilm searches. She was pleased knowing that she would have everything photocopied within a few hours and be on her way. There were more smiles in this lovely old building than in some of the stops she had made along the storm path. The staff was proud of their collection of materials, chatting on about how the History Channel producers and researchers from Paducah NOAA had often scrutinized every carefully organized detail of the storm. Paths of researchers from all over the country crossed inevitably in Princeton. It was an important town. Elena was feeling the tiring effects of days of work and travel. Her back ached and she squirmed on the rigid, oak chair seat. Nevertheless, she relished the opportunity to get back home where she could peruse the details of the file while resting by the fireplace. The 4,000-mile trek was quashing her enthusiasm. She needed a break again. A ride in a '53 Vette would do it.

In the middle of sifting through folders and files, Elena paused and opened her tri-fold wallet. The stiff, white business card with the distinct NOAA icon in the corner took her to a brief respite. Memories of laughter and stirring conversation evoked an awareness of mutual respect and warmth with a stranger. It had been so much fun to meet all the thoughtful people that stretched from Ellington, Missouri, to Princeton, Indiana. Now it was becoming apparent that the wistful longing for home was mixed with a little melancholy. The playful part of research was coming to an end. Hours and hours of studying, sorting, organizing, drafting, and rewriting lay ahead. As rewarding as the final product was, the process of feature story writing had its moments. Burying herself in a cubicle at the *Sentinel* was the downside of the job. Yet, she was lucky. The beauty of writing in an electronic age was that she could transfer information from her home office to the *Sentinel* database with a flick of her pinkie on the mouse. That was a huge benny compared to the old boys' days when they slept on cots, trying to get out breaking news, big stories, and special editions. Elena knew she would never want to change anything about work. She wondered how many people wander through life thoroughly disenchanted with their lot. She would settle for nothing less than fulfillment. So far, so good.

Just as Elena slipped into a deeper daydream, Franny plopped a hardback book on the table. It was a collection of black-and-white photographs that had been turned over to local collection of photographs that historians entrusted with their preservation for posterity. The Photographs of the Princeton Tornado, not the Tri-State Tornado—the Princeton Tornado—was an archive to beat out all others.

"Oh! Sorry, Franny. I was just thinking about some storm research I got from NOAA recently," Elena blurted.

The slender librarian smiled and proudly began pointing to key

pages she had marked with small yellow Post-it notes. Images of the
Heinz plant and its greenhouse and office building stood out on the
glossy white-and-black pages. Elena thought back to all the weenie
roasts at Tabor. Grandma Kizzie would sway back and forth in a sturdy
black rocker that had been placed for her beside the crackling bonfire.
No one had a picnic at Tabor unless they packed the Heinz Ketchup. As
a kid, Elena never gave ketchup a second thought. It was a staple. It was
served at every meal for one reason or another. Grandma Bessie made
homemade catsup, and so did her sister, Edna. Pint jars were stored in
stone cellars that had been dug into the hills beneath the farmhouses.
Each cool room contained meticulously lined rows of beans, tomato
juice, peaches, grape juice, and catsup. The reporter's mouth watered. She
came back to the present. Time for lunch.

"Thanks so much, Franny. Tell you what, I'm going to leave the files
here and run out for a bite to eat. I'll be back in an hour or so. I should
be able to wrap up this work pretty quickly. I do appreciate your help
so much. This storm is a mystery, even after all these years. And, I have
to admit, I'm intellectually pulled into it, almost as though it happened
yesterday."

"You and a few other people have said that. I've talked to a few old-
timers around here who went through it, but most of 'em would rather
not dredge up the memories. We've done the best we can to preserve the
history."

"And, you've done it well. Your files are the best I've seen for the last
two hundred miles."

Elena nodded with total sincerity as Franny blushed a modest smile
and stepped backward. It was true. Except for the Jackson County
Historical Society book and the files of the Murphysboro library
staff, Elena had not seen work so painstakingly safeguarded as it was
here. Princeton was a good stop at the end of the research road. There
was good reason for the hard work. The town had suffered losses as
gruesome as any.

She slipped the long strap of her bag over her right shoulder and briskly climbed the basement steps. At the top, she paused briefly, staring at the open doorways of the rooms on the main floor. What was this presence she could not articulate? Somewhere here, broken, mud-caked bodies had been laid in dire need of comfort and healing. Blood had stained the floorboards beneath her feet. A silent shroud of pain hung here. The cries of suffering victims whispered from dark wainscoting all around her. Elena gulped as she finally stepped into the sunshine. No journalistic standard existed by which she could conceivably report the presence of ghosts. This was a library. But on a few days in the early twentieth century, it had been a hospital.

42

4:14 p.m., March 18, 1925, Princeton, Illinois. It was Bargain
Day uptown. Shoppers, including hooky-playing schoolchildren, were
sorting through collections of clothing, hoping for new duds to wear on
Easter Sunday. It was always good to get to the stores early for the best
bargains, but the shopkeepers had been busy pretty much all day. Old Ben
Franklin's "penny saved … penny earned philosophy" was the rule in most
Princeton households. Ladies fingered bolts of fabric and calculated the
number of yards needed for the girls' dresses and boys' shirts. Sales were
brisk. Neighbors greeted each other on the walkways leading from the
hardware store to Miss Emily's Finery for Ladies. They had no reason to
suspect this day would not be like the days before or the ones after.

At the Heinz Plant in the southern part of town, seventy-five men
and women toiled at boilers, tended sprouting tomato plants in the
company's new greenhouse, manipulated the Granell sprinkler system
above hearty green plants, and prepared tomatoes for the last batch of
tomato paste. Mashers converted firm red tomatoes into a gooey pulp
for storage in five-gallon cans on the main floor. Containers of Heinz
pickles, ketchup, sauces, and soup were toted from the main building
proper to the newly constructed storage building. Clerks in the office
building carefully penciled numbers on order forms and bookkeeping
records. In the garage, the company mechanics replaced broken machine
parts in the truck engines, cars, and canning equipment. It was work as
usual at the Heinz Plant.

Schools were dismissing, and students were gathering their
belongings for the walk home. At the Baldwin Heights School,
children were soon streaming out the door and dragging sweaters and
coats behind them while clutching books and swinging satchels. They
chattered about basketball games and what they hoped their mamas
were fixing for supper. They made plans to meet friends at designated
fields, lots, and lawns after evening chores were out of the way.

Once outside the building, the children clamored and scattered in every direction. Laughter flew on the March breeze like bubbles scattering on a gust of warm breath spewed from the puckered lips of a giggling towhead. Not a single student was unhappy when the final bell rang at 4:00. Unrestrained joy always welled in the hearts of children of Baldwin Heights whether or not it had been a good day for lessons. The chatter of friends, hollering to meet up later with playmates, welled into screeching crescendos. Clamoring, goose-like squawking rode on waves of excitement. Then it quickly ebbed, as children separated onto different paths toward home. They hardly noticed the snapping force of winds that forewarned of darkened dust rolling along the ground in the southwest.

Teachers scurried out the large double doors as quickly as the children. They had a little time left to peruse the sale items on the town square. The ladies bustled along the narrow walkways of Princeton, chatting about opportunities to buy the latest fashions, and giggling not so much unlike their youthful protégés. In a matter of minutes, clustered groups of maiden educators joined in the search for the best bargains in the shops along Main Street. The ladies had unanimously agreed to convene their faculty meeting the following day in order that they would not miss out on the shopping excursion that drew so many Princetonians uptown. They nodded to friends and neighbors who stirred through hats, gloves, beads, and bangles. Smiles and soft discourse bounced like gentle echoes through the shops. Each teacher had a ticket for the drawing, and each teacher failed to notice the darkened skies that were approaching their beloved school in the southern part of town.

In mere minutes, the Baldwin Heights School would be disemboweled by wrenching blasts of air. Nearby, workers at the Heinz Plant would run for sturdy shelter or drop flat where they were in anticipation of the blows to follow. That afternoon, the men of the Southern Railroad shop flung their arms over their heads as the brick walls imploded from the unforeseen assault. In only seconds, the third floor disappeared into ravaging winds, and futile cries of pain failed to penetrate the roar of the assailing cyclone.

Uptown, Miss Harkin had been selecting three lace-trimmed handkerchiefs from a stack of personal linens just as she overheard a familiar voice saying she had skipped school to go shopping. Out of the corner of her eye, she caught a glimpse of the swishing shadows of two girls. There was something about the self-declared truant's voice that got her attention. As she turned half-circle to identify the graceful, half-galloping, fifteen-year-old girl, she slowly sighed. Corean Amy was too far away for the dedicated teacher to call out. It would be too boisterous and impolite to shout across two aisles. Corean had been one of Miss Harkin's favorite students in elementary school. The teacher always missed her former students, wondered how they were doing, and spoke enthusiastically to them when she saw them around town. Obviously, Corean was well enough to have attended school, and the dedicated teacher was disappointed to realize that the high-school student had played hooky. She nodded and returned to her shopping, reminding herself that one never knows what the circumstances might be when it came to pupil absenteeism. Corean was a pretty girl, and she had always been conscientious about her studies. It was uncharacteristic of her to sneak off, despite the fact that it was Bargain Day.

Corean stepped quickly, knowing that she should try to make it home by her normal time. Occasional absences were not called into question at the high school, but her time spent looking through sale dresses and lockets was time she needed to keep secret.

Dad had been plenty frustrated that morning when she fussed about wanting to buy a new Easter coat after school. He had pulled out his pocketbook, showing her a single, ten-dollar bill that was all he had until payday. He had a soft spot for Corean when it came to sparing money for something as special as a new coat, but food needed to be put on the table, and bills had to be paid. He and Corean's mother tried to keep their tab at the local stores as low as possible. The coat Corean had was good enough for Easter. When she grew out of it, there would be money for a new one.

The young woman tucked long hair strands behind her ears as she walked along Gibson Street. Her head was tilted down as she wrestled with increasingly powerful wind gusts. Suddenly, an indomitable, engulfing roar overtook her. Corean knew she was in trouble, but there was little she could do about it. In the time it took to barely comprehend the danger, the high-school student's feet were lifted into the air. Her arms flailed wildly as she instinctively reached for anything that could hold her to the ground. Her legs stung with repeated jabs as boards, metal shards, and sticks pummeled the skinny extremities. Then the unbelievable happened. As quickly as she had been whisked upward, her feet touched down on a porch. She quickly crouched, gasping for breath, and then crawled toward the front door. As polite girls always do, she knocked. No one answered.

By the time Corean clutched the doorknob, she was wrestling with all her might to escape the grasp of the tornado. A man across the street was yelling at her, but the tornadic noise was all encompassing. She had no way to know what he was saying. She needed to get inside the house. Just as she opened the door, a yanking force plucked at her as though she were nothing more than a down goose feather. She had no intention of being stuffed into the black cloud against her will. The door slammed into the parlor of the two-story house just as she grabbed the door casing for stability. The door frame held steady, but the wind thrashed Corean back and forth as though she were a limp bullwhip to be cracked against the board floor below her. She groaned with fierce determination, never letting go of her hold on the oak trim.

Two chairs inside the house were hurled toward the opening. Corean was hardly aware that they smashed into the wall just inches from her head. A small table tumbled toward the corner of the room and figurines were fractured into hundreds of pieces as they smashed into walls that strained under the blasts of black air. Finally, her grip eased as she mustered the strength to crawl on her belly into the parlor. Everything was a wreck. Shattered glass, shards of porcelain, garments, and broken furniture was strewn in the most unlikely places. A gray, striped bed pillow lay at her feet, and a pot from the kitchen stove was pressed against her neck.

This mess was her fault. If she had not come into the house, leaving the front door open, these precious pieces of property would never have been damaged. The woman of the house would be very angry. Corean hardly knew what to do next. She guessed that the only honorable thing to do was to own up to her mistake. Once the roar outside eased, Corean lifted herself on her elbows. She looked toward the west window, searching the air for flying pieces of wood and other debris. The tornado had passed. She choked back tears and made plans to find her family in the middle of the aftermath. She was half-stunned and half-energized by each breath she inhaled. She had to get home. Just as she stood and faced the gray doorway, guilt swept over her again. In the doorway stood a middle aged woman. Her dark-eyed stare was fixed on the shaking fifteen-year-old. For a moment, the two women were silent, unable to speak a word. The older woman choked on welling tears as she uttered a pathetic plea.

"Could you go to the school and look for my little girl?"

"I'm sorry! I'm sorry! I can't. I have to get home," Corean blared.

It was all too much for the two Princeton women to comprehend. The woman of the house looked down at the rubble on the parlor floor. She had taken shelter at her neighbor's house while Corean invaded hers. Now, none of this mattered. She was too numb with shock to know which way to turn. The shaking truant ran past her, wondering what to do next. All she could do was run.

At the time Corean had braced herself against the winds on Gibson Street, two little sisters a few blocks away huddled in play on the hallway floor of their home. They giggled and tugged at tiny dresses, which they pulled over the heads of their dollies. They had no way to understand why the room grew darker and darker by the second. Four-year-old Ada McClurkin was rolling her eyes mischievously, and her sister, Harriet, pretended to walk her small porcelain doll toward the kitchen. Ada stopped moving her eyes. She paused and turned her head curiously. Instead of smoke going up the chimney as it should, it was coming down into the front room.

In the kitchen, Mama was humming and stirring a hot pot of soup on top of the stove as Grammy Miller swished melting butter over the freshly baked bread loaves. Eight shoebox-size clumps of golden-crusted bread were neatly lined atop cotton tea towels on the worktable in front of Grammy. The aroma of Mama's white bread was soothing and inviting. Ada wiped slobber from her chin as she imagined the taste of sweet apple jelly on her bread at suppertime. Harriet secretly hoped Mama had saved enough dough to make one long, brown sugar roll to slice for their special treat after supper.

Little did it matter. In a heartbeat, the tornado slammed the southwest wall of the house with such force that the walls collapsed before five-year-old Harriet could look up. Three bricks caught her arm in midair, and the pain became her center of focus even as walls caved in on the four ladies of the house. A wail pierced the air as the roar overtook the small abode. Sweet Ada never knew what hit her in the face; in a second, she was unconscious. The swelling of her cheekbone was instantaneous. When she came to, she could see piles of rubble through only one eye. She was partially blinded by one blow from the monster that crushed Grammy and Mama somewhere underneath the pile of rubble in the kitchen.

When the sisters were carried from the rubble of what had been their home, they did not realize that Mama and Grammy would not be going with them to the Methodist Hospital. A kind lady spoke soft words, assuring Harriet that her arm would be all right. Ada swooned in and out of gray consciousness, as two men lifted her onto a makeshift stretcher. All along the ride uptown, she felt that she could see if she could just open her eyelid. But the swelling was so profuse, that each attempt she made to see through the puffy lid was futile. Harriet held her little sister's hand and prayed that Mama would come get them soon.

By the time the girls were washed and dressed in clean, white, ruffled sleeping gowns, Aunt Katie Miller was on a cot beside them and unwilling to take her eyes off them. She was conscious but in much physical distress. Ada and Harriet were snuggled close beside each other in one narrow bed when Aunt Katie uttered her first words.

"Girls, I'm goin' to be right here with you. Don't you worry none. We're safe and the nurses will help us."

Harriet knew without being told that Mama was not coming. But she and Ada would be all right. Aunt Katie was here. The storm had passed. Nurses were scurrying in every which direction. Loud voices clamored in the corridor where lights suspended from high ceilings dangled at the ends of linked chains. The bustle through the hallway signaled the arrival of more patients than the Methodist Hospital could handle. Ada and Harriet were aware of the turmoil that spun around them in the hospital ward, but their focus was on the eyes of their favorite aunt. She looked sad, and the trio understood that they were all feeling pain they would rather not have. But Mama always taught the little girls and their brother Morton to be strong and brave when things were difficult. So they mustered all their strength and comforted each other for days and years to come.

In the hours after the cyclone, doctors would stress the urgency of removing Ada's injured eye. But Aunt Katie and Great-Uncle Sam McClurkin would have none of it. They felt intuitively that the little girl's eyesight would be restored in time. Within hours following the tornado, reporters from regional newspapers were sifting through human wreckage. They searched for exclusive moments of inspiration and firsthand accounts of the living terror that had destroyed south Princeton. The earliest printed reports would hail Bargain Day for saving the lives of so many people who traveled from the southern end of town to find a bargain far greater than the ones they expected to purchase. Life itself.

When a reporter from the *Princeton Clarion News* spoke with little Ada and Harriet, it was four-year-old Ada who summed up unimaginable beauty in the midst of heart-wrenching pain. She smiled sweetly at her sister, nodded at her aunt, and then stuck her chin out in absolute resolve.

"Harriet will be my eyes, and I will be her arms."

43

Elena stood in the middle of the dirt road a hundred feet or so below Mount Tabor Church. It had been a week since she had returned home from the journey along the tornado path. Charles was pleased with her research and had laid out an unprecedented storm series for the *Sentinel*. The writing had come together sooner than she had anticipated. The story would run in ten Sunday sequels. It was more than a coincidence that the plans for publication would represent the most in-depth report of its kind to date. The deadliest tornado in the history of the United States had enveloped her. Yet something else was at work here.

The facts were clear. The Tri-State Tornado account was a powerful story that spilled over into countless lives nearly a century after its destruction. If the Associated Press picked up an excerpt from Elena's feature story, as Charles believed it might, the story would impact many more people than Elena had imagined when she first started her journey. She squirmed. Something bigger than a *Sentinel* series had affected her along the path she had traveled.

The story about Sam Flowers' lonely journey into night's abyss was haunting. An indefinable alluring quality about Sam and his horse lingered in her thoughts. Prevailing was an ethereal image of Joker racing maniacally through howling winds, then snorting, sweating, and gyrating at the front door of the farmhouse near Ellington. The story was a song for all the children who could never fully understand the terrific force that crashed into their homes and schools. The black thundering cloud lingered in nightmares of all who managed to live another day. Even more basic was some profound effect the crisis had on Elena's sense of being. She was moved by a newfound, keen appreciation for the goodness of people who respond to Disasters. The National Guard. The American Red Cross. The Salvation Army. And nameless volunteers who rush into danger with no thought for themselves, propelled with no thought of acknowledgement. How many victims waited for the rescuer who never came? What hope is there for today's victims of disaster? The questions resonated inside Elena's brain. Some foggy notion about progress and applied scientific principles captivated her. Hope lay always with disaster relief agencies, but it lay also in the most secretive heroes of the twenty-first century: the men and women of NOAA. Response time was improving markedly with each new analysis of storm development. Local and federal authorities were striving for safety on all fronts, especially since the Katrina debacle. The outcry of the American people was heard clearly, and the press played a demonstrable role in efforts to protect people who might otherwise be storm victims.

That was all well and good, but Elena still felt a nagging personal connection that eluded her. She studied the wavy windowpanes of the church and imagined a skinny, curious Garnet leaning against the glass when the thunderbolt exploded from the heavens. She wondered which way the men beneath the bell tower had run. The answers to every question about what had transpired here were buried with the souls at rest in the iron-gated cemetery beside the church. Elena wondered why the questions mattered at all. The story was simply a revelation of a string of natural events here and along the storm path. It was life. It was death. And so much in between. What pulled her, she wondered. What real purpose had this trek laid before her?

The young reporter turned toward the dirt road, eyeing the general direction where a schoolhouse had been. She could almost hear the cheering and the laughter of children tossing the softball at recess as Ralph chased Hiram toward home plate. She could nearly see Lois and Jesse sitting on the velvety moss-covered bank below the school. Princesses. Planning to rule the kingdom of Mount Tabor Ridge as soon as they mastered readin', writin', and 'rithmetic. Piano and violin practice filled late afternoons while their mamas stirred up supper, and their papas tended livestock in the barns. Bursting yellow blooms of dandelions and daisies had blanketed the meadows and lawns on this ridge for decades. This place was the children's kingdom. Elena was trespassing.

Suddenly, the sound of tires crunching on gravel awakened Elena from the daydream. Greg pulled his blue Celebrity onto the brown spot at the edge of the church lawn. Her heart raced momentarily, then sank as fast as it had rushed with anticipation. He opened the door slowly, then ambled up the bank toward her. She could see it in her fiancé's eyes before they ever had a chance to exchange words. He saw it in her eyes too. For what seemed to be a frozen space in time, they stood facing each other. Elena tilted her head in a downward gesture, as though she could find the right words in the grass beneath her feet. Greg gently wrapped his arms around her shoulders and spoke softly.

"I know. You don't have to say anything. I already know," he whispered.

She glanced up at the man who had tutored her through college physics, comforted her through stressful deadlines at the *Sentinel*, and laughed with her over mustard-covered hotdogs at the Carmichael Drive-In Theater. They had been longtime extraordinary friends, with abiding loyalty that would throw either of them into fierce battle to defend each other when threatened. But, at this moment, they were both aware of some irrevocable change that was separating them. Plans for an autumn wedding dissipated in an instant on the lawn of Mount Tabor Church. Their life together was swept away as easily as a leaf whisked across the ridge by a light breeze. Suddenly, time sped at an unprecedented rate. Before Elena could truly believe the engagement was broken, she found herself eyeing the old blue car as her best friend drove down the narrow road toward Wise Run. It was the same road where the Thomas and Porter children had walked to the one-room schoolhouse. It was the place where Grandma Kizzie Tom told the story underneath the maple trees as Elena and her cousins gathered around. The legacy was here. Elena's life had changed in the quest for understanding.

She fumbled through her fanny pack, unzipping the small inside pouch. The NOAA business card was slightly crumpled, but legible. She clutched it in her right hand as a smile edged across her skinny face. She would be heading off to Paducah as soon as she could wrap up her work at the *Sentinel*. She would assure Charles that she would continue to submit feature stories from the road, and he would agree to a compromise that would provide guaranteed, continued friendship and hard work from the young lady he hired fresh out of WVU's School of Journalism. Life was taking a new road for Elena. It was a bittersweet, albeit exhilarating, moment.

The wind picked up, stringing golden threads of hair across her face. She started the walk down the road, contemplating one last story that had to be told here. It had been one of Grandma Kizzie's last, sweet moments in her final days at the log house in Wana. Nellie King was almost old enough to need a caregiver herself, but she did her best, watching out for the white-haired lady in her last years. She caught up with Grandma Tom by the pear tree stump at the edge of the yard. Cars swished along Route 7. Nellie gasped for breath, trying to figure out how to turn the old lady around.

"Grandma! Where ya goin'?" she asked.

Kizzie Jane looked toward the hills above the road and shook with concern that was as clear in her mind as it had been six decades earlier. She could not look at Nellie or the log house. Her purpose was intense and unequivocal. Nellie clasped her forearm, nudging her to return in the general direction of the kitchen porch.

"Where ya goin', Grandma?" she asked again.

Kizzie's response was clear as a bell. Clear as a school bell.

"I'm goin' after the children! They're out in the storm."

PART II

STORM ON TABOR RIDGE

44

March 19, 1925, Thomas Family Farmhouse, Western Monongalia County, West Virginia. The smell of bacon fat warming in Kiz's skillet had the younguns' up without coaxing by anyone. Fried bread from the ebony pan was calling the four children to eat before they needed to hurry along for school out the ridge. Even Bess and Baby Carl tiptoed across the wavy linoleum floor, finding a place at the breakfast table where the first golden slab of homemade toast brought slobber to their grinning mouths.

"You two make room for the others. They need to get to school on time, else Miss White will mark them tardy in front of all the class." Bess wondered what "tardy" was anyway as she nudged Carl to scoot a bit. Kiz flipped over the first two servings of toast sizzling in the finest cured skillet on Tabor Ridge. She smiled at the thought of her skillet cookings compared to those from any pan on Punkin' Run all the way to the ridge top and on down to Camp Run. How many meals had she stirred for Sherman and her growing brood? Busy little bunch they were, with hearty appetites to fill.

Upstairs Lois tugged at her blue-and-yellow calico dress.

"C'mon Little Bit of a Thing!" Fern fumed. "You get more poky every day."

She reached over to help the first-grader with the button underneath her wavy, brown hair.

"Thanks," Lois murmured, twisting calico folds around in the front. "When I grow up, I'm going to make beautiful dresses with buttons down the front!"

Fern was not so sure about her little sister's claim. She frowned in silence as she buckled the skinny sibling's hand-me-down leather shoes. The tiny feet of the future seamstress would need another pair before much longer.

Clomping, heavy, boy feet bolted down the stairwell, two steps at a time. Once again, Ralph was going to make it to the table before the others. He could pack away more grub than ten half-starved pigs rummaging through Dye's General Store. Fern mumbled something about "never seen anyone eat so fast or eat so much so often."

Downstairs, Edna moved calmly around the kitchen. She and Mary Porter could catch up with the Little Ones about the time they made it to the one-room schoolhouse. She pulled the cold, tin pitcher from the icebox and poured milk halfway up six empty jelly jars. Aunt Lilly's rose dinner plates were lined up beside the iron skillet. Edna glanced at her Mom who was spreading butter on both sides of eight slices of bread. Kiz methodically slipped four pieces at a time into the pan. The sound of sizzling bread slices crackled through the kitchen as the smell of quickly fried, hand-churned butter filled the farmhouse.

"Can we ride Old Sam to school?" Lois beamed.

"Gracious, no!" Kiz smiled. "The weather is looking very nice out there today. See the sun peeking around the clouds up there?"

As she pointed, she noticed her index finger was just beginning to show signs of a hard life. By the time she was fifteen, Kiz was scrubbing floors at the Edwards Hotel in Wadestown, plowing rows for summer crops, toting berry pails, and cinching saddles for every ride to the next destination. So much work. In later years, with six younguns and needy neighbors and kin, there was always hard work for her bony fingers. On some days, she was so tired she could hardly move. Every knuckle ached. When it rained, swollen, crooked fingers distracted her from heavy chores. She wondered about the throbbing joints today. It did not look stormy outside. Yet, Kiz clutched her fingertips, gently rubbing up and down, as though the pain would ease with the slightest caress.

She paused to smile at the children, wiped her hands on a feed-sack tea towel, and gestured for them to come closer to the window. Gazing toward the Mason-Dixon Line marker in the field, Kiz reassured them, "See. That sun is tryin' to break through those clouds to give you a nice warm mornin' to walk to school. Sam doesn't need to be tied up to the hitchin' post all day. Let's let him stay in the field to rest."

Her soft voice was all the persuasion Lois needed. With a half-hour for her to sit before the walk out the ridge, Lois plopped herself onto a kitchen chair, determined to save her strength for the long road ahead.

"OK, Mom. I can do it. I can walk the whole way and not even stop once to rest."

Beside her, Ralph gulped the last of his milk, wiped his mouth on his sleeve, and jumped up to take a look for himself. His expression was less conciliatory.

"Those clouds look like they're movin' in. We might be up for a rain," he asserted.

Many a time he had studied clouds from his stance on the Model T running board from where he pumped air into the gas tank. Traveling hills to Wheeling required lots of work for the oldest son. Two days to make the jerky, bouncing trip along rutted roads required Ralph's strong muscles to force air-catapulted gas through the wobbling vehicle's fuel line. There was no other way to power the Ford over the winding ridges. Also, it was often necessary for the boisterous Thomas boy to tear into the running-board toolbox for wrenches to fix problems with the combustible engine. Pumping up flat tires was always a given. Ralph could do it all.

They were never sure when the Tin Lizzie would stop or be delayed on the trip. But the Thomas clan always set out with the expectation of making it to the bustling town on the Ohio River. Stormy weather was common, and when a shower blew up quickly, Sherman headed for the nearest covered bridge. With chilling wind and rain spraying through the cracks of the bridge walls, Ralph and his Dad snapped side curtains to the windshield frame and doors of the Ford. Ralph knew how to study the sky and could almost always predict exactly when Dad needed to head for the shelter of a bridge. Most of the time they succeeded in encasing the car with the Cello glass-windowed cloth before anyone could squeal about getting wet. Ralph always worked hard to figure out what the sky held in store, and the family trusted his assessment of encroaching bad weather.

"Mom," he said, "there's a storm a-comin.' I'm pretty sure of it."

"Maybe so," Kiz paused. "Now you children just remember, if there's lightning, go to the closest house as fast as you can. You know what happened to Uncle Tumps' mule."

Solemn eyes of the two small, curious youngsters looked at each other with understanding. Everyone knew what happened to Uncle Tumps' mule.

45

"Tell us the story again," Bess pleaded. Her sparkling eyes and sweetly curved smile were more than Mom could resist. With a sigh of concession and warmth welling within her, Kiz continued her morning tasks and began to tell the Mule Story for the umpteenth time.

Garnet was just a little girl when it happened. It was a perfect spring morning at the Mount Tabor United Methodist Church. The six-year-old stood on tiptoes in her favorite pew beside the window. From there, she could watch arriving neighbors tie their horses to the hitchin' post. Church would be starting in a few minutes. Latecomers scurried across the lawn toward the white clapboard chapel.

Uncle Tumps had quickly flung the reins around the post as Garnet pulled herself closer and closer to the window. Oh, to be outside playing on the grass instead of twisting back and forth on that hard church bench. Well, if she couldn't be outside, she could look outside. The lawn was nicely trimmed. Daffodils and phlox edged the bank beside the tree-lined ridge road. The smell of fragrant flowers was mixed with the unmistakable scent of the sweating horses that were hitched nearby.

Uncle Tumps' oak wagon was plain and useful in the country. It was not one of those fancy Sunday surreys with fringe dangling from a canopied cover. Garnet liked the sturdy old wagon and wondered how tired the two mules were, having lugged the wagon so far up the winding road.

What was it like to be a mule? She knew they could be feisty and cross as a bull with its tail caught in a barn door. She knew to keep her distance and let the mule-tenders like Uncle Tumps rein them to and fro. For the moment, the mules seemed quiet and glad to rest at the edge of the grassy knoll. They looked strong and sure of themselves. She knew they would step on her and squash her if she got in the way. Despite her trepidation, she had a keen regard for the hardworking animals. How many times she had heard the Tabor men gathering around, talking admirably about a hardworking field hand who was "strong as a mule." It was strength she doubted she would ever know.

But, of course, there was the other side of the mule's character: that irrefutable reference to some ornery scallywag, like Sherman's brother Uncle Linc, who more often than not was "sly as a fox" and "stubborn as a mule." Now that was a quality Garnet thought she could muster. She smiled and wondered if God would be mad at her if she decided to become as stubborn as a mule. Maybe it was all right to be set in one's ways sometimes. That would be a good question for the preacher today.

Boisterous men clamored underneath the bell tower. Garnet glanced quickly at the gathering parishioners, trying to figure out how soon she would have to sit down in a quiet spot on the oak seat. Uncle Tumps was scuffing his feet back and forth on the rag rug, and the bell rope was being pulled slowly up and down by the callused, tan hands of the Superintendent. She had one last moment to see the mules. They stood only a few feet away from the little girl. A ripple of old glass separated their eyes from hers. Worshipers were at their assigned posts.

A ping resounded on the wavy windowpane. A second drop of rain splattered in front of Garnet. The storm was moving in quickly, and she was so glad that she would not get her new dress soaked. The shower would probably pass over by the time she was out of Sunday School.

But, as children are inclined to do, Garnet studied the mules and wondered if they minded getting rained on as much as she did. Mama had told her that most farm animals are better off inside a barn during bad weather, but their tough hides and coarse hair were something like good coats on people. It was all right for folks to be out in the rain occasionally just as long as they had a nice topcoat to protect them until they could reach shelter. Garnet breathed a sign of relief and smiled at Uncle Tumps' old mules. Their coats were nice and thick enough to protect very well against the rain that was coming. The mules would be fine. So it seemed.

Suddenly, an explosion of white light overwhelmed Garnet. She was stunned by the whiteness that enshrouded her from every direction. An accompanying deafening blast from Heaven itself shook the church and rumbled the pew where the little girl stood. The trembling six-year-old felt as though she had been hit in the face, and briefly, she could see nothing at all. Some awful power had reached into her eyes and heart. She shook all over but continued gazing straight ahead, eyes fixed on blank air where the hitching post had been. Then she saw. There in front of her, one of Uncle Tumps' mules wavered for a moment, and then crashed to the ground with a deafening thump.

In later years, she would recount, "That mule just dropped dead right there. I was so afraid of storms after that."

One single bolt of lightning had taken away the strength of the towering, strong work animal. And, it changed the life of Garnet Tennant forever. No one took shelter faster than Garnet when storm clouds approached. At the first sound of thunder, she would admonish her playmates to run inside as fast as they could, and on stormy nights, she hunched underneath the quilts, hiding from the white light that almost took her sight away.

Kiz and Sherman had told the story many times and warned the children to respect all God's forces in nature. Taking shelter quickly at a neighbor's farmhouse was a lesson as common as ciphering in the one-room schoolhouse. All the Thomas children listened attentively when Uncle Tumps' mule was mentioned in parental instructions.

Kiz moved the skillet to the back burner as Bess rolled her eyes toward Lois. The older kids clamored near the doorway as the silent, young sisters held each other's gaze. Garnet might be by tomorrow to help Mom with the spring cleaning. They would ask her more questions about the day that God came to church to get Uncle Tumps' mule.

"All right, you young whippersnappers," Kiz teased, "time to get out the ridge."

Lois had almost forgotten about the long walk ahead of her. The petite first-grader hopped off the chair and bounded out the door. She was sure they would have time to rest along the way if she just got too tuckered out. Her *McGuffy Reader* was strapped with a special leather cinch that Dad had made just for her books. She swung it back and forth, and glanced over her shoulder. The youngest schoolgirl beamed her biggest smile in the direction of the lady waving from the doorway.

"Bye, Mom."

Fern fumed a little more, "Come on, Lois Nell!" she urged.

Kiz winked at the two girls, "Patience, Fern Elizabeth. Patience is a virtue, don't you forget."

"Yes, Ma'am … uh … I'll try … it's just so hard to keep her on time. I'll try to be patient."

Kiz' waved her weathered hands, and Lois smiled a silent one last, "Bye."

Kiz whispered too low to hear, "Bye, Lois Nell."

46

Ralph took off lightning fast, thinking that he and Hiram Basinger might have some time to play softball before Miss White rang the bell. He hesitated just long enough to caution the girls, "Stay together all the way to school. Jesse will be along soon. Fern, you watch out for them two girls."

Fern sighed, knowing that she was always responsible for the Little Ones. Truth be told, she and Edna were the "other" Moms in the Thomas household. It was true that Ralph had hard work at the barn and in the fields. She understood his chores were difficult, but what she wanted more than anything was to run to school by herself. She craved the idea of a few quiet minutes alone underneath the maples. How she would relish a morning pause to catch her breath and dream of days ahead. She had peace and quiet a few times on any day of the week. She was always surrounded by little people. Wishing otherwise would not make it so. She smiled at her little sister and breathed in the crisp, mountain air. The two of them would have their own time to play, all the way to school.

Fern plopped her feet methodically on each walkway stone, but she was a little too fast for Lois. The tiny girl looked all around for the earliest signs of spring. Golden dandelion crowns poky-dotted the banks just below the road. Birds sang morning wakeup calls from branches that arched above the rutted, dirt drive beyond the barn.

"Look at Mom's roses, Fern Elizabeth," she said. Her fragile little hand was gesturing toward the arbor at the end of the walk. She quick-stepped two paces for each of Fern's strides.

"Yes, yes, I see," Fern agreed.

She smiled and paused. Patience had found a place in her for the moment. How Mom loved her flowers. The entwined green strands over the wooden trellis were budding nicely this year.

"Won't be long 'til we see beautiful pink flowers all around," she whispered to her petite sibling. Lois giggled, knowing that she was getting the appropriate amount of attention now. Fern clasped Lois' skinny fingers, smiled an even bigger smile, and waited for the squeaky voice of the younger sister. "Come on! We'll be late for school!"

Stick-like legs moved side by side beneath floral, feed-sack dresses. The two youngsters peered intently at the funny looking clouds above the isolated marker in the field. The sky-pointing stone pillar marked the place where King George III of England had sent his trusty surveyors to settle the disputed land border of the New World. On the mark, precisely between West Virginia and Pennsylvania, the gray, chiseled column denoted the famous Mason-Dixon Line. Kiz had told the children that the line ran smack-dab through the middle of the Thomas house. Fern was not sure whether she were a West Virginia resident or a Pennsylvania resident. Lois did not care. When the hay was mowed and harvested in the summers, the Thomas kids would chase around the stone pillar playing Prisoner's Base with the Porter children and some of the Watson cousins that came down from Wheeling. Extra kids came and went in the summers. For all the hard work on the ridge, lots of laughter filled the fields and farmhouse. On cool summer nights, Sherman and Uncle Ray would load their shotguns, leash the hounds, and head off past the Mason-Dixon marker to hunt coon.

Before the harvest, Edna, Lois, and Fern would gather wild daisies near the marker and braid them into beautiful hair wreaths, which they wore proudly to the supper table. Even Baby Bess would tag along to be sure she had a daisy crown of her own. When Bess's asthma acted up, the bigger girls crossed their arms to make a chair for her to ride back to the farmhouse, daisies piled high in her lap. They were also sure to have a big bundle of daisies for Mom's glass pitcher on the worktable. Good times were generously shared in that field, but today peculiar clouds were looming overhead. Lois squinted and curved her pursed lips, but said nothing about the sky.

Fern and Lois knew they were certain royalty to walk where King Charles II of England granted lands to the Calvert and Penn families in 1683. Now, the land was proudly owned by the Thomas clan. Princesses they were: Princess Fern Elizabeth and Princess Lois Nell, walking toward the one-room schoolhouse where they would read and cipher numbers. But deep inside, they knew the day would come when they would know reading and writing and arithmetic. Time would come for them to reign over the majestic kingdom of Mount Tabor Ridge. In the meantime, they guessed they would have to continue with their studies and music lessons in preparation for their exquisite work in the mountainous woodland of the Thomases, Whites, Porters, Clovises, Basingers, and many more.

Shortly, they would meet one of their royal subjects, Lady Jesse Porter, and the three of them would stroll along the wagon-wheel and Tin Lizzie ruts, hoping they could remember the words for the spelling bee and taking care not to twist an ankle along the way. It was too early to look for daisies, but a few dandelions were popping up here and there. Mom would soon be making dandelion jelly, and much to Dad's consternation, rumors would be whispered in the school yard about who on Camp Run was making dandelion spirits. None of that sinners' drink would touch the lips of any of the Thomas kids. Not if Dad had anything to do with it.

Lois did not understand all the talk about liquor. She just knew that Dad loved to tell a story about Uncle Linc being out on the ridge one day without an outhouse in sight. Something made Linc woozy just as he stood at the edge of the hillside, and he tipsied over face-forward, tumbling down over the hill. One night last June, she had been playing on the back porch when she caught the first telling of the tale. Uncle Ray was in the yard, barking the story to four coon hunters, as they loaded buckshot shells in their coat pockets. The ruddy-faced storyteller roared and bellowed his declaration that Linc was so useless, he couldn't even take a piss right. Baudy laughter had filled the night air.

Lois did not think it was good manners to laugh about someone falling down a hill. She did not think it was one bit funny. And, what did dandelions have to do with that anyway? Sometimes grown-ups were so confusing with all their talk about, "Don't do this, don't do that!"

She could not very well keep from doing something when she did not know what it was. She guessed she was not supposed to fall over the hill if she could not find an outhouse.

"Here she comes!" Lois cheered.

She pointed toward the bend in the road and skipped toward Jesse.

"Ralph says it might come a storm," she warned Lady Porter.

Jesse smiled at her best friend. She nodded sideways and quietly began to study the boughs of large, sugar maples and skinny, sugar tree saplings.

"Look, Lois, those leaves are turning upside down. Papaw says upside-down leaves are a sure sign of rain coming."

Lois halted her tiny, rhythmic pace and looked up into the canopy of limbs that loomed over the royal trio. She abruptly planted her fists on her waistline and listened to the symphonic rustling of the woods. The calico-clad girl was puzzled.

"I don't know, Jesse. Mom said the sun was coming through the clouds to shine on us today. It was pretty sunny over on our porch. Why do leaves turn upside down anyway?"

Fern caressed her little sister's hand again, gently tugging her toward the bend in the road. "Leaves turn upside down because the wind pushes them over. The wind blows in the rain, and it blows Ralph's underwear upside down on the clothesline."

Fern winked and the brigade of silly princesses exploded into a silly song of, "Oh! Oh! Oh!" Such silliness indeed. Mom would probably not want them making fun of Ralph's underwear on the clothesline. But they would not tell her. That was for sure.

They laughed and continued the walk along the narrow roadway between the maple, oak, and birch trees. Fern slowed down to remind them, "Listen for thunder. Mom told us to run to a farmhouse if we are going to get caught in the storm before we make it to the schoolhouse. Maybe we better walk a little faster."

"OK," Lois responded.

"OK," Jesse replied. "I'm sure we'll make it before the storm."

47

Back in the kitchen, Edna finished clearing the table and wiped the oilcloth cover with wet cheesecloth. Behind the pantry door, four thread spools had been nailed to the wall. She eyed the spool closest to the door and hung her apron beside Mom's sweater. With open palms, she pressed the front of her dress and tidied the skirt gathers to make them as neat as possible. Curtains on the windowed door fluttered back and forth, and the clear taste of cool dampness was apparent in the spring air.

Edna moved gracefully alongside the basin and picked up her geography book which was laying beside the butter churn. She had studied the countries of Europe the night before while sitting on Mom's stool and turning the wheeled paddle through the milky mixture in the glass jar. Two oblong mounds of fresh butter were in the icebox. Not only had she prepared new butter for the family's morning toast, but also she believed she had successfully memorized the capitals, mountain ranges, and rivers of Europe. All the Thomas kids learned their lessons quickly, and Edna was a fine example of what every family's children should be: hardworking, smart, responsible, pensive, respectful, and talented. She was a good listener too, and she had not missed Ralph's storm admonition, despite his boisterously typical-boy behavior.

"Mom, it looks like Ralph was right. We're in for a shower, I think."

A gentle knock on the doorframe caught their attention. Kiz moved toward the porch door. It was Mary. She was a little early this morning, and Edna wondered if her friend might have hoped to get a small serving of homemade butter on skillet-fried toast.

"Hello, Mary," Kiz said.

"Good morning, Mrs. Thomas. I got my chores done quickly this morning and thought I'd just come on over early to visit until Edna is ready. Here, I brought you some of Mom's peach cobbler she made last night. She knows how much you like her cobbler."

Kiz reached for the brown paper package.

"Why, thank you, Mary. Tell your Mom how much I appreciate you sharing with us. When I get my spring cleaning done, I'll be sending over some jelly and pone. How's your family?"

"Oh, we're all doin' fine. Jesse had an earache last night, but Papa blew some pipe smoke in her ear. Mama put some warm drops of castor oil in her ear too, and she went to sleep on a heated pillow. I think she is doing better this morning. She dressed for school and said she was determined to be there for the spelling bee championship. You know how she likes to spell, more than anything else in school."

"Yes," Kiz chuckled, "she is always asking Fern to give her words to spell. It's good that she likes school. So many children just think it's so hard to work on their lessons. She might grow up to be a teacher. Jesse isn't afraid to try new things, is she?"

"No, I don't think she is afraid of much of anything … well … almost anything," Mary acquiesced.

Kiz studied the wavering trees down across the meadow.

"I think you girls better get on out the road. Edna, I'll finish your chores. The rain may come pouring down on those Little Ones pretty fast. Maybe you can catch up with them and shoo them into a neighbor's home if you have to. I'd hate for them to be alone, even if it's just a spring shower."

"All right, Mom. "We'll try to catch up with them, but they got a pretty good start."

Edna moved to the parlor to get her sweater and satchel. She glanced at the piano and wished she had taken time to study her scales before breakfast, but she had no time now. She would work on her music lesson when she got back this afternoon. Golden forsythia blossoms blew into the windowpanes of the parlor. Edna thought there was something odd about the blooms loosening from the bush by the side porch. Something about it felt strange and unsettling. She hurried back to the kitchen and reassured her Mom that they would catch up with the children. The two friends would be sure that Fern and the Little Ones did not get drenched before school. There was still a lot of time before the opening bell assembly. Even if they were delayed 15 minutes or so, they would all make it to school with time to spare.

Edna was a towering, surrogate mama. As firstborn, she had become the "keeper of the house" whenever gardening or tending to chickens, cows, sheep, geese, and goats pulled Kiz away from the household. Long ago, she had surmised that the Little Ones were far better off with so many grown-ups watching out for them.

Fern had her share of chores for certain. With Sweet Bess tagging along everywhere and with Lois asking questions over and over, Edna could see how Fern was drawn into the mama's role too. Ralph was down at the barn every chance he got to bring the cows in and to curry Old Sam, Rhoda, called "Rodie," and Lark. Once a year, he sheared wool from Mom's pet sheep, Babyface, who was kept only for wool sales in the spring. No mutton was ever to be eaten in the Thomas household. More than once they heard the admonition, "No sheep-eatin' in Kiz's house!"

Edna sighed. She missed being little. In fact, she could hardly remember being a child. Every day she had so many chores. Yet she knew her daily tasks were important to the family. There were also moments when music from her piano-playing and squeaky, violin-stroking in the parlor gave her great satisfaction. She knew she was fortunate to learn music, and she was much better off than Grandma Thomas.

Poor Grandma Thomas lived in a shack along the creek called Honey Run. Edna dreaded visits to the house in the wintertime. The wind whistled between newspaper-covered boards, and a small coal-stoked fire was the only heat source for warming the place during freezing weather and snowstorms. Edna could not retreat soon enough to the shingled home on the ridge. With gas stoves, gas lights, and plenty of quilts and wool clothing, it was much more comfortable than Grandma's house. Edna knew she had well-defined advantages in her Tabor home, even though she wearied of so much work every day.

"Edna! Edna!"

Small hands tugged at her hem. It was Bess. Edna smiled, knowing she had no time to brood when curious eyes looked up for answers. She did not know what the question would be, but she knew the tug was a signal. Carl and Bess believed their sister was the source of all knowledge. Edna chuckled softly. If only the two little whippersnappers realized how much she did not know.

"Edna," Bess whispered seriously. "Do you think this is a day like the one when God took Uncle Tumps' mule to Heaven?"

"I don't think so," Edna spoke reassuringly.

She patted the silky, chopped hair of the youngest sister.

"Don't you worry. You stay inside the house and you'll be safe. I'm going down the road to make sure Lois, Fern, and Ralph are safe too. Don't you worry. I've been through lots of storms, and I know what to do."

Edna patted her Mom on the arm and repeated the reassurance.

"I'll take care of the Little Ones. We'll be fine."

Mary held the screen door as Edna stepped across the threshold. A gust of wind caught strands of Edna's hair and whipped them into her face. Something about this experience felt alarming. She was a little apprehensive, but the children and her Mom were counting on her to be in charge of the situation. She tucked her brown hair behind her ears and turned up the collar of her coat. It was time to find her young siblings and Mary's little sister. She knew her Mom was worried. She knew also that once again she was responsible for the well-being of the Little Ones.

48

The door had just closed behind Mary and Edna when Kiz felt a tightening sensation in her throat. Nervousness was taking hold, and she fought to stay calm for her children's sake. She tugged at the apron strings and hung it over the chair beside the stove. This was not the same air she sensed in showers and storms close to planting time. A glance toward the garden revealed clotheslines whipping up and down as T-shaped end poles wavered in what usually were perpendicular positions.

"Mom," Bess whispered, "are Fern and Lois safe walking outside? Is the storm coming like Ralph said?"

Kiz leaned over and fixed her eyes on the little girl's face. She smiled and scooped the youngest daughter up into the air. Then she reached inside her dress pocket. Slowly she pulled a closed hand up toward Bess' face. The little moppet head began to giggle. She knew what was next, and up came her pointy finger. Tap, tap, tap. The finger motioned for the fist to open. Kiz's bony hand uncurled. In her palm lay a round pink lozenge. Tiny fingers grasped the mint candy, and Bess eagerly pushed it toward her wide grin.

"Now, don't you worry. When children are as old as Edna, Ralph, and Fern, they know how to stay safe. The walk to school isn't very far, and neighbors are out there watchin' out for anyone who needs a hand. Lois can count on the others to keep her safe. And once they get to school, Miss White will watch over them. They will take just as good care of them as I will of you."

Kiz tapped the nose of the puckered-face child, and Bess wrapped her skinny arms around her mother's neck. She hugged her mom so hard, Kiz was compelled to mimic a slight groan.

"Oh, my! That's the biggest hug I've ever had!" Kiz said.

A gentle tugging motion pulled on the waist sash of Kiz's dress. The pull was so firm, she nearly lost her balance. Down at her knee, Baby Carl was insisting that he have some attention too. Kiz leaned over with a pink candy for him, and then she pulled him up to the side opposite Bess.

"Yes, Carl. I'll take care of you too!!"

Just then the screen door on the side porch slammed against the southwest wall of the gray house. Kiz lowered the children to the kitchen floor and moved through the parlor. As she opened the windowed door, her smile faded. She halted dead in her tracks.

The ridges miles away were covered with looming, black clouds, darker and more ominous than any she had ever seen. Day was turning into night. Stepping onto the porch, Kiz's gaze was sustained on the distant hills as she reached methodically toward the screen door. The stretched out spring had slipped off the catch and was dangling uselessly against the warped door edge. Kiz had no interest in putting it back in place. Ralph could tend to that later. She quickly grasped the hook latch and pressed it firmly through the screw eye on the door frame.

Pushing the main door closed, the willowy mother looked toward the kitchen floor. Carl and Bess were playing with the butter paddle and one of the croquet balls. They were well distracted now and had little concern about approaching bad weather or Uncle Tumps' mule. Thoughts of what to do raced through Kiz's head. Sherman had left early for the brass works plant in Brave. He had ridden Rhoda down the hill. Even though the Model T was out in the shed, it was of no use.

Edna was learning to drive the wobbly vehicle, and Ralph knew all about its parts and mechanics. But Kiz left the learning and driving to Sherman and to the older children. She had her hands full, taking care of kids on the trips in Lizzie. Kizzie did not have enough time to learn how to drive. Besides, few women in the mountain community had shown any interest in driving. That was men's work. Kiz was all too happy not to take on any more chores than she already had.

When there were moments to catch her breath, Kiz would smile as she realized how much Sherman enjoyed driving the family all the way to Wheeling in two short days. In the back, Lois sat on Edna's lap, Bess sat on Fern's lap, and Carl crunched between the older sisters on the velvet seat. Sherman manned the steering wheel, and Kiz cradled Bess or Carl when one of them began to squirm. Ralph would usually be hanging onto the running board, waiting for Dad's instructions to pump air into the gas tank. They were fine trips, and the family always made do whatever way necessary.

Years before, the family had taken fewer trips. Traveling on horseback and in buggies, they would plan overnight stays for two or three nights before pulling into Delphi's tree-lined road just outside Wheeling. The Watson family greeted them with smiles, hugs, and lemonade. Nowadays, kids sprang out of the automobile and ran helter-skelter across the lawn, laughing and squealing with the chance to play freely in the open air.

Kizzie had a flicker of awareness of those happy days of beautiful weather, but today was nothing close to those moments. No one was here to drive the Ford, and no laughter came from children frolicking on the lawn. There was only the quiet play of two younguns rolling a croquet ball across a linoleum floor. They were unaware of any danger. Mom was there to take care of them.

For a moment, Kiz regretted her inability to operate the T, but she let the thought pass. It did no good to worry about things that could not be remedied at the moment. Even if she could drive, she was not sure it would be wise to pack the smallest children in a vehicle as shaky and prone to breaking down as that contraption anyway.

Sam and the surrey might be a way to go on hunt of the children. But Sam could be skittish in the midst of storms, and it was more than she could manage to load up the surrey with the smallest children. The conditions were too threatening. It did not seem wise to take Bess and Carl out into the storm as bad as the one hovering a few miles away. Gusts of wind suggested that the ebon clouds would not linger for long on the distant horizon.

Kiz murmured in frustration, "Why didn't I pay attention to Ralph's warning about those clouds? He's a smart fellow when it comes to the outdoors."

She hushed and glanced at the two giggling children edging toward the archway between the two rooms. Certainly, she did not want to upset them. Her job was to stay calm and make them feel safe and protected. There were no inquiring interruptions, so she knew that her obtuse thoughts were indeed her alone. But one quiet, internal voice repeatedly whispered in her heart, "I should have kept the children home. I should have …."

Kiz sighed and sank into the rose brocade chair. She stared at Bess and Carl. There was no place they could go. The closest neighbors were the Porters, and they were down the hill a mile or so. Kiz felt helpless. She would have to trust the older children's good judgment to care for themselves and for each other. The Thomas children were smart.

"They will know what to do," she whispered.

49

Mrs. Porter had placed the eggs back in the icebox and turned to her oldest son, Harry. He was pulling on a second four-buckle and was ready to head down to the barn. Just as he reached for the milk pail on the porch, a firm clasp of Mama's hand crushed the lanky farmer's shirtsleeve. She was frowning. Mama was usually talkative and opinionated, but not inclined to lean on others for assurance. This morning, Harry was disconcerted by her behavior. Harry could not put his finger on it, but he recognized his mother's tendency to exaggerate trouble as something that was terribly frustrating for him. He understood Mama's best intentions, and he had learned to listen with an air of skepticism, being careful not to hurt her feelings.

"Harry, have you looked at the sky? Don't those clouds look peculiar to you?"

"Mmmmm … don't know," he mumbled. "I guess we might be getting a storm. Best maybe that I leave the cows in the barn for a time, till this passes over."

She nodded agreeably, "That's probably a good idea. Leave the horses in too. The way this wind is blowin', they'd probably get spooked in the field. You can turn them out later."

Harry plodded down the path, past the chicken coop, swinging the bucket while gazing at the ridge top. He had tended to the animals on many a stormy day, and it looked as if today would be one of those days. He hoped that Jesse had started off to school a little bit early. How many nights had she cried on the floor beside her bed, frightened of thunder and lightning? Most of the time Mama could comfort the first grader, but it was lots of work for the whole family. Dealing with a frightened child was almost as terrifying for Harry as the storms were for Jesse. Luckily, Mama was always there for the girls, and he did not have to do much except pull down the blinds.

Sometimes he would hang the wool Army blanket over the window in Jesse's room. Minute holes were evidence that hungry moths had slipped into the hall closet from time to time. Flickers of lightning flashes would sparkle erratically across the heavy dark cover. But it was the best he could do when Jesse was scared. Distracting her from the sight and sound of a thunderstorm seemed to be the best remedy for her fear.

Even Harry noticed that his breathing slowed and a safer feeling took hold of him somehow. He would watch Mama gently brush Jesse's silky hair with one hand while rocking her back and forth. Leaning against the open doorway, he would think how lucky they were to be cared for by such good parents. Work was hard on Punkin' Run, and getting the food to the table was often a day's work by itself. Grandpap had always reminded them that "A day's work yields a day's grace." Harry was not sure what Grandpap meant exactly, but he reckoned it had something to do with the need to work for the food on the table and a roof over their heads. It seemed to be the order of things. And that order did not change much on the farm in the shaded hollow. Chores started with feeding the livestock, milking, gathering eggs, and working in the fields as seasons changed. There always seemed to be shingles on the roof that leaked or hinges on the barn door that screeched as metal rasped against metal. So much work. But so much safety too—around them all.

Mrs. Porter would hum softly, almost at the very interval when thunder would follow the lightning. Harry did not know how Mama figured out exactly when to vocalize her unspoken lullaby. She had this uncanny ability to supersede nature's own exploding voice and to mask it with a tighter hug and reassuring murmurs straight from her heart. He could almost feel the hugs from where he stood across the room. Yes, he did feel impatient at times, but he knew some folks were a whole lot worse off than they were. Mama and Pa had done their best with next to nothing but the Old Home Place and a few head of cattle. Harry never complained.

Oh, when he went down to Hundred on Saturday night, some of the boys would banter about who had it the hardest that week and who was better for it. But Harry was never sure whom to believe. Some of their tales were nothing but yarns designed to get the attention of pretty girls lined up at the picture show. And he was just as likely as any of them to get carried away with complicated stories about carpentry, cattle-tending, timbering, and harvesting, all at the same time. Not a farmhand in the country could come close to the feats he claimed to have achieved.

On the other hand, Mama would remind them from time to time to be thankful for beans and corn pone, even if that was all they had had for two weeks straight. She would be off around the ridge some days to care for neighbors when they were sick or just in need of a little extra help, no matter what it was. Old Mrs. Evans was as tough as jerky for all she had been through. Mama would gather torn overalls and worn-out socks and take them to the widow lady. She would tell the mother of five younguns that she needed help with some mending. She could not pay Mrs. Evans to fix the clothes, but she would bring her a pan of mush or pone if that would be acceptable pay. It was a fair exchange, and the grateful seamstress would work diligently to earn the bartered food.

Sometimes Mama would send Harry over with food, and he would watch the neighbor lady slide a jelly jar into the worn-out heel of a white sock, preparing to darn it by weaving a patch of thread inside the space filled by glass. He was not sure, but he thought he walked into the parlor one time and saw Mama rip a hole right down the back of Grandpap's trousers. He guessed he knew what was really going on there.

On one occasion, he strapped a basket of eggs and meal onto the horn of his saddle to take out to the Evans' place. Mama was having one of her headaches and was laid up with a cold washrag on her forehead and the blinds pulled. On that ride, Harry had not imagined all that he would learn about making do with the best one had. As he arrived at the homeplace along the run, he noticed the frail neighbor coming out onto the porch toting her 12-gauge. He shouted out that Mama had sent some eatin's over for her and the kids. He asked if she might have time to weave some of their rag strips into a rug for their front room.

"Why sure. I'm pretty well caught up with my work. Is your Mama in a hurry for the rug?"

"Naw," he shook his head. "She told me to tell you to take your time. It was just that her ragbag was filling up, and she needed to do something to make room for other things."

Mrs. Evans' eyes lowered as a sense of calm came over her. It was clear that she was very tired. She leaned the barrel of the shotgun against the windowsill and went out to meet Harry on his horse, Thunder.

"He's a strong friend you have there, Harry."

She stroked the nose of the black steed. Thunder jerked his head back, and Harry yanked the left rein with a reprimand, "Here! Here! Easy, boy. Would it be all right if I got him a drink from your pump, ma'am?"

Mrs. Evans nodded. Harry dismounted and walked with the lady toward the pump. Her head was tilted downward as she explained their plight. Appreciatively, she began.

"Tell your Mama how much we appreciated you thinkin' of us. The pantry is getting low. Just a few canned peaches in there. We're gettin' by all right, but it's good to have some fresh eggs to fry and some meal for mush. The kids will be so glad to get a taste of somethin' new. I've been doin' a little huntin' for meat. Growin' kids need meat on their bones. For the last couple of weeks, all I've caught is possum. When you don't have nothin' else, possum tastes awful good. Your Mama is a good woman, Harry. It's awful easy to forget about other people's eatin' sometimes. Your Mama never forgets."

Harry did well to be reminded of this. Some of the other boys near Burton were starting to show up in Hundred on Saturday night, driving their Model T's they got for forty or fifty dollars. Thunder was Harry's ride to the picture show, and it did not look as if there would be an automobile for him anytime soon. But with Pa's work in the fields and his own work with the animals, there always seemed to be plenty of eggs, milk, and crops to trade for just about anything they needed at Dye's General Store in Jolly Town. The Porter children always had a little money left over for penny candy. There was not enough to buy a Ford, but they never ate possum.

He knew also that if Mama did not take time to send him off to the Evans' place, he would likely not have thought about going there. Just as her ability to know when thunder would clap, Mama knew when other people were in need. And she always had a solution that kept their pride in place. Everything Mama did, even her exaggerated talk, had a purpose that others might not see until much later. She could calm Jesse in a storm, and she could calm a hungry neighbor miles away. Harry did not think he had what it took to see how to do it all the way she did.

Harry knew that Mama's words and actions had a place in this world that was part of some "order of things." Sometimes he wondered why he missed the opportunity to see further than pulling a blind, rounding up cattle to get them out of the rain, or pounding a nail into a roof shingle. Even her music had a purpose that he did not fully understand.

The wind was gusting as he walked toward the barn. He glanced over his shoulder at Mama. Without a moment's hesitation, he began whispering one of Jesse's favorite songs.

"Now the moon shines tonight on pretty Red Wing, the breeze is sighing, the Night Bird's crying. For afar 'neath his star her brave is sleeping while Red Wing's weeping her heart away..."

Harry's musical interlude was audible to him only. He paused and looked toward the ridge where Jesse met the Thomas children each morning on her way to school. She should be at their back porch by now if she had not dawdled too long beside the road. Their sister Mary would be finishing her morning chores soon and would catch up with the little girl. Jesse's stride was half that of her siblings, and she loved having a head start on the two-mile hike. A peculiar thought crossed Harry's mind. His gut churned. Something was wrong. He was singing Jesse's favorite song.

50

Ralph's legs were strong and lean, so he could save lots of time running along the ridge. If he waited on those giggling girls to lollygag with every little flower by the side of the road, he would never have a chance to play ball before school. And by the time school was out, he had to hurry home for evening chores. Recess sometimes gave all the kids a chance to run bases on the gentle slope beside the school. But more often than not, Ralph had to stay inside the school to work on lessons he never seemed to have time to do at home.

"Just not enough hours in the day," he would mutter while poring over numbers and reading.

Dad had told him that he must have a good foundation for managing life, and that foundation included all his lessons inside and outside the one-room schoolhouse. In trying to follow his father's advice, Ralph had even found time to study violin. But he seldom spoke about his discipline where music was concerned. He would play at the church socials and for the family, and with years of practice, he knew he was a fairly good musician. In spite of the spark he felt when he played "Old Susanna" and "Carry Me Back to Ol' Virginny," it seemed as if the outdoors were always calling him louder than the indoors.

So here he stood near the white birches, expecting Hiram any minute. The two of them could get in a few hits of the partly unraveled, leather ball, and then Miss White would shake the bell so loud that the folks down at Wadestown would think the ringing was for them. Sweat moistened the underarms of his cotton shirt, but the run from home was only a small example of stored energy in the oldest Thomas boy. He had plenty of power to swing a bat, run to catch a fly, and laugh as lanky Hiram lumbered up the hill searching for the surefire, home-run ball that Ralph hit every single day they played ball. Ralph wondered why the heck Hiram never got tired of chasing his three-base hits, but he always appreciated the loyal effort put forth by the buck-toothed friend.

Poor Hiram was the butt of jokes all over. The kindest folks said he was a "little slow," and too often the kids took advantage of his gullibility. When some prankster put thumbtacks on Miss White's chair, the deviant thought far enough ahead to put thumbtacks inside Hiram's desk also. Of course, it was Hiram who stood in the corner while kids laughed at his punishment. But Ralph knew that the raggedly clothed boy was an innocent dupe, without enough courage or admiration to protest injustice. He just took it. The switch had flown more than once in Hiram's direction for something some ill-natured classmate had done.

Even when Ralph intervened on Hiram's behalf, no one listened. Somewhere along the way, he just figured that the best for the both of them to do was to play ball and stay away from the troublemakers. Most of the time, things worked out pretty well, at least until some bully started the name-calling.

"Hillbilly Hiram has no sense! Can't even climb a two-foot fence! Dummy Hiram's a scaredy-cat! His head is filled with lard and fat!"

Mom had reminded Ralph to hold his temper, but at times a good bloody nose was the only way to handle the no-account mockers. It did not matter that they were a head taller than Ralph. He would take on the biggest one without so much as a flinch. When his temper exploded, his fists flew harder and faster than any other boy's. He could stop a taunter dead in his tracks. Bullies were learning to think twice before picking on Hiram, especially when Ralph was around.

Of course, with splattered blood on his shirt, Ralph was always in trouble when he got home. Mom would fret about why her oldest child was fighting again. But when Dad sat him down for one of those stern family lectures, Ralph heard more than harsh words. There was the reminder that responsibility for other people supersedes what otherwise might be seen as wrong. Mom's whispers of shame echoed in Ralph's heart, but it was Dad's words that resounded loudest when faced with unfairness in the school out the ridge.

"When you can help someone who cannot help himself, it is your job to do it. We do our best to work out our problems without fightin', but some folks don't know nothin' else. The Bible says that man hath no greater friend than he who would lay down his life for another. Take up for the Hirams in the world. Best to try to stay clear of those who make trouble. But don't let innocent people pay for the wrongs of others."

Ralph wrestled with his Mom's lament and Dad's reassurance, and he tried to figure it all out from time to time, especially when he held his temper as long as any reasonable person could. Yet today something else was stirring in the mix. Hiram came straggling along the row of trees by the road. Normally carefree and oblivious to danger, even Hiram had an expression of concern on his face. The wind whipped his coattail until it was sticking straight out, parallel with the road. Hiram leaned forward to balance himself against the strain of blustery weather. His brown eyes squinted, and his nose crinkled in response to the odd gusts. Bony fingers pressed down on the top of his head, holding onto his hat. Stringy strands of bowl-cut hair jumped back and forth under the edge of the black wool cap.

"Hail, Ralph! This wind is somethin' ain't it? I saw smoke just startin' from the stove pipe. But there's no other kids around as far as I can tell."

Hiram froze in place a couple of feet in front of his loyal friend. His dark brows crunched a deep wrinkle above long, wispy lashes. He looked more determined than scared. Thoughts about what to do scrambled his brain something like Mama's eggs stirred in a fry pan on the wood stove. No one would call him a scaredy-cat today if he had his way about it. Within a moment, he thought what should be done.

"S'pect' we oughta get into the schoolhouse. There's somethin' funny about this mornin' wind."

Ralph nodded his head but stared down the road. He wondered how far behind the princesses were, and whether they had lost time dillydallying with dandelions and imaginary tea parties on some moss-covered, rocky ledge. As far as he was concerned, those girls were a lot more trouble than any boys would ever be. At least, that was Ralph's assessment. He was certain he had lived long enough to know what made life easier some days than others. Should he go back to check on them? Or would Edna and Mary be along fast enough to get them to a neighbor's house if need be? Edna was the smartest of them all, and she was, without a doubt, the most responsible. She would probably do her best to catch up with the younger children, and they would be all right.

"I don't know, Hiram," Ralph pondered. "The girls are behind me on the road, and they won't know what to do if lightnin' and thunder starts. Jesse's brother told us once that she is not afraid of much of anythin' … except storms. You know how it is, when one person gets scared, everybody else gets scared and all mixed up about what to do. I stayed all night at the Porters' place one time, and Jesse's Mom had to sing to her and rock her to get her to calm down, right smack-dab in the middle of thunder and lightnin'. Even Harry said he felt better when his Mom sang. 'Course, their house is old and rickety; I could swear I felt it shake in the wind. I wanted to go out to the barn to sleep, but thought I'd look like a yellow-bellied sapsucker if I ran out of the house. So I stayed. Just didn't feel none too safe. Maybe we should go after them. They're just girls, and they'll get all mixed up about what to do if the weather gets worse."

"Boys!" Miss White's voice strained from the open door of the school. "Get in here! You're going to be drenched in a few minutes. There's a storm coming! Can't you see?"

The tall, willowy maid clutched the doorknob in one hand and pushed thin hair strands away from her forehead. Her eyes made piercing contact with Hiram's. Her gray skirt fluttered erratically against the door casing, but the starched, high collar of the blouse seemed to be frozen, in spite of the wind.

Obedience was the first rule at school, and Ralph had learned a long time ago not to argue with the teacher. Arguing never did any good, and it seemed as if most often it made matters a whole lot worse. Surely, Miss White would understand his concern once he had a chance to talk to her beside the warm coal stove, and they were all safe inside.

Reluctantly, the two boys scuffed their feet along the stone path as they moved toward the small building. Ralph hesitated, looking over his shoulder. He thought maybe he would catch a glimpse of the princesses scurrying along the dirt road. But there was no sign of them yet.

"C'mon Thomas!" Hiram yelled. "C'mon … or Miss White will whoop us good!"

Hiram knew better than most how the stinging hickory stick would crack on his skinny rear end, sometimes making it too sore to sit and read the Sears and Roebuck catalog in the outhouse. Not that he did that much reading, but he liked to look at pictures of shoes, shirts, hardware, and wagon parts he dreamed of having one day. Of course, Miss White barely touched his trousers with the stick. She just made it look worse than it really was. But other grown-ups swatted hard enough to bring tears to the rims of his eyes. Still, Hiram did not care to have the other children laughing at him while he felt so foolish. And he knew the tall, skinny teacher would wait till the other kids got to school to "make an example" of him.

"We're a-comin' Miss White," Hiram shouted.

He swung his spindly legs awkwardly across the stone-tablet walkway. The homely boy resembled a swatted, crippled spider trying unsuccessfully to rush along a windowsill. Hiram had probably been swatted one time too many.

"We're a comin'! Whatcha think about this wind, Miss White?"

The poor boy's toothy grin was winsome and bothersome both at the same time. Hiram tried his best, but it never seemed good enough to please anybody. Nothing he said mattered to anyone except his friend, Ralph. He could always count on Ralph.

"Get in here, you silly boy. I think the wind is bringing a lot of rain and lightning with it. That's what I think! Come on, Ralph. Hurry," the schoolmarm demanded.

Just then Ralph spotted dark trousers and a second calico-clad figure moving hurriedly toward him. It was Simon and Margaret Ann. They lived just down the holler from the school and always arrived at school about the same time as the Thomas girls.

Ralph cupped his hands around his mouth and shouted, "You see my sisters anywhere?"

"Naw. We ain't seen no one."

Ralph stared at Miss White, and she immediately recognized his thoughts even without a word being spoken. As he stepped into the coatroom, she grasped his shoulders.

"Where are the girls, Ralph? How far behind are they?" she implored.

Simon and Margaret Ann stumbled through the door, panting and wide eyed. They scuffed their shoes back and forth on the braided rug. Ralph glanced at them and then turned toward the teacher. He looked seriously into her blue eyes.

"They're back that away, but I don't know how far. They're waitin' on Jesse. I need to go look for them. That's what Dad and Mom would want me to do. I'm the oldest, and I know about storms better than anyone else in these parts. I'm also the fastest, strongest runner on the ridge."

Miss White peered through the smoky glass of the southwest window. Everything Ralph had claimed was true. He was indeed the fastest runner. Ralph won every Mount Tabor footrace, whether he ran it with or without shoes. He also knew when to round up Little Ones to get inside before a storm moved in, and long before anyone else could pick up the scent of rain in the air.

"All right. Go," she affirmed.

As Ralph tore through the doorway toward the embankment above the road, Hiram ran hot on his heels. Before Miss White could think to say anything, the two boys were out of shouting distance. She watched them shrink smaller and smaller in the distance, and then she closed the door quietly. With fluttering, gentle sweeps of outstretched hands, she shooed the children like chicks into the inner sanctum of the school.

51

Mrs. Porter eyed the field from her stance on the porch. Harry had yet to come back from the barn. It would be time soon to sow seeds for summer harvest, but today was not a day for turning soil. The family's work would be confined to the house and tending to animals sheltered inside the barn. With only a couple milk cows, it usually did not take long for Harry to finish up his morning chores. He would throw down a few pitchforks of hay and scoop some grain for the cattle and horses to eat. The wooden barrels were well stocked with oats and barley. No trip to the feed store at Hundred would be necessary for at least a week. Collecting the eggs took only a few minutes with Harry scurrying around the chicken coop gently placing fresh eggs inside Granny's old wooden basket.

With the cows in the stalls longer than usual today, Harry would need to get the milk and eggs back to the house and then return to the barn where he would clean every stall with the thick rake, old hoe, and shovel. Tossing refuse onto the manure pile out back was his least favorite chore, but he did it with the best disposition he could muster. Much of the time he would distract himself with thoughts of beautiful Helen Rose who lived in Burton. Would he see her Saturday night at the soda fountain in the Hundred pharmacy? Would she go to the movie house with him if he asked? Daydreaming was a good way to pass time in the barn.

Still, shoveling dung worked up an appetite, and Harry would think about talking Mama into baking a peach pie. The cellar shelves were well stocked with Mason jars of peaches and cooked apples. Mama liked to use up all the year's produce to make room for the autumn harvest. Harry could easily persuade her to fire up the stove for making a pie or cobbler.

In the middle of her own morning chores, Mama Porter plopped down on the scrolled oak chair next to the washtub. She wiped her hands on her apron and wondered if the day had something different in store for her family. Charcoal-colored clouds in the sky were askew. Something she could not put her finger on continued to make her heart beat a little faster than normal. Even the two calico cats were snuggling close to her ankles and meowing for admittance to the kitchen. Harry would be sure to pour them a saucer of warm milk from one of two pails. But unquenched thirst for fresh milk did not seem to be the reason the feline twins were whining. Poky Dot and Tabby's purring was curiously absent. So was Mama Porter's sense of well-being.

"Maybe I should give Kiz a ring, just to see if the girls got off to school in plenty of time," Mrs. Porter whispered to herself. "Oh, all right you two."

She scratched the nape of Poky Dot's neck with her index knuckle. "You can come in for a bit, and then you'll have to go off to the barn when Harry is finished with his work."

She swung the screen door open, and the two cats rushed across the threshold before the space was wide enough for Mama Porter to get through. Her toe caught Tabby's back, and she steadied herself with a quick grasp of the door casing. She had nearly stumbled over the frantic felines.

"Tarnation mousers! What has gotten into you?"

The cats peered from beneath the wooden cupboards hanging next to the fireplace. Mrs. Porter shook her head and turned toward the crank telephone in the hallway. The battery was almost down on the phone, but Harry and his Dad had placed the battery inside a tin coffee can of water on the floor. Harry had promised to trade some eggs and butter for a new battery at Hundred Hardware on Saturday. Every Saturday, he had a pencil-scribbled list of bartering goods tucked in his shirt pocket. It was little trouble to trade produce for hardware when his real motive was to see Helen Rose. Until Saturday though, he thought there was plenty of "juice" for any telephoning that needed to be done.

Mrs. Porter pulled the heavy, black earpiece from its hinged lever and reached for the crank on the right side of the oak phone box. With a confident jerk, she twisted the "spinner," as she called it.

"Ring, ring, ring, riiiiiinnnnngggggg," she cranked with the determination of a meat grinder. She let off the lever and moved her lips close to the protruding mouthpiece. She paused and waited. Nothing. Again, she jerked the rotating knob with three shorts and a long, beckoning Kiz to answer her call. Of all times to need a battery, this was it. But needing it and having it were two different things. Wanting something would not make it so.

In the Thomas' house, Kiz had moved upstairs to gather the overnight jars for dumping. The two youngest children were rolling a croquet ball on the linoleum floor from one to the other, giggling when they "caught" the ball. As the familiar ring blared, Carl and Bess tired of their game and ran toward the crank phone. Bess stood on her tippy-toes and did her best to reach the earpiece, but she just could not do it. She nudged behind one of the kitchen chairs and started scooting it across the rippled floor. Climbing precariously up the spindled sides, the little girl rested her knees on the chair and grabbed hold of the wooden talk box. By the time Mama Porter rang the second signal, Bess lifted the earpiece from the brass cradle.

"Hallooo." Little Bess imitated the finest telephone greeting.

"Bessie Virginia, is that you?" Mrs. Porter queried. "Is your Mama there, honey?"

"Yes. And I'm here with Carl too," Bessie yelled into the black, shallow mouthpiece. "Who are you?" she asked with a high-pitched, curious voice.

"This is Jesse's Mama. Please get your Mama to the phone. Can you do that?"

While Bess began chatting incongruently about the day Uncle Tumps' mule died, Kiz hurried down the staircase, clutching the banister at regular intervals to steady her quick descent.

"Here, Little One," she gasped.

Her bony fingers wrapped around the earpiece while she wrapped her right arm around the little girl's waist. Bess's face lighted with glee as her Mom swung her around in the air over Carl's head. With one half-circled swoop, Kiz displaced the youngster and sat her on the floor beside her feet. Bess ran toward the side-porch window and looked for anything interesting she could see. She wanted to go outside to swing on the stuffed feed sack dangling from the oak tree, but she first had to ask Mom if it was okay. So she waited quietly while Kiz talked to Jesse's Mama. She wondered if Mama Porter had ever heard the story about Uncle Tumps' mule. The little girl was proud that she had told the story so well.

"Kiz, this is Emmie. Did Jesse get there all right for school?"

"Yes, the girls left together, and Edna and Mary are not too far behind them. They should almost be to school, but you know how those girls are. Miss White has told me over and over that those girls are late because they lose track of time when they stop to play. I'm here with the babies, and I don't think I should take them out in this weather."

"I know how you're feelin'. I'll talk to Harry …."

Suddenly, there was complete silence in the earpiece. Kiz strained to hear her neighbor's voice, but she might as well have been listening to a Mason jar. Nothing was coming through.

"Emmie? Emmie?" she pleaded.

There was no sound of a connection. Nothing.

At the Porter house, Emmie's frantic fingers shook the telephone battery that sat in cool water in a Maxwell House coffee can. Mrs. Porter did not know if any juice were left for talking, but she would try again. Cranking the spinner, SHORT L-O-N-G, she waited anxiously for some sound. She pleaded for an answer. But, there was nothing. The connection to the Thomas' farm was gone. Harry would now be the one to summon.

She heard him stomping his feet around back. Looking at the porch, she saw the pails of warm milk and half-dozen eggs stacked carefully in Granny's basket. The hens should have been laying better than that, she thought. However, she quickly shifted her attention to the approaching storm. Thoughts of lollygagging girls nearly had her in a frenzy.

"Harry, I need your help," she said.

Harry sighed, wondering what Mama was fretting about now.

52

Mary and Edna took long strides, knowing that the weather could change very quickly. The smallest children would be easily frightened. The slender eighth graders marched in double time, looking ahead for the girls, and particularly checking the princesses' favorite play areas along the road. A short distance beyond the Thomas' fence line, they looked at the "Bishop's Table," where tea parties were held on warm summer days. The mossy, flat rock was a perfect velvet throne for the finest young royals and their court. But Lady Porter and the others had not stopped for long, if they had stopped at all today.

"Maybe they've gone straight to school ... for a change," Edna said. Mary smiled.

"Well, I have my doubts, knowing those girls. It doesn't take much for them to get off track and before you know it, they have wasted time needed to get there before the tardy bell. I think that's why your Mom starts them out a little early and counts on us to hurry them along when we catch up with them. They get a little time to play, and we still make sure—most of the time—they make it to school without being tardy."

A gust of wind snapped Edna's skirt like a bullwhip cracking at the Wadestown Fair cowboy show. She pinned the fabric against her thigh with a firm, flat hand and pointed with her free hand to the horizon.

"Look ..." she whispered.

Mary turned to see looming, rolling, dark clouds engulfing the wooded valley near Brave. She halted abruptly, entranced by a brooding sky that boasted horizontal lightning in the distance. She did not remember having seen anything like the sky that day. Years later, she would attest that she had never seen anything like it since.

"C'mon, Edna. Let's hurry! We may not make it. I can't even hear any thunder with that lightning. That doesn't seem right to me. Maybe we still have time to catch up. Have you ever seen lightning go sideways?"

Her chattering was wearing on Edna's nerves. The senior Thomas girl was struggling to figure out what to do. Edna stared at the horizon and thought she saw something like a dirty cloud, but she was not exactly sure what she saw. Day began turning into night directly in front of them. Clearly, they had to find shelter and make sure the other kids were safe. Mary paused and twisted sideways to catch Edna's eyes. Edna turned and shouted, "Run!"

Startled by the ominous shout and threatening sky, Mary picked up her right leg and frantically stretched it out in front of her. But when her foot touched down, it slid off the edge of one of the skinny Model T ruts. She went down with a screech.

"OW…EDNA! Oh…"

Mary wailed as tears welled in her eyes.

"My ankle! I … I turned it!"

Edna reached a hand toward her friend but soon realized that pulling her to her feet was futile. Excruciating pain was etched on Mary's distraught face. She leaned over and wrapped her arm around Mary's back, securing her by the armpit and lugging on her until she could stand on one foot. Mary's injured foot dangled a few inches from the ground, and she looked down at the uneven road that triggered the fall.

"Tarnation! Tarnation! This stupid road! I'm so mad I could spit!"

Mary glanced at the horizon and then peered at Edna. She had temporarily lost her wits. The duo had to figure out what to do, and figure it out quickly.

"I'll try to walk on it if I can," she declared.

But with tentative pressure weighing down on the swelling ankle, Mary's face tightened, and she grimaced with pain. She sighed and breathed in short, shallow gasps. She wobbled from side to side while remembering that Mama too often fainted dead-away when she breathed in short spurts. Mary closed her eyes, slowed her breathing, and inhaled in steady rhythms. She regained her balance and sure-footedness with the one good foot she had. She looked over her right shoulder and saw the old Throckmorton farmhouse abandoned in the field. That was where they could go. Or, at least she could stay there while Edna went on ahead for the Little Ones.

"I can't walk, Edna. Just help me over to the Throckmorton place. I'll stay there until the storm blows over. You can go after the girls."

Mary's head was as clear now as it had been all morning. It was the best plan she could think of, and Edna agreed.

"Lean on me. We'll use your left leg on the outside and you can swing the right leg as I step. Use me to balance you," Edna directed.

But the twosome found the erratic pace to be entirely too awkward. As they moved off the road into the meadow, it was next to impossible to proceed toward the gray, windowless building. In frustration, Edna threw her books on the ground and grabbed Mary around the thighs.

"Hold on," Edna yelled.

She moaned and lifted with all her might, pulling Mary onto her bony hips. Mary clung, piggy-back style, to her best friend. Her arms dangled around Edna's neck and they set out once more for safety. With fierce determination, Edna managed to tote Mary like a sack of potatoes thrown over her shoulders. The two friends lumbered through the high grass toward the shelter of the empty farmhouse.

Edna was surprised by how strong she felt, and she knew they could safely make it to the impromptu shelter. Mary winced with each jerking movement by Edna, but she did her best to hold in the pain. What a stupid thing to happen. They walked on those rutted roads every day and had learned the hard way to look where every step was placed. It was just too easy to sprain an ankle if walkers were careless. She had picked a bad time to be careless.

"Don't worry, Mary," Edna offered. "We're all right. We'll be safe here. Ralph probably kept an eye on the sky and went back for Fern and Lois and Jesse. He wouldn't forget to watch out for them, even if he could play ball in a thunderstorm. And I know Miss White. She isn't letting him play ball this morning. She definitely isn't letting crazy Hiram play ball either!"

The two girls smiled as they imagined seeing the skinny, hayseed

Hiram swinging a bat while lightning bolts crashed to the ground around him. They did not know who watched out for Hiram when Ralph was not around. Maybe some angel kept him safe every time he was in a predicament that would kill most people. That made as much sense as anything.

Mary thanked her friend for her help and encouraged Edna to go ahead after the girls. Edna paused for a moment and concluded that going ahead would be a good idea.

"Well, you'll be safe here. Just cuddle up here at the back of the house."

Edna eyed the root cellar. It was partially underground, just off the kitchen.

"It has a strong foundation, you know, like that man that built his house on the rocks. And the winds came, and the house stood strong. The root cellar is dug back into the hill a little. It has a good rock foundation … safe place to rest. I'll come back for you or send someone as fast as I can. Don't be scared. I won't forget to come for you."

"I'm not afraid," Mary spoke assuredly. "Get out of here. I'm all right."

Edna glanced at the open doorway, but hesitated. She pulled her long stockings off and quickly made a bandage around Mary's foot to immobilize it. She had watched Doc Steele wrap ankles more than once, weaving loops back and forth around the heel and across the top of the foot.

"Now put your foot up a little. It might help to keep the swelling down. I'm not sure, but it might make some of the pain go away. It won't hurt, and I've seen turned ankles tended to this way lots of times."

"All right," Mary murmured.

She clasped her hands underneath the knee of the injured leg and judiciously raised it atop an old stool that Edna had uprighted from its topsy-turvy position. It seemed as if the pain was letting up a little.

Edna ran to the window facing Brave as she prepared to venture on in search of her younger sisters and neighbor. Suddenly, a strange and paralyzing power grabbed her throat muscles from the inside out.

Her hands began shaking, and her knees melted into the consistency of butter in Mom's iron skillet. What was happening?

Slowly, she backed toward the root cellar. Not sure of what to say, Edna simply snuggled up quietly beside her friend. Thuds of what sounded like rocks pounded the corrugated tin roof. Boulders from Hell were threatening to crash through the upper floors and onto the girls' heads. Outside it looked as if it were snowing. Mary stared into Edna's eyes. The two friends cowered against the cool stone wall. Edna contemplated her next words.

"I've never seen hailstones that big before."

53

Ralph hurled his lanky legs through the air. As soon as he touched one foot on the dirt road below him, the opposite foot lifted off at breakneck speed. This would be the fastest race he would ever run. His floppy pant legs whisked against each other, sounding like parlor curtains flapping together from an open window. But the air today was strange. The oldest Thomas boy strained to move his strong extremities effectively in the blustery weather. The wind kicked sideways and back and forth, throwing him off balance to the point of nearly stumbling. But he managed to stay upright in spite of the whipping gusts.

"Hey, Ralph! I'm comin' too," his homely companion yelled.

Hiram suddenly had become slightly more coordinated with his running than he had ever been in any Mount Tabor races. Kiz often said what a "good soul" he was, loyal to friends and completely ignorant of his enemies' unkindness. His determined pace was evidence of a good heart and a deliberate focus on the quest to help the smaller children. He did not truly understand the urgency of the "race," but if Ralph could talk Miss White into letting him leave the school, it must be important. So he ran with all his might, swinging his arms wildly while keeping his eyes on the friend ahead of him.

Ralph hesitated for a moment, glancing over his shoulder at Hiram.

"Okay, come on. I'll have Mom bake you one of her custards if you can keep up with me. This here wind is just blowin' so bad, it's hard to cut through it to get anywhere right now! The girls can't be much further down the road, and they're probably scared out of their wits! Your Mama and mine wouldn't want them to be alone and scared."

"I'm a-comin'," Hiram panted. And so he closed the gap between himself and Ralph, thinking, as he slobbered, how good that custard would taste coming straight out of Mrs. Thomas' stove.

Loose leaves and twigs brushed against the boys' pant legs. Tall sycamores and oaks swayed like wispy willow trees above their heads.

Even as Ralph and Hiram peered down the ridge, they realized that the force of the wind was formidable. Little Lois Nelle would not be able to walk through all this commotion. The other girls could hardly do much better. After all, they were just girls. Maybe they had stopped at one of the many rock ledges where they played "Queens and Princesses." If so, that would give them a little protection from all the scattering twigs which would sting bony shins through thin stockings.

Suddenly, a loud snapping sound crackled over Ralph's head. He jerked his head upward and instinctively raised his right arm for protection from the wood assailant. A silver maple branch swung viciously through the air, aiming squarely for Ralph's face. The boy could sock the school's biggest bully right in the nose even after he himself had been punched a good wallop. But he was no match for this brawling storm. With immediate self-preservation at the heart of each movement, Ralph flattened himself in the road. He hardly even realized what he had done as the scraggly branches brushed against his back and shoulders.

Hiram let out a squelching holler, and his brown eyes looked as though they would pop right out of his skull. With his mouth agape, Hiram stared at the attacking limb and then looked down at Ralph.

"Hey! Did you see that?" he yelled. "I didn't see it comin'! Did you? Almost hit me! I didn't see it comin'! Did you?"

Ralph inhaled a long breath and briefly closed his eyes. Maybe it was not such a good idea to have Hiram along to "help" him, but there was no sending him back now. He guessed he would have to watch out for Hiram and himself. Maybe the awkward companion would come in handy if things got much worse. Ralph silently hoped Hiram would be more of a help than a bother.

"Keep your eyes peeled, Hiram," Ralph instructed. "These old trees don't seem to be strong enough to stand up against the wind. And for that matter, neither do I."

Suddenly, Ralph felt the earlier surge of strength evaporate from his legs. Exhausted and scared, he sat down in the middle of the road, looking ahead for the sisters. It could not be much farther, and he would just have to muster up some more energy to find them. He glanced at Hiram and marveled at the fearless expression on his face. Hiram seemed intrigued and energized by the danger of their surroundings. He did not seem to have enough sense to be scared. Ralph was not sure if that were a good thing or not.

"Okay. My eyes are peeled," Hiram blurted. His eyes were fine slits of fiery determination. "Ya think we'll have another branch comin' at us?"

"I don't know. Just be ready to duck if you have to," Ralph sighed.

Ralph's arms were wrapped around his rib cage, and for the first time, he was aware that his sides were aching as labored breathing seemed to pound his lungs right into his bony chest frame. That did not matter now. He looked around, watching the wind tear through what usually was a passive grove of maples, sumacs, oaks, and sycamores. The boys had no time to deliberate. They would just have to keep an eye on everything in front of them and be aware of flying tree limbs behind them. Ralph's head was lowered defensively as he stood against the blustering gales.

"Come on, Hiram. We're close, and we need to stay together. Now, listen. If one of us gets hurt or anything, the other one is going to have to find the girls. You got it? That limb almost hit me, and I think it could have knocked me out cold if it had."

"Yeah," Hiram responded curiously, "I got it. Stick together. Sure."

Ralph nodded his head, not knowing whether Hiram understood much of anything, let alone what kind of damage this storm could cause. He grabbed Hiram's coat sleeve and motioned him in the direction of the road home. For a brief moment, Ralph felt his rib cage shake and his hands tremble. It felt as if he and Hiram were responding to the crisis in slow motion.

"Let's go. Watch out," he warned.

Side by side, the two ball players began to walk quickly again. And soon the attempt to run through the forceful gusts resumed. Ralph tried to run and simultaneously listen carefully for the high-pitched voices of Fern and Lois. The sound of the voracious, howling wind prevailed. Even eyesight was compromised as rain, wind, and wood particles were hurled into the boys' faces. The girls had often been told to get to a farmhouse if they saw lightning, but long stretches of road extended between houses along the ridge. Could they have gone off the road for shelter? Maybe they were together in the old Throckmorton place, or maybe they ran to the Taylor Farm down the hollow apiece. Ralph surmised that they probably just kept going along the road and found themselves in trouble before they had time to take shelter.

"Hey, Ralph," Hiram yelled, "what's that?"

Ralph stopped dead in his tracks. Some awful vision of black and gray was heading up toward the ridge from the direction of Brave. Chunks of brush, leaves, and soil were being pulled upward by a dark, gray cloud. Ralph had never seen anything like it.

"What's that, Ralph? Hey … what's that?" Hiram yelled.

"I don't know," Ralph asserted, "I don't know, but it's comin' this way."

54

"I feel like I'm gonna blow clean over," Lois said.

Her hand was tugging at Fern's gingham skirt tail. The tiny girl was not as frightened as she was curious. She looked around in all directions while trying to walk pretty much straight ahead with the two playmates. Her eyes were tiny slits, squinting to see what all the ruckus was about.

Jesse and Fern had begun to walk a little faster, and the laughter about Ralph's underwear and goings-on in the Ridge Kingdom had subsided. Fern's eyes continually monitored the sky. Jesse was entranced by the jerking branches of trees that canopied the road.

"I'm glad we didn't stop at the Bishop's Table," Jesse commented. "It looks like we need to get on to school lickety-split!"

Fern nodded. "Uh … I think so. Ralph was right again about the sky. Problem is we have a ways to go. We could get back to the Throckmorton place. It's the closest place to get in."

Jesse urged Fern on, insisting that. if they went backwards they would just have that much farther to go when it was safe to move on toward school. She squinted her eyes until they were nearly shut. Fern moved her face close to Lois' grimaced lips. She encouraged her younger sister to try to walk a little faster.

"I think I can go faster," Lois beamed.

Then Lois mustered a pretentious frown and said, "You just remember what my Mom always says. My legs are littler than yours, so I have to walk twice as far as you do in the same time."

"True, true…," Fern smiled. "We'll do our best to keep that in mind."

A brisk gale caught Lois' curls, surprising her as brown strands jumped in front of her eyes. She halted abruptly and tried to push the hair away from her face. Already she had stopped the faster procession before they hardly got started.

Fern looked back over her shoulder to see what the holdup was. Even Lois must understand that they had no time to dillydally. On the other hand, Fern quickly realized that it is pretty hard to walk when you cannot see in front of you. She reached into her side pocket.

"Here," she directed.

Her left hand pushed a clump of Lois' locks back to the side. She separated the bobby pins with her front tooth and hurriedly lined up a tousled clump of hair above her baby sister's forehead. With two quick clips, the hair fasteners secured the curls well enough that Lois could see to walk again.

"We're going to have to get Dad's sheep shears out again to snip your hair off," Fern chided.

Jesse stared wide-eyed at Fern, finding it inconceivable that anyone could cut a child's hair with sheep shears. Putting a china bowl on top of Harry's head was the most peculiar thing she had ever seen, and at their house, the sheep shears stayed in the barn … for the sheep! Maybe she should have a talk with Sherman Thomas about using plain old sewing scissors like her Mama did. Perhaps no one had told him not to use sheep shears on a girl's hair.

Fern smiled and winked at her sister. She was doing her best to convey calmness even though her heart paced a little faster than the walking alone would demand.

"Thank you," Lois chimed. "Now I can see."

The girls knew they were only about fifteen minutes away from the school, if they strode briskly. But this morning, they were not moving along well at all. The wind with its generally discordant directions kept interrupting the trek.

"It's feelin' a lot cooler, Fern," Jesse said.

"I know," Fern agreed. "It's times like this when Ralph claims he can smell a storm in the air. I suppose he is at school. It sure would be nice if he were here to carry Lois. But, if he is over there playing ball with Hiram, Miss White wouldn't be about to let him leave to come on the hunt of us."

Jesse felt her heart pounding harder than she thought it should, and she was unsure about what to do. She began to feel as it this were one of the times when Mama could reassure her that they would be all right. However, Mama was too far away. The three girls were counting on each other to make the right choices for dealing with the weather. If they had a scary situation with which to contend, it did no good for either Jesse or Lois to get upset. If Lois got scared, Jesse would follow suit. They would both start crying for their Mamas, and no one could think what to do when that happened. So far, petite Lois did not seem to realize fully that decisions had to be made quickly about what to do.

A raindrop spattered on Fern's cheek. Suddenly, dark clouds tore loose overhead, as though ripped apart by cumulative, sagging tons of water. Rain crashed down on top of the threesome. The girls might as well have been walking directly underneath a tipped washtub with no way to escape. In an instant, stinging chunks of ice jabbed their arms and faces. They were thoroughly drenched in a matter of only seconds.

"Oh, no! I'm getting wet! I'll be soaked all day at school. I hate my clothes sticking to me from the rain! Ouch! It hurts!" Lois protested.

"I know, Sissie," Fern replied. "Let's get close to the edge of the bank. We'll try to use the trees like big umbrellas. There doesn't seem to be any lightning, so Dad's lesson about staying away from trees doesn't matter right now. If you two hear thunder, let me know. We'll have to do something else."

"Oh, all right," Lois fumed.

"But, this daggone wind," Jesse said, "it's so … so … hard to walk, and now the rain too! If lightning starts…"

Her lower chin began to quiver. Mama was not here to sing and wrap her in the wool blanket, and Fern did not know what to do any more than she did. Lois was slowing them down, and she could see no house to run to as Mrs. Thomas said. They were between houses. There was not even an old barn to get to. Fear had taken hold of Jesse, as in so many other storms. She wanted to run in every direction at once. She spun around in the road, trying to figure out the safest place for them. Jesse knew they were in trouble. So did Fern. It was just that the Thomas girl managed to stay calm in spite of the blustery conditions.

"Fern! Fern! I don't know what to do!" Jesse cried. "I'm scared. And we don't have no place to go to be safe. What do we do? I want to go home."

Fern whirled around, grabbed Lois and Jesse's hands and stared unwaveringly at Jesse.

"Now listen. We've been through lots of storms on this ridge, and this is just another one. Nothing is going to happen to us except we're getting a little wet. Our clothes will mostly dry out if we sit by the stove when we get to school. Besides that, Miss White sometimes has extra clothes in the coatroom, just for days like this. Once we get to school, she'll take good care of us. Till then, we're smart enough to know how to take care of ourselves. Jesse, we'll be all right. We've been through lots of storms, and you know it. And I've been through a lot more than you have, so I know what to do!"

Lois was beginning to shiver, her little shoulders quaking slightly. Fern did not know if the dampness on her cheeks were from tears or rain or both. Fern's stomach flip-flopped with a flicker of self-doubt shattering her confidence. But her personal tremor was quickly quashed by her fiery temperament in the face of adversity. No storm was going to scare her. Not today anyway.

Suddenly, Lois wrapped both arms around Fern's skirted thighs. She hugged as hard as she could, hoping she would feel safety in her big sister's gathers. Her courage had dissipated at the moment Jesse began crying. She did not know what to do either, and the wind was blowing harder and harder.

Fern stooped down near the ground and enveloped Lois in her arms. She hugged with all the reassurance she could manage. Rain and sleet pelted their heads and faces as the youngest schoolgirl asked the inevitable question.

"Is God coming to take us to Heaven with Uncle Tumps' mule?"

"No," Fern insisted, "Don't you worry. There isn't even a single sound of thunder anywhere. I promise I'll take care of you and Jesse even if it does start to lightning."

"Promise?" Lois pleaded.

Fern hugged the shaking sibling extra hard.

"Don't worry. I won't leave you."

55

Mrs. Porter clutched the wooden frame of the screen door. Her tearing eyes said as much about her concern for the children as any words could ever convey. Harry's impatience waned as he too felt some profound sense of harm encircling the rustic, hollow home. He knew that it would be his responsibility to remedy the problem of the children's whereabouts. The sky darkened in the distance, and it was clear that today was a serious storm day on Tabor Ridge. Miss White would watch out for the schoolchildren once they arrived at the clapboard edifice atop the ridge. Her pupils would be well cared for, no doubt. But where they were at the moment was difficult to say.

"Don't worry about the younguns, Mama," Harry said. "I can go after them."

Mrs. Porter smiled slightly and breathed deeply as she realized that Harry was a responsible young man who would do his best to take care of his family and neighbors. She could do little more at this point except to trust him to reach the children and find shelter for them until the rain blew over. Her hand gently caressed Harry's forearm, and she shook his lanky extremity while admonishing him to hurry and go on hunt of the girls.

"I just talked to Kiz, but that telephone battery ran down. I tried ringin' her again, but it was no use. Before we lost the line, she said the youngest girls had gone on ahead of Mary and Edna. Knowin' those younguns' habit of playing along the ridge, it was hard to tell how far they'd gone before your sister and Edna started out after 'em. Maybe they made it to the Throckmorton place and got under roof for shelter. Maybe…."

Harry tilted his head sideways into the wind, peered in the general direction of the church, and clenched his jaw. Time was short to make it out the ridgeline for the girls. He thrust the egg basket into his mother's arms. He sprang from the wood, porch floor and sprinted toward the barn. His shirttail flopped crazily beneath the hemline of his coat. He glanced backward at his mother.

"Don't worry, Mama! Me and Thunder will catch up with 'em. I'll get the girls!"

His heart thumped, and his lungs strained for each breath. Both the wind and the fear of stinging weather with lethal lightning troubled Harry. This was no time to be scared. He had time only to find a safe place for the children. All the nooks of rocks along the ridge came into focus as Harry imagined the safest places to wait out the storm. One by one, he plotted his course from the gray house of Sherman and Kiz Thomas all the way along the road, trying to imagine where the girls would be if they got scared. The Throckmorton farmhouse, a couple of cow barns on Wise Run, the old Thomas family log house among Punkin' Run maple trees, and several rocky precipices near the school, the cemetery, and the church were all possibilities for shelter. The first thing he would do would be to ride straightway to school. If he did not find the girls there, he would backtrack to the adjoining farms and roads in the hollows below Wadestown. They could not be too far ahead of him. Common sense told him he would catch up with them in a matter of minutes.

Harry tugged at the barn-door latch, releasing it from the rusted clamp. The heavy door was held taut by the wind. Harry pulled with all his might to reposition the door until it slammed backwards against the south side of the barn. Hanging on the half-wall of the second cow stall was the horse blanket, saddle, and reins. Thunder was moving restlessly around the floor of the third stall, and he stomped with increasing nervousness when he heard the barn door smash into the outside wall. He whinnied loudly. Harry responded with soothing murmurs that contradicted the reality of the moment.

"Easy, Boy! Easy ..." Harry called.

He grabbed the halter with his right hand and stroked the white blaze of Thunder's nose. He moved steadily closer to the frisky companion, continually whispering, "Easy, Boy! It's all right. It's just some rain and wind. Easy ...."

The spirited equine continued to stomp the straw-covered floor. Harry smiled, feeling enormous pride in the beautiful black horse. Many neighbors, young men in particular, had offered a fair price for Thunder, but Harry was not about to let his friend leave the Porter farm. The young horseman and black stallion would travel many miles in the days ahead of them. Harry was going to hold onto the one sure thing that made his life happy. Thunder.

Once the ebon companion settled, Harry gently slipped the halter over Thunder's ears, and down along the wide nose. He hung it on an upwardly turned nail on the beam outside the stall while continuing to speak soothing words. Gusts of wind whistled between boards and underneath the tin roof of the old barn, but Harry only faintly heard the signs of adverse weather. He grasped the bridle that had been draped over the stall, positioned the bit between Thunder's teeth, and gently maneuvered the leather straps around the horse's head. By then, Thunder was calmed and prepared for a ride with his master. Little did he understand that this ride would be quite different from the ones he normally experienced with the young man.

Harry reached for the blanket and slowly pulled it toward him. He stroked the coarse mane, and he patted Thunder's neck while laying the wool covering over the slight sway of the horse's back. With one hand over Thunder's strong neck and one hand pulling at the blanket, Harry lined up the tan wool cover in preparation for the saddle. He was working as quickly as he could while trying to maintain as much calm as possible, but somehow the process was taking too long. Time was of the essence. Thunder was already spooked by the storm, and Harry's effort to control the situation was nerve racking.

The black, riveted saddle came next. Mama had sold her Mother's sidesaddle and old treadle sewing machine to get enough money to order the slick, new, black saddle from Sears and Roebuck. It was the nicest Christmas gift ever given to any of the Porter children. Mama made no promises of anything so grand in the future. It was a Christmas that Harry would never forget. He polished the saddle with oil and rags every time he came back from riding, and the silver rivets were polished with the finest, silver-polishing cream Charlie Dye could order. For months, Harry had worked secretly and doubly hard on Saturdays doing chores at Dye's General Store. He had saved enough to get Mama a new sewing machine. Someday he would replace the sidesaddle too. But Mama had insisted that he save his money for the future. She expected that she would develop a liking for a new Model T. Sooner or later, horses and carriages would not be necessary for the trips to church, or to Hundred, or for excursions with the family.

Harry wedged the saddle slowly over Thunder while holding the reins in his left hand. Then he reached for the cinch dangling beyond the horse's underbelly. Slowly, too slowly it seemed to him, he threaded the cinch and pulled it to a firm hold as Thunder winced from the squeeze. Harry momentarily laid his head against the warm neck of Thunder, and with his arm crooked overtop the neck, patted the horse with long, firm strokes.

56

Whistling gusts of wind circled the stovepipe above the potbellied heater. Miss White had moved the coal bucket close to the stove and instructed Simon to keep tossing lumps of coal on the fire and to stir the embers at the bottom of the stove every five or ten minutes. Dampness was pervasive, and a chill from the sudden cold front was distracting and uncomfortable for the school inhabitants.

The door swung open. There stood wide-eyed Bonnie with her sister, Gladys, and cousin, John. The trio dripped rain onto the pine floor, and all three seemed too fatigued to speak. The willowy teacher noticed Bonnie was shaking particularly hard, but she could not tell if it was from the chill in the air or the schoolgirl's fear about the weather. As the other children huddled on a bench near the stove, Miss White moved briskly toward the arriving pupils.

Simon's attention was drawn to the noticeable absence of half of the kids who should have been there. Hiram was always there early, and sometimes the schoolmates had time for a quick game of softball or Prisoner's Base before lessons started. Hiram was not Simon's favorite friend. That was for sure. But when there was no one else around, Hiram would do. It seemed that Hiram hardly ever missed school because of sickness. Even when he was sick, he came anyway, just to make people mad. Or so it seemed. Many a day, Simon had to help Hiram with his lessons, because Miss White always picked one of the boys to be the "Hiram Helper." No one liked being the "Hiram Helper," but it was either being that or missing recess. No one wanted to miss recess.

Miss White paused for a moment before speaking. She wondered if those children could be realizing, too, that her first obligation was to care for the students in the schoolhouse.

Although it was nearly time to start arithmetic class, the neatly printed, chalk fractions on the blackboard remained unattended. Alone, the slender teacher would have to decide what to do about school and the storm outside. She was very experienced and moved ahead with new responsibilities quite well compared to many of the community women. How many of her women friends seemed easily taken to fainting and crying during difficult times. She reckoned it was her calm nature and a little bit of a fiery determination that worked well in the position of teacher, disciplinarian, and caregiver for the kids at Tabor School. She whispered a silent reminder to herself to stay calm. No other response was appropriate. She smiled confidently at the threesome.

"Hiram is out looking for Jesse and the Thomas children. He and Ralph ran back out the ridge to help them. They'll all be here soon. Now you children pull off those coats and move over toward the fire. Gladys, you hand out the *McGuffey Readers* to everyone. While you're sitting by the fire, you can work on the next lesson in the *Reader*. John, those pant legs are soaked. Go out to the coatroom and grab a pair of pants from the hook nearest the road. Bring your pants in here next to the stove to dry out. No one will look. You can lock the front door for a moment for privacy, if you like."

"Yes, ma'am," John replied with his head down.

It was a little embarrassing to take his pants off at school, but Mother had always told him to follow the teacher's instructions "to the letter." He guessed she knew what was best even though he had played ball, run races, and played Hide-and-Seek in the rain lots of times before. The first grader moved out into the coatroom, pulled the curtain over the wooden dowel rod, latched the deadbolt, and unbuckled his belt. The pants hanging by the door looked way too big, but he reckoned he could use his belt to hold them up. And the legs could be rolled up three or four times to keep him from tripping.

Miss White counted on the students being distracted by the *Readers* while waiting for the storm to pass and for the other children to arrive. She stepped close to the window, studying the sky as inconspicuously as possible. In the distance, she saw some movement of wind and rain like none she had ever seen. Dusty, charcoal-colored wind filled with specks of tree branches and dirt hypnotized her where she stood. Her slender neck stretched forward toward the pane and she squinted, trying to figure out what the commotion was.

None of the old folks ever talked about wind like this on the ridge. It certainly seemed to be the worst natural phenomenon she had ever experienced. The school had no crank phone to call anyone, and clearly it was not safe to leave the shelter of the sturdy old school. She imagined it would be best to stay as close as possible to the center of the room. Certainly, they needed to keep clear of the windows. There was nothing to say, except to the extent that talking itself might be the best diversion for everyone there. Slowly, she sashayed toward the reading group and watched them closely. Her hands were clenched behind her as she made a concerted effort to conceal here own alarm. She forced a smile and wondered if she looked reassuring.

"I have an idea. Let's play a game," she asserted. "I'll start a story with a sentence and we'll go around the circle with each of you adding a line to the story. The object of this game is to be as funny and silly as we can be. You will all decide what happens next in the story. I won't give you a grade on grammar or anything. We'll just see where this story goes. All right?"

Eager to have some fun, the young students clapped shut the *McGuffey Readers* in near unison. The older children's eyes drifted toward the windowpane as the younger ones cheered.

"All right."

"Now, let's see," Miss White began, "there was an old lady who lived with four pigs."

"And they danced at the fair doing old Irish jigs!" Bonnie giggled. She bounced off the bench and stomped a few steps on the boarded floor. She rigidly folded both arms over her chest and tilted her head to the left in her best imitation of an Irish dance. "My Pa taught me this!" she bragged. The group clapped and laughed as they tried to imagine pigs dancing at the fair.

The oldest children managed half-smiles at the silliness and reluctantly fixed their gaze on the next storyteller, Gladys. For the moment, the howling wind seemed to quiet a little, and they joined in the fun as John entered the room in drooping, oversized pants.

"But the problem with pigs is there's no pants that fit 'em," John added to the story.

"So they went to Charlie Dye's to get plaid, Irish pants," Margaret Ann chimed.

The teacher rolled her eyes with approval and winked. For the time being, this story creation would be an excellent distraction. If necessary, she knew she could defend the change in the day's curriculum because of the unusual circumstances outside and the unavoidable absence of half the students. But she knew that when the story ended with two rounds for each child, she would have to move on to another activity. Perhaps math, which required a good deal of focus by everyone, would be the next thing to pursue. Could she find a funny way to do math? Maybe they could calculate how much material would be needed to make the pig pants and how much it would cost off the bolt at Dye's General Store. Two-and-a-half yards of plaid cotton at $0.50 per yard. Yes, she knew many ways they could stay busy by adjusting the classroom activities during the storm. Students always liked a break from routine ciphering, and today, more than most days, they needed a change.

Without any warning, tears welled in the teacher's eyes. She did not imagine she could ever forgive herself if anything happened to those boys out there looking for the girls. Miss White lowered her head and cleared her throat. Her eyelids batted quickly and she felt a nauseating pang of doubt as her throat tightened. It was the most hopeless feeling imaginable. But a grin returned to her face as she realized that something more was unimaginable than the fear that engulfed her. It was four pigs wearing plaid cotton pants made with material from Dye's General Store in Jolly Town.

57

Jesse trembled and tried to move ahead with her companions, but she was so scared that she could hardly focus on the roadway. All she could see were whipping tree branches. She tightly scrunched her eyes, trying to protect herself from pelting rain which was blowing in every direction. For the moment, Fern sounded as if she could figure out what to do. Jesse knew she would have to trust her friend at this point. But the crying was hard to hold inside. The smallest Porter child began to moan in low tones that matched the wind as nearly as she could manage. Maybe Fern would not hear her if she cried just a little. Who cared anyway? God must have given them tears to use for something. This seemed like as good a time as any.

"Fern, I think we need to get some place safe now," Jesse insisted.

Fern listened quietly to Jesse's plea. She looked around and surmised that, indeed, it was time to find some kind of safe shelter, whatever it might be. It was too difficult to continue under the harsh conditions. Their clothes were soaked. Their wool coats weighed down on their shoulders making each step twice as difficult as it had been even minutes beforehand. Their heads were sopping wet; strands of hair stuck to their cheeks. They did not need anything else to slow them down.

"Let me think a minute," Fern commanded.

She wrapped her arm around Lois' shoulder and pulled her as close as she could. Lois again stood up tall, stuck her chin out in a ferocious gesture, and waited to hear what Sis would say to do next. Jesse moved closer without commenting that she too wanted to be hugged until they figured out what to do.

"Uh," Fern began, "the Throckmorton place is too far back. We need somewhere close to wait until we can go on to school. The old White home place is through the woods over there, but the house fell down a long time ago."

Jesse's thinking became a little clearer as she too tried to imagine the safest place for them. She did not know much about the farm Fern was talking about, but she did know that all the big farmhouses and even some of the small ones had cellars to save preserves and potatoes through the winter months. Root cellars consisted of enclosed walls, which were usually made of fieldstone and built back into a hill to get the cool earth temperature to work something like an icebox. Jesse had often wondered if the name, root cellar, came from the idea that the cellar was "rooted" into the ground, something like a carrot or potato. She would remember to ask Miss White that question later. Right now they needed to be rooted themselves.

"Fern, maybe there's a cellar we can get in," she yelled.

"Good idea, Jesse. C'mon. We can get over there in a jiffy," Fern replied.

Secretly, she was relieved that Jesse had thought about the good possibility of a stoned fortress that probably was still intact. She was running out of ideas, and she was as scared as Lois and Jesse put together. Clenching Lois' hand, she stepped across the roadside ditch and led the way through saplings to a heap of half-rotted boards. She knew it was a snaky place and copperheads and spiders could take shelter there. But they would deal with that. Today seemed too cool for snakes to be much of a problem, and she just did not know about the spiders. They had no better choice than the cellar. It would be best for her to keep her mouth shut about snakes and spiders. Maybe Lady Jesse and Princess Lois would not think about those possibilities. Perhaps they would just be relieved to sit down and not have to fight the rain and wind for a while.

As the girls approached the fallen house, they searched around the foundation for a place that looked like a cellar. The uneven ground and scattered debris made it difficult to surmise the existence of a root cellar if a cellar had ever been there at all. Lois' small feet wobbled, partly from the rough ground and partly because her shoes were feeling very tight on her toes. She looked earnestly for the cellar and wondered if they would find a nice jar of grape juice to drink while they rested.

"There's nothing here!" Fern cried. Her voice was shaking and she blubbered in frustration as tears finally ran down her cheeks too.

"Now don't you worry none," Lois shouted. "There must be some place where they kept their grape juice. That looks like pieces of a grapevine trellis like ours. The grape juice must be here somewhere."

Fern looked down at her feet and howled with laughter, certain that the prospect of finding grape juice was decidedly slim. Lois' observation was a good one. Narrow lattice boards in the distance did look like pieces of an old trellis. But was it for grapes or for roses? It was hard to say. Possibly, old Mrs. White had canned grape jelly and grape juice, and the odds were that there was a better chance of food being raised on that trellis than roses. Fern clenched her jaw trying to reason that if she built a house here, where would she put a cellar? Glancing off to her left she saw a small moss and leaf-covered hill. It was close enough to the house foundation to serve as a cellar but just a little farther away than Fern would have guessed. Without a word, she tugged at Lois' hand and began marching in giant steps toward the embankment. Sure enough, as they got closer, they saw a dark indentation in the hill. It looked like a cave. Slate-gray orbs were barely visible through the moss and decaying leaves. There it was: the root cellar.

A few large, warped boards had been placed up against the bank, and it appeared that they had been put there fairly recently. Unlike the house siding and stonewalls, these boards were lighter in color and showed few signs of aging and weathering. It was odd for someone to have put boards on a bank out here, but that mattered little to Fern and Jesse. Fern motioned Lois off to the side of the slope, and in mere seconds, she and Jesse pulled the improvised doorway away from the cellar opening.

Inside, the cellar was fairly clean. The floor consisted of smooth, red clay, and sufficient overhang to provided a room-like enclosure. Fern pulled Lois inside and the trio moved toward the back of the ten-by-ten man-made cave. Fern's mouth fell open as she laughed at the sight of something gleaming in the corner. A round, tin container with copper coils on top was conspicuous among the weeds and stones. Beside it were kindling wood and box-crates where someone had neatly stored clear Mason jars. The jars were clean, and it was obvious that they had been placed there within the last few days or so. No signs of dust or cobwebs were anywhere to be seen. Jesse pulled her wet hair back on her neck and breathed out a huge sigh.

"Thank goodness, we're inside. Thank goodness!"

"We'll be all right, now," Fern agreed.

Lois stood very tall and pointed to the corner.

"See … there … IS grape juice in this cellar! I was right!"

Jesse and Fern smiled at each other, clenching their teeth trying not to laugh. Only a second passed before the two friends burst into laughter. For the moment, the storm was not a problem at all, and the innocence of the little girl was a source of tremendous relief from the difficult morning.

"Can I get a little drink of grape juice, Fern? I'm awfully thirsty from all this fast walking," Lois pleaded.

"I'm sorry, Little Bit of a Thing. This grape juice belongs to someone else. If we drank it, we would be stealing their … uh … juice," Fern said. She did her best to sound serious so that Lois would not think she was making fun of her.

"Here," Fern said.

She released the latch on the cinched schoolbooks and removed a sheet of notepad paper. She slowly folded the paper into a small square shape, stuck her index finger into one of the folds, and popped out a little reservoir. She extended her hand outside the cellar and caught a small pool of raindrops. She handed the makeshift cup of water to Lois.

"This will tide you over until we get to the pump at school."

Lois gulped the rainwater and seemed to be satisfied with the gesture. Somehow, the grape juice in the corner looked better than the rainwater, but she knew Fern was right. They were not allowed to steal. It did occur to her that they might borrow a jar and replace it with Mom's juice from home. Lois wondered why Fern did not think of that.

"Look!" Jesse yelled, "White stones!"

Bits of hail had begun to pummel the glen, and the girls moved closer together, knowing that they had found a safe place just in time. The tension that was so apparent when they had been outside had begun to dissipate. But once they had stopped walking and stopped talking about what to do, they began to shiver. The cool temperature of the half-underground shelter intensified the cold as the three hugged each other for warmth. Jesse glanced at the Mason jars and knew what would take away the chill.

58

The girls stood mesmerized by pummeling hailstones. It was almost like winter, but the icy crystals had a magical effect on the shadowy, woodland floor. Bouncing, white pebbles were being sprinkled on wet leaves like sugar candies on Kiz's chocolate cake icing.

"Look at that!" Lois exclaimed. "We're sure lucky to be inside here. I'm cold, but I feel better being in here with the grape juice and you."

She squeezed Fern's hand, affirming her statement, and she noticed that Fern was grinning that funny smile she did not always understand. Her lower jaw continued to quiver and the threesome quietly pondered what to do next. Clearly, the weather was too bad to go on with the walk to school. Would they return to the Thomas farm after the storm cleared or hurry on to school? Miss White would mark them tardy if they arrived at school late. Losing recess because of tardy marks on the blackboard was worse than just missing a day of school. Lessons could be made up quickly most days, and the teachers usually knew that if a student missed school, it was for a good reason. At least, most of the time, it was for a good reason.

"Fern," Jesse whispered, "we're shaking pretty bad, and the … juice … in the corner could take the chill away a bit until we get warm clothes."

Fern's eyes rolled slowly toward her young friend, and she shook her head slowly. The possibility of breaking into someone's moonshine was not even a consideration. If her Dad found out that they had been "sippin' shine" on the ridge, they would never get out of the house again. She was certain of that. And with Lois with them, the secret of shine-stealing would be quickly blurted out at the dinner table. Fern remembered Mom telling her about Doc Steele using a whiskey plaster on Bess as a baby. It cured her croup. The smelly concoction had saved Bess's life, most certainly. And everyone old enough to understand how easily babies died in the farmhouses of Appalachia knew it was all right to use whiskey and the likes at appropriate times. Fern thought carefully and decided that for the moment, this was not the appropriate time. She shook her head thoughtfully, looking straight into Jesse's eyes, and said nothing.

"Hey, someone's over there!" Jesse yelled.

She pointed her index finger toward gray figures moving quickly near the bank above the road. Before Fern could respond, Jesse bolted out of the root cellar into the hail and rain. She threw her right arm overtop her head and bounded through slick leaves and branches toward the boys.

"Hey! Hey you!" she yelled at the top of her lungs.

But, the wind and stirring branches muffled the girl's voice which carried no more than a few feet in front of her. She halted dead in her tracks and mustered all her energy into one bellowing salutation.

"Hey! You over there…" she insisted.

She took off running at lightning-fast speed. The boys were almost to the bend, when she caught up with them. She grabbed Hiram's coat. The bug-eyed boy jumped nearly a foot off the ground.

"Whoa!" he shouted, clearly alarmed by the surprise of someone behind him.

"Ralph, help! Help! They got me! They got me!"

"Oh, hush, you silly goose!" Jesse chastened. "It's just me. What's the matter with you anyway? Don't you know a girl when you see one?"

By then, Ralph had turned around a few yards ahead of them. He stared at Jesse. His beanpole arms stretched out from his shoulders as he moved quickly in her direction. He flung the palms of his hands upward and frowned at the petite neighbor.

"Where's Fern and Lois? What are you doin' out here?" Ralph demanded.

"She's out here in the storm with us, Ralph," Hiram explained sincerely.

"Yeah, yeah … I know that," Ralph responded.

The prize-winning runner was amazingly patient, even in the middle of frightening circumstances. He had heard Hiram's curious assertions so many times before, he had no room for surprise or criticism. It did no good to tell him not to be so blamed stupid. Besides that, it always seemed to hurt his feelings, at least a little, even though ten minutes later, he had forgotten the snickers and was right back to his stupid declarations.

Jesse caught her breath, holding her sides with wool-covered arms. She doubled over slightly, fixing her clasp above each knee, trying to speak through the howling woods and gasping breath.

"We ... we ... had to get in outta the storm. We found an old root cellar over there by the White place. Fern and Lois are there," she said.

The two boys turned in the direction of the White farmhouse foundation. They saw nothing more than high grass, loose boards, and trees in the area Jesse cited. Hiram gawked through the trees, unsure of the whereabouts of the other girls. He scratched his wool cap, as though the gesture could improve his eyesight. Ralph grabbed Jesse's arm and yelled.

"Show us!"

She stood up from her half-crouched position and turned toward the collapsed buildings. She could not remember ever having been so tired and so strong at the same time. It did not seem to matter at the moment, just as long as she could get back inside the cozy room with the girls and the whiskey still.

The three stumbled across twigs, leaves, planks, and debris, doing their best to run along the rugged terrain. As they reached the open doorway, Fern's eyes appeared wider than any girl's eyes could be without falling out of her head. The boys and Jesse hurled themselves through the doorway and collapsed onto the dirt floor. They were exhausted from fighting the wind and hail.

"Those ice balls really hurt my face!" Jesse blared.

"Let me see," Lois insisted. With her best mother-hen imitation, she studied the red, wet face of Jesse and reassured her.

"You're not cut anywhere. You'll be all right. Now don't you worry none."

That was the standard response when the Thomas children tripped over jagged wire along fences, slammed their fingers with the barn door, fought off attacks by the old hissing gander, or tripped over a milk stool at the barn. They were a hardy bunch, determined to pick themselves up and keep on going, regardless of a few little bruises or cuts. There was never time to fuss too much about being hurt. Doc Steele was always summoned when someone was seriously injured.

"We won't need to call Doc Steele today," Lois concluded in a serious tone.

"Good thing!" Jesse yelled, "He couldn't get through this dadburned weather if he wanted to."

Ralph moved to the doorway beside Fern. They stood speechless and motionless. The overpowering sound of some awful stirring outside was nearly deafening. A mile or so off the ridge, they could see a large cloud carrying bits of wood, dirt, and what looked like fence posts through the air. Violent clutches of wind grasped treetops, and even with bare eyes, the brother and sister could see the effects of the storm that had more power than they had ever imagined possible. They were alone and would have to watch out for each other. Mom would be worried sick, but they could do nothing about that now. Dad was all the way down at Brave at the brass plant. Jesse was right. No one could get through the storm to find them. Except for not knowing the whereabouts of Edna and Mary, Ralph felt relieved to have some shelter with the girls, safe in the root cellar. Edna and Mary might have had time to get back to the Throckmorton farm before the weather took a turn for the worse. Or maybe they had stayed home, knowing they could not make it to school in time. He wondered where they were, but he knew it was a waste of time to dwell on it right now. They would have to take care of themselves.

"Back in the cellar," he motioned to Fern. "Let's get pretty close to that back wall there."

"We have grape juice in case we need to stay here a day or two," Lois bragged.

Ralph looked at the tin apparatus in the corner and realized that the little sister was partly right about what they had. It was juice, so to speak. He wondered how long it would be until the storm passed over, but he understood, too, that they would not be there very long. It was just a matter of waiting for a break in the rain. Then they would make a run for the schoolhouse. Miss White's room was closer than the nearest farmhouse. Obviously, it was the only logical place to take shelter once they had a chance to make it there. Ralph would not admit to the others that he really wanted Miss White to tell him what to do next. He certainly could not tell the girls and Idiot Hiram. It was one of the few times he would have welcomed his teacher's admonitions and advice.

"All right, listen here," he instructed, "we're gonna wait here until the rain lets up a little. Then we'll make a run for the schoolhouse as fast as we can. Miss White will get us dried out by the stove. She always does that. And Lois, we won't have to stay here for days and drink juice."

"Are you sure?" she asked with her curly, mop head tipped sideways.

"Yes," Ralph replied, briskly tousling her wet curls with his callused hand.

For a few minutes, they all seemed to rest collectively. The children said nothing as they huddled together in the dim refuge. Pellets of ice had transformed into slushy wisps of rain, but the wind continued to blow horizontally through the trees. Lois wondered why it was raining sideways, but since everyone else was quiet, she thought maybe she should be quiet too. Even as a first grader, she had learned not to talk too often or too loud. As a general rule, she had learned to talk when someone asked her to speak. Anytime she offered an opinion, she was open to the possibility of a nasty encounter with impatience, laughter, or mockery. Besides, somewhere she had heard that children should be seen and not heard. She thought that was the rule, especially in the company of grown-ups and older siblings.

Gradually, the wind calmed. The eerie presence of the dust cloud in the distance had dissipated. Although a good downpour was continuing outside, the chilling roar of wind eased substantially. Ralph stood up, and Hiram immediately imitated his steady friend.

"It's a good time to make a run for it," Ralph said.

The younger children were not sure of what to do, but Ralph saw no sense arguing about it. He was the oldest, and he was always in charge of weather and shelter when the Thomases traveled in the Model T. So he must know better than they what to do now. Ralph pulled wet, stringy hair back from his brow and thought carefully about how well they could stay together as a group. Lois and Hiram were the two in the group who needed the most help. Even so, Ralph had to admit that he had been pretty impressed by Hiram's speed and determination while accompanying him on the road. As long as Hiram could stick with the four of them, he would be all right. On the other hand, Lois was too big to carry and too little to run very fast. He thought it best that they stay together, even if Lois slowed them down.

"Fern, how 'bout you be sure to watch out for Lois? Keep hold of her hand, and we'll stay together till we get to school," Ralph said.

Fern nodded and gripped Lois' hand, and the children stepped out into the rain once again. They walked hurriedly through the wooded plateau and soon found themselves on the road to school. Hiram was feeling mighty tired. But, like Lois, he knew this was a good time to keep quiet and concentrate on making it the rest of the way to school. Jesse had said little since the ice had battered her cheeks. She was feeling very peculiar. The sudden burst of energy she had experienced was gone as quickly as if the wind had carried it away.

The view of the path ahead was amazing. The roadway leading to Tabor School was unexpectedly out of kilter. Hundreds of twisted and broken branches were scattered in every direction. The children walked slowly around the bend and saw logs, branches, boards, and leaves scattered helter-skelter across the road. Even some farmer's old shirt was draped unnaturally across a white birch limb. Suddenly, they heard the sound of wind picking up. The rain pelted the children with ferocity. Once more, they felt the dizzying effects of a revived storm. The violent, terrorizing impact of wind, rain, and hail was destined to leave a mark that would be remembered for a lifetime.

Jesse moved as fast as she could, but her head was down. She stumbled through the debris, trying to keep up with the boys. She needed to go faster, but she was exhausted and frightened. Tears cascaded down her cheeks like a personal waterfall. An exploding thunderclap above their heads was all it took to break the stride of the group. Jesse screamed. Her wail pierced the gray air like a razor blade slicing unprotected skin. Lois was startled by both the thunder and Jesse's outburst. Panic found its hold.

"Run! Run!" Fern blurted.

"RUN!" Ralph echoed.

The five children took off toward the shelter of the nearest building: the Mount Tabor Grade School. They ran about a hundred feet when a humongous oak tree was uprooted in front of them. It crashed to the ground, narrowly missing Ralph's head. The road was completely blocked. Hiram and Ralph heaved themselves over the hardwood trunk. Fern was close on their heels. She had released her clasp of Lois' hand. Once her feet were planted on the road opposite her sister, she heard Lois scream. The little sister was stretching her sticklike arms over the downed tree. As hard as she tried, she could not surmount it.

"Aaaaeeeooogh! Aaaaaeeeoogh!" Lois yelled. "I can't make it! I can't make it!" A flash of lightning and a second explosion of thunder sent chills through each child.

Screams filled the air. Even Ralph let out a low-pitched wail in a fit of anger. Leaves whirled into their faces, and again the Heavens were dumping thousands of barrels of water on them. Fern tried pulling Lois over the oak tree, but the smallest girl was stuck. Cries of the thoroughly drenched children blended with high-pitched winds and bashing limbs. Which sound came from where was hard to say.

"It's scratching my legs! It's hurting my legs," Lois cried. "I can't make it!"

59

Kiz stared out the window. She rested her bony right hand against the pane. The wind howled like a wandering ghost that was hell-bent on taking possession of the porch. The house would be next. Bess and Carl had successfully distracted themselves, playing near the upright piano. They had no idea how worried their Mother was. The silence and inevitable solitude was strangely deafening by itself. The dark clouds and accompanying billows of wind hung like a gigantic, whipping shroud that engulfed the Mason-Dixon marker. It seemed that just moments ago the marker cast faint shadows on the soft, sunlit, brown and yellow meadow.

Kiz removed a crushed hankie from her dress pocket and discreetly dabbed her eyes, making sure the children did not notice. She looked around at the twosome as they giggled and played peek-a-boo through the claw-foot piano legs. Kiz aimed a faint smile in their direction. The farmhouse windows rattled mysteriously as rain beat against the side of the home. Mother Thomas knew that she must keep the brother and sister away from the windows and hope for the best.

She whispered, "God, please watch over the children in the storm. I'll tend to these younguns', but I can't be with the others."

It was that simple. Kiz inhaled deeply, relaxed her shoulders, and took playful, bouncing steps toward Bess and Carl. She stretched her thin arms underneath the piano keyboard, as though to chase Carl away from the musical centerpiece. Carl giggled a toothy grin and rolled backwards onto the thick rag rug. Bessie Virginia squealed like a piglet running for slop, and Kiz sat down on the floor laughing too. The piano was against the stairwell wall beside the fireplace. That seemed to be the best place for them for right now.

"Mama, can you play with us?" Bess pleaded.

Ordinarily, Kiz would shoo the twosome away until lunch. On any other day, she would continue to do chores. There was almost more to do than one woman could accomplish. Washing dishes, mending clothes, making beds, baking bread, and doing laundry were at the heart of her homemaking. She decided that she could work doubly hard later in the day, if necessary. For now, all three of them could use a little more laughter to keep their minds busy. Storms that blew up this fast had a way of passing over fairly quickly. Kiz had learned that one of the best ways to deal with times like this was to sing and stay close to kin. She scooted the piano stool from underneath the keys, spread out her skirt, and tapped her toe on the right pedal. Their willowy Mother winked at Bess as Carl came running from his tumbled state.

"London Bridge! London Bridge!" Bess began.

Before Kiz could find the keys to the familiar tune, Bess began showing Carl how the bridge fell down, singing and clapping rhythmically while repeating, "London Bridge is falling down … falling down … falling down …"

Carl and Bess bounced their bottoms on the covered oak floor as their Mother found the keys and began singing with them. She stopped playing and sang a cappella while she pushed the babies' hands together to form a small circle between them. The brother and sister spun around faster and faster until they got dizzy. They were doubled over and giggling when their knees buckled unexpectedly. The duo began swaying erratically from side to side. Once again they reeled backward, pounding backsides onto the brown floor.

"Whoa!" Carl shouted.

He lay on his back staring at the ceiling. He tried to guess why the light above him was wobbling so much. Was the light wobbling? Maybe it was his eyes that were wobbling. It seemed as though the whole house were turning around. The only way to make it stop was to close his eyes.

"All right, we better sing another song that won't make us so dizzy," Kiz insisted.

"London Bridge! London Bridge!" Bess demanded.

Kiz could have sworn there were stars sparkling in her sweet girl's eyes. She was determined that the children curb the whirling, or they would fall and crack their heads on the piano leg. She bit her bottom lip as she contemplated the next song. But Bess was distracted. She clasped her Mom's right hand and pointed to the window.

Tiny pings were echoing each other on the porch steps and tin roof. It sounded as if Ralph were dropping his cat eyes into the washtub at the corner of the house. For an instant, Kiz imagined how nice it would be to hear Ralph's marbles clanking on the tin and getting on her nerves.

"Look…it's snowing," Bess chimed.

"Snowing," Carl repeated.

The trio automatically rushed to the window to see what the crazy weather was doing now. Kiz pulled the children back close to her but stood hypnotized by pea-sized hail. Snow, with its drifts against the house, would be a welcomed sight compared to this. This seemed like one of those Bible stories where houses crashed to their very foundation because of shifting sand. Snow in Monongalia County had its drawbacks, but if the roofs were kept clear, sturdy homes like the Thomas house were not likely to collapse.

"No, Bessie," Kiz explained. "It looks like snow, and it's cold, but it's called hail. Sometimes we get hail when rain comes in the springtime and summer. I'm afraid you children won't be able to ride your sleds today if that's what you are thinking."

Images of schoolchildren riding red, wooden sleds down the embankment above the schoolhouse flickered in Kiz's memory. Bess imagined that if she had just enough hail, she could slide down the bank at the edge of the meadow. Ice was like snow, and snow was like ice. She would surprise Mom. This would be the day they would sled ride on hail. She hoped so.

The white stones grew larger and larger until Kiz could almost swear they were the size of the biggest brown sugar lumps in her pantry. She was certain they would leave bruises if they hit a person's head or arms. For a fleeting moment, she thought that her plan to stay sheltered was the wrong decision. She could bundle up the children, put egg crates over their heads for protection, and pull them in the milk wagon down to the Porters.

Once they were safe, she could go on hunt of Ralph and the girls. One minute the thought occurred to her, and the next she realized that it would not be a wise choice. Kiz's eyelids sagged because of worry. The stones grew even bigger.

The wind speed was picking up, and the air flowing through the vents in the attic were whistling all the way to the ground floor. The rain was falling in peculiar erratic patterns. Kiz frowned, realizing that none of this seemed real. For the most part, the screen door remained flat against the side of the house. The forsythia blossoms darted through the air like lightning bugs. It was almost dark enough for lightning bugs to come out, Kiz thought.

Boughs of trees along the yard stretched in opposing directions. Kiz stared as the children's sack-swing was tossed violently in the wind. Suddenly, the large maple tree was blown sideways. Its roots were pulled out of the earth. Before Kiz could catch her breath, budded limbs scraped the porch floor as the old sugar tree and its sister maple smashed into the gray wall below the boys' bedroom window.

As strange as the storm was to the Mother and her Little Ones, the effects of its force held their attention. Kiz wondered if they were in more danger than she had realized. Another maple was jerked out of the ground. Kiz collected her thoughts. She grabbed Bess and Carl under each arm and hastily pulled them back toward the fireplace and piano. Bess seemed undaunted by the commotion and continued to enjoy her Mother's close attention and the opportunity to play.

"Great big trees are falling down…falling down…falling down…" she sang.

Kiz tried unsuccessfully to muffle an overwhelming moan from a heart that had been breaking ever since Edna and Mary headed out the door. She huddled near the fireplace, embracing her youngest babies. Her breath quaked as she kissed the tops of the sibling mopheads.

"Mama, what's wrong?" Bess asked.

Carl wrapped his arms tightly around his Mama's waist.

Kiz stared at the distant window and whispered.

"This rain is pretty bad. I'm a little bit scared 'cause I don't know where Lois, Fern, Edna, and Ralph are. And, I don't know where the other children are either. We'll be all right. We'll stay inside here until the sun comes out again."

She sighed, trying to convey a comforting smile.

Bess frowned, realizing for the first time that the children might not be with Miss White at the school. She hardly ever saw her Mom upset, and she never heard her talk about worrying. Carl failed to register any cause for alarm. He sneaked under the piano and giggled as he tried to hide from his big sister.

"Where's Lois?" Bess asked.

Kiz hugged the little girl tightly and replied with the utmost truth. "I don't know."

60

Fern yanked up her skirt and threw herself headfirst across the fallen tree toward Lois. She patted the little sister's arm while scrambling awkwardly to the opposite side.

Lois smiled in the middle of the confusion, knowing that she would not be separated long from the others. The wind howled louder, adding confusion to the situation. It was hard for the young students to tell which way was which. The noise and frantic cries of the quintet were muffled by terrifying gusts that fired dirt and twigs into their faces.

"Hurry up! Hurry up!" Ralph commanded in Fern's direction.

"Yeah, come on! Let's get outta here!" Hiram yelled.

Fern mustered incredible strength in the middle of the chaos, wrapped her arms around Lois' knees, and heaved as the little girl hugged the downed oak's trunk. The next thing Lois knew, she was rolling over the top of the tree and Ralph was helping her down the other side. Fern scrambled back over the tree as Ralph patted Lois' shoulder. The tall brunette planted her feet on the earth beneath the oak and balanced herself against whipping winds as she turned to move on with the group.

"Let's go!" Hiram yelled again. "We can't stay here!"

"All right. All right." Fern answered.

But something was wrong. In the middle of the confusion, reality hit with such impact that they might as well have been leveled alongside the oak. Jesse was gone.

"Where's Jesse? Where's Jesse?" Lois shrieked. A terrified scream followed.

Eight eyes looked back to the road that paralleled the White farm's fence line. Jesse was nowhere to be seen. Ralph spun around to see if she had made it over the tree before Lois became entangled in the leveled branches of the oak and debris of shrubs.

Maybe Jesse had run ahead of them. But as far as he could tell, no one was farther down the road than they. Leaves and dirt were stirring through the mist and rain. Visibility was seriously compromised, and he had no way to tell which way Jesse had gone. Grit and hail began pounding the children's faces again. Lois doubled over and collapsed on the ground, not knowing how to make it to the school and feeling too weak to try. Fern wrapped both arms once more around her and hugged her tightly.

"Come on, Lois. You're stronger than you think, and we're almost to Miss White's room. We can make it together, and Miss White'll take care of us."

Fern was not sure that she believed they could make it, and fatigue was taking its toll on her too. The way she reckoned, they simply had no other choice. Somehow, they would all have to get to the school together. Her heart was sinking into its own state of confusion; not knowing which way Jesse had gone was an aggravation that chiseled away at common sense. Maybe she had managed to get ahead of them. Knowing how Jesse hated storms, maybe she was running like greased lightning to the safety of the teacher and the one-room building. Possibly, she was just out of sight through the rain, and the time it took to get Lois over the tree was sufficient to give her a good head start.

"We have to get to school," Ralph asserted. "I'll go back for Jesse when the wind lets up a little. Right now, we have to stay together. Don't let anyone outta your sight till we get there. She may already be at school."

Fern tugged at Lois' arm, clutched her skinny fingers, and looked her straight in the eyes.

"You can do this. We're almost there. Try! Try!"

Lois bit her bottom lip and nodded her head up and down. She blew a long breath upward, flinging her bangs through the rain. Then to the surprise of the other children, she began running as hard as she could into the wind. Fern's eyes widened with disbelief. She smiled a confident grin and leaped ahead of the boys, being sure to hold Lois' hand for the final sprint to safety. Ralph pointed for Hiram to go ahead.

This time, Ralph was going to be sure to watch all the kids ahead of him, so that whatever had become of Jesse did not happen again.

The children ran at Lois' pace which clearly required the most strength that any of them could muster. Ralph's breathing was hard and raspy. His legs had begun to ache, and he realized that the effort to find the girls had nearly depleted his ability to continue.

Hiram was too dumb and scared to know how hard he could run. He yanked his head upward in spite of the blowing debris and in spite of the fact that it threw off his pace for the desperate race to shelter. The tree branches above them, which they usually associated with safety, shade, and play, had become sinister and foreboding. Hiram was waiting for the next branch to come crashing down on his head, as though expecting it would keep it from happening.

Fern managed to move along steadily, holding Lois' hand, and determined that they would not let her be hurt, whatever the cost. The retreat in the stone-wall cellar had given them enough rest to regain the energy needed to press on through the storm. She barely noticed the sound of thunder, but she could not stop thinking about Jesse.

A voice inside her kept whispering, "Go back and look for Jesse. Go back. She's lost in the storm."

Choking back tears, Fern knew they had to get on to the schoolhouse. They could not imagine even the possibility of remaining outdoors in conditions such as these. During many a storm like this, Dad and Ralph had gone on hunt of newborn calves and their mothers while Mom waited nervously at the back porch door for their return. It was always a crisis to protect the animals in harsh weather, and it was often done at considerable risk to the men in the family. Even Mom would leave the children with Edna and head out to help get the livestock into the barn. It was just as much her job to protect the cattle and horses. The protection of a good milk cow was always an urgent matter.

The butter, cheese, cream, milk, and cottage cheese, as well as the sale of calves at the livestock auction or to neighbors kept the family supplied with food. The family had enough money from sales and swapping of eggs and cheese to Charlie Dye to buy shoes for the fast-growing feet of the Thomas children. Mom had never had to cut the toes out of her children's shoes to make room for their growing feet. Fern always appreciated that.

While Fern and Lois ran in a nearly synchronized pace, they wondered silently if Mom had already started out into the storm looking for them. Fern's heart sank as she realized that the babies were too little to be left alone. Probably Mom was confined to the house, unable to locate the whereabouts of anyone until the rain, lightning, and wind subsided. They were on their own, but daggone it anyway, they had been all right so far.

They could make it the rest of the way. These siblings with their homely friend could do whatever they set their minds to, and that was that. There was nothing to worry about—except Jesse.

"Look!" Lois hollered.

The threesome with her had hardly realized exactly where they were. There ahead of them was the school. Solid as a rock, it stood by the maples and sumac, waiting for their arrival and looking mighty good.

Hiram let out a squall of relief that sounded something like a cross between a pig squealing for its slop and a braying donkey voicing its protest of a farmer pulling its rein. Ralph instantly reacted with a boisterous laugh. Hiram's outburst was positively peculiar. All of them laughed as Hiram continued braying like a jackass. They were never completely used to it, and Hiram was none the wiser. It did not matter. It mattered only that they were quickly approaching safety. Fern and Lois made it first to the door. Turning the knob, the princesses found themselves in yet another panic.

"It's locked! They've gone home and left us here!" Fern yelled.

Ralph and Hiram were pulling up the rear, and Fern's protest had not clearly registered with either of them. Ralph knew she had to be mistaken, so he did not give it another thought. Just as he catapulted himself forward toward the white porcelain orb, the door swung open.

"Children!" Miss White exclaimed.

For a fleeting moment, it looked as if the teacher were about to break down crying, but before she had time to do so, she reached out and wrapped her arms around Fern and Lois in one embracing sweep. The next thing the girls knew, they were standing in the coatroom, dripping water on the floor. Lois hoped they would not get the hickory switch for tracking mud and rain into the school.

Ralph and Hiram were close behind the girls, jerking off their coats and tossing them onto the brass hooks of the hall tree. Hiram was out of breath, but somehow it did not matter now.

"Children, have you seen Jesse? Where are Edna and Mary?" Miss White asked.

"We don't know," Fern responded. "Edna was helping Mom with dishes when we left."

"But, Jesse. Where's Jesse?" Miss White demanded.

She knew the three girls were inseparable friends, and something was terribly amiss. Lois lowered her chin. She shook from the chill of the rain as well as from fright. Her shoulders were slumped and she looked intently up toward the towering teacher. She burst into tears, sobbing right smack-dab there in front of everyone.

"We don't know where Jesse is!" she blurted. "She's lost in the storm!"

61

"Edna, I think I want to try to make it to the school," Mary said.

The weather outside the abandoned Throckmorton place was calming down considerably. Hailstones dotted the walkway and yard. The rain was steady but less threatening. Mary's ankle was tightly wrapped, and she was feeling as if she would much rather hobble along the way to school than sit alone in the abandoned house. She had an uncomfortable suspicion that rats and snakes would come after her eyeballs if Edna left her alone. That fear would be left unspoken.

Edna stood up and walked toward the gray glass panes nearest the old chicken coop. She had no particular notion about going outdoors, given the ferocious torrent that had ripped through the wooded upland. Her first inclination was to stay put, at least until the sun came out. However, she realized that other things were more important to consider. No one knew where they were, and she had considerable misgivings about where the smaller children were. If the Princesses had not stopped to play at Bishop's Rock or the moss-covered bank, they could have made it all the way to school. The prospects of their walking straight to school were never good even on the best of days.

Edna and Mary needed to get moving. The schoolhouse is where everyone would be looking for them. Mary looked around the pantry and kitchen searching for anything that would aid her with walking. A rickety pram, covered with cobwebs and dust, had been left askew against a closet doorway. With a missing wheel and broken spindles jutting outward, it was obviously of little use. Then Mary saw it. On a nail hook, just inside the closet door she spied a thin leather strap. She leaned sideways and saw that it was attached to a hand-hewn walking stick. Old Uncle Seth always kept a walking pole handy for trips to Hundred and Jolly Town. If a crippled, old man could walk with the aid of a stick, she was absolutely sure she could also.

Mary pushed herself forward, bending her arms so as to leverage herself against the cool stone-and-oak wall. Her swollen ankle throbbed, but she was determined not to be left alone after such a frightening downpour. Some neighbors had insisted the old house was haunted. She clenched her jaws to the point where she thought she might break a tooth. She half-walked, half-hopped toward the closet.

"What is it?" Edna asked.

"Look," her friend replied. "I think it's a walking stick."

Edna grabbed Mary's elbow and slid her hand underneath Mary's armpit. Edna was going to do everything possible to lighten her friend's load for the brief walk to the closet. When they reached the dark opening, Edna cautiously extended her arm toward the stick. Cobwebs stretched out like pulled cotton candy as she lifted the cane from the hook. The walking stick was made of solid oak. It was as strong today as the day it was made. Some old man's cane was a sure-fire blessing for an injured schoolgirl. Edna did not want to be held back by Mary's limited mobility, but she knew she would not want to be alone in that old, dingy farmhouse if she were in Mary's place.

"What do you think?" Edna asked.

"This will work. I'm sure I can lean on it and make it down the road. I'll do my best."

"All right," Edna nodded. "Let's get out of here."

Edna stayed by Mary's injured side and directed her gently through the creaky front door. Once outside, their mouths fell open. Not only had maple saplings been brought down by the storm, but also full-grown sumacs and oaks had been wrenched from the earth with as much ease as Carl knocking down a tower of toy blocks.

Neither girl had ever seen such a sight. Rain continued to fall, and drops ran down their cheeks like a gush of irrepressible tears. For a moment, Edna thought she would cry, but she could spare no time to bawl about things they had no hand in controlling. She bowed her head momentarily and tried to sort through thoughts that were operating somewhere between a mode of silent prayer and a muffled cry for help. Mary's hand shook involuntarily atop the curved handle of the walking stick. She swayed back and forth from the shock of it all.

"We're all right," she said. "The storm is over, and we can make it to school. I know we'll be all right."

Edna thought her tall, skinny body would crumble. She worried that she might pass out. Never in her life had she fainted over anything, and she was not about to let these circumstances scare the wits out of her. She reasoned that if she spoke, she would stay conscious. So the next thing she knew, she was jabbering about all kinds of things, some of which were important and some of which made little sense. Move. Move. Find the girls. Get to Miss White. Run down past the school to ring Mom and see if they were safe at home. See what Miss White needed her to do to help with the children. Check the horses at the hitching rail to see if they were hurt. Get the children dried out so they would not catch their death of cold. Tend to Mary's ankle. Get it up in the air again to help minimize swelling. Stir up some sassafras in the kettle on the potbellied stove. The brew would warm up the children. On and on she prattled. Mary was beginning to wonder how in the world she could get in a word edgewise.

The two friends did their best to walk quickly to the road with Mary leaning heavily on the cane. They had to concentrate very hard on walking because of all the scattered leaves and tree limbs. The twosome climbed over a huge fallen oak, and Mary gently positioned her good leg for support at a strategic point on the ground. She looked down to make sure her foot would not roll on a branch or on one of those dadburned Model T ruts. And there it was.

"Look here," she directed Edna.

Just in front of their feet were deep, footprints in the mud and clay. The tracks were fresh, and it was clear they were not far behind the girls. For sure, the younger children had made it this far. Suddenly, Mary found her ankle to be less of a problem than it had been just moments ago. She thrust the cane forward in synchronized rhythm with the wrapped leg and took a gigantic step. Her little sister was out there in the middle of all the commotion while she had snuggled safely in the old house. It was time to stop thinking about her twisted ankle and find the others. The pace of the two friends doubled, and they hurried toward the school building.

They saw no sign of the Little Ones, and the closer Edna and Mary got to the school, the faster they walked. Mary made it to the porch a couple paces ahead of Edna. The eldest Thomas had been walking near Mary's side, watching to be sure she did not slip again and slow them down more. They reached for the knob simultaneously.

As the door swung open, the two eagerly looked around the cloakroom. There stood Lois. She was still shaking from chill and fright, and her hair was stuck in thick clumps against her scalp. Fern was close beside her, looking like the mother hen with an outstretched wing protecting Lois from more trauma.

"Girls!" Miss White said. "Girls…get in here!"

She stretched out her long arms for the young ladies just as she had reached for the little sisters earlier. A great sense of relief quietly overtook the small room, and a few smiles were all that needed to be communicated to the worried friends. Edna dutifully wiped her feet at the door and smiled at her baby sister.

"Why, Lois! You look like a drowned rat!"

"I do NOT!" Lois protested, thinking that a drowned rat would not make for a very pretty little girl. "I do not look like a drowned rat. I'm just wet. And that's all there is to it!"

Miss White counted heads and reached the same conclusion that the others did. She leaned against the wall and checked around the group a second time, thinking maybe she was mistaken. Eleven children. Not twelve. Not her Lucky Dozen as she sometimes called them. Fern's eyes were locked with Mary's. She spoke softly.

"Did you see Jesse?"

"No," came the curious reply. "What…"

Mary hurried into the open room. She briefly stared at Hiram who was crouching on the bench beside the potbelly. He was rubbing his hands together and toasting his shoeless toes by the base of the iron stove. Mary looked from side to side. A wave of nausea hit her like a sledgehammer. The expectation of finding her little sister safe inside the building had vanished as quickly as frost melting from a splash of hot teakettle water. She barely felt Lois' cool hand touching her fingers.

"Jesse's lost in the storm," Lois whispered.

62

Jesse's heart was pounding so hard she felt as if it would jump clean out of her rib cage. She breathed in nervous, airy gasps, each of which was followed by low moans of distress. She believed the deep pitches of desperation were coming straight from her heart. The youngest Porter child scurried lightning-fast along the crooked roadway. She winced as dirt and leaves were hurled into her tear-stained face, and she wondered if her friends were close behind her. Jesse had no time to stop to take account of the other children. Her eyes were fixed ahead. She needed to find familiar trees and fences.

Safety was ahead. She was sure of that. How she wished they had all stayed in the old White farmhouse. It was cold there, but safe. Now she had to find safety again. If she could just run at her fastest speed, she knew she would be all right. She whispered to herself. Run. Run fast.

"Mama! Mama!"

She cried and shouted for help although she knew that no one would hear her. Her words came without any regard to common sense. She steadied herself with a realization that she was unharmed, so far. Everything she had done had protected her from tumbling trees and lightning strikes. Surely Uncle Tumps' mule did not need a little girl to tend to him in Heaven. It was pointless to think about that stupid mule. Even as panic threatened to overwhelm her, Jesse thought that recollections of the Mule Story had nothing to do with her plight. For the time being, she must run as hard and fast as possible. Her legs were strong from jumping rope with Lois near the Bishop's Table. Little had she realized how much the competition between princesses had prepared her for the day. Her legs were her way to safety, most definitely. In spite of the choking fear, Jesse kept telling herself, "You can do this! You can! Run!"

Farther out the ridge, Harry coaxed Thunder up the steep, narrow driveway at the Porter house. Harry studied each step the horse took while trying to sustain his balance in the saddle. He rode carefully into what was the most violent weather assault he had ever experienced. Looking back over his shoulder, he saw Mama peering at him through the kitchen window. She eyed the horseman's every movement and prayed that he would find the children safe. Harry imagined how awful the feeling would be to send a child into a storm after other children. He knew very well that he was no child, but he understood that mothers never accept adult titles for their offspring. Adult children were still children. At the moment, Harry was curiously sensitive to the fact that Mama was seeing all her children threatened by a deadly force no one could control. Such a lonely feeling that must be.

Emmie stared unwaveringly in his direction. She spread her fingers against the gray pane. Her knees buckled. Almost certain that she would succumb to the weight of despair, she clutched the sill in an effort to steady herself. Then she saw his arm. Harry was waving in a gesture of determination that was intended clearly for her.

What a good, young man he was. He would do his best. Mama Porter had no doubt about that. She stood tall again and found herself waving a strong salute to the oldest child, knowing that he would indeed take care of little Jesse, Mary, and all their friends. She whispered a thankful prayer and stayed faithfully at the window. Harry and Thunder's silhouette became smaller and smaller as they crossed the top of the hill.

She grabbed a straight-backed chair near the hall tree and pulled it close to the window. Plopping herself down, she was determined to stay within view of any movement near the house. Lightning be damned, she would be there when Harry returned with the children.

She wondered about Kiz, Bess, and Carl, alone in the gray house up the road. Should she have saddled up with Harry and at least ridden that far? Should she wait and see if Kiz would ring her with good news? What if … the children … lightning? The thought of the girls being scared and likely to be injured under these conditions held a steady place in her heart. But the hope that they were safe was holding its own. Much of her hope lay in the knowledge that Harry was strong and fierce. He would search until every girl and boy was rescued. Even the horse could be counted on in these circumstances. Thunder was a strong and obedient ally of the Porter family. He was surefooted and familiar with all the trappings of rutted roadways. Thunder would take each step with precision and unwavering loyalty. Nothing would stop Thunder, just as nothing would stop Harry.

On a curious impulse, Mama Porter stood and moved toward the Victrola. Jesse loved cranking the music machine when the family gathered around on Saturday evenings. They had only a few recordings. The thick-grooved, black records were gifts from Aunt Martha who passed away in November. The old lady had very few possessions, but the music machine and her small music library were prized sources of happiness. Mary loved Chopin's Fantasia in F Minor. Every time she played it, the family reminisced about how much fun they had had at Aunt Martha's house. They would munch on apple sugar cookies and watch the old lady sway back and forth.

Auntie smiled and tapped her toe as she perched on her oak sewing rocker. Jesse always waited to see if she would fly away like a graceful bird. When Martha died unexpectedly, Mary believed the silver-haired lady was gently lifted to Heaven. Music carried her to the angels. Martha's single-story house had been left to Uncle John and their children. The Victrola was bequeathed to her beloved Porter nieces and nephew.

Alone in the storm, Mama Porter turned the brass and porcelain knob on the crank that wound the turntable. She placed the needle arm at the shiny edge of the black record. The music wafted through the parlor, and Mama Porter returned to her chair. She was determined that when the girls walked through the door, they would find hot tea, a warm embrace, and Aunt Martha's music playing. They would celebrate their safe homecoming. The teakettle whistled at the edge of the gas burner. All that was needed were the girls.

Harry turned back around in the saddle, leaned forward, and

nudged Thunder's flanks to move ahead. Out of nowhere, a tiny figure emerged through the rain and fog. A foggy shadow of a child was dashing toward him. Harry whipped the reins, urging Thunder to pick up the pace.

"Harry! Harry!" Jesse screamed.

The oldest Porter youth jerked the reins toward his chest. He pulled his right foot abruptly from the stirrup, swung his leg over the horse's rump and leaped to the muddy surface. The reins dangled and then fell into the mud as the big brother lunged toward Jesse. She flung her arms upward, and he picked her up. He held her tightly against his chest.

"Harry! I'm scared! Harry!" Jesse screamed.

Harry felt tears choking his eyes. His throat tightened while he held on for dear life to the trembling girl. He pressed his right hand against the back of her head and began to shush her in an attempt to instill calm.

"It's all right, Jesse. You're safe. You're safe. It's all right," he asserted. "Let's get you to the house."

He grabbed Thunder's reins with his left hand and hurled his frightened sibling into the saddle. Pausing just long enough to see Jesse grab the saddle horn, he pulled Thunder's head sideways and motioned the beautiful equine toward the house. Mama was already halfway up the road. She was soaking wet and running with all her might.

"Mama!" Jesse blared.

"Jesse! Jesse!" Mama yelled.

The distraught Mother leaned against the little girl's leg, kissing the drenched skirt and then reaching upward to help Jesse from the saddle. The storm seemed to dissipate. The mother and daughter cried together. In the meantime, Harry scanned the rumbling sky. He kept his senses and reminded Mama to get to safety.

"I'll go on ahead for the others," he said. "Get back to the house, Mama."

Mrs. Porter nodded while reaching to squeeze Harry's forearm.

"Jesse, where is Mary? Where is Edna?" Harry asked.

"I don't know," she tearfully replied. "The tree came down and there was lightning. I came home. Mary and Edna were not with us. The others ran to the school, I think."

Once more, Harry was back in the saddle, ready to ride on until every Mount Tabor child was found. He hesitated just long enough to be sure that Mama had regained her senses. She moved straightway to the kitchen porch. The gentle sounds of the teakettle whistle and the sweet notes of Chopin pierced the kitchen air. Jesse was home. Harry and Thunder faded into the rain near the ridge top.

63

Mary's eyes were fixed on some invisible horizon as she quickly sat down beside Hiram. Normally, she would have chosen a seat considerably farther away from the goofy boy. Rumor was that he had cooties, and all but Ralph would start itching no sooner than Hiram came within spittin' distance. At the moment though, Mary was barely cognizant of his presence. Catching cooties was the furthest thing from her mind.

"This here fire will toast your toes for ya," Hiram said. "That rain out there sure has a sharp edge to it, don't it?"

"Yeah," Mary said.

She stared at the raised lettering on the top section of the cast-iron heater, not registering exactly what the letters spelled. Lois snuggled close to Mary, partly to get warm herself and partly to take on the role of Little Mother to the obviously distraught friend. For a few minutes, no one spoke at all. The chill and the fear which had Lois quaking was slowly displaced by the warmth emanating from the brown stove. The little girl turned her toes up toward the ceiling, trying to dry out the bottoms of her tiny feet. Dad had always said that drying the feet was the first thing to do to prevent hypo something. Hiram was spinning around in his seat, first front, then back. Then front again. Just when he succeeded in warming one side, the other one got cold.

Mary nodded as she felt Miss White gently draping a brown wool cover around her shoulders. The girl crossed her chest with her arms as she tugged at the Army blanket edges, pulling it as close as she could get it. The matronly teacher patted her shoulder before heading out to the coatroom to beckon the soppy students. Slowly the octet of friends shuffled toward the center of the classroom. The sound of wood scraping on wood permeated the air as stools and benches were dragged across the oak floor. A silent circle of shivering children said all there was to say for the time being. No one cared a whole lot about talking. Lois' lips were a peculiar shade of deep navy blue, almost as if she had been whacked in the mouth with the ball bat at recess. Miss White clasped the little Thomas girl's hand and motioned her toward the front door.

"Get behind that curtain there. You're too cold with all those wet clothes. I have a sweater you can wear, and here…" Miss White said.

Once in the private makeshift closet, she reached underneath her long black dress and pulled out a cotton petticoat. The puckered waistline was not skinny enough for the child, but the ribbon underneath Miss White's dress collar worked well as a belt.

"And let's get those socks off you," she continued. "Let's see. This will sound funny, but how about if you wear my new gloves on your feet while we dry out your clothes on the stove? We'll make this a great adventure that you can tell your grandchildren when you're as old as I am."

She winked. Lois smiled a self-conscious grin and ducked her head in embarrassment. She was not sure if the other kids would laugh at her, but if Miss White said to do it, then she had to do it. That was the rule. Besides, the dry clothes had a wonderful warm feeling, and she already felt much better. She was not sure she cared a hill of beans worth what the others said. Miss White was a smart lady, and Lois reckoned she was pretty lucky to have such a good teacher. The schoolmarm rolled up the dangling sleeves until Lois' forearms peeked out. The sweater hung almost down to her knees, so the other students would hardly know she was wearing a petticoat.

With floppy-gloved fingers preceding every step she took back to the circle, Lois waited for the hoots and hollers to bounce off the walls and blackboard, amplying her embarrassed state. But no one laughed, no one stared, and no one pointed fingers. Edna smiled and hugged the baby sister. Fern scooted out of the way, so Lois could get close to the fire again.

Simon scooped two big lumps of coal out of the bucket and flung open the stove door with the poker rod. Faces squinted from the engulfing heat, and Simon threw the shiny clumps inside the red-hot caldron. He slammed the door shut with the iron, flipping the latch to the locked position. Then he leaned over and stuck the rod inside the oval opening at the base of the potbelly. Jabbing and poking ashes and embers, he forced the new fuel and the yellowish embers into a tumbled state. Air moved through the oblong slit, producing an inner burst of flames and a surge of heat through the outer walls of the heater. The children leaned back in near unison, knowing that the wave of heat would subside shortly. No one spoke a word.

Simon rammed the rod back into the oval bucket and began pacing nervously. He could not think straight. The sound of thunder and wind howling like a wolf at the door added to his jitters. No one was saying anything, and something had to be done to find Jesse. Miss White was always the calm and confident leader who knew exactly what to do, and yet she seemed to be immobilized. At least that was how he saw it.

In the meantime, the teacher pondered the severity of the situation and knew the older children could watch after the younger ones. Edna and Mary were always reliable aides with instruction, but Mary was noticeably shaken by the morning events. With Simon tending the stove and with Edna's eye for safety, it would be possible for the teacher to go on hunt of Jesse. No more children could be sent outside, especially under such dire circumstances.

"Miss White!" Simon demanded. "Jesse is out there. We have to do somethin'."

"You're right," she said. "I think it would be best if I leave Mary and Edna in charge, and I'll go on hunt of her. Edna, you are to be the teacher while I'm gone, and all of you children are to mind what she says. Is that understood?"

"Yes, Miss White," they spoke in unison.

"Simon, I want you and Ralph to tend to the stove. Keep the kids warm and watch out for their safety. You know enough about fire tending to be safe. Keep the school warm and keep the children close to the center of the room. There's plenty of coal, and you don't have to go out to the coal pile to fill the bucket. If the winds pick up again, move everyone toward the hill-side of the building. Put all the coats close to the group. No one leaves this school until I get back. Is that understood?"

"Yes, Miss White," they recited.

The teacher stared at the frightened eyes fixed on her and tried to think where the little girl could be. Simon was still pacing and clearly unnerved by the events. Ralph was staring at the floor, frowning as he twisted the toe of his shoe back and forth. He had done his best, but it was not good enough to make sure that everyone reached safety. From his way of seeing it, he had failed to do any more than could have been done if he had not tried to help them in the first place.

"Ralph," the teacher spoke. "You did a very good job getting these children here. I've never seen anything like this weather in all my years on the ridge. You're not at all responsible for Jesse. She probably just got confused from all the wind and lightning and there was nothing more you could have done. I'll find her. You help watch after the others here. I need you to do that, all right?"

"Yes, ma'am," he answered. He still tilted his head downward, and he was not so sure that he had done his best.

"Yeah, Ralph!" Hiram blurted. "You couldn't have done better if you'd had a team of horses to haul 'em here in a wagon! I know. You did good. You told the girls to stick together, and Jesse didn't do it. These dumb girls just don't listen ...."

"Hiram ..." Miss White cautioned.

Hiram had seen that stern look before and knew it was time to keep his mouth shut. He puckered his lips, widened his eyes, and ducked his head. The dunce cowered to one side and waited to be walloped with the back of a hand. The blow did not come, and he decided just to sit on his backside and keep his mouth shut. That way he could avoid a few more clouts. He just did not know what in tarnation was wrong with his mouth, but it always seemed to run faster than his brain could think. Just last week, Pa had told him he had diarrhea of the mouth. The senior Basinger walloped him good, but hitting the boy did no good where his prattle was concerned. Maybe there was a tonic that could cure it.

Hiram thought he better ask Doc Steele about it the next time he saw him.

A slow smile replaced Ralph's sour expression, and for a moment, he felt some reassurance that things like this happen, even when people do their best. He would try to keep reminding himself of that. In a few days, it would all be forgotten. Jesse was probably all right. She would be happy to be found, even if Ralph had managed to lose her in the storm. He did not lose her on purpose.

Miss White started toward the door, when all of a sudden a flash of a boy's silhouette raced past her. Simon's legs flew across the stone path. Before the teacher could pull up her skirt to chase after him, he disappeared into the thicket and fog.

"Simon!"

No response.

"Simon!"

Her chest felt heavy with a suffocating sense of breathlessness. Feelings ranged somewhere between fury and total despair. But she knew she could not be too angry with him. They all were terrified, but more than fear, they all wanted Jesse safe and sound. Of course Simon felt he was doing the right thing. She would keep that in mind when they talked later about his disobedience.

She whirled around and reentered the wooden structure. All the students were staring at her when she stormed toward them. She pushed loose, brown strands back across her ears and fussed with the bun at the nape of her neck. She repositioned hair pins that secured the rolled mane. She hesitated, trying to compose herself in preparation for what would be said next. It was clear that she was on one of her stampedes, and the Mount Tabor children had better get out of the way or else her fatal stomp would finish them all off. At this point, the best they could figure was that they would all be better off if they were out in the storm with Jesse.

Lois jumped off the bench and ran to the willowy lady. Donned in the petticoat/sweater attire, she was a peculiar but sweet sight. She knew it. Miss White grimaced in an effort to suppress riotous laughter lest Lois feel she were making fun of her. No one could melt a heart as fast as Lois. Often the children would use her as a diversion when something troublesome happened on the playground. Miss White was on to their little tricks. Even so, she knew the ploy might serve the brunette punkin' head well down the road. What now?

"Yes, Lois?"

"Don't be mad, Miss White. Simon can run faster than you in your skirt. He's just goin' to help Jesse. That's a good thing, isn't it?"

"Yes, Lois. It is indeed a good thing. You're right," she answered.

With that reassurance, Lois went back to the huddle of her companions, stood on her tiptoes to get on the bench, plopped herself down, and conspicuously pressed the petticoat with her hands. She looked at the teacher and winked. They were all saved again.

64

Mrs. Porter glanced out the window while tugging at Jesse's drooping coat. The little girl's sobs had subsided into barely audible whimpers. She tried as hard as she could to make her shoulders calm down, but fierce trembling shook her all the way down to her knobby knees.

Just as Mama took one final look toward the road, Harry yanked the storm-drenched reins and turned toward the family home place. Looking back through the sumacs and maples, he craved one final assurance that his baby sister was safe inside the house. Thunder stomped his hooves nervously, and mud splattered his steely forelegs.

"Will Harry be all right?" Jesse pleaded.

Mama cradled the little girl's cheeks in her hands and made a determined effort to comfort her.

"Don't you go worryin' yourself none. Harry is as tough as nails, and Thunder is the best horse around. The two of them'll be just fine."

Her voice crackled slightly, but Jesse's tiny smile was sufficient to convince her that the youngest Porter was feeling safer by the moment.

In the meantime, Harry proceeded along the ridge peering through dark boughs and urging his horse across strewn leaves and branches in the road. Not far beyond the first bend in the road, a black dangling object caught Harry's eye.

"Whoa," he ordered. "Easy boy …."

Harry patted the neck of the restless equine as he slid hastily from the saddle. Twirling the reins in an arc over the horse's head, Harry wrapped the loose ends around a nearby sapling, securing Thunder with a hastily tied half-hitch. He hooked his arm over the horse's neck and patted the coarse black mane with four successive slaps.

"Easy, boy. Easy," he spoke.

Thunder's ears perked forward, he whinnied defiantly, but he responded with eventual resignation, head down while Harry moved away from him.

The swatch of cloth was snagged on a single barb of partly collapsed fence. The dye had not been faded by sunlight over time, and scuffed trenches from recent footsteps in the mud suggested that someone had been there while the storm was in progress. He wished he had paid closer attention to Jesse's coat. He snatched the wool from the fence and studied the weave, trying to remember exactly what kind of material her coat was made of. Tarnation, if only he could remember! At any rate, she was safe with Mama.

Whether the other kids were safe was hard to say. Harry looked around trying to ascertain whether the children had taken shelter nearby. Periodically, the rain diminished until it was nearly a drizzle. Just when he had begun to relax, he was blasted by a gust of wind seeming to come out of the blue.

The children were nowhere to be seen, and as best as Harry could tell, there was no reason to panic until there was good cause to do so. Mama had always said, "No news is good news," and Harry had always tried to keep that in mind when faced with a crisis. He was also certain that Mama sometimes said things that, in her heart, she did not really believe.

Thunder jerked his head nervously, rolling his eyes toward the dismounted rider. The frantic steed was bending the skinny tree sideways. Harry glanced cautiously in the direction of the horse but paused to contemplate his next move. Could the kids have cut through the woods looking for shelter, or would they have stayed in the rutted road while moving toward the safety of the schoolhouse?

Harry pivoted slowly on one heel as he scoured the horizon for some sign of the children's whereabouts. With uncanny timing, the unthinkable happened. The black silhouette of the animal lunged toward the bank, and rain-slicked leather unwound from the makeshift hitching post.

Before he realized what was happening, Harry was moving through the thicket in a futile attempt to retrieve the horse. He had never seen anything quite like it. Thunder was not easily spooked. Harry also knew that this was the most peculiar weather either one of them had ever experienced. Harry was not nearly so mad as he was desperate. He knew better than to have reined his horse in such a sloppy matter. Too much was on his mind and too much was going on to know exactly how to do everything right.

The shadowy image of the horse faded through a thick haze, blanketing the tree line. With a sharp pain tearing his side and his heart pounding wildly, Harry doubled over to catch his breath. He muttered a half-spoken curse, secure in the belief that neither Mother nor the Preacher would ever know about his blasphemy. He was somewhat secure in the belief that God would forgive him anyway. Under the circumstances, a little profanity made sense.

He scrunched his eyes while clasping his knees for support. Apple-red blood trickled across the knuckles of his right hand, and he realized that his torn skin smarted from thorns stuck through tanned flesh. He could hardly think straight. He winced, slapped his thigh, and then stood up straight. Nothing else could happen that would make this search more difficult. That was his thought, until he heard the godforsaken roar.

65

Simon was shaking like Sam Collier's arm at the Hundred Saturday Night Auction. The harder he tried to steady himself, the harder he shook. His spindly legs wobbled with each long stride he took toward the wooded hillside below the school.

Jesse had to be there somewhere, and he knew the other kids, including Ralph, were just too tired to do any more searching. It was up to him to help his little classmate. However, he knew also that probably no one in the immediate vicinity was available to help him. He was on his own. Doubts about his own safety came creeping into his muddled brain. He reflected on Miss White's calls through the mist as he hurdled branches and ruts leading away from the school. Maybe he should have stayed there.

No. It would not have been the right thing to do. Sometimes a man has to do what is right, despite the best intentions of others. That is what Pa always said. And that was what the eighth grader intended to do.

He could see the old Hostutler horse barn through the trees, and he made up his mind to look inside the rusty-brown structure to see if Jesse might be there. It was a good strong building that would give ample shelter to frightened girls. From Simon's way of seeing, it was the logical place to go. No horses were in sight near the barns, and Simon figured Old Man Hostutler had taken the horses to the lower pasture. There were haystacks in the valley that provided sufficient nutrition until spring grass turned green. Simon guessed that the animals would be moved to higher ground within a couple of weeks.

The large double doors banged back and forth in the wind. The hinges creaked loudly, even through the howling wind. He must look inside before going any farther. This was probably the end of the search. Jesse would be inside, cowered in one of the straw-bedded stalls. She had to be there. Suddenly, a gust of wind blasted against the door. The lever latch caught Simon's hand, slitting a huge gash below his right thumb. Simon doubled over hollering like a cat caught in a Sears Roebuck wringer washer. The only benefit he could see to this new situation was that his shaking had finally stopped. He could concentrate better on what needed to be done.

He yanked his red-and-black handkerchief out of his hip pocket and balled it up in the palm of the injured hand. An unpredictable sense of strength and pure rage exploded in Simon. He clutched the door handle. With a ferocious jerk, he tore into the door as though he were a strong man in a carnival sideshow. To his amazement, the door was easily pulled away from the building. The next thing he knew, he was standing on the stone-and-straw floor inspecting his wound.

"Dadblast it anyway!" he shouted.

The kerchief had sopped up a lot of blood, but there was something more needed to be done. If he could just remember when Pa was in the hayfield. What would Pa do with a cut as bad as this one? Simon choked back tears and tried to think rationally about his dilemma. Pressure. He needed to put pressure on the cut. Just last week Mama had sliced her finger with a recently honed hatchet. She washed out the wound under the hand pump at the sink. Then she poured a slopped measurement of hydrogen peroxide into the cut. She put a big pad of gauze on the cut and double-wrapped it with a rag strip she kept in the cupboard ragbag. He was not sure, but he thought he had heard her whisper some curse words when she thought he could not hear her. With her hand raised over her head for a little bit, she seemed to be all right, enough to go back to her chores.

Simon looked around the barn. Obviously, no hydrogen peroxide was to be had. He could not see a pump. He mumbled, knowing that if he were building a barn, he would never do it without procuring water for the horses. Yet the schoolboy knew the inherent dangers of an open wound, especially around a barn. He briefly imagined how suffering with lockjaw would be the most terrible death imaginable. It happened from time to time. The grown-ups had sometimes talked about Old Man Smith dying of lockjaw after getting cut on a rusty tedder last year.

Simon was not going to die that way.

He caught a glimpse of a water barrel outside at the fence line above the barn, and he thought he remembered seeing a skinny pipe feeding spring water into the barrel. Peering through the small, window in the wooden door of the barn, he did indeed see a steady flow of water pouring into a sawed-off barrel. That must be where the horses drank. Good sense told him to wash out his wound. He needed to cover it until he could get home to Mama's medicine cabinet.

With his right shoulder braced against the barn door, he wedged his way through a nine-inch opening and loped toward the trough. Pulling the bloodstained cloth away from his right hand, he aimed the cut for the stream above the barrel. A sharp pain surged through his right arm as the cold water hit the wound, but Simon clenched his jaw and held the hand in place for afull minute. Certain he had done the best possible, he lifted his arm high and ran back to the barn. Adrenaline was still his ally, and he confidently moved back inside the building with what seemed to be little effort.

Now he just needed a sterile bandage. The kerchief was soiled and blood-soaked. He decided against using it again. The only thing he had that was close to being very clean was the new undershirt Pa had brought him from Dye's Store. He yanked off his long-sleeved, blue shirt. Then he slowly removed the thin undergarment. Wadding it into a tight ball, he cushioned the cut hand with the outside of the shirt, assured that it was the cleanest cloth he had available. Next, he tied the handkerchief around the back of his hand, looping it again before tying it off with his teeth and left hand. That was the best he could do. And it was time to resume his search for Jesse.

"Jesse!" he yelled at the top of his lungs, "JESSE!"

He stared at a loft that was suspended above the back two stalls. He wondered if she had curled up there on some loose hay for warmth. Most of the children on Tabor knew that it was important to get warm as fast as possible whenever a rain came up unexpectedly. Knowing how warm the hay made them feel when they worked the fields in the summertime, it made sense to crawl into a big pile of hay to take the chill away when the occasion warranted it.

"Jesse? You up there? It's Simon!"

To his dismay, Simon heard nothing more than the wind whipping around the building. The noise escalated as a roar welled in the distance. He frowned. Hundreds of rocks were slamming the tin roof. The lost girl was nowhere to be found inside the barn. Now all he concentrated on was the crazy weather.

Staring at the tin sheets over his head, he was puzzled to see round indentations forming. A feeling of terror and loneliness overwhelmed him. He wondered if the Last Days were here. He was going to die alone. Simon gritted his teeth and spat on the floor. He did not want to die that way either.

"Oh, tarnation! Stop making this stuff up!" he growled, "Stay calm!"

He took a deep breath and tried to figure out what to do next. There was nothing else to do except to go on hunt of Jesse. He was rested. It was time to continue the search.

As he turned to force the door open, an abrupt silence fell over the building and surroundings. Nothing. No wind. No rain. No rocks hitting the roof. Something did not feel right, and Simon stopped dead in his tracks.

Simon reached toward the door but suddenly jumped back. An explosive roar like nothing he had ever heard hit him out of nowhere. He had seen a biplane take off at the Hundred Airport in October. The noise that was blasting him at the barn door was even louder than roaring engines on the mountaintop landing strip. Once more, he stood on tiptoes to peer out the nine-inch window of the first milking stall.

"What the …."

He had never seen anything like it. It was not a cloud. It looked like smoke from a mine fire. He recalled seeing an open, ground portal ablaze once. The billowing smoke was gray and black as it rolled from the walk-in shaft at the back of the Lough farm. But there were no open portals on the Tabor. Nothing was outside the barn that could catch on fire suddenly. Simon froze. Nature had induced a hypnotic trance. He was unable to control his legs, arms, or anything else for that matter.

Above the tree line, he saw fence rails and tree limbs sailing through the sky. Even whole trees were flying through the air at the edge of the cloud. Survival instinct finally kicked in, and Simon ran to the back of the barn. He crashed facedown on the stone floor and covered his head as though the biggest school bully in the world were about to beat him to a pulp.

The roar was deafening. Although Simon groaned in fear, the sound of his voice was barely audible inside his skull. All he heard was the roar. A minute passed before the exploding wind subsided.

When calm returned, Simon sat up. He saw that boards from the side of the building had been pulled outward. Some planks were completely missing. A strange sight overhead vied for his intention. All but a few strips of the tin roof had been pulled from the barn. It had happened faster than Doc Rose could pull a bad tooth! And Doc was pretty fast, when he was not drunk.

Poor Jesse. Simon wondered where she was when the unrelenting storm tore across the ridge. He stood quietly, looking around at the destruction. His ears were working better than they had ever worked. He listened intently for more signs of the roar. It was quiet. He was safe at last. Wherever Jesse was, she would need help now more than ever. She was all that Simon could think about now. No one was out there to help her.

Simon ran to the door, lunged against the reinforced oak boards, and hurled himself into the gray space outside. He surveyed the horizon, taking in the view of uprooted trees. He was sure that some of the downed trees were a hundred years old.

The road was buried beneath brush and boughs.

"Best to stay on the road," he muttered. "That's where Jesse would be."

He looked over his shoulder at the barn and scanned 360 degrees of terrain. In a heartbeat, he realized that he had been in the path of a twister. He was certain that the danger had passed. With renewed confidence and fiery determination, Simon strode to the bank by the road.

"Jesse! Jesse, can you hear me?"

He would find her one way or another.

66

Simon skidded down the muddy bank. He flung his arms in a futile effort to balance himself. The next thing he knew, he was slinging mud and twigs off both hands and shaking his head, wondering how disappointed Mother would be when she saw his clothes. There was no time to think about that. He had to find the little girls. Certain they must be terrified, Simon swallowed hard and choked back tears of terror and desperation.

Suddenly, a distinct rhythmic thumping resonated through the glen. Simon was startled by a frantic, black horse barreling toward him. Without hesitation, he jumped to his feet, waved his arms, and soothingly called out, "Whoa, Boy! Easy, Boy ... easy ...."

Thunder jerked his head back and for a second appeared to be more alarmed by the erratic movement of Simon's outstretched arms than by the storm events of the last few minutes. His front quarters were caked with mud, and his mane was tangled with leaves, mud, and grass. His nostrils flared suspiciously, and he eyed the stranger. The horse wanted only to find safety, and he spun nervously away from the boy. Simon bent his knees, lowered his arms, and reached out toward the frightened animal.

"Easy, Boy. I won't hurt you. Easy. It's all right. We're all right now."

Simon squinted momentarily, trying to think whose horse that was. It was not any of the Thomas' riding horses. But he thought he recognized it. The saddle was slightly crooked. Muddy reins dangled from each side of the blazed face. It would do both of them well for Simon to control this situation and see how the riderless horse came to be isolated in the middle of the storm. Slowly, he stepped toward Thunder and gently closed his fingers around the left rein. He whispered comforting words and extended a slow stroke across the white streak of the horse's face.

"All right, fella. Where is your rider?" Simon said.

He continued stroking the horse while looking around the glen.

Simon searched earnestly for some sign of a thrown rider. Broken boughs, uprooted trees, and a heavy gray mist over the woods made it difficult to see much at all. If an injured rider were on the ground, it would take a considerable amount of time to find him. Simon and Thunder made curious companions. Caked with mud and drenched, they were a sight to behold; yet, no one would see them in the middle of storm debris.

"Hello!" Simon yelled. "Anybody out there?"

Thunder jerked again, but Simon had taken tight control of the reins and patted the horse's neck in a gesture of reassurance.

"HELLO!"

Silence. No one could hear him. Or, maybe someone could hear him but could not respond. The wind had died down. No birds were chirping. It was an eerie phenomenon. A violent shudder momentarily took over Simon's whole body. He imagined being left alone in this foreboding set of circumstances. Were people hurt? Were houses able to withstand the relentless assault by the wind? He did not know what to do.

A nudge of Thunder's nose shook Simon back to the reality of the moment. They were both unhurt. Obviously, they could continue the search with no immediate fear of Black, engulfing clouds and flying trees. Simon was unsure about mounting the stallion.

For the time being, it might be best just to lead the horse. When a barn could be found to board the horse temporarily, Simon would get him inside. Heading away from the school and on toward Punkin' Run, Simon found sure footing with each step he took. He coaxed the nervous horse with each stride. This complication was slowing down his search for the girls, but Simon could not bring himself to tie the terrified animal to a tree. They would stick together. If the absent rider or playmates were hurt, they could be carried to safety by the stallion.

In the meantime, Harry was stomping furiously along the rubble-strewn road. He choked back tears. What in the world would he do without Thunder? What if a tree had come down on the girls? For a fleeting moment, he remembered something about levers from his science studies at Tabor School. Maybe he could pry a tree loose with a fence post or something. Thoughts of despair and emergency engulfed him even while he chastised himself for letting his horse go into the storm. What about Thunder? Was he hurt in the midst of so much destruction? Could Harry have taken better care of his loyal friend? It was too late to fret about things that could not be undone. The most important matter now was to press on in search of Jesse's friends.

He hurried along the narrow road, looking around quickly for any sign of the girls. A wide path of uprooted trees and brushless banks struck a strange note with him. He had never seen wind do so much harm in one place. It looked as if a monstrous scythe had torn through the woods, leveling the strongest oaks and uprooting bushes and grass as it went. At the same time, other parts of the woods seemed barely affected by the forceful onslaught. He had not heard of any tornado in the Wadestown area. He reckoned that life was much more than just that which he had seen during his first twenty years.

Then he saw a horse and boy walking toward him.

"Hey yuh!" Harry shouted.

"Hello," Simon replied.

Both boys picked up their pace toward each other, grateful to be alone in the godforsaken woods no longer. Harry smiled from ear to ear, thankful to encounter both his horse and a rescuer. His mouth fell open and disappointment crept into his eyes.

"I'm lookin' for the girls, Mary and Edna. Fern and the others. You seen 'em anywhere?" he asked.

"Yeah, they're back yonder at the schoolhouse. But Jesse got lost somewhere, and nobody knows whereabouts she is!"

Simon dropped his shoulders, realizing that between the two of them, neither had seen a sign of Jesse. She must have been killed or blown away. That was all he could imagine, and he cried spontaneously. His efforts had been in vain. Maybe if he had gone out sooner instead of huddling by the potbelly stove, she would have been all right.

Someone should have been looking for her sooner. His knees

buckled, and the next thing he knew he was kneeling in the middle of the road.

"Hey!" Harry yelled. "Jesse is home with our Mama. She got scared and ran back home. It sounds like everyone is all right. I must say, you look like somethin' the cats drug in!"

Simon stared at the tall boy's face, trying to register the information. Then he looked at his clothes and hands. He tasted the unmistakable grit of mud on his lips. Laughter exploded from his gut, and he could only imagine how he must look to someone else. The two young men laughed like hyenas. The fact that they both looked like vagrants who had not had a bath in a year did not help matters.

"I think this is your horse?" he asked.

"Yep," Harry answered.

He reached out a hand to help Simon up and secured Thunder's rein in his left hand. Simon shook his head from side to side and marveled at what they had been through.

"Did you see that wind?" he shouted.

His eyes were wide and his face animated as he handed over the mud-caked horse to his owner. Simon shook his head and elaborated even more.

"Have you ever seen anything like this?"

"Naw," Harry answered. "It's really somethin'! What's all that blood on ya'?"

"I'm all right," Simon replied, "just a cut from a barn-door handle."

"Get on," Harry motioned toward the saddle. "You look like you're worn out."

Simon lifted his left foot for the stirrup and gratefully nestled himself into the curved, black saddle. Harry kicked the stirrup back toward Thunder's rump and slung himself over the horse's back. They rode slowly along the debris-strewn ridge. Today was not a good day for school.

67

Miss White lifted the curved lever of the potbelly stove door with the poker. The red, hot cinders were settled below the rim of the cast-iron bowl. It was clear that the heat was fading and chill was taking a toll on the students. The teacher glanced at Ralph who was twisting his feet around the bottom of his desk. He was scratching white figures on his slate. For the time being, the multiplication table was diverting his attention from terrifying events of the morning. She hesitated to remind him that it was his job to keep the fire stoked and maintain a good supply of coal for the heater. Knowing that the oldest Thomas boy had to be exhausted, she decided to tend to the stove herself. The children were settled for the time being, but she sensed uneasiness in the midst of quiet study.

Keeping the children calm, safe, and warm was foremost in her thoughts. She placed the poker across the square base of the stove and quietly moved the bail of the bucket to an upright position. She looked directly at Edna, silently signaling her to be in charge of the room while she went out to the coal pile for more fuel. Miss White grabbed the square shovel from the corner and stepped precariously toward the door. Edna nodded, and the teacher gently opened the door. Outside, the winds had calmed to near stillness. It was enough to get to the stockpile and back. She looked back at the classroom to ensure that the children were minding their lessons. Then, Miss White stepped across the threshold.

For a brief moment she froze in place. Branches, saplings, and leaves were strewn erratically as far as she could see. Even lumps of coal had been dislodged. Normally, a neat cone-shaped stack of coal was about twenty yards from second base on the ball field. She wished the children could be out playing today instead of cowering in silence. That would come another day. For now, lessons were obviously not so important as Jesse and Simon's whereabouts. For a second, the maiden lady doubted her decision about managing the classroom. She could hardly act as though nothing had happened. The children knew she was doing her best, and her best meant keeping the fire going. She needed to keep her own feelings under control. The well-being of all the children was paramount.

However, a gnawing whisper played over and over in her mind. It was she who had been responsible for Simon when he went on hunt of Jesse. It was also her responsibility to account for his whereabouts, just as much as he hoped to account for Jesse's. She would have to build up the fire and leave the oldest children in charge. No one else would know two children were still lost in the storm.

Miss White heaved large scoops of black-diamond chunks into the bucket, filling it to the top. The supply would be more than enough to keep the students warm. She clutched her black skirt, whirled around, and again grabbed the shovel in her left hand. Swinging the load of coal against the counterbalance of the shovel, she took long steps toward the school she loved. The old maid, as she knew the children referred to her, glanced at her dapple mare, still tied to the hitching rail. The old gal seemed to be fairly steady despite the wind storm. The two oldest females on the ridge were doing very well for the moment.

Once on the steps of the porch, the teacher set the load down with a thud. She turned around one last time to examine the area. Perhaps she would see Simon and Jesse coming through the trees. A thick, charcoal-gray fog hung over the school like a foreboding shroud. The building was a strong shelter for the young people of Mount Tabor. Cupping her hands around her mouth, she yelled for the missing students.

"Simon! Jesse! Are you out there?"

She could hear nothing except a whisper of a breeze brushing a broken branch against the stone path. It was a lonely moment.

"Simon?"

"Jesse?"

Reluctantly, she lifted the bucket. The load was a hundred times heavier than it had been a few moments before. Determined not to add to the students' fears, she mustered a smile that she hoped was reassuring. She lugged the coal into the classroom. Miss White tipped the bucket forward and shook a mound of fuel into the belly of the heater. Silently, the schoolmarm grabbed the poker and jabbed the pile of coal and embers. She dueled with the coals as though she were fighting off a dozen bobcats. She rammed the rod underneath several lumps of coal at a time, allowing air to feed the flame and dissipate heat to the inner walls of the iron belly. Finally, the teacher wedged the door of the stove away from the outer stove wall and slammed it shut. In less than a minute, she stuck the poker into the coal bucket and wiped her hands on the hearth rag.

"Children, you are doing a good job with your work. I congratulate you for being very disciplined. Your parents will hear about how good you have all been today. I know you are worried about Jesse and Simon, and I'm worried too. I'm afraid we're the only ones who know they're out there in the woods trying to find their way through the storm. Ralph, you and Hiram have done an outstanding job getting the younger students to school. And it is no one's fault that Jesse got lost. So don't even think that way."

The thoughtful teacher looked slowly at the sea of quiet faces and wished she had time to hug every child in front of her. Miss White had no time for sentiment, so she continued with her instructions. Lois was winking at her again.

"With everyone dry now and lots of coal in the stove, I think it is a good idea for me to go look for the children. I'll go to the neighbors' houses and get help. We'll look everywhere for Jesse and Simon. Edna will be in charge here. I need to remind Ralph and Hiram to tend to the fire while I'm gone. I'll come back to school as fast as I can. I promise. You'll be safe here. Is everything clear?"

"Yes, Miss White," they responded.

"Are there any questions?" she asked.

Scared faces stared inquisitively at her, but no one raised a hand. No one needed to ask questions. Nothing else could be done. Even Lois understood that she would be safe if she stayed inside the schoolhouse with the other children. She looked down at her makeshift skirt and warm sweater. She thought Miss White would get awfully cold without her petticoat. But her sagging blue-floral dress in the coatroom was not dry yet. She wiped her hands across the black gathers of the petticoat. She smoothed the skirt over her knobby knees and bit her lip. The next time she looked up, Miss White was closing the door.

The teacher stood at the edge of the porch. It made sense to think about Jesse's well-being first. Simon was old enough, with sufficient common sense, to protect himself better than a six-year-old. Of course, in a panic, the conscientious bookworm could be in serious trouble just as easily as his small friend.

Miss White would need to get help from the closest reliable neighbor. That would be the Smith family down on Wise Run. It might take some time to get to them, but John and Ervin would be the best companions for the search. The men were strong young farmers and they knew these parts as well as anyone. They would make intelligent assessments of the dangers that children would face in a storm of such magnitude.

Riding Rosie through the mess of tangled branches would be challenging, but Miss White knew it would behoove her to save her strength for the considerable length of time she would need to scour the landscape between the Porter farm and Tabor. The gentle mare would be her ally for the next few hours. It would be prudent also to make a trip to the outhouse before embarking on any search. That was not to be.

Miss White grimaced when she saw the upset toilet. She would have no personal break today. The toilet looked as if it could fly down into the hollow as slick as a greased sled in January. Only the double-hole seat remained intact, and there was no possibility of a lady with a scant of modesty doing her business here. She would just have to hold it until she reached the Smith farm or a thick patch of bushes.

Suddenly, movement of leaves on the bank caught her attention. Her heart jumped as she hoped to see Jesse and Simon coming up the path. Changing directions, she lifted her skirt to midcalf and galloped across the stone path. Her breathing was so intense, she could not speak. She saw an outline of a horse and wondered if the children had borrowed the steed to ride to safety. A lanky arm pulled a limb away from the jagged, gray steps below the lawn. The teacher realized that it was the appendage of neither Jesse nor Simon. She slowed her pace, knowing that what she had hoped would be was somehow amiss. She needed to be careful not to slip on the wet flat rocks. There was still a lot of work to do.

"Miss White!"

Simon's squeaky voice pierced the fog with a croak that imitated neither child nor man. Finally, the crisis was coming to an end for the children of Mount Tabor. Little did they understand the day would be a memory that would linger a lifetime. This day would never go completely away. Miss White welcomed a good sign. She hoped that Jesse was tagging along behind Simon.

"Miss White!"

Her throat tightened. For a fleeting moment, she could not articulate a single sound. She blinked several times, trying unsuccessfully to choke back tears which inevitably streamed down her cheeks. Jesse was not with the ragtag boys. Still, she felt hopeful.

"Simon, are you all right? Are you hurt?" she asked.

"I'm fine, ma'am. Just a little cut on my hand. And Jesse is fine too. She ran back home to her Mama. Miss White, there was something dark and awful blowing through the woods. I was in a barn, and all I could do was wait till it stopped."

"That's all right," she said. "It was very brave of you to try to find Jesse. I'm so proud of all you children."

In a gesture of relief, she wrapped her arms around the gangly youth and smacked him hard a couple of times between the shoulder blades. Simon was stilted by the unexpected assault, and wondered if his permanent teeth would be knocked clean out as the result of the old maid's blows to his back. He looked toward the ground, not knowing what else to say. Fortunately by then, the teacher was directing her acts of aggression toward Harry. Simon just hoped he could stand the whacks to his back, shoulder, and anything else she hoped to beat up. Where was she when the bullies from Hundred tore into the Tabor boys on Saturday night? They could sure use her pitchfork-tossing thrusts then.

"Harry Porter! What in the world are you doing out here in this weather?" she asked.

"Ma'am, Jesse did make it home all right, but Mama and I were not sure about the other children. Thunder and I came lookin' for 'em. Did everyone make it to school before the worst of it came through?"

"Yes. Yes."

Her face took on a blank expression. Her overtaxed brain was just beginning to put together the facts. Everyone was accounted for, and the worst was over. She clasped Harry's forearm, thanking him for all he had done.

"Come on, boys, let's go inside. What a terrible morning this has been. Harry, were there signs of anyone hurt along the way?"

"Not that I could see nowhere," he answered. "There sure is a lot of trees damaged, though."

"There sure is," she agreed.

She winced at his poor grammar and wondered why she had not done a better job before he dropped out of school in the eighth grade. But, today, she was determined to forget the words and all the rules that went with them. There was a time and place for everything. Today was not a day for English and recitations. This was a morning for rest and calm. This was a morning to dismiss school.

Harry hung his head sheepishly as he stood at the front of his old classroom. Miss White and the students cheered and clapped together as she announced the greatest news of the year. School was dismissed for the day to give everyone a chance to let their families know all was well. It would be a day to tell their grandchildren about, she insisted. But none of the classmates were thinking about grandchildren. The good thing was they were going home.

"Mr. Porter has offered to go with you to your homes to make sure you are safe. Simon, I'll accompany you and Margaret Anne down Camp Run. All of you leave your books in your desks. There will be no lessons tonight."

Echoed squeals of total delight bounced off the blackboard. The teacher paused and smiled patiently until the children settled down again. Lois was giggling and jumping up and down. The others were waving their arms and clapping, knowing that they had lots of time to play and realizing that once again everyone, including Jesse, was safe and sound. Now, it was a good day for everyone.

"You children stay together and don't run ahead of the younger ones. Ralph, you and Hiram are expected to stay with Mr. Porter all the way home," she directed.

"Yes, ma'am!" the boys replied.

"Line up for your coats," Miss White said.

Dutifully, the children of Tabor stood in a perfectly straight line with Lois at the front and Hiram wobbling at the rear. He was nervous and ready to run as fast as he could, but he fought as hard as ever in his whole life to wait his turn and go with the group. Maybe there would be another storm next week, and they could go home again. Maybe not.

Miss White removed Lois' clothes from the nail above the shovel. In all the confusion, her dress had not been placed by the fire, but enough time had passed in the coal-heated room for the calico to dry. All children seemed to be dry enough to send out. It was cool and misty but definitely not too cold to worry about a little dampness until they all got home. She crooked her index finger in the direction of the youngest student, and the tiny Thomas girl left her place at the front of the line. In minutes, she had changed into her own clothes. Miss White smiled as Lois handed her the neatly folded petticoat and sweater.

Wearing the petticoat had not been a problem. None of the classmates had made fun of her. In fact, she had felt special, wearing the teacher's black apparel. Mom never let her wear black. It was not an appropriate color for little girls. The teacher beamed with gratitude as

Lois whispered a cordial, "Thank you."

"All right, children. Remember, no running today, watch every step you take, and stay together. Mary, do you think you can make it home? If not, you can take Rose and bring her back in the morning."

Mary gratefully acknowledged the generous offer but said she was doing much better. If the ankle started hurting too much, she would climb on Harry's horse and ride the rest of the way. She waved the old cane at the teacher and straightened her posture so that she was as tall as Hiram in front of her. Satisfied that the group would make good decisions, the teacher opened the door for the small, exiting figures.

The orderly line became jumbled about halfway to the path as youngsters looked around at the damage to the landscape. A buzz of "look over theres" passed through the group like wind passing through high grass in July. They stood a little closer than usual, and Miss White noticed that some of the girls were reaching for friends' hands.

The air close to the school was gray and foreboding, but it was nothing compared to the billowing force of the ravenous monster that had touched down on the woods, farms, and meadows of the peaceful community. Damage to buildings and land could be repaired with some good work teams and a family full of farmhands. That was not a problem that even crossed the students' minds. Hot, sweet custard from the oven, cups of sassafras tea, and tomato gravy on biscuits would pull the families together at the dinner tables. The children would be safe on the walk home.

The glee that Lois had demonstrated by jumping inside the schoolhouse abruptly vanished as she studied the ruin around the building. She nuzzled up close to Fern, making sure not to lose sight of the big sister. She looked up with tear-filled eyes.

"We're all right," the older sister smiled, "The storm is gone."

Up ahead, Harry twisted in the saddle, counting heads of younguns as Miss White pulled the school door shut. Harry nudged his heels against the rain slicked sides of the confident steed. He looked backward as much as he looked forward.

"You younguns' stay together now. I'll take you home."

Black-stockinged, skinny legs shuffled through slate-gray clouds that touched the road home. The children stared at fragmented boughs and scattered leaves as far across the ridge as they could see. Mud-speckled, calico, feed-sack skirts hung in disarray, and trusting eyes moved back and forth, counting every friend. Lois tugged at Fern's fingers. The two ragtag sisters interlocked each other's fingers as Lois whispered.

"Don't worry. I won't leave you."

Part III

A New Path

68

Elena had driven hard on her return trip to the Ozarks. The final copy of the feature story on the storm was complete. She had delivered her feature article files and hard copy to *The Sentinel's* octogenarian editor, Charles. In one morning, she had cleaned out her desk and piled her personal belongings into three cardboard boxes. Charles had decided he would run the storm series early in the spring. The first piece would be published on March 18, the anniversary date of the Tri-State Tornado.

The old man was saddened by Elena's letter of resignation, but he respected the reporter's decision to move on to new horizons. Looking back on his younger days, he knew he would have done the same thing. The young woman was creative and unrelenting in her quest of a story. He would have a difficult time filling her shoes.

Once she walked out of her office at *The Sentinel*, Elena was restless. She had a final meeting with her mentor. She and Charles shared hugs and tears as they ate one last Blue Plate Special at Miss Blue's Diner in Hundred. They had driven up to Tabor to visit the Porter family marker in the cemetery on the hill. The two newspaper colleagues walked along the dirt road where the Thomas children encountered the twister. Both tried to imagine whether they would have known what to do at such a young age. The storm had hit the farm community eight decades earlier, but it felt as if it could have been yesterday. It was a good story that would affect many lives. Now it was time for Elena to move forward.

A compulsion to go back to Sam's grave spurred Elena to make the cross-country drive to the Old Redford Cemetery. The Tri-State Tornado research had changed her. Now she was simultaneously contemplative and alarmed by every forecast that warned people of adverse weather. This visit would be the last time she would pay respects to the farmer, but the memory of his ordeal would invariably hover like an angel watching over her.

It was a warm, sunny day when she pulled the Windstar alongside the rows of granite markers. She was surprised to see that the grass was high. No one had mowed the lawn in weeks. The Old Redford Cemetery sign was on the ground by the gate. She wondered if the wind had brought down the painted boards. Elena sensed that Sam's final resting place could easily be overshadowed by weeds and brambles. She had seen many old markers that were crooked slabs of stone, tipped haphazardly in wooded areas and unkempt fields. No one could guarantee that burial sites would be eternally tended by concerned locals. Once the years pass, too many graves are of little consequence. Children move on, grandchildren lose interest in their predecessors, and cemeteries fall into disarray. It was a fact of life. And death.

Elena clutched a dozen, red, silk roses in her left hand. She walked toward the double headstone. The course of plotting the story had been a curious journey with unanticipated outcomes. She did not know why she had returned. She simply had to be there one more time. The journalist had traveled an ethereal circle from the hills of Appalachia to the hills of the Ozarks. The truth she discovered was undeniable. Lives are fragile. Time is precious.

She whispered to herself, "The good we do for another is a gift that blesses everyone along the way."

Sam Flowers died alone in a gulley. He was alone when the angels lifted his soul to the heavens. Sam left behind a wife and family, a farm, a horse named Joker, and a legacy to be cherished by the good people of Reynolds County. In 1925, *The New York Times* referred to him only as a farmer near Ellington, Missouri. Elena gave him a name.

Sam's place in history had been a catastrophic moment filled with anonymity. So were the countless numbers of anonymous people who disappeared from the face of the earth on March 18, 1925. The exact death count was never known. Children's graves and names were mixed up with each other. Little boys were identified only by marbles or pen knives in their pockets. Cat eyes. Shooters. A Buck knife. Some unidentified Negro woman was buried in an unmarked plot. A mass grave of nameless remains was shoveled over by exhausted volunteers, who had cried as though it mattered.

Elena had wiped away her share of tears. Never had she grieved for those who died before her time ... until now. There was awesome power in the wind that blew across the fields of Redford, Missouri. There was awesome love in the hearts of neighbors who rode into the night in search of Sam. There was glory in the selfless work of two thousand Boy Scouts who descended on Murphysboro, Illinois. There was hope for a father who found his daughter alive after he buried someone else's child. There was goodness in National Guard troops who organized searches. Quests to find and rescue injured neighbors had extended 219 miles across the Mississippi and Wabash Rivers. People came from every direction. The Salvation Army. Nurse volunteers. Doctors.

Local churches. The American Red Cross.

On a ridge called Mount Tabor, a West Virginia farmer rode his horse into treacherous weather in search of children lost in a piece of the dissipating storm system that started near Ellington, Missouri. Like one of Kizzie's patchwork quilts, it was the people along the way who pieced together the whole story of March 18 and March 19, 1925. The names would live on. The legacy was its own gift. It started with a farmer and his horse in the Ozark Mountains. It ended with a farmer and his horse in Appalachia.

Elena rested the roses on the grass in front of the Flowers' marker. She stood staring at Mary and Sam's names, wondering where on earth her next story would lead her. She wanted to stay in the warm meadow of the Ozarks, but she knew she had to press on to new horizons. A young man in Paducah, Kentucky, had invited her to a severe weather conference. She would begin her new quest there. She looked around to make sure that no one was watching her. Then she spoke her last words in Redford.

"Sam, the day you died, you thought no one would remember you or what happened. You were wrong. You are remembered."

Out of nowhere, a blast of wind hit Elena's chest so hard, she lost her balance and stumbled backward onto the grave. She jumped to her feet and ran like a crazed banshee for the Windstar. As she barreled down the road, she tuned the radio to 106.7 FM, KAUL Ellington. The regular program had been interrupted by a familiar message: "The National Weather Service has issued a tornado watch for the southeast Missouri Counties of Iron, Madison, Wayne, Reynolds ...."